I0562256

UNTIL ALL THE STARS ARE FOUND

Katelyn Costello

1

Until All the Stars are Found

Copyright © 2021 Katelyn Costello

All Rights Reserved. No part of this publication may be reproduced, stored, or transmitted in any form or by any means, electronic, mechanical, photocopying, recording, scanning or otherwise without written permission from the publisher. It is illegal to copy this book, post it to a website, or distribute it by any other means, without permission.

This novel is entirely a work of fiction. The names, characters, and incidents portrayed in it are the work of the author's imagination. Any resemblance to actual persons, living or dead, events or localities is entirely coincidental.

First Edition

ISBN: 978-1-7369598-0-0

Cover Design: Jane Farrell

Also, by Katelyn Costello

The Frituals Saga

The Frituals

Rebellion

Until All the Stars are Found

DEDICATION

Thank you to my love for pushing me to work, even when I didn't want to, and for answering my eighty-bazillion hypothetical medical questions with every book.

To Mom and Dad for introducing me to Science Fiction as a wee baby.

Until All the Stars are Found

Contents

Chapter 1

Running without gravity is really fucking weird. If I didn't have this harness on, who knows how far away from this wall I would be? It's one of several thoughts I have to push away along with what would happen if I hit the button for my GRAV boots? What time does Karrie think I can do? Do I love or hate gravity? I still don't fucking know.

Running without gravity is, without a doubt, harder than running with a weighted backpack. Sure, running for ten kilometers on the road is hard. Your body gets tired of the thud of the bag against your back, the repetitive impact of your feet striking the ground over and over and over again. But without gravity? Your balance is shit. You constantly search for the ground. You don't have to worry about that with regular running.

"Let's go, Gomez, four hundred more meters then you're done for the day," my trainer yells from the floor below me.

I glance down to the floor and see her standing in line with the other mentors. I don't have long to look at her face before I zip past her with the rest of the pack, but I can't tell if she's pleased or not. I look down at the track lanes. The LED lights that illuminate my feet are bright lime green, letting me know I'm on track for whatever pace Karrie wants me to run. The neighbor to my left has a track that turns a bright yellow, letting him know he isn't running up to par.

"Come on, Gomez!"

Four hundred meters. Then I can take this goddamn harness off. I don't know when it happened, but my shirt has slid up over the harness again. Leaving the course nylon to rub the same spot it had two days ago. The raw skin burns with the friction and the sweat dripping into it.

Someone hits a button, and a glowing ring three meters in diameter slides out of the floor off the edge of the track. The pack surges forward for the last hundred meters, our uneven breathing and my heartbeat pounding in my ears moments before we go airborne. I hit the button on my side, and the harness releases its hold on the track, and soar through the air, pinwheeling in a mass of arms and legs with my peers before I hit the mat wall with a thud.

I brace for the impact and grab the handholds, scurrying as fast as I can, my legs floating off the wall as I pull myself down. With a grunt, I pull my legs down against the lack of gravity and hit the GRAV lock button, slamming my feet to the ground. I move away from the other recruits, and I put my hands on my knees, trying to catch my breath.

"Nope. Up, walking, let's go," Karrie says, walking past me. I stand and move to the line where the others who already finished wait. We watch, backs stiff and at attention, while the others finish, their tracks in a myriad of red, yellow, and green.

I peer up at the screen above our heads, where the scoreboard will update in a few moments. This scoreboard is how the Galactic Garrison tracks people's progress through ranks. When the last person hits the wall, all the mentors tap their tablets, and the numbers change. I watch as my name turns green and shifts slightly up the chart.

ADA GOMEZ +2

Someone taps out a command, and gravity returns. My thick ponytail falls to my back, the black hair sticking to the sweat across my shoulders.

"At ease, soldiers. Good work today. We will be back here tomorrow at 0500."

There is a mixture of sighs of relief that we are done for the day and groans of disgust at how early we'll have to be out of bed to make it here in the morning.

"Fuck me," I breathe, trying to contain my hair. On the final twist, the hairband breaks, snapping across the back of my hand, leaving a nice red welt. I sigh and reach into my pocket, pulling another hair tie out as Karrie walks over to me.

"That wasn't bad. How did your ankle feel?" Karrie asks, scrolling through the stats on the tablet. She puts her hand out, and I hand her the data chip that syncs her tablet to my harness. While the harness I wear keeps me from flying away, it also scans my heart rate, pace, cadence, and a slew of other data I don't understand.

"Fine, I guess, I don't think it was my best go, but it wasn't my worst," I say, unbuckling the harness and hanging it up on the wall.

Karrie smirks and looks back down at the tablet. "Okay."

I pause. Karrie usually has more to say than that. "Okay?"

"Okay." She turns and walks toward her office.

My brain spins. "Just okay?" I call after her. *Is she pissed off at me? But she smiled. Did I fuck up?* "Karrie?"

"Go shower, then meet me in my office," she says, heading out of the training block.

"Fuck," I mutter to the empty air. My brain spirals through all the potential outcomes.

I met Karrie three years ago. They sent me to her not long after my parents died. I was acting out in school; the school didn't know what to do. They didn't have the capacity to deal with someone who lost both parents at once, was in the foster system, and not doing okay. So, like most of the adults in my life did, they passed me off to someone else. Someone handed me a pamphlet and suggested I check out the Garrison as a way to 'deal with all the feelings'. It was

4

a youth system that was meant to help us become "vibrant young leaders in our community." I thought at first it was stupid. That was when Karrie came into my life. Sergeant Karrie Lima is my mentor. She listened, helped me to figure out a plan. And what I wanted for me. She helped me out of a dark time and set me back on track. With her help, I graduated their program and diverted my training from on-world service to off-world.

I follow the other Fems to the locker room and strip down, throw the borrowed fatigues in the laundry bin, grab a towel, and head to the showers. I scrub down quickly, the scalding water wicks away the sweat, but burns where the harness rubbed against my side. I get out of the shower, towel off, and pull on my civilian clothes—a pair of ripped black jeans and a thin blue t-shirt. My sneakers have a few holes that are only apparent when you step in a puddle, and the rubber bottoms have almost no treads left.

I wring as much of the water out of my hair and search in vain in my bag for another hair tie to make a neater bun. But this is my last one. *Maybe I can find one at home tonight after Jaxon goes to sleep.* The other girls pull on their civilian clothes. The holes in their jeans are fashionable and on purpose. Mine are holey because I've worn the same pair of jeans for three years now. I sling my small backpack over my shoulder and head out of the lockers into the hallway.

At the third door on the right I pause, "Sergeant Lima, may I enter?" I step back and look down the hall. Normally by this time on a Friday afternoon, the training center's halls are empty, and the lights are turned down. Today, however, the space is still brightly lit with LEDs and a man waits down the hall. From this distance I can't make out the rank patch on his sleeve, but his tight stance clues me in that he must be some sort of officer. He looks up from the tablet he had been reading at me and nods. I nod back and turn to the door.

Karrie opens the door and beckons me inside. In contrast to the bright hallway, the office is dim, and the sole light in the room comes from Karrie's tablet, and the projector shining on the wall. Karrie sits back down behind her desk and pulls up a graph on her tablet and sends the data to a projector. I stand tall, hands behind my back, waiting for Karrie to ask me to sit. Retired or not, Karrie has specific standards she wants me to meet.

"So," Karrie says, turning back to me. "Sit on down, Ada. How are classes going?"

I want to roll my eyes but don't. If Karrie is asking something, there's a purpose. "My classes are going well. May I be candid?" I ask.

"Yes, Ada, you may always be candid with me," she says.

"I don't see the point in them anymore. I know, I know." I put my hands up. "I know I need them to qualify. I am doing my best with them. I passed that mech test last week with a b-plus. But the summer classes at the college so far are nothing. I am the only one doing anything. And then going the training base six days a week, I just feel run down."

Karrie nods. "That makes sense." She taps something on the tablet, sets it down, and looks at me. She steeples her hands and doesn't speak for a moment, just watches me. I do my best not to squirm. "Do you realize what today is?" Karrie asks.

I try not to grin. "As long as all of my paperwork went through on time, this weekend should be my rank approval."

Karrie nods. "Today was also the last day to qualify for the next shift to go off-world," Karrie says, pulling up a chart with the requirements. These are all stats I have seen and memorized over the last year.

One-mile run (Earth): 7 min cut off

One-mile run (Zero-G): 9 min cut off

60 sit-ups: 2 Min

60 pushups: 2 Min

Most of these are things that I have already passed, and if I haven't yet, I'm within one to two points of each. Karrie grins. "Over the last few days, the other mentors and I have incorporated the parts of their specialized training requirements into the group sessions."

"Oh? How different are those requirements?" I ask, trying not to sound too eager. Two more taps and the comparisons are up on the screen. The most significant difference is the mile times, the Earth mile is still seven minutes, but the gravity-free mile is a whole minute faster. "Damn," I sit back in my chair. "So, what do I need to change to make the next cut off?" I try to think of where I could scrounge up some extra time to have a few additional training sessions with Karrie.

"Nothing." With one more tap, my stats are up on the screen.

My eyes fall to the gravity run, and my mouth drops open. The needed time was eight minutes—I made it with ten seconds to spare. "That can't be right." I say, "There is no fu—there's no way. How?" I catch myself mid-swear and run over the rest of the sentence, hoping she won't notice.

She shoots me a look that says she did notice but doesn't admonish me. "The harness doesn't lie."

I've read countless news articles about people that have tried to claim they had done better than the harness said, but the harness was always the one the officials looked to. The belt has a ninety-eight point eight percent accuracy.

"So, what do I do now?"

Karrie taps the intercom button and says, "We are ready for you, Staff Sergeant."

A moment later, the man that I saw in the hallway enters the room. I jump to my feet and give a salute.

He nods and settles into the chair next to me. "At ease, Private Gomez. I am Staff Sergeant O'Malley. I work for the Galactic Garrison and assist in the recruitment of the specialized operations

8

division. Sergeant Lima here tells me you have some interest in joining our division."

I nod. "Yes Sir, I have looked at what it offers, and I would like to study in either the Jumper or Fighter lines and Medic practices. I know for sure I want to go as a Medic."

He looks me over. "You are small, but that can be good in a Fighter, and we are always looking for Medics. Too many teams don't take care of their Medic." He looked up at my stats. "Sergeant Lima sent me your paperwork before today's deadline. After reviewing them, I think you would be a great fit for the special op's division. I am sure Sergeant Lima told you that today was the last day to qualify for the next draft. Did she explain anything else?"

Karrie shook her head. "No, Sir, I figured it would be better for you to explain the next steps."

O'Malley nodded. "Right. Well, you may or may not know that we recently moved our special operations base on-world to Houston."

My mouth goes dry. "Houston? It's not right outside New Seattle anymore?"

"No, we found too many from New Seattle ended up not passing the second round of testing, so administration demoted the location to a basic infantry station. That change occurred in the past few weeks. It may not be public knowledge yet."

"Oh, okay, that makes sense," I say, thinking of Sarkus. *If I have to leave for Houston, who will be there for him?* I wonder.

"Is that an issue?" the Sergeant asks.

"Oh, no. No, just surprising, but it's fine."

Karrie, knowing that I'm thinking of my brother, gives me a sad smile.

"Alright," O'Malley continues. "You will be tested once you arrive at Houston to see if you are ready to go off-world. If you pass those tests, you will move up to the space station. Should you fail, we will send you to do more infantry work on-world. You can try for spec ops twice in your career."

I nod as he speaks. Most of the information are things I already know. "Thank you for explaining all of that. My main question now is; when would I have to report for transport?"

"If you are ready to move on, report to the base in New Seattle by 1300 to catch the eco-train to Houston. Before your departure there will be a short test to determine if you really deserve to go to Houston," he says.

"At 1300?" I glance up at the clock on the wall. It gives me less than twenty-four hours to get everything together and get out the door. "Okay, what sort of paperwork would I need to finish?"

"You need your identification cards, and a signature of clearance from your parent or guardian."

I try to keep my face clear, but I share a glance with Karrie. She is just as surprised as me, the thin lines around her mouth in a small frown. "Even if she is over eighteen?"

"Yes, this is required. Will this be an issue?" O'Malley asks, interlacing his fingers.

I hate the way he asks that. 'Will it be an issue?' Each time he does, it feels like a challenge, one I'm not meant to meet, it makes my skin crawl every time.

Karrie gives me a nod, encouraging me to say my piece. I clear my throat. "Honestly, Sir, it may be. I have recently grown out of the foster system; I don't have the best relationship with my foster parent. I don't know if I will get him to sign off. If he is home during the next few days, he most likely will be blackout drunk." I glance at my hands uncomfortably, considering my options, and look up. "I have a meeting after this with my social worker. Could she sign off? She has been helping me get ready for the transition out of his home."

"I think that should work, let me make a quick call to verify." He pulls out his phone and steps outside.

I spin around to face her as soon as he steps out of the room. "Karrie, is this really going to happen?"

"Yes, Ada, you will go off-world! You didn't want to know how you've been doing compared to the mark, but you've ranked past it for weeks now!" She laughs. "I told you! You train with me, and you would make it! I didn't go through all that training for nothing," she says, spinning and pointing to her medals on the wall.

"I know, I know, but I still didn't believe that I could do it. There has just been so much happening."

A soft knock at the door puts a pause in our celebration as O'Malley reenters the room. He glances between Karrie and me. His brow furrowed for a moment in disapproval of our antics. "They said that you could get your main signature from your social worker, but they would also like you to attempt to get a signature from your foster father. Just in case."

I sigh. "Okay, I'll try." I turn to Karrie. "Could you forward the forms to me?"

She nods. "Of course. Thank you for stopping by Sergeant O'Malley. I will make sure Ada is all set and on her way to you soon."

"Thank you, I look forward to seeing you on our base in a few days."

I stand and shake his hand. "You as well, Sir. Thank you for this opportunity." I follow him to the door and slowly close it. Craning my neck, I watch him got down the hall until I know that he is far enough away, and he won't hear me. "Great expanse, Karrie! I am going off-world!"

She squeals and jumps up, rushing around the desk and hugging me. "I am so proud of you, Ada." She taps down the screen, and the projector goes black. "Okay, now we need to talk about what you are going to need to do over the next few days."

The sobering reality of the ticking clock on the wall floods back. "Right. Less than twenty-four before I have to go."

"Exactly. First, they are saying you need to be there at 1300. But that is wrong. You need to be there closer to 1100. The train will leave at 1300. If you get there that late, you will miss the train and be screwed. Especially if they are adding a 'little test'," she says, using air quotes. "How are you going to get to the bus station?"

"I can walk, it isn't too far. I just need to make sure I get up with enough time. Jaxon won't care when I leave. I go scrapping at weird hours all the time." I look at the tiny screen of my watch, and I pull up my bank account and check out my credits. "Do you know where I can get a cheap tablet?"

"Maybe why?" Karrie asks.

"I have a hundred credits. I told Sarkus I would get him one for his birthday or before I go, whichever came first. So, he can still talk to me sometimes." Karrie opens her mouth to say something, but I cut her off. "I've already told him it most likely will only be once a week if that. It's mainly for messenger. And only when I am off-duty."

"Okay, hit up this guy, he should be able to give you a decent enough tablet. Do you have a large backpack you can put your stuff in?" She shoots a contact to my inbox.

I think for a second but shake my head. "No. Jaxon got rid of the duffel bag I moved in with."

Karrie sighs. "Of course, he did. Because why would the man want to keep a decent piece of equipment?" she grumbles, going into her closet and pulling out a medium-sized duffel bag. "You don't need to pack much—basic toiletries, a few outfits for when you are on off-duty. They will give you anything else you need. You will also need your identification cards."

"Thank you," I say, pulling up the list on my watch screen and rotating the dial to scroll through the contents. "You don't know how much all of this means to me. You're helping me so much."

She shrugs. "Don't get sappy on me now, Gomez. You still got a ton of work to do." She glances at the clock. "Go, you don't wanna be late again."

I follow her gaze. "Shit." I jump from my chair. "Thanks, Karrie. Seriously." Then scooping up the bag run for the door. I glance over my shoulder as the door closes and see Karrie smile and shake her head.

Chapter 2

I glance at my watch when I get outside the training center, mentally calculating how long it is going to take to get to the city bus. The stop is three blocks down the road. It's 2:45, and the bus comes at 2:50... and it's at least a seven-minute walk. *Shit shit shit.*

I hike my bag higher on my shoulder and take off down the road. This section of the city is dead around this time, but if I don't get my ass down the road faster, I will get caught up in foot traffic when the school releases for the day.

I weave in and out of the parents waiting in front of the school and dash around the corner. *I can't be late for another appointment,* I stress, spotting the stop not far down the road. I skid to a halt by the sign and glancing back and forth, the bus nowhere in sight.

"Did I miss it?" I wonder, glancing at my watch again. 2:49.

"Did it come early?" I look down the road, trying to see past the sea of school buses floating in front of the school.

"Ah, Miss Ada, just leave your training?" a voice asks before slipping a hand in the crook of my arm.

"Emma!" I jump, turning to the elderly lady at my side.

"Who else would it be? Do you let other old ladies grab your arm?" She grouches as I lead her to the bench next to the sign.

"I don't let anyone grab my arm." I laugh. "I guess if you're here, I haven't missed the bus yet?" I ask, praying that it hasn't come.

"No, Ma'am, here it is." The bus appears around the corner like she magicked it into existence.

"Right, of course, it is," I sigh. I didn't miss the bus again.

"How is your training going?" she asks. "Did you reach your goal yet?"

"Which one?" I laugh as the bus stops in front of us with a whoosh.

We sit near the front, with Emma, on the outside since her stop comes first. "I don't know what your main goal is. Have you made it to that yet?"

I smile. I see Emma about once a week. She is always waiting for the 2:50 bus, while my training times vary throughout the week. But every time she sees me, she asks how my goals are going. It helps to keep me accountable. I never want to tell Emma I've failed to make progress on my goals. I hold back a grin, barely able to contain my excitement. "Emma, I have definitely made progress on my goals this week." I glance around. "Do you want to know a secret?"

"Of course, I do. You should know by now that you should always tell your secrets to old ladies. You never know when we will die, and then your secret will be safe with us."

I laugh and lean in. This close, the smell of Emma's lavender perfume and hairspray fill my nose, and I breathe it in, knowing I will miss these moments very soon. "So, there are only two people that know this so far, one of which is my trainer Karrie, and a staff sergeant."

Emma's eyebrows shoot up. "A staff sergeant? Why were you talking to one of those?"

"Well—" I wiggle my eyebrows "—I may or may not have been smashing my goals. You know Karrie, she tells just enough that you think she told you everything. But she left out just how much I've been improving."

"Well, I won't be here on this Earth much longer! What happened?"

I laugh again. "I won't be either! I passed the test to qualify for the special operations division. I get to go to Houston, then off-world!" I grin with pride.

"You did!" She claps. "Oh my gosh, Ada, this is amazing! We

have to celebrate!" She turns to her bag and digs around, looking up at me and then back down into the depths. "Aha!" She whips out two bits of chocolate candy wrapped in a delicate pink foil. The bus shudders to a stop and the air releases the bus back down to the Earth. Emma fumbles for the chocolate, and I just barely catch it. "See! This is why you would be a great addition to the special operations. Your reflexes are great," Emma coos, patting my arm.

I pop the chocolate into my mouth, savoring the flavor as it melts. "Thank you, Emma, this is a great way to celebrate."

"So—" she grabs my hand; her wrinkled skin feels soft and cool in mine "—when do you leave?"

"Very soon." I smile sadly. "This is probably the last time you'll see me for a long time. I'll be shipping out to the on-Earth base in Houston in a little over a day."

"Does Sarkus know yet?" she asks as the bus slows down again.

"I'll see him in a few hours. I have some other stuff I have to get ready first," I say.

She stands and pulls her purse over her shoulder. She waves to the driver bot at the door before turning back to me. "I wish you the best of luck, my sweet Ada. You will be great. You've been working for this so hard. I am very proud of you." She plants a wet kiss on my hairline. "Make me proud. I expect to still hear from you."

I squeeze her hand. "Thank you."

She heads for the door. "I am serious. I better hear from you, miss. I promise I will actually check my messenger now," she says with a wave before stepping off the bus.

I scooch over to the window and watch as she toddles off down the road. As she slips out of view, I feel a slight pang in my chest. I haven't had a chance to think about the goodbyes I will have to make. Emma's words have warmed me since my parents died—she was one of the few people I could turn to for support. I've only really considered how hard my goodbyes would be with Sarkus, and now that time was coming up.

I glance above my head at the display that informs riders of each stop. Next to the stop number is a rotating information section. I rarely notice the ads, but this slide catches my eye. It's another missing person's report.

Child

Male

Age 7

Name: Yang

Last seen walking home from school

Next to the text is a rotating photo of the boy.

I wonder what happened to him. These reports started last summer, with one boy who was nine, a few months later six-year-old twins. From there, it escalated to the point where it seems like every other day there's a new report. Once I'm an officer, I'll make sure someone looks into this.

The bus stops two more times before I climb off. The New City

Hall stands in the center of New Seattle. Officer's cars fly overhead, and people scurry everywhere, bumping into nearly everyone they pass. I have been coming here since Mom and Dad died three years ago.

I buzz in at the door and hurry to the front desk. "Hi, Adaline Gomez, I'm here to see my social worker Shaelin Denmark. She has an office on the second floor," I say, sliding my ID card across the counter to the secretary bot behind the desk.

I glance around, waiting while the bot scans my ID, and verifies that I do, in fact, have an appointment. "Thank you, A-da-line, your appointment is running be-hind by fifteen minutes. Please use the fourth elevator to head up to the second floor."

I take the ID back and slide it into my bag. "Thank you, have a good day," I say and hurry on to the already stuffed elevator. The doors slide closed, and I lean against the wall as the box flies to the second floor, faster than it ever needed to, in my opinion. I push my way out of the elevator and smoosh past people down the hall. Shaelin has a small office, with a single couch outside for the people waiting. A mother and her small child have taken up the couch, so I slide to the floor beside it and settle in for the wait.

I pull up the list of supplies that Karrie had written up, and the form Sergeant O'Malley had given me. The formal document was one that would release my parent or guardian from any responsibilities, essentially giving me over to the Galactic Garrison for the next year. I guess since I just turned eighteen, it still considers me a child. Which is kind of annoying? This entire process would have been a lot easier if I didn't have to worry about trying to get Jaxon to sign this doc. *Maybe I could forge his signature?* I quickly dash that thought away. Jaxon barely ever wrote anything down. It would be pointless. Come to think of it, I don't know if I had ever seen him actually write anything.

The door opens to Shaelin's office, and she leads a little boy out. The boy reminds me of Sarkus with his short black hair, it's like how Mom used to cut his hair when we couldn't get to the hairdresser. He wears a green polo with thin blue stripes that is just a bit too big on him. His eyes are ringed in red and glassy from tears. I look away as his adult rushes to his side. I know all too well what it is like to feel vulnerable when leaving my social worker's office.

The boy's sniffles echo down the hall as he explains to the adult in his life how his appointment went as they move toward the elevator.

Shaelin watches him go with big, sad eyes. It's something that I both appreciate and hate about her. She is always full of understanding or pity, whether or not I want to feel it. "Hi, Ada," she says, turning back to me, hand on the doorframe of her office. "Come on in. Sorry for the wait. I just have to clean a few things up."

I enter and sit in my usual chair. Two chairs face her desk, I always take the seat on the right, closer to the door. When I have meetings, and Sarkus is here, he always takes the left side, so he can hold my hand, and if I ever need to sign any docs, he doesn't need to let go. "It isn't a problem," I say.

Shaelin goes around the room, quickly tossing toys in a bin. "Right," she says, settling in the chair across from me. "How are things? You look very sprightly today."

"Sprightly?"

"Well, yes, you seem extra happy today. Has something changed for the better at home?" She asks, looking over her glasses. The question is almost a jab at my usual sullen demeanor. I can be a real bitch to her.

"You and I both wish. No. Jaxon is just as much of a lazy drunkard as he was two weeks ago. No, this is something better, bigger, more important." I beam, pride making my heart squeeze with joy. "I passed the basic spec ops test! I can go actually start training, and then I'll be able to claim custody of Sarkus!"

"That is a great, Ada," Shaelin says, but something in the way she sets her shoulders says she isn't as excited for me as she would like to be.

"What?" I ask. "You aren't saying something. Does it have to do with that message you sent me yesterday morning? Why we had to move our appointment up? I am glad we did, cause it definitely helps with stuff, but I feel like something is wrong." She turns the big pity eyes on me.

"Ada, now I don't want you to be upset."

"You realize that whenever you say that to me, I end up absolutely pissed, right?" I say, leaning forward, narrowing my eyes. She can be hard to read sometimes.

"Well, I just want to forewarn you that this may put a damper on your good news." She spins her stylus between her fingers before tucking it behind her ear.

"Already has," I grumble, thinking of Emma's exuberant reaction.

"Well, Sarkus' foster parents came in yesterday. It turns out that Melody is unexpectedly pregnant."

I let the words sink in for a moment. Melody and Bryan Blain are nice people. By far, the kindest foster parents Sark has had so far. They have two other children. One is Sarkus' age, while the other is around fourteen. "So, they're giving him up because they want to make room for a new baby in a few months," I say, my voice coming out deadpan. But inside, I am *screaming*. I can't believe that they would do this. They had said they would be willing to keep him for another year at least.

"That is correct," Shaelin says, waiting for me to react more.

"When are they kicking him out, then?"

She sighs. "They aren't kicking him out. They have put in for him to have a transfer."

"Well, how long until that transfer gets processed?" I ask.

"I've already approved it. He moves tomorrow afternoon," she says, passing a tablet across the desk to me.

I scan the doc quickly, already knowing what most of the information would be, having been through plenty of my own transfers. I would gladly go through twenty transfers if it meant he wouldn't have to go through one more. "He is moving out of the city?" I ask, looking up. "I thought we made it clear on his paperwork he had to stay in New Seattle?"

Shaelin takes the tablet back from me. "Yes, and if I had another family who would take him, I would send him there in a heartbeat. But most either want babies or have a track record of being like Jaxon."

I growl my disappointment but don't argue anymore. "Will they allow my visitation rights before he moves? I leave in less than twenty-four hours for Houston. I told him I would do my best to say goodbye to him before I went, whenever it happened."

She shakes her head. "They don't want you seeing him. He is already very upset, and Melody thinks seeing you would make it worse."

"Well, can you at least call her and let her know what is happening now? Maybe she will make an exception because we will both be leaving New Seattle?" I plead. "I need to see him before I go. I don't—" I stop and take a breath. "I don't know when I will be

24

Earth side again if I make it through the training. I don't want him to think I've abandoned him."

She reaches across the table and writes a note. "Yes, I will call her after we are through here. And I will send you a message as soon as I have an answer. Just promise me you won't try to sneak over to see him."

"I won't," I lie. "I know I need to respect their choices." It's bullshit. "They have to do what's best for their family."

She nods slowly, as if she doesn't quite believe that I am being agreeable. "Yes, well, what do you need to do for Spec Ops?"

I email her the doc. "I need you to sign this. They want me to attempt to get Jaxon's signature tonight. I am going to try, but I doubt it is going to happen."

She skims it before grabbing a stylus. She signs below the line labeled guardian and writes the social worker below it. She taps around her tablet before sending me a copy of my birth certificate. "I see you also need this?"

"Oh, thank the expanse you have one. I wasn't sure what file I saved it in."

"Well, they should be able to access a copy of that in their Database, but you never know when a file will corrupt."

"Yeah. I mean, at least they keep hard copies of all legal documents, even if we aren't allowed to use paper for anything else."

"Hard copy is always better," Shaelin agrees. "Now, can I do anything else for you today? I mainly wanted to make sure I talked to you in person about Sarkus."

I shake my head and stand up. "I don't think so, I just needed your approval to go. Especially if I can't get Jaxon to sign."

"Do what you can, but don't push him. The last thing you need is him taking a swing at you right before you leave. Because that paperwork *will* take you more than twenty-four hours to get together." She strides to the door and opens it for me. "Good luck, Ada." She pulls me into a stiff hug.

"Thanks, Shaelin. Please take care of Sarkus and let me know as soon as you can of any changes in the future. I want to get him out of this system as fast as possible."

Chapter 3

My bus ride back to the apartment is long and quiet, giving me plenty of time to plan what to say to Jaxon. I get off the bus just up the road from "home" around seven, well after rush hour traffic. My stomach is screaming for food at this point. And the granola bar wrappers in the bottom of my bag are a tease. Though there likely isn't going to be much to eat waiting for me in the apartment either.

Peering up at the windows of my apartment high above, it looks like no one is home, but you never know with Jaxon. I honestly don't know how he passed the tests to be a foster parent. His ex-girlfriend Leslie had at least been a decent human. But she deserved better, and she left within four months of me moving in. It was a rough couple of months after she left, Jaxon was even more moody and thought everything was a personal attack on his character. Not that he has much to begin with.

I grab the rungs of the fire escape and haul myself up to the first level. I figured out pretty quickly when I moved in with Jaxon that it was best to put all my things down and remove any trace of my day before approaching him. Today, I'll need a different tactic.

I quickly and quietly scale the stairs to the third-floor window. I wipe my hands off on a towel I've tucked in a small box. The fabric is stained a burnt copper color from the flakes of iron on the rungs. I replace the towel to its nook and turn back to the window. My life would have been ten times easier if the landing led right into my bedroom, but no, this window leads into the hallway right outside my room. It looks down the hall to the living room and Jaxon's big armchair, where ninety percent of the time, he is passed out drunk.

I stand at the edge of the window frame and peer down the hall, ready to jump back and run down a flight of stairs if I need to. Jaxon hates that I come in this way. He has tried to lock the window in the past, but I figured out a way to undo the lock from the outside. Great for sneaking in, shitty for home security. He isn't smart enough to nail it shut.

I never know what sort of mood Jaxon will be in when I get home. He has gotten a lot worse lately now that I'm eighteen. Nearly every conversation we have is him asking when I will be leaving now that I have aged out of the foster system. My answer has been the same every time. As soon as possible. He technically could have kicked me out on my birthday, however the contract he signed when I got transferred stated when I left it had to be moving to another stable environment. Because I haven't had anywhere to go, he would have been hit with a nasty fine if anything had gone wrong. Besides, the lazy ass wants to keep me around because he can't take care of himself.

I peer down the hall. Jaxon lays in his chair, feet splayed out in front of him, and he loosely holds a can of beer. Keeled over to his side, I can't see his face. I grip the frame and slowly raise it a few inches. I crouch below the window and strain to hear any noise coming from the apartment. Aside from the muffled voices from the television, all is quiet. I can't hear him snoring. Keeping my eyes on his legs for any sign of movement, I lift the frame the rest of the way open, thankful yet again that I remembered to oil the frame and hide any squeaks. I quickly climb through and shut it behind me. I spin back to the hallway, take the two strides into my room, and close the door with a soft click.

I press my ear flat against the door and listen for thirty beats. I sigh, hearing nothing, and sink to the squeaky mattress of my bed. My room is small. I'm pretty sure on the floor plan it was a large closet for the master bedroom across the hall. But when I was placed here, Jaxon had already furnished it for me. So, kind of him. I have the bed, a standing lamp since there are no overheads, and a dresser. There's no window. That was the biggest hint to me that it was a closet. That and the fact that I can't lock the room from the inside, but he can from the outside. I barely have space to open the bottom drawer of the dresser. But I don't have that many clothes, anyway.

I empty the drawers of the dresser, laying the few clothing items I have out on the bed. By now, most of the clothes don't fit anymore or are so worn out I don't see any point in taking them with me. My go-to clothes are the green cargo pants I wear ninety percent of the time, and a few black shirts; black is easier to layer and doesn't show wear and tear as quickly. I wear something until it's see-through.

Socks, bras, and underwear all make their way into the bag too. I lift the false bottom I installed in the of the drawer and pull out my sentimental items: a necklace my mother used to wear, but I never have for fear Jaxon would pawn it, one of my father's ties, and a single photo of my family screen-printed on a piece of sheet metal a few inches wide. I lay them between my clothes for padding and turn to my bed.

I lift the mattress and pull out the bag of food and a few bits of garbage I stashed underneath, I shove the trash in a pocket of the duffle bag to dispose of later and sort through the food. I probably won't be able to take it with me. But I need something for dinner tonight, and breakfast. *Maybe Sarkus can use some of it?* Tossing a stale granola bar and other expired snacks in the garbage pocket. Lastly, I pull my pillow from its thin case. I needed a way to hide any credits I earned scrapping from Jaxon. I learned the hard way he liked to go through my stuff. So, I created a small slit in the pillow that you can't see when it is in the fabric case. I shake the pillow and out falls about fifty credits. I split a pair of socks and shove most of the money in them, putting some in my backpack to have handy.

I press my ear to the door. The show sounds louder. Which means Jaxon is probably up now. I pull the form up on my watch and take a deep breath. *He needs to sign it. But if he refuses to, I have Shaelin's signature,* I remind myself.

"Hey, Jaxon," I say, coming into his domain. My room is neat and clean, mainly due to the lack of things, but the living room is trashed. I step carefully around piles of cans and bottles trying not to topple the precarious stacks. I look at the bits of metal, wondering if it would be worth staying to clean them up a bit—I might be able to sell some of them for scraps to get a few more credits for Sarkus.

"What do you want, Ada?" Jaxon says, crushing the can in his hand it sloshes across his lap and onto the already stained carpet. "Shit. Ada, get me another." He slurs.

I hold my breath in the kitchen. The smell of rotten food is overpowering. I can't clean it. He thinks I would be too loud, and I honestly wouldn't know where to start. I pull open the fridge. Like usual, it is crammed full of cans of alcohol, but I managed to squeeze a few containers of food in the back, none of which I can grab now.

I bring him back the can and stand off to the side as he opens the drink with a crack and a hiss and takes several large gulps.

"So, you know how my birthday was a few weeks ago," I say. It's a statement. We know it occurred (see above all the conversations about me leaving.)

"Yeah, when did Shaelin say I could kick you out?" Jaxon asks, turning back to the game on the TV. I start to answer, but he screams at the bots fighting on the screen. "Fuckin' A' they made him last week! Why did you think you could beat him? His tech is brand new!"

I wait until the round is over. "So, kicking me out isn't quite the wording I would use, but—" I tap a few buttons and send him the doc for him to sign "—if you sign this doc, I'm released from your care. You claim no rights to my welfare. It would all be over."

He picks up his cracked tablet from a side table and scans the doc. He blinks a few times, trying to focus on the small print. "So, where'd you get this?" He reads it again, "Really? The Galactic Garrison, you think you are good enough for them? They really want you?" He tosses the tablet to the couch on the other side of the room.

I shrug. "I guess so." I leave out the part about me already passing the tests or the fact that he knows I enlisted and have been training for nearly three years now. "Sign the doc, and even if they kick me out, I won't be your problem anymore. I'll be on my own." I cross my arms, waiting.

He scans me up and down. "No. No, I won't sign it." He turns the TV back up.

A spark of anger bursts in my chest. "What? Gonna get all sentimental now on me?" I say, my voice dripping with sarcasm.

"No. I think it's a waste of time. They won't even let you out of New Seattle, let alone off the world. There's no way they'd let you in."

"Well, that's your opinion. I'd like to get theirs."

"What's the catch?"

"There is no catch. If you'd read the damn doc—"

"Don't you swear at me, bitch!" Jaxon says, launching the half-full can at my head. I duck away, and it ricochets off the wall spraying my back with cold alcohol. "I said I'm not signing it. Find another way to get out of my house. I want you gone by the end of the week."

"Sign the doc, and I'll be gone in twenty-four hours," I repeat.

"I'm not fucking signing the doc. Get the fuck out of my face. Get out."

I retreat down the hall and slam the door. I slide down the door to the floor and rub my eyes. I knew that would happen. I wipe off my watch, now soaked in alcohol, and tap out a message to Shaelin.

ADA: I tried to get him to sign. He threw a beer can at my head. Told me it was a waste of time because I won't be good enough to get in. Said he wants me gone by the end of the week. I guess it is a good thing I'll be gone tomorrow.

I hit send and lay back, waiting for her to respond.

SHAELIN: Did he hit you with the can? Let me know if you need any support, I can have someone come around. I'm sorry Ada. I will send a message to the Galactic Garrison and let them know you were unable to get his signature.

SHAELIN: Still waiting to hear from Melody.

I scroll over to the doc from Sergeant O'Malley. It lists some benefits and flaws of being in the military. I scroll down looking to see if there is anything else, I need to get before I leave, but this signature was it. I glance at my duffel where I know a pile of money sits, though maybe not enough for a decent tablet for Sarkus. I need to sell a few more items.

I do one last check under and around my bed, making sure nothing else is left in my room, before heading out into the hall. I don't worry about sneaking out, I walk right out the door. When Jaxon calls to me, I keep walking, knowing he will follow for a minute, screaming. He will get fined for breaking quiet hours and for some health code violations while acting as a guardian to a foster child. I grin and speed up. *Serves him fucking right. Good luck with that, buddy.*

Chapter 4

The building across the street has been abandoned for years now. The signs listing it for demolition have faded, the dates long past, making the entire building a scrap heap in its own right. I shove aside the metal panel I keep in front of the door and move inside the dark interior. In the corner closest to the door is a pile of scrap metal that I've collected over the last few weeks. This building was picked over long ago, so I've felt pretty confident no one would come through again.

I sift through the pieces of metal, appraising each by its color, thickness, and overall look. I have pipes, pieces of hardware from outdated machines, and sheets of metal cut into weird shapes by prior owners. Most of the parts have bits of rust, but one sheet of copper catches my eye. I've been saving this piece to sell when it got colder. Most people still use copper piping, even though the element is so rare now. When it gets colder here in New Seattle, pipes burst all the time, leaving people scrambling for the metal. I was saving it, but since I am leaving, it will probably get me the most cash now.

I slide the pliable metal away from the wall. The piece is three-feet by two-feet and will probably get me somewhere around 175 credits. I just have to hope that plus the other money in my bag will be enough for a tablet for Sarkus. I don't have long until The Market closes. I thread my arms through the handles of the duffle bag, turning it into a rough backpack that digs into my shoulders and carry the piece of copper in front of me.

I hurry through the streets. It's dark—the time of day where you don't want to linger. The shadows grow long, and the floating solar streetlight flickers to life. But this is also the perfect time for a sale.

When I was little, I would go out with Dad, a bundle of metal sheets and pipes between us as we headed to The Market. Mom and Dad would spend all day when Sarkus and I were in school searching for metal, and Dad and I would go sell it while Mom stayed home with my brother. He taught me all his for tricks to make the haggling process quick and to the point, every time playing to my advantage.

Then Mom and Dad died. I was watching Sarkus at home, but we heard the blast. Gang violence was and is nothing out of the ordinary, so we didn't think anything of it. We had just gotten off a video call; they had just finished a sale and were coming home. They were meant to be back in five minutes. Sarkus and I had made cookies, and they were excited to get the cookies while they were hot.

Someone must've thought our car was someone else's. It was four hours before I called the police. Twelve hours after the blast when the officer came to our door. Sarkus and I woke up to the officer standing over us in the living room. On the table was a plate of cold uneaten cookies.

I started selling the rest of the scraps Dad had in the stash two weeks later. At first, people didn't take me seriously. But they recognized me. A lot of the sales I got that year were pity sales. I had to be careful though—the foster parent Sarkus, and I lived with didn't like me going into The Market. But we didn't want to ask for anything. The third time they caught me with scraps was when they had us re-homed. They screamed at me for getting into gang violence. But I never sold to the gangs. Not at first. The next home was pretty much the same; no one understood my need to keep selling. I didn't really understand it until recently. I needed to do it because it made me feel close to Dad.

I have to make this last sale a good one. One that will pay off for years to come.

I turn into the dark alley and pass under the arch. Blasters power up nearby, a threat and a promise. Not everyone who sells in the Market is affiliated with the mob. But the Market is owned by the mob, and the mob must protect its property, which includes the vendors that pay them to be there.

A monitor flashes, and my face appears on the screen. "Ada Gomez," I say, waiting for the voice tech to recognize me.

"Welcome, Ada." It intones, and I hear the weapons power down. "Is there anyone you would like to meet with today?"

The monitor lowers to eye level, and a list of other patrons of The Market show up on the screen. "Tortie, I want to meet with Tortie." The other names flash away, and Tortie glows white. They send the message to him, and when my request is met with an answer, the name turns green.

The monitor pings. "Tortie has agreed to meet with you. He is in Bay 9. He will expect you in five minutes. You will have ten minutes for your sale. Do you accept these terms for your meeting? Please note that this does not guarantee a sale."

"I agree to the terms," I say, and wait for the message to be passed along.

"Welcome to The Market, Ada." The monitor lifts away, and a doorway slides open. I hurry down the passage and into the general sales area. Bay 9 is, of course, the farthest away from the entrance. But Tortie would do that. He and his cronies need time to get out when The Market is raided. On a quiet day, it can still take up to ten minutes to get through to Bay 9, and today it's packed.

I force my way to the edge of the large room and push my way along the wall, passing the other bays. Vendors bark at me as I shove behind their stalls, but I just keep going. I can see Bay 9 with its glowing number over the heads of everyone. Luckily, the closer I get, the more the crowds thin out. This is where the pricier sales go down and few people can afford to be down here anymore. I could quickly get fifty, maybe even one hundred credits for my sheet of copper in the general sales area, but a sheet this big is a rarity. Something I know Tortie will value. And he won't try to swing any bullshit with me, because he knows I won't with him.

I am passing Bay 7 when I see the first of Tortie's men. Their skin is a deep orange—in the right lighting, it looks like it could just be a bad tan, but their eyes, vertical slits like a goat, give them away. They glue themselves to me like shadows. Protecting both me and the item for sale, while also appraising me and whether or not I'm a threat to Tortie. I recognize the gentleman who flanks my right side and nod as he approaches. The guy to my left is new, jumpy. His hand hovers at hip height, ready to grab his blaster. "Your buddy gonna shoot me?" I ask, keeping my gaze locked on the sign for Bay 9. Out of my peripheral, I see the one I recognize wave the other down.

"Sorry, Ada, he doesn't know a lot of people 'round here yet." I nod and try to pick up the pace. I'm running out of time. I hear a squawk and the sound of Tortie speaking in his native Plutonian. The guard responds, then calls to me. "Ada, he will wait for you. No rush."

I nod and take a deep breath, slowing my pace to a brisk walk. My heart is pounding as if I just finished my gravity run. Tortie expects a lot from his clients. Whether he and my father were friends, I still need to prove myself to him to get this sale. Bay 9 looms overhead, and I slowly raise my hand to the sensor. It scans my palm print before blinking green, and the door slides open. Knowing the protocol, I wait for my shadows to step behind me. One takes my duffle bag to search, while the other takes the sheet of metal from me. I step forward into the room and put my hands up. A third guard in the room steps forward and pats me down.

"Ada! Baby, how are you?" Tortie calls from his seat on the far end of the room.

I smile, "Hi, Tortie, I'm doing pretty good today."

"Blowing off another guardian's rules?" he asks, waving off the guard. "She's clean. Ada would know better than to bring any dirty shit in here." He says, "Right, Ada, baby?" The words are sweet but carry an edge of malice. People have approached me more than once to snoop on Tortie. I let him know every time, and he took care of it. I don't know exactly how he and Dad connected, but Tortie is a powerful ally. I don't do runs for him, or snoop for him, but I will tell him if people come to pry. Does that make me a rat? Maybe. But it keeps people away.

"Of course, Sir, I don't deal in that," I reply, glancing at the guard going through my bag. He holds up the wad of credits I put inside. "If any of that goes missing, can I clock him?" I ask Tortie as he waves in the guard's direction. The Plutonian glances down and quickly shoves the money back in the bag, and Tortie and I laugh.

"Ada, baby, come, come, sit with me."

I slide onto the couch and sit next to Tortie. He puts an arm around my shoulder and draws me close to his side. His skin is cold. I hate the way it feels. He does this every time I come in. It makes my skin crawl. But I know better than to resist him. I need him. Especially with me leaving. I need that layer of protection to cover Sarkus.

My watch buzzes, and I glance down at it, a message from Shaelin.

SHAELIN: Update on visitation. The family said no. I'm sorry. Melody insists that it would be too upsetting for Sark.

I sigh and sit back. "Shit."

"What's wrong, bug?" Tortie asks, continuing with the pet names. He blinks a few times, his goat-like pupil dilating.

"Sark is being moved again, and the family doesn't want to give me visitation before I go," I say, trying to keep my voice neutral.

"Go? Where are you going? Do you know where he will be moved to?" Tortie turns more to me, thankfully moving his arm off my shoulders.

"I don't know where he is going yet. Shaelin said he was

assigned but didn't say where, just that it would be outside of New Seattle. I'll be going to Houston, then hopefully off-world." My frown turned to a grin. "I made it through the first step of getting into the program." My smile falters. "I just hope that my plans work out, and I'll get to see Sarkus soon."

"Why don't they want you to see him?"

I shift. "I think it's mainly, so he isn't super upset when I leave, coupled with the fact that he is being re-homed. It was tough when he was little, but he has been better now that he's older. He used to make himself sick. But I *am* going to see him tonight. I *need* to see him. I promised him I would say goodbye."

"Well, I am proud of you. If you want, we can keep an eye on him while you're gone." He waves over one of his guards and tells him something in Plutonian. "We can put a tail on him if you want, give you updates where he's going if they don't give you any."

"I would appreciate that," I say. "When I see him tonight, I'll let him know that he may see some of your guys. I think he'll remember who you are."

"Good. Now, what brings you here? You aren't here just to tell me you passed a few tests," Tortie asks. I nod and point at the sheet of copper. He gets off the couch and takes the copper sheet from his man. "This is a beautiful piece. What are you selling it for?"

I tuck my feet up, feigning confidence. "I wanted to get it out of my stash, it would be a shame if someone stole that while I was gone, but using the credits in there—" I nod at the bag "—and the credits I make from this I am going to get Sarkus a tablet so we can communicate when I go off-world." I drape my arms on the back of the couch, mimicking the relaxed position of the Plutonian mobster. "That is my next stop, I was given a contact."

Tortie grins. "Well, I can fix that, no problem No need to see anyone else." He snaps his fingers, says something in his garbled native tongue, and a few moments later, someone brings him a tablet. "Here, give this to little Sarkus." He hands it to me. "For real, my gift to you for passing the test." He pauses and turns back to his man. "This is clean, right? One of the new ones?" They nod, and he grins. "Good."

I'm dumbfounded for a second. I turn the tablet over and over in my hand, glancing at the serial number on the back—It's one of the newest releases. "Wow, that—thank you, you really don't have to, but I truly appreciate it. Thank you. I don't know what to say."

"Say no more, babe, it's a gift to you. From your favorite Plutonian." Pulling the tablet from its case I see this thing is in mint condition. The charging pad doesn't even have that many scratches, like it hasn't been used at all. "Now, what do you want for that piece?" Tortie asks, turning the sheet of metal over in his burnt orange hands.

I look over the piece again. "I'm looking for a hundred and seventy-five credits."

"One seventy-five, really?" Tortie says. He looks at one of his men. They cock their head to the right. He turns back to me. "One fifty."

I scoff. "One hundred and fifty, really? Oh no, for that, I'm bumping it to two hundred." I lean forward on my knees, enjoying the rise and fall of the bartering game.

"Hm. Nah, let's do one hundred eighty." He says, stroking a coarse beard.

I wave him away, and he scowls. "You do realize that winter is coming to New Seattle in just a few months? Think of all the burst pipes, all the repairs that could be made with that single piece, let alone welding it with others. It's worth at least two hundred credits."

He nods along. "Okay, baby girl, I see what you're saying. I see you." He hands the copper sheet back to his guard. "Okay, okay, one hundred ninety."

"Done!" I put a hand out, and we shake on it. Someone comes by with the contract on a tablet, and I quickly fill out the information and sign it. While I do, Tortie waves a hand, and one guard takes the piece of copper away, the other transferring the credits to my account. I twist the dial on my watch and view my account—the numbers on my account rise by the agreed one hundred and ninety credits. "Always a pleasure doing business with you, Tortie."

He leans back against the couch and takes a big swig of his drink. "Uh-huh. You are going to make me go broke, girl."

44

I laugh and toss my ponytail over my shoulder. "That may be, but that's because I always bring the good stuff that you can't pass up."

The Male growls, but this time there is no anger in it. "You know, sweetie, you are so right. I can't even be mad." He pulls me into a hug. "You know your father would be so proud of you?" I feel a lump form in my throat and nod. The Plutonian laughs. "Well, he may not have been too happy to see you coming to me to sell shit. But you best be sure he and your mama would be proud to see their baby girl going places. I know I am." He plants his cold lips on my forehead, in an attempt to emulate the human kiss. "I know I am. You are going places, baby girl. Just don't get so good at your job that you get a stick up your ass whenever I call."

"Never," I laugh. "Thanks, I'll see you around."

"Yeah, you will. Good luck and tell Sarkus I will see him around too. We'll keep an eye on him for you." I give Tortie another quick hug, nod at the guards, and head back out the door.

Chapter 5

I look at the screen of my watch, the message icon pulses. I scroll over to the notification again.

SHAELIN: Update on visitation. The family said no. I'm sorry. Melody insists that it would be too upsetting for Sark.

I look up the road to the apartment complex with Sarkus inside.

The cameras around the complex aren't the best. There are a series of blind spots, I press myself into the brick wall across the street as long as I stay along the wall, I'll stay out of the camera's sights. Keeping my eye out for cameras, I turn away from the gatehouse. If the family said that I can't see Sarkus, they most likely told the gatehouse not to let me in. They've done it in the past. I don't know what Melody's problem is with me. I guess I should've seen this as a red flag.

This gated housing facility is beautiful. But like most things that come with the upper crust, there are cracks in the armor. The chink in this piece of armor is a broken section in the back wall of the fence line. I found it just after Sarkus moved in. The corner of the wall had fallen out into the street, making a small pile of bricks for me to climb. This back section isn't traversed often by the public, so if it was ever reported, the community didn't care enough to fix it.

I move through the edge of the hole and glance around. This side of the wall has no cameras because why would they ever expect someone to actually get in.

Sarkus' house is right here by the corner. Which again makes it super easy to get a hold of him. But I climb the fire escape quickly and press myself against the wall next to the sliding door. The last thing I need is for the motion sensor to go off and the door to open. It wouldn't be the first time. I will never understand why Brian doesn't lock the back door.

The light in Sarkus' room is on. I lean out toward his window. I can't hear Melody or Brian moving around the room, but I hear quiet piano music. Meaning he has been put to bed and is likely reading quietly. I reach out and tap the window lightly a few times and wait a few minutes, my heartbeat pounding in my ears. I want to speak to him, but my stomach rolls at the idea of telling him I am leaving. I tap the glass again, three times leaning close to the glass I hear a faint rustle from inside. The curtain shifts, and my brother's little fluffy head looks out the window.

I tap the side of the glass, and his head snaps in my direction.

His eyes grow wide, and a massive smile breaks across his face. He reaches up and taps the button next to the window. It brushes open with a soft hiss. "Ada!" He reaches his hand out to me. "I thought Melody said you weren't coming today," he says, his big brown eyes like saucers.

My heart constricts. *You have to tell him. You promised you would tell him.* I smile tightly and press a squeeze into his fingers. "Why do you think I'm on the fire escape versus coming in the front door?" I glance behind me to the door. Sarkus jumps, looking over his shoulder to his bedroom door. "Hang on," he whispers loudly. He jumps down from the window and hurries to his door, pressing a button to lock it from the inside. He tiptoes back across the carpeted floor. He leans out the window, catching my hand again.

"Good thinking. How are you?" I ask.

He leans farther out the window, "I am kinda sad, cause I wanted to stay here. I like it here. But I understand. I'm not actually their son, and they need my room for the baby when it comes." He looks around his space like he is trying to memorize every bit of it.

My heart squeezes at his words. My little twelve-year-old brother shouldn't be used to this and understand that his space isn't his own. He shouldn't have to feel like his time anywhere is temporary. "I am so sorry, Sarkus." He rubs his eyes. "Buddy, part of the reason that I'm here is also not very fun. I mean, it's good, but it's also sad for us."

He looks down at our hands, then back up at me. He smiles, but his eyes bubble with tears. "You got in, didn't you?" I nod. "I—" He stops and sniffles. "—I am happy for you, Ada. You wanted to do this for a long time since Mom and Dad… yeah." He pulls his hand away from me and disappears inside his room. The curtain falls back into place, obscuring my view.

"Wait, Sarkus!" All I can hear for a moment is his heavy breathing as he tries to control his emotions. I lean back against the wall, letting my head tilt to look at the stars. "Sarkus?" I ask quietly.

He stays inside, and he blows his nose before coming back. "I just needed to blow my nose," he doesn't look me in the face or put his hand back out to me. "So, what happens now?" he asks, hugging himself.

I sigh. "Life has horrible timing sometimes, bud. Let me just say that, okay? I found all of this out today. I'm sorry this is happening all at once." He nods and rubs his nose. I wait until he meets my eyes, waiting until I know he's ready. "I passed the test today, and I have to head out tomorrow morning."

He finally reaches out to me again. "Where do you have to go?"

I squeeze his hand. "I'll be leaving from the base here in New Seattle, they have a train scheduled already for Houston. If I make it through that round of testing, that is when I will go off-world to train on the space station." I lower my voice even more. "Remember what Shaelin said last year, as long as I get a job with a salary, I can have you come stay with me. It will be a few months at least, maybe a year, but I promise Sark, I'm going to work so hard. We will stay together. We may have to move around a lot, but you'll be with me. That'll be okay right?" He nods. "I love you."

Tears roll down his cheeks. "I love you too, Ada."

"Now." I drop his hand and start digging around in the bag. "I'm not leaving you completely alone. I got this for you. I set up the apps you'll need to talk to me. I get one for enlisting. You can message me. I'm not sure how often I'll be able to answer, but sometimes we could video chat. I won't be far away."

He hugs the tablet to his little chest, arms squeezing the metal. "I promise to keep it safe. I love you, Ada. Thank you."

"I love you too, Sarkus." I turn and look to the stars, searching for the moving lights. There. "Can I show you something?" I motion for him to bring the tablet closer

"Yeah?" He says, following my hand as I tap the tablet on and move to one of the apps.

It takes a moment but the starry sky appears on the screen, clearer than any stars we could see above us. "You see that ball of light that's moving across the sky kind of fast?" I ask, trailing my hand across the screen, following the trajectory.

"Yeah? I see it," he traces its path too.

"That's the space station. I'll be up there soon. It goes around the Earth several times a day. If you can find that, you can find me."

I watch him as he follows the space station until it disappears off screen. He tries to follow it zooming out the screen and quickly sliding it over, but it is already gone. I glance over my shoulder again at the sliding glass door. "I have something else. You will really have to be careful with this. Only use it if you need it, okay?"

He looks at my bag, apprehensive. "What? What is it?"

I pull out the money from my backpack. "Here, I got this from scrapping, it isn't much. I really wish I could give you some more, but as soon as I start getting paid for my service, I will wire you money."

He counts out the 200 credits I pulled from my bank account. "Ada, what would I need this for?"

I squeeze his hand. "I don't know. But that's the point. I don't know what will happen to us over the next few months, but I want to make sure you're set. That you will still be able to do all the clubs you want to in school or to buy ice cream, whatever you want." I smile, and my eyes start to burn, but I don't want to cry in front of him. "I want to stay longer, but we shouldn't push your luck. I should go. You need to get some sleep. You have a big day tomorrow."

He puts the tablet and the credits down and reaches as far out as he can. I can't hold him as tight as I want to but my shirt still grows wet from his sniffles. I look up to the stars, hoping that this is the right thing to do. I stay like that until he releases me.

"I love you so much, Ada."

Deleted Draft Email 11:48:04   August 10th, 2228

Hey bud,

I love you a lot. I wish I could help you without having to leave our planet. I slept on a bench last night. It wasn't the first time I did. It probably won't be the last. But I would do it again and again if it meant that you wouldn't have to. I am so sorry about Melody and Brian. This is the worst time for me to leave. And I am sorry I don't want you to be stuck like this anymore. Moving from home to home. You deserve so much more. It's my fault we aren't together now. I promise to work as hard as I can every day when I do this training. The harder I work, the sooner I'll see you again.

Chapter 6

I made the train with no issues this morning. My back is stiff from the bench outside the train station I called home for the night. My ticket was more expensive than I would have assumed for a trip to the base, but it was a necessary evil. It was only a forty-five-minute ride to the army compound outside of the city. It still has an old-fashioned look from when all our battles were on Earth. It has high brick walls, turrets, and barbed wire fence but it's been retrofitted for space fighting with laser cannons and enough solar panels to power the entire city and thus had enough capacity to power the jump platforms and a series of tunnels that branch out several kilometers around the base. Or so I read in the articles I found on the way over.

The sun was near to its zenith when the train finally buzzed to a stop right outside of the compound. I'm one of only three that get off the train and the only girl.

I hold my head high; I have a right to be here. The two boys are broad, both wear obnoxiously tight t-shirts. I never understood why guys wear shirts that look like they will tear off their bodies if they move wrong.

"Oh, babe, I think you got off on the wrong stop. The mall was a few back, don't want to miss the meeting with your girlfriends." One guy says as he fist bumps the other. They push in front of me and stride through the doors.

Right, this should be fun. I pass through the gate and stop behind them.

"Name?" a guard at the gate asks, lifting three gate keys on lanyards. He spots me and skips the two guys. "I assume you are Adaline Gomez?"

I take the key from him and slip it over my neck. "Yes, Sir." I fall into attention, waiting for orders.

The sentry guard looks me over and nods. "Right, Gomez, please go through this gate. They will begin your intake procedure."

I nod and push my way through the two Males, who don't step out of the way. I smile at the scowls they shoot in my direction as I go by, annoyed that I could go right past them. "Sorry, boys, I think the bar was a few stops back. You don't want to miss your meeting with your boys," I simper. I step up to the sliding door and wait until it buzzes open, and closes behind me.

I enter a long room. Benches are lining the edge, and there are three piles of shirts, pants, and boots. I quickly grab the shoes and try to find the pair closest to my size. I can deal with a shirt that is too big and possibly pants, but boots? That would be a nightmare. I find the smallest pair of pants and a shirt. Before the other two come in, I strip down and pull the new clothes on. I shove my personal items in the bag and work on lacing the boots.

"What?" One says, grabbing one of the remaining pairs of boots. "My feet won't fit into these!"

"A small shirt? What do they expect?"

I read somewhere that this was one of the first tests. They put only a few items that would fit some. Your options were to either grab what would fit you fast and get out and deal with the wrong size or fight for something better. I am smaller than both guys, they probably have a good forty pounds of muscle and five to six inches on me. I inch my way down to the next door while they argue over who should get what pair of pants. The door whooshes open behind me, and I turn and step through.

A stern-looking woman sits at a card table. "Ah, Miss Gomez, come sit. We shall continue with your processing. I hope you could find clothing to your liking?"

"Yes, Ma'am," I say, sitting across from her.

"This process is private; we will lock the two other recruits out until it is their turn, so please speak freely." I nod, and she clicks on a file. There is a small photo of me holding Sarkus in the corner. It looks definitely looks like a surveillance shot. I blush at the sight of it and the idea that someone has been watching me. "Is your full name Adaline Sierra Gomez?"

"Yes, ma'am."

"And you prefer to go by Ada?" she says, sliding a finger across a line of text.

"That is correct, Ma'am, I have always gone by Ada."

She writes a note. "Is there any particular reason for that?"

"I feel like Adaline makes me sound very prim. Nothing about me or my life has ever been prim or proper. So, the name doesn't feel like it's mine."

She writes another scribble in the corner of my file. "And you are eighteen years of age, and have one brother, Sarkus Manuel Gomez, age twelve? And your parents died in 2225."

I feel a lump form in my throat. "Yes, Ma'am, that is all correct."

She sits back, placing her stylus on the table. "Now, remind me why you want to be in the Garrison and why you specifically want to get off-world and do special operations training?"

I pull a hand through my ponytail, realize I am doing it, and push my hand into my lap. "Well, Ma'am, you see, Sarkus and I—my brother—we were put into the foster care system when our parents died. We were together for a while but—I got us separated. My actions—my social worker decided I put Sarkus in too many high-risk situations—I got money as a scrapper. My biggest fear is my brother being taken away from me and not knowing where he went. Now that I'm eighteen and have aged out of the system, I want to get a steady job and take him far away from what happened to us. Our parents were scrappers, but that isn't consistent; I can't use that as proof of income. So, I want to get a job, a good job, and bring Sarkus far away from all of our issues. I hope that the Galactic Garrison can give me the skills to do that and to give my brother and me a better life."

The woman eyes me before pressing a button on the side of the table. "She checks out. No lies here. Pass her on."

I look up, and a light on the panel next to the third door flashes to my right. "What would have happened if I didn't pass?"

"That door," she says, pointing at the door behind her, "would have taken you right back to the train station." She points at the door she first showed. "You better hurry. They'll be waiting for you."

I want to stay and ask who will be waiting for me, but the faster I move, the faster I will get an answer. I step up to the door, and nothing happens. Looking at the panel I see a small opening, about three inches long. I look at my ID card; it has my name across it and a bar code. I pull the card off my neck and slide it in the hole. The light goes dark for a second before flashing green. The door slides open a moment later. It leads to a small, dark, circular room. It is a dimly lit elevator. I step in and stand on the circle in the middle of the floor.

Another light flashes, and a robotic voice says, "Please listen for instructions. Please hold your arms out at a ninety-degree angle, and your feet on the edges of the circle on the floor." A light flashes on my bag and turns off.

"Please place all personal items at the door." The blue light cuts into the darkness once I put my bag down, illuminating the room with a grid-like blue glow. It scans me head to toe three times. "Thank you, Private Gomez. Please place your hands on the two wall monitors." Two glowing blue handprints appear to my right. My hands are much too small for the monitor's actual shape, but it can still get a read on my hands. The console beeps and goes dark, "thank you, Private Gomez. In the future, your handprint will be used at all biological scanners for access. Do not give your handprints to anyone."

I wouldn't even know how to if I wanted to. I say, "Thank you. What is the next step of my intake process?" My voice sounds strange in the empty room, but I make sure I am speaking loud and clear enough for the computer to pick up my question.

A tunnel opens in front of me its walls a smooth chrome, with minimal manufacturing marks. "Your next step is to go down the tunnel. It's a two kilometer journey. Make it fast."

If I didn't know that it was a computer and computers don't have emotions, I would have thought there was a touch of glee in the last bit of the sentence.

Fun, I think. *A two K jog with all of my stuff—what a way to start my training.* As I step out into the tunnel, I feel a buzz pass through my body, and my feet float off the ground. This isn't just a happy little jog. This, like the other things, is a test. I glance down at my watch. It is a bit after noon. With or without me, that train will leave for Houston at 1300.

I push my arms off the ceiling and thud down to the floor. I have a split second to react and push myself forward before the lack of gravity puts me back into the ceiling. I struggle to keep moving forward and to slip my arms through the duffel bag and make it yet again into a makeshift backpack. And then I take off. Well, as much as I can when I'm already free-floating. I press off the ceiling, trying to angle myself forward with each movement. Something we could never replicate in Karrie's training facility. The tunnel has curved to the right, and I have probably made it about four hundred feet down the tunnel when I hear the door slide open far behind me.

"Shit," I curse, and push off harder. My wrists bark at the force of the impact as I hit the ceiling. But I don't care. I pick up the movements, sweat dripping down my back. I can't let either of those guys catch up to me. They probably think me getting my key card first was a sexist advantage. But it was just a simple deduction. I'm the only female in our little group.

My arms burn, but I keep on pushing down and forward. Up and forward. Again and again, pushing my body forward. This messy movement is nothing like the tailored gravity runs Karrie had me do.

In the distance I hear the whoosh of the door opening a third time and a cry of surprise as the person hits the lack of gravity. Someone either hasn't practiced enough or never experienced zero gravity unharnessed. *Thanks, Karrie.*

I move quickly, and while it isn't pretty, I feel like I've gotten a pretty good rhythm going. Looking ahead, I feel a spike of panic shoot through my body. I scream, flailing to stop my momentum. A large hole has opened up in a ring around the hall, the gap a black hole. Gravity or something like it pulls at my body trying to suck me into the depths. I cling to the edge of the void, tucking myself in and push off hard, gliding across the gap. My torso crosses over, leaving my feet and knees exposed to the hole. I struggle, the boots like a heavy stone in water wanting to drown me into the nothing. I press down and catch the smooth surface of the floor.

"There has to be a better way of doing this," I growl. Then I see it. On the edge of the floor of the next section is a switch, a small black toggle laying flush against the wall. I aim for it, hoping it does something helpful.

My hand catches the switch, and my body, only a few inches from the floor, drops. I exhale as I do, so the air isn't forced to make a harsh exit from my lungs. The others behind me aren't so lucky. As the floor merges closed, I hear the hacking and coughing of someone behind me. I can't help but grin. I climb to my feet and run trying to put as much distance as I can between us as the boys recover. I've made it past the last uneven section and hit a straightaway. I peek over my shoulder and see that the gaps in the floor are opening back up, and my strides send me higher with each step. "I guess it was only temporary."

In the distance I can see a door and run harder, my chest heaving with exertion. I push off one more time, sending my body forward the last few meters to the door. A framed outline of a hand sits on the wall. I reach for it before pressing my hand flat against it. The door whizzes open and sucks me in. I don't have time to prepare for the sudden gravity and thud to the ground, the air pushed rudely from my lungs.

"Fuck," I groan, struggling to sit up. There is a screen above the door, reading 12:37 PM and lists:

Gomez 10:17

Steele + 1:30

Keller +2:45

The two boys' time continues to tick downward. Realizing that the screen is listing my lead time, I struggle to my feet. "What's next Ada?" I ask aloud, glancing around the room.

There is only one more door, so I go for it. I roll through the door, hands up in fists, ready to jump into action.

"Ah, Private Gomez. You are a few minutes ahead of schedule.

Good job, please continue down the hall, and you can board the Eco-train to Houston."

I slowly lower my hands. "There aren't any other tests?" I glance around, but the man leaning against the wall, holding a tablet, is the only one left.

"I suggest you keep moving." He says vaguely.

Readjusting the straps of my bag, I hurry past the man. I press my hand to the bio scanner and, when I do, a door that wasn't there before opens. I run down the hall I need to move.

I push my legs harder. The only sound in the tunnel is that of my boots smacking against the floor and my breathing. My hair whips against the bag on my back, and my pulse pounds in my ears. As I run, my chest feels tighter, like the air isn't quite enough to fill my lungs. It's too difficult considering the endurance level I know I have.

I pass an air vent and something, makes me turn back. Pressing my hand to it, I feel a steady suction. *The oxygen.* I look up, trying to see the end of the tunnel. It still looks just as far as it did when I first started. Knowing I don't have that much time, I take off again but take slower, deeper breaths. I try to slow my heart rate and conserve oxygen, even as I move faster. "Fuck," I breathe. I wipe away the sweat that coats my face.

My head spins. Reaching out, I catch my hand against the curved wall; I lean against it but keep moving. Always moving down the hall. *Make the train. Make the train*, I think, again and again, chest heaving in vain.

The drumming in my ears is louder and louder, muffling all other sounds as my vision closes in around me. "Fuck!" I shout as I fall to my knees, using up another bit of precious oxygen. I crawl forward, my arms buckling. I try to move until I can't anymore. It's like I have no energy anymore. Like I've run a marathon.

I lay flat, panting. "Shit, the train." My unresponsive arms feel like lead. Black spots blink in front of me. I don't know if I am moving in the right direction anymore. I press my body forward, my skin skidding across the floor, pulling in tight lines of pain are like a distant memory.

Hands grab me under the armpits and lift.

I try to thrash and fight, but it's like I am moving in slow motion.

"It's okay, Private Gomez. You're done." I slump in relief. "Great job, Private. You've shown you have dedication; you went until you had nothing left. You have earned your ticket to Houston," the voice says.

My head rolls on their shoulder. "How-how much farther did I..." I pant.

"You made it to the door. You went farther than the required distance."

We pass through a door, and I am hit with a blast of cold air laced with blessed oxygen. I take several deep breaths before sliding from the person's hands to hold myself up. My world spins, but I don't ask for help. "Thanks," I cough out, using the wall to steady myself. I open my eyes to see the train, waiting right there for me. "Fuck yes." I stumble toward the train.

Chapter 7

It took the boys five more minutes before they made it to the station. Both were carried out like me. But officers didn't say whether they made it to whatever line that deemed whether or not we passed the test. We stand in a line, waiting to be told what to do. I glance down at my watch. *It's 12:56. Someone back there said something about needing to make it through in a specific time?* We must be waiting to find out if we made the right cut off. A screen above our heads shows our times.

HENRI STEELE 20:43.6

ADALINE GOMEZ 21:40.37

SHAWN KELLER 26:17.56

A woman steps off the train. She looks at the three of us, then up at the screen. I shift slightly to stand straighter. I press my hands into the side of my thighs, so the fatigue making my hands shake isn't visible.

She puts a hand to her ear. "This is it?" she asks. She brings her hand down, and I see a small silver earpiece. She turns back to us. "Thank you for your application. I am afraid not all of you have passed the test to make this train."

My heart squeezes a bit in fear. *What was the minimum?* I glance up at the board. I don't think I am the one cut based on the numbers but you never know.

I try to keep my eyes forward, looking strictly at the woman, or the train, but my eyes drift to the two other applicants beside me. The guy who came in right after me, who I think is Steele, stands farther off. He has long blackish brown hair that swoops low in his eyes, and curls around his ears. *That is going to get the chop.* The shirt he grabbed is much too small exposing a thin line of his stomach.

The woman steps forward and sizes each of us up. "Keller."

"Yes?" the man to my left says, he shifts and I have to hide a smirk.

"Yes, Ma'am," she corrects. She steps in front of him. "Why do you want to be in spec ops?" He turns his face, and she snaps. "Look at me when I am talking to you."

"I-yes, Ma'am. I want to be in spec ops."

"That was not the question, Private Keller," she snaps. She is all edges, standing tall and strong.

"I-no, Ma'am, I'm sorry, Ma'am. I want to be in the spec ops because my grandfather was. My father was a cadet before he died. He didn't have time to be a spec op. But I want to continue the tradition."

She cocks an eyebrow. "You do?"

"Yes, Ma'am," he replies, but he doesn't sound like he believes the words.

"Hm." She moves on to who I assume is Steele. "Why do you want to be in spec ops?"

"I don't want to be. I was told I had to be." He pauses, "Ma'am."

She scowls. "Hm. And why were you told you had to be in spec ops?"

He shrugs. The woman opens her mouth to say something, but he cuts her off. "I was told I was too good to be in a regular platoon. They told me I needed to find something else."

"Ah, you are one of those recruits." She walks up to me. "And you—" she glances up at the wall "—Gomez. Our only female recruit this quarter."

"Ma'am." I nod in respect. "I am joining Spec ops to better my family." I nearly cringe the words sound so arrogant.

She nods and taps a button on the wall. A slit opens, and a touch display pops out. She taps a few keys, and a red line appears on the screen.

CUT OFF TIME: 23 MINUTES

Keller sighs and steps out of line. "What do I tell my

grandfather?"

The woman smiles sympathetically. "From your records, you seem to be improving. Just keep working. Reminder, you only have one more attempt to join the Spec Ops team." I look over and catch Steele looking at me. I look away as the captain brings her attention back to me and Steele. "As for you two. You may proceed onto the eco-train. It will take you to Houston to continue your training. You should arrive at the dinner bell." She taps another series of commands on her tablet, and the door to the train slides open. "Good luck. And may your training serve you and the Galactic Garrison well."

I step up aboard the train first. I sit on a bench and lay my bag on the seat next to me, and rub my shoulders trying to work some of the tension away. Steele sits a few rows up leaning back casually in the seat. A light flashes, and the train quickly accelerates down the track. I scoot to the window, blinded for a second by the afternoon sun that streams through as we come out from under the compound. From this angle, I can see two other cars. Presumably for storage or cargo—since there are only two of us—they would have wanted to make sure the trip was worth it.

A screen slides down out of the ceiling. "Thank you for boarding Eco-trains, your journey has been paid for by the United Nations of Earth. You are on your way to Houston, specifically the Johnson Space Center. There you will go through a few tests that simulate space travel. Should you pass these, you will be sent off-world to the Intergalactic Space Station for the duration of your training. If you fail, you will be sent on to Fort Bragg to serve your tenure for on-world service."

"These videos are all very repetitive," Steele says. He runs a hand over his hair. It's long enough that it stays brushed up, with a few stray bits falling in a disheveled mess.

"How have you gotten away with having your hair that long?" I blurt out.

He freezes, his hand falling away from his head. "My hair. We just went through all those tests, and the first thing you want to talk about is my hair."

I shrug. "We both took the test. We know what was on it. What is there to discuss?" I look out the window.

"You did good back there."

I glance over at him. "And how would you know that?"

He gets up and sits in the chair across from me. "Well, I did just finish working a term of on-world service. And I've been off-world. And you're one of the few Fems who I've seen do that test well."

"Have you seen many people do the test?" I ask, turning away from the window, cocking an eyebrow at him. *Why would someone who has served off-world come back and do the test? Unless he got demoted and is trying to work his way back up.*

He shrugs, flipping the lock of hair out of his eyes. "Well, no, but I have heard of the test. At least bits and pieces of it."

I roll my eyes. "So, you can't say I am one of the few females you have seen do well, because you haven't seen *anyone* do it, let alone females." He opens his mouth to make some sort of smart reply but promptly snaps it shut with an audible click. "That's what I thought," I say with a grin.

He flushes pink. "You know what, bitch?" he snaps, getting up.

"What? What are you going to do about it?" I cross my arms. "You Males and your attempts at flirting or whatever you want to call it. You never can stand when you get caught in a lie." I stare him down, and he flushes an angry red.

"Fucking bitch."

"Really, we go from I'm a good Fem to a bitch because you got called out?" I scoff and lean back against the window. "Typical Males."

He doesn't talk to me for the rest of the ride. I watch out the window as the world I know quickly slips away, replaced within minutes by mountains, and snow, followed quickly by deserts, and a wide green prairie, each slipping by like they each had places to be, and they were late.

I don't know what I expected Houston to be like, but the buildings are more spread out than what I am used to seeing, with low flying cars sailing easily over the buildings. A low tone buzzes through the cabin pulling my gaze from the window as the train comes to an abrupt stop. Steele gets off first, rushing ahead of me, his wounded pride hanging from his shoulders.

"Hello, my name is Staff Sergeant O'Malley, and I am tasked with showing you to the barracks, shortly thereafter will be dinner. Your simulation training will begin first thing in the morning at 0600. Any questions?" He asks, leading us to a bus.

"No, Sir," I say, taking the first seat I find. Unlike the train, this car is full, forcing Steele to sit next to me. He leans into the aisle, trying to get away from me. I have to roll my eyes at the sight. The effort Males will go to when their pride has been hurt is ridiculous. One more short ride to the barracks, and I can finally drop this fucking lead-like duffle bag. I don't have that much stuff. But when forced to carry it for hours on end, I just want to get rid of it.

"Fems are on the right, Males to the left," O'Malley instructs when we get to the barracks. "Any bed with a black coverlet is up for grabs." I find a bed and sink down onto it. The mattress has to be twice as thick as the one at Jaxon's. It feels like heaven. "Keep your bunk clean, and you won't have any issues. Don't get into any fights with your bunkmates. Keep your hands to yourself. You know, basic adult things we all should know but are rules that get broken all the time so I have to repeat them." He drags. "Just don't be a shithead. You should be off-world in the next day or so anyway, so you shouldn't have any issues."

I unzip the bag. "Right, thanks. Any tips you can give me on acclimating?"

O'Malley pauses, hand on the door. "No, it's a different process for everyone. Don't be obnoxious but find yourself an ally. That never hurt anyone."

I nod, and he leaves. Reaching into my bag, I pull out the metal plate with the photo of my family. I have an ally. But now he's a few thousand kilometers away, soon to be much farther. I slip the photo under my pillow. Remembering how O'Malley said that black meant the bed was free, I quickly flip the blanket to the colorful side, claiming my new temporary—as everything seems to be in my life—base.

A long bell tone cuts the air, signaling my favorite time of day. Dinner.

Chapter 8

I follow the line of people heading down to the mess, and much to my chagrin, find that we're separated by rank and purpose. Which meant that I got to sit with my *favorite* person and a few other Males. I grab a tray and flop into a chair, and devour the food in front of me. Because it is like actual fucking food!

"So, it looks like we'll be stuck together for a bit, Gomez. It's going to get boring having to call you Gomez all the time," Steele says a fork partway to his mouth. When I don't answer, he says, "My name is Henri Steele. I figured I would introduce myself since we will probably spend most of our time here together."

I look him over and swallow, then nod. I see his face fall as I leave him hanging for a moment. *This is too fun.* "I'm Ada," I finally say, and I see him relax a bit. "Which you would know if you read the stats in New Seattle."

"Right." He pauses, "Ada. Is that short for something?" He asks, digging more.

I down my orange juice, shuddering at the sour tang. "Yes, but no one calls me by it unless it is for legal reasons," I say, hoping that is enough to end the conversation.

His eyebrows pinch together. "Does that happen often?"

"More than I would care to admit."

"Oh, so you're a rebel? That why you're in the Garrison?" He asks.

I glance up and hope I give him a look that translates my pure confusion.

"Well, cause you said people only call you your full name if you get into legal trouble?"

I put down my fork. "I never said trouble. You added the trouble bit. I only get called my legal first name when I meet with a superior who doesn't know me well or am in court because I am, or was, being re-homed. I am a recent 'graduate' of the foster system." I do jazz hands. "Yay me."

Steele seems to take a moment to process what I mean by the foster system. Another free bird who never needed it. "You were in the foster system? How did you get through it? Is that how you cut your eyebrow?"

I look at him over a bite of food. "My eyebrow?" I reach up and touch it, feeling the groove where a thin scar cuts through my eyebrow, I usually forget about. "Oh, I mean sorta. It happened while I was in the system. How did I do it? I mean, I did it. I didn't have any other choice in the matter. It wasn't like the good officer was going to let me and my brother live on our own without adult supervision." I say bitterly. "I'm sorry, I'm rambling." I glance up at him, but he doesn't look up from his food anymore. I can't tell if he is contemplative or just doesn't know what to say. I wouldn't either.

We finish our food in silence. I spend the time I have looking at everyone around me. Impeccably groomed, toned, hard, and yet empty. Most people here look tired; they look like they can't wait for today to end. Maybe for their enlistment to end. I'm sure I will look like that sometimes, but I have a bigger purpose that puts me here. I think of the stories of soldiers before the Tech Wars that used to carry photos of their loved ones printed out. I wish I could do that with Sarkus. But we don't use paper. Maybe I can get a hologram of him.

"Gomez, Steele!" A voice barks, and I jump out of my chair and to attention. "We would work on that, Gomez, but we don't have time. Perhaps Steele can show you sometime." Steele shoots me a brief grin, and I adjust my stance to mirror his. "Have the two of you finished eating?" the officer asks, glancing down at our plates.

"Yes, Sir." Steele and I bark in unison. It wouldn't matter if we hadn't finished eating. We were now.

"Good. We have had to rearrange our schedule for the next few weeks. As you both have scored exceedingly high in past tests, the higher ups have decided to make an exemption. If you wish you may stay and do the additional training, or you may take the test tonight without that training." He pauses and waits for us to make a decision.

I step forward. "Sir, I would like the opportunity to try tonight."

"Me too," Steele says.

"Understood. In order to get through the test, and any additional paperwork you will need to take your tests now. Should you pass, we will jump at 1300 tomorrow."

I nod, still tired from the last test, but ready for the next set of criteria.

"Right, head to room 402. You will have thirty minutes to complete a written test. You will find your next steps after that portion is complete." Steele and I look at each other again. "You have thirty minutes." The officer repeats. "Your time has already started, so I would get a move on."

"Thank you, Sir." I jump, giving the officer a tight salute. *Shit* The door to the mess hall has a number 105 on it. I run out the door and round the corner. Steele is a few steps behind me. I push to the end of the hall. *Corners usually have stairs*. I grab the handle and yank. The movement against the rigid door wrenches my arm. "Fuck," I let go. I spin around and take off, looking for another way up. Steele slides past me and pulls again, and the door opens. He shoots me a wicked grin and bolts through. "You fucker!" I yell after him, struggling to change my trajectory.

"I opened that for you." He laughs, his voice echoing up the staircase.

I take the stairs two at a time, praying to whatever being lives in the heavens that I won't trip and fall flat on my face.

My legs burn from the use of a different muscle, one rarely worked with Karrie. I avoid stairs like the plague, and here I am, sprinting them. We hit floor four at the same time. And burst through, searching for the first door we can see. "446," Steele pants. "We're on the wrong side of the floor."

He hangs off a door, and I don't wait for him. "What? Tired from the earlier test?" I call over my shoulder, attempting to pretend that I'm also not completely winded and dying and dehydrated, especially after passing out earlier.

He lets out a weird growling roar and pushes past me. He sprints down the hall and rounds a corner. I am just arriving at said door when he comes barreling back down the hall and heads the other way. A door at the end of the hall has the faint numbers 402 on the bottom right corner.

"There!" I shout and point at it.

We hit the door at the same time and blast through. There are two desks and two tablets. I grab the one and sit, trying to catch my breath. I push a button. Then another, and another, hold down the button, and it slowly lights up. "Really, they couldn't even have the test booted up for us?" I look up at the walls, looking for any clues when I see it. On a tiny, three-by-five-inch screen in the corner is a clock slowly ticking down the minutes we have left in this test. "Shit, we only have fifty minutes left."

"I found it. It is in the top right corner of the home screen."

I finally get the screen up and stab the file with my finger. A pdf file with ten bullet points opens.

1. First, find your stylus.

I drop to the floor, crawling all around under desks and tables looking for the stylus. *I could do it without it. Do I have to have it?* I grab chair legs and table legs looking for a false opening. I glance at the clock again and let out a growl of frustration. Ten minutes have slid by and I haven't even answered one question on this damn test.

There is a counter that runs around the edge of the room. Leaning against the wall in the corner is a little analog clock. The arms of the clock are suspiciously large: both happen to be the same length. I leap from my spot on the floor, knocking several chairs out of my way as I do. I grab the stylus and fling one to Steele, who is in a cabinet. "Thanks," he says, scooping his tablet up again. I bring my stylus up, ready to answer all the questions.

Once you have found your stylus, answer the following questions.

2. When did the first manned space flight take place?

April 1961 by the USSR

3. Who was the first person on the Moon?

US Astronaut Neil Armstrong

4. Who was the first female into space?

Valentina Tereshkova of the USSR

6. What race did humans first contact?

The Capmings on Mars in 2056

7. What does ISS stand for?

International Space Station

8. When was the Galactic Garrison Founded, and by whom?

The Galactic Garrison was founded in 2107 by Ethan Facri.

9. What is the Galactic Garrison' slogan?

We will fight for peace and safety through the galaxy until all the stars are found.

10. What are the five types of Spec Ops classes you can enter into?

Medic, Fighter, Jumper, Espionage, Tech

I fly through the questions, sending a silent thank you out to Karrie for her random fact drills during our training runs. I glance over at Steele; he is staring hard at the answers, his face screwed up in concentration.

I glance over the test again and see tiny letters near the bottom. CLICK ME. I glance over to Steele, but he hasn't noticed it yet. I click the hyperlink, and a little text box appears on the screen.

Once you feel you have completed the test, place the tablet on the podium. Then please proceed to room 327 to begin the next steps. You have twenty minutes.

I quickly scan the room and find the podium. I make sure I type in my name at the top of the test, turn off the tablet, and get up.

"What are you doing?" Steele asks, glancing from his screen to me.

I place my tablet on the podium and turn back to him. "Just following instructions." I head for the door.

"Wait, how do you know? How are you already done?" He asks, frantically scrolling through the test.

I laugh as I head out the door. "What's the matter? I thought you already went through basic once on-world. It shouldn't be that hard. Should it?"

"These are different questions!" He says before the door clangs shut.

Chapter 9

I jog down the hall and head down one flight of stairs. I take a quick break on the landing. The lack of sleep is gnawing at me.

I take a deep breath, and I pop open the door and check the numbers. 303, 305, 307. I jog through the halls, counting the numbers as I pass them, searching for number 327. I finally find it at the end of the hall. I catch a glimpse of a large gym with a shooting range at the far side before I step into the room, and the lights go dark. The door seals shut behind me with a soft hiss.

I drop to my knees and close my eyes, making my five-foot-four frame even smaller. A few seconds later, I open my eyes, letting them adjust to the gloom. I am nearly blind, but faintly, in the distance, a dull light shines on the floor. Staying low to the ground, I walk slowly, moving my legs in sweeping movements. When I looked into the room, it seemed mostly empty.

I move toward the light, trying to keep my breathing even,

straining to hear anything besides the slide of my boot across the floor.

I reach out and am just able to touch the light source. I crouch over it. It's a panel box, the cover shifted slightly out of place. I lift the piece of metal, and the light spills out, the edge lined with small LED lights, illuminating a bundle of wires and a screen. I lift the screen out of the cabinet. It looks like the old tablet I used to have before Jaxon snapped it. Maybe a few models newer, but this one has been adapted with additional ports for the wiring and cables. I tap the screen a few times, but it doesn't come to life. I turn it over, and on the back is a single word etched in sharp lines.

FIX

"Fix it. Okay, I, uh, I can do that." I rotate the tablet, looking for the seam. I glance down into the bundle of wires. *If they want me to fix this thing, there have to be tools, right?* I lay on the floor shifting the wires, exposing the lights. I squint into the darkness around me looking for the reflection off a toolbox, or something. My hand catches on the pointed top of something and I pull my hand back in surprise. What was that? I pull the wires up and see the edge of a handle. Grabbing it I pull out a slim Phillips head screwdriver and, wedging it into the seam, I gently pry open the casing. The inside is a mess of tiny filigree wiring, and the memory board. I take a moment to stare in confusion at the technical innards. I glance down at my watch—time is ticking—and I need to figure this out. I follow the different wires and try to find where the issues lie. Then I see a small wire has been cut. I turn back to the panel looking for more tools, I set aside a wrench, a small pair of pliers, and a hammer. Using the pliers, I strip back the plastic from the wires, twist them together, jumping a bit as it sparks. I loosely put the back on the tablet and tap the screen. It slowly comes to life. "Yes!" I press the casing back together and wait while it slowly boots up. The screen lights up with a message.

GOOD JOB, ADA.

"Thanks."

YOUR NEXT TASK REQUIRES A BIT MORE SPEED.

"Okay, well, what do I need to do?" Slowly, the lights come up around me with a dinging sounds off to my left.

The ringing tone calls me over to the shooting range. One gun on the wall sits in a holster with a flashing green light on it. I slowly lift the weapon, testing the balance.

The moment I lift it from the holster, the sound stops, replaced by a buzzer alarm. "Shoot," An artificial voice says before targets start moving on the range. "Do not hit the people." The moving items are a mixture of cutouts of various species and four targets. I widen my stance and look down the sight. Taking a deep breath, I fire once, twice, pause, fire again, once, twice, and lower my pistol. The targets fall, and the cutouts keep moving. A buzzer goes off again, and the targets, now with a few satisfying burn marks, rise again and move faster than the last round. I take another deep breath, and watch the beat of the moving targets, willing my heart to slow, to keep my hands steady. I fire twice. One target falls, as does one cutout.

"Shit," I breathe and feel my heart rate pick up. "No," I relax my shoulders, roll them back and fire again; a target falls. I pause again, wait, then fire. The last target drops. The buzzer sounds, and as expected, the targets rise again, but this time only three. *I'm going to have to do this until I miss four times.* I shake out my arms, letting blood flow into my fingers before lifting and firing again. This time, all three targets fall without issue. The buzzer sounds, and the targets and cut-outs move again this time, so fast it's hard to see where they start and end their movements. I fire three times, and two targets fall and a cut out of an alien falls. The buzzer calls, and knowing I can't perceive the movements, I fire at will. I can't tell if I made the shot or not, but the buzzer makes a longer tone, and all moving objects drop.

"Please replace your weapon, Private Gomez." I do so. I turn back to the room and a series of pulsing lights beckons me out of the shooting range. I wait, in silence, for my next command and am met with the sound of machinery powering down. The lights around me fade to black, but I hear a door open. I turn to the sound, but I can't see anything in the gloom. "Please fight." The robotic voice orders.

Please fight? Looking up toward the speakers. *What am I*

fighting? I strain to hear in the darkness but can't hear anything from where I stand. I step forward and wince at the sound of my boots squeaking across the floor. I move across the floor, hands curled into fists. Every few feet, I stop and hold my breath, listening for any other sounds.

I see a very, very faint glow in the distance. It looks like the edging they used to put in the aisles of school auditoriums but in the shape of a circle. That's when I see the target. The light is blocked by their feet. I raise my arms, ready to fight. If I can see the target, they can see me, when I break the line of lights.

I move forward to engage. It is too dark for me to make out the details of the person, but their silhouette is tall, hunched over, ready to fight but protecting themselves. The lights reflect dully off their boots giving away their position. I move forward on tiptoes, ready to jump. When I am a few feet away from the ring, the opponent turns. I jump at them and swing. The person gives a shout of surprise but leaps back and ducks. I swing again and feel the satisfying connection of my fist to their face as they come back up. They grab my wrist and pull me toward them. They elbow me, the blow connecting with my shoulder and knocking me back, my teeth clash together.

They wrap me in a massive bear hug. And not the good kind. I beat my fists back, but it does nothing. They shift their position and put me in a headlock. I cock my leg up and kick them just above the knee as hard as I can. They drop me and I roll away, rising into a crouch. Before driving my shoulder into their stomach. Already off-balance from the kick to the knee, they stumble back. I rain down a series of punches, most of which they block, until they hook me with their foot and send me tumbling.

"Fuck," I say, holding the back of my head.

"Ada?" My opponent asks dropping their fists

"What?" Wiping my mouth, I taste copper on my lips. I keep my hands up, ready to launch myself back in.

"What are you doing here?" Steele pants.

The lights clang on, blinding the two of us for a second. He looks rough, a large red welt that I'm honestly proud of blooms across his eye. "What are *you* doing here? You were the one that came in here." I snap, wiping the blood off my chin from where he elbowed me.

A door whisks open, and an officer steps into the light, pristine in his fatigues. Steele and I jump to our feet and salute. "At ease." We relax. "Very well-done Private Steele, Private Gomez. Please get cleaned up at the infirmary, then head to the barracks to wait. You will learn your scores shortly."

"Sir, if I may," I say respectfully. He nods, and I continue, "Sir, could we please know what the baseline score we need to pass and go off-world would be?"

He pauses, then, putting his hands behind his back, says, "You need to pass each area with at least a seven out of ten and a thirty overall." Steele and I nod. "If there are no other questions, you are dismissed. A change of clothes will be waiting for you. Make yourselves comfortable."

"Yes, Sir," we intone.

Chapter 10

My body is growing stiff: from the tough work out with Karrie at the training ground, the night spent on a bench, the traveling, to everything we did today. It feels great to just lie in a bed for a few minutes. And one that doesn't have springs that poke and prod me when I move.

I wake up to Steele poking me with his bony ass finger. "Shove it," I say, rolling away and swatting at him.

"The corporal is on her way. And a good thing, too. You could make an avalanche happen with those snores," Steele says, backing away from my swings.

I groan and sit up. My ponytail sits unevenly on my head and loose bits of hair tickle my nose, Steele snickers, and I shoot daggers in his direction as he moves to the door. I get up and throw my hair in a messy top knot and start frantically cleaning my bunk. I've just finished making my bed when the corporal enters. Steele and I snap into a salute.

She gives us a once over, and I pull down the edge of my rumpled shirt. She nods before saying, "They have sent me to inform you of your testing scores. As you were told earlier, we require you to have scored at least a seven in each category and a thirty overall to pass and move to our off-world training facility aboard the Intergalactic Space Station." She taps the screen, and a hologram projects our scores.

ADALINE GOMEZ
WRITTEN TEST 9
TECHNOLOGY 7
SHOOTING 8
FIGHTING 8
FINAL SCORE ACHIEVED 32

HENRI STEELE
WRITTEN TEST 5
TECHNOLOGY 7
SHOOTING 9
FIGHTING 8
FINAL SCORE ACHIEVED 29

The corporal turns to me. "Congratulations, Private Gomez. If you would please gather any belongings you came with and follow me, we will move on to the jump gate for your immediate departure."

I seriously want to squeal in joy. I settle for a large dorky grin. "Yes, Ma'am."

 Steele doesn't look as pleased. "Ma'am?"

"Yes, Private Steele?"

He looks down at his boot laces then takes a deep breath. "Does this mean I'm out?" My smile falters. It feels rude to be excited when he didn't pass. These tests aren't meant to be easy and who knows how long he prepared for it.

The corporal taps a button, and the scores disappear. "I am afraid so, Private Steele. You have done phenomenally well in all categories but the written test. As stated, you have to pass all categories to make it off-world. You will have another opportunity to take the test in three months. This does not completely set you back to square one."

He takes a deep breath and swallows hard. "Thank you, Ma'am. I look forward to that opportunity."

"Agent Gomez—" the corporal says pausing over the new title I have earned with my progress to the space station "—Please gather your things and meet me outside."

"Yes Ma'am."

Steele and I wait until the woman leaves before moving. He sighs and sits down putting his head in his hands. I throw my few belongings in my bag. "So, I'll see you soon up on the station?" I offer trying to sound optimistic. "You will be great for the Garrison."

He looks up sharply like he expects me to be joking. But his face softens. "Yeah, I'll be up there. Might not make this class, but I will be with the next for sure."

The corporal comes back into the room. "Ready?"

"Yes Ma'am." She nods and takes off in a brisk walk. Forcing me to take two strides for every one of hers. I glance over my shoulder as I leave the room and see that Steele has slumped back in the bed looking up at the ceiling.

"Ma'am?" I ask, jogging to catch up with the woman. "How exactly do we use a jump gate? I've only ever done simulations."

Glancing over her shoulder, she says. "It's simple enough. We have one gate, so we type in the coordinates of a known gate, they connect, and you walk through."

That's it. Obviously. You just walk through. It's easy Gomez, just walk.

The corporal stops in front of a doorway lined with red lights, presses a button on her tablet, and a secure screen pops up. She lays her hand flat, and the screen scans her hand. The light around the door turns green, before opening inward and she waves me in. Across the room is a ring with a turbulent surface, like it's made of liquid silver. She goes to the wall, and a holo display and a keyboard come out. She taps out a few keystrokes, and the liquid in the ring goes smooth.

"Oh before you go up—" she reaches into a pocket and pulls out a small case "—Nearly everyone on board will speak Gian to a point, but many of your peers will have learned Gian as a second or third language. This—" She hands me the device "—will translate in real time for you. It will also connect you to the stations main frame should you require anything technology wise. You will just need to set it up once you get settled." I slip the device into my pocket eager to connect it once on board. "Right, now you just need to step through. The shipment will come through right after you, so we can't delay."

I nod, trying to ignore the nervous excitement in the pit of my stomach.

"Just so you know," she adds, "it is not uncommon for people to feel sick after a jump. Especially if you have never jumped before." She glances down, "Okay, they have given us the all-clear; please step up." I move to a yellow line on the floor, "Agent Gomez, you are cleared to jump. Please proceed to the station."

I close my eyes as I step through. It feels like cool air slips over my body and a slow current draws me forward. After a moment, a force hooks me and wrenches me across the space between the two gates. My eyes flutter open and spot the ripple of the other gate. I step through and onto the space station. My stomach rolls and I press a hand to my mouth, and swallow the bitter bile back down. I force myself to stand up straight and grab my bag.

The soldier operating the jump gate gives me a sympathetic grin. "It gets better. Please follow me."

"Right," I grumble around the bile in my throat.

I follow him, slowly as my eyes rise to the ceiling. Thick panels of glass are all that separate me from the open vacuum of space. I slow to a stop. The Moon floats closer to me than I have ever seen. I can see every detail, all the small craters and holes from asteroids that have marred its surface. I turn and see my home. I've seen pictures of Earth from space, of course. It looks so soft, so innocent, and unassuming. But this is not the same beautiful bluc-green marble I grew up seeing pictures of. This orb looks like a more muted, dirty version, filled with deep swirls of browns. I've pictured this moment, seeing my home world time and time again. I imagined the pride, and the joy, and awe I would feel seeing it compared to the vastness of space. And I do still feel that little jolt in my stomach, but the garbage that surrounds it is devastating. And yet there is still beauty in the various shades of brown, and the way the clouds pillow over the ocean. It is what it is mean to be. *It's so fucking beautiful.*

Chapter 11

"It's cool, isn't it?"

I spin away from the brownish-green blob of my home to see a deep blue figure in front of me. "What?" I freeze, mouth agape.

Standing in front of me is a beautiful blue Fem. Her skin is sapphire blue like the gemstones I've seen in pictures, cut through with thin white stripes rippling up her arms. Instead of hair, she has a clump of tentacles that lay slicked back but squirm at the tips. "Seeing your planet for the first time is so cool. Don't you think?"

"Yeah, yeah, it is," I'm not sure if I am talking about her or the planet. I occasionally saw people on Earth that weren't human, but outside of Tortie and a few other vendors in The Market, I never had the chance to interact with any of them.

Her cheerful voice has a clipped, short way of forming the words. Her smile is so bright in contrast to the dark blue of her skin. "Oh, you are *new* new," she laughs, reaching out a hand; even her fingernails are a deep shade of indigo. "My name is Dita. I am a Ganymede. I come from the Jupiter quadrant. I came here since my base was full, and the Earth quadrant has the next best program."

My brain is bouncing from point to point as she rapidly describes herself. I scan her fatigues: they are like mine, but they have a few different patches on them, one of which I can't wait to have. It has a picture of the milky way galaxy and the Earth. I have wanted that symbol ever since I started looking into the Galactic Garrison. It is the badge that a soldier is awarded when they arrive at the Earth station. Once we have earned our Special Operations rank, we will receive one that also depicts the solar system. "Wait, wait, you get sent here if your base is full?"

She shrugs, and the tentacles on her head lift and make a shrugging move too. "It isn't super enforced; you could go wherever you want if it got approved. But it wouldn't really make sense for you to come to Ganymede or Titan for basic. You wouldn't be able to breathe unless you were always in a suit. Kind of hard to train that way." She points to a small device that sits under the edge of her shirts neckline. "This helps my body not to be overwhelmed when I don't have access or can't be in a suit that moderates my levels."

I look back to Earth. "It isn't what I expected it to look like, but I guess it would reflect what it looks like on the planet, huh?"

She sighs, "You aren't the only human I have heard say that since getting here. I guess your ancestors really screwed it up for you. Someone always says something about a blue marble. But no one can show me a marble. I don't think they know." She grabs my arm. "Come on, I will bring you to do your intake."

I can't help but grin at her babbling. *I like this Fem.* I follow her through the halls, taking in as much of it as I can. I have devoured as much research on the International Space Station as possible in the last few years, but it doesn't look like the messy, cramped, wire-filled pods I had seen. "Are we on the new ISS?" These walls are smooth gray with recessed panels for entrances to lifts or rooms. Everyone is in uniforms similar to Dita's: a green shirt with three-quarter length sleeves, their rank and class patches on their bicep, and tapered black cargo pants. "This doesn't look like the photos of the ISS I saw growing up."

"We are in pathway seven now. Headed for node twenty-three. Some older areas have been shut down and are primarily used for storage."

I wrack my brain, trying to think of the maps I had seen, and where we were on the ship. Over the years, scientists kind of just kept building more and more replicas of the International space station on top of each other, connecting them with a series of rings or tunnels. It is honestly a mess. But they must have found a decent enough way to make it work.

"How long did you say you've been here, Dita?" I ask.

She slows, "Oh, I don't think I did," she puts a blue hand up to the wall, and a door slides open, revealing a lift inside—a few agents exit. One is more humanoid, another is small, bald, and green, the last has the darkest skin I have ever seen, black as pitch, covered in spines. I glance at them as they go past but do my best not to stare. Dita hits a button, the door slides shut, and we rise. "I have been here, I think, for two weeks now. It hasn't been too long. But I've been in the military for three years, four months and eight days. That is in your time."

"Nice. What do you think of it so far?" I say.

"It's been going pretty well. We've been waiting for some other agents to get here before we get started on training. So, it has just been conditioning." She says, "You humans train really strangely."

"How so?"

We step out of the elevator onto a packed floor of people of many species. "Holy shit," I murmur.

"Oh, I would have to argue, none of the shitty people in here are holy," She grins, "I learned that joke right before I came. I have been dying for someone to say it!" She trills, and I roll my eyes. "Come on, we need to go this way." I jump as she grabs my hand and pulls me on the outside edge of the room. "You humans focus so much on conditioning your... aerobic system? I think that was what the instructors called it. You have to train your body to use the oxygen you need to like to survive. That seems odd. Shouldn't you be able to use it fine without having to condition your body?" I open my mouth to respond, but she continues on, "I mean we have to do conditioning on Ganymede, but that was because we have to train our bodies to use oxygen better because we have so much less. But you have all the oxygen you could ever need. Why would you need to train yourself to use it? I don't know, you humans are weird."

I sigh and let her ramble. My mind floats back to what O'Malley said in Karrie's office. Soon after arriving, we would need to decide and let the administration know what specialty we want to go into. I always thought I wanted to be a Medic. Karrie tried to teach me little bits and bobs about the human body. But I don't think I processed that I may have to heal people of other species. That would mean there would be at least half a dozen species I may need to learn about.

"You good? You look like you just saw a joly." Dita asks pulling me into the hallways.

I snap out of it, "I'm sorry, a what?"

Dita looks at me like I am the crazy one. "A joly, a spirit, like your friend died and came back?"

"A ghost?"

"No, a *joly*."

I laugh. "No, I mean, we call a *joly* a ghost."

"Oh, well, why do you look so scared?"

I sigh, "well, I just thought how I always figured that I would be a Medic, but I never thought I would need to worry about keeping people alive that have completely different anatomy than my own."

She nods, "Yeah, I knew someone that used to be a Medic. They said it was a lot, but that it was really fulfilling. I want to do Tech Espionage."

"Nice, I am thinking either Medic Fighter, or Medic Jumper."

Dita stops in front of a door. "Here we are! I'll meet you back in the barracks. You should be able to ask them some of your questions. They need to make sure your file is completely up to date now that you are here." She waves, as do all the tentacles on her head.

When I step into the room, all the chairs are taken, and a few other people are standing against the wall waiting to be called. I step to the right of the door, and I almost bump into another humanoid figure. He gives me a slight nod of acknowledgment when I hurriedly step out of his space. I step up to the woman at the desk. "Uh, hello, my name is Adaline Gomez. I am signing in for the rest of my intake process.

The person taps a screen, and I see a photo of me whiz across the screen. She compares the two pictures and then nods. "It will be a bit of a wait; you are one of several agents that came in today. Please find a place to wait."

I turn back and sit against the wall before tucking my feet up so no one will step on me.

Here on the floor I have a different vantage point. The ticking hiss of claws sliding across the floor draws my eyes up. I slowly take in this creature that looks like a monster out of a film. "I am Edonne. I need my clearance." His long snout is full of teeth and the arms that lean on the counter end in three clawed fingers.

The Fem at the desk does the same as she did with me, looking up their name and letting them know there would be a wait.

"Are you serious? I need to get this done." Edonne hisses.

The Fem's pure white eyebrows pinch in an annoyed glance. "And you don't think everyone behind you also needs to get checked in? You need to wait just like them."

"Well, they should allow me to go first."

I scoff. I've seen people like this in The Market. They just assumed that because they perceived everyone else to be less and thus had to cater to them. It hardly ever worked in their favor. And when it did, it was because they threw a major fit and nobody wanted to deal with them anymore. They always took it as a win, but I, for one, did not.

"You have something you would like to say?" the pompous alien asks, spinning around to face me.

I look around at those around me. "You mean me?" Out of the corner of my eye, I see the guy I had bumped into when I came in rub his temple, while everyone else minds their own business. *What is his problem? I didn't do anything.*

"Yes, I mean you. What have you got to say that you would like everyone to know?" Edonne hisses.

The officer at the desk snaps, "Agent Edonne, find a seat or leave."

Edonne ignores her and stalks up to me, towering over me from where I sit. "Well, you wanna say anything?"

I am already small, but I had learned long ago not to let bullies think you were any smaller than them, so I rise to my feet, shoulders back, head high. "The same thing all of us are thinking. The same thing our superior already told you. Wait or leave."

"Really?" Edonne hisses again, balling his claw-like hands into fists.

"Edonne, stand down. Gomez, back off." The Fem orders. I take a step back, acknowledging the order, but I do not turn my back away from the Male. I lean against the wall, crossing my arms.

"Really, you can speak for all the people here, huh?" He spits. Bits of his saliva fall on my face, and fuck it stings. The alien's eyes shift to the spots on my face. *He knew that would happen.* I fight the urge to scrub my face. I lived with Jaxon long enough to know better than to show any reaction to the things he would do.

"Well, I can't fully speak for everyone, but I'm pretty sure our superior would agree. And ya know, you should listen to them. They can make your life hell."

"I will make your life hell." He growls.

I see the Fem behind the desk speak into an intercom before

moving across the room.

"Is that a threat?" The Male I bumped asks, stepping up and pushing Edonne out of my face. "Shove off. Gomez is being soft with you. "

"Edonne, I gave you an order. Follow the damn order. Wait or leave. Gomez, Torrac, back off." I startle for a second, wondering who this Male is and how he knows my name. *Did he hear the officer say it?* Again, I move to disengage from the enraged alien but find the wall is much closer than I thought.

"What need big Rogues to protect you, little human?" Edonne cackles.

I step around the Male, not allowing him to use his larger frame to protect me. "On the contrary, good Sir," I preen. "This Male is making sure I don't kick your ass. But I will save that for training."

"Attention!!" We all snap to attention. Two soldiers flank the Fem who spoke. "Edonne, go sit your ass in holding room two since you can't seem to wait nicely. Gomez and Torrac. Please step into holding room four. An officer will be there to meet with you shortly." The woman at the desk stands tall, her white hair standing on end in anger. Edonne opens his mouth to hiss something out again, but she snaps, and her hair pulls together into spikes, not unlike a porcupine. "You would do well to learn to listen to your superiors. You will spend a lot of time running chores if you don't." Edonne glares at Torrac and me and stalks away, his talons clicking on the floor.

Chapter 12

I glance at the Male named Torrac, and head down the hall to the waiting room. Everyone stares at us as we pass. I feel both embarrassed and strong at the same time. *Great. You have been off-world for less than an hour, and you already fucked up.* I inwardly groan. *Well, did I really fuck up or just stand up for myself?* I guess it will be up to the officer that comes to speak with us.

The holding room is cramped. With the ends of a bench and a table pressed against the wall leaving a small walk space around the perimeter. I sit on the bench and scooch over, giving Torrac room, but he doesn't sit down. "That was sorta badass of you."

"What do you mean?" I ask, pulling at the sleeves of my t-shirt.

"Well, I mean that guy is literally a foot taller than you and a massive lizard." He laughs, "I mean, did you see his feet? They were like talons. Corcians are crazy mean, and you did not care." He looks at my face. "Your face has red splotches all over. Did he spit on you or something?"

"Yeah, he was spitting when he was talking. I don't want to smear it; it'd get worse, wouldn't it?" I take the edge of my shirt and dab at one spot on my chin. The stinging returns and bites deep into my skin. "I just really hate bullies. I had to deal with enough of them on Earth. It would be nice not to have to deal with them here too."

"While brave, it was also ridiculously stupid." He laughs. "I'm Kathel, Kathel Torrac, I'm from the Kuiper Belt." He says, putting out a hand.

"Ada Gomez, Earth," I say, shaking his hand.

Kathel and I jump to attention as a man strolls in. His skin is a deep burnt orange with black spots falling down the back of his shirt from his hairline. He has his head buried in a tablet and barely looks up at us. "My name is Agent Androna. Agent Gomez, I see here you got into a scuffle with a Corcian, I want you to go down the hall to the Med Center as soon as we are done here to get that skin checked out. The last thing you would want would be those spots to scar. And Agent Torrac, you did you get spit on?" He asks looking up from his tablet. He glances back down, "So. You are the two recruits from Earth?"

"If I may, Sir, I'm from the Kuiper colony," Kathel says, shifting. If Torrac is from Earth, I would eat my shoe. He is no Corcian with claws and acid spit, but he isn't like Dita either. I'll give it to Agent Androna, that Torrac looks "more human" than most, but his white hair, and nearly translucent pale skin, definitely stand out next to the olive tones of my own.

"Steele didn't pass the test." I offer.

The officer turns and picks up a tablet from the desk; he flips through and scans it for a moment "ah yes," Androna turns back to me. "I would highly suggest you don't engage with the Corcians again. They're the kind of people that will hold a grudge for a long while. I am sure this will come back up. So just mind yourself. You definitely made your mark. We need people like you here. Just don't do that again. Clear?"

"Yes, Sir," I nod. "Crystal clear."

"Good, the two of you are dismissed. You both should be seen shortly for your final check. They start to serve dinner at 1700." He stands, and we give a salute before following him out. I glance at Kathel, and we share a smile before I split off and head down the hall, following the signs to the infirmary.

There are a few nurses bustling around, and I cut through to what I hope is the main desk. I stand for a moment unsure if there is a button I should push when a Fem walks by. "Hello, miss. What can we... Oh, your face! How did you do that? Is that what you are here for?"

I nod. "Yes, I'm Agent Gomez. I am not sure if anyone said I would be coming or not. I got into a bit of an argument with a Corcian, and he spat on me."

She ushers me over to a table and pulls over a cart of medical goodies. "I will send someone over to get you fixed up right away." Sitting down I get to observe the organized chaos of the place. It's oddly quiet for how active it is. Nothing like the loud hospitals on Earth where people cry, and sometimes scream, where there seems to be a constant barrage of information over the loudspeakers. Here, you hear the quick footsteps of the nurses and doctors, the squeaky wheels of medicine carts and quiet conversation.

"I'm Doctor Skovnia, I believe someone did mention that you were coming. Let's look at this." She dampens a cloth in a green liquid and dabs at the spots. I flinch back, "I am sorry," she dabs again, and I hold myself as still as I can. "What were you doing getting in a fight with a Corcian? Few people will do that."

"Maybe that means more people should," I say. "He was an ass. And I made a noise when he was throwing a fit. He got aggressive and then got pissed when I didn't rise to his level. Then, he spits all over me, trying to get a reaction. Clearly, it worked so well for me."

"Well, I give you props." She looks at me over the edge of her glasses. Just like Emma would. She rinses the cloth and squeezes a bit of ointment into a cup, then taking a cotton bud dabs it over the spots. "This is a burn cream. You should be all set after tonight, but if you have any other issues, let someone know, and we will get you sorted."

"That's it?"

"That's it." She smiles. "Go on, finish up your intake."

I hop off the table and head back down to the first room where I had the pleasure of meeting Edonne. Kathel and one other are the only ones left.

"All fixed up?" He asks, sliding across the bench for me to sit.

"Yeah, they gave me a burn cream, said if I need more, I can get a refill, but that I shouldn't need any after tomorrow."

"Nice. I've noticed that the med stations here on the bases are pretty efficient."

"Yeah," I say. We sit in silence for a minute. They call the last person back. "Thanks for, you know, telling him to back off. I didn't say that before. But that was cool of you. I was annoyed at first, but I appreciate it."

He clears his throat, "Yeah, no problem. Like you said, bullies shouldn't be allowed to be shit on people. Especially people they just met." He pauses, "You should be a Fighter. You seem like you could hold your own."

"I was thinking of it." I shrug. "I may want to be a Jumper too. Though the jump in may have changed my mind. I don't really know yet."

"Me too. I wanna be a Fighter and Jumper. Why can't you do both?"

"Well, I also want to be a medic, or at least I did before I got here and saw all the different types of people I may need to learn about. It just seems overwhelming."

"It may be, but it would also be pretty cool. I know they're always looking for medics."

"Well, yeah, because they die a lot." Silence stretches between us. "Sorry, that was kinda morbid—just the statistics. Medics are often Medic Techs, so they aren't prepared and get picked off like nothing. I just don't want to end up another statistic. I've beaten most of them."

"Torrac," A voice calls, and Kathel gets up.

He pauses in the doorway. "You're going to keep beating them. I just have a feeling." He smiles and then moves into the room. I wait a few minutes before I'm called.

"Gomez?"

"Over here," I get up and hurry toward the doorway.

A Male who must be the same race as Dita holds a clipboard in one hand, with a stethoscope, syringes, and vials in his tentacles, waits for me in the hall outside the waiting room, "Ah, Agent Gomez, nice to meet you. If you will, please follow me." We make our way down a long hall full of side rooms before getting to the correct one. "Now, Miss Gomez, do you like to go by Adaline?" He motions for me to sit.

"Ada, please, Sir. I go by Ada."

He makes a note on his clipboard. "Alright, Agent Gomez, now, I'm sure you know from going to doctors on Earth that you have full doctor-patient confidentiality with me, correct?" He looks up over the edge of his thick-rimmed glasses at me, waiting to answer so he can mark it off.

"Yes sir, but I didn't really go to the doctor on Earth," I rub my shoulder, feeling my cheeks warm. "At least not for the last few years."

"Oh, did you go to a doctor off-world? Who did you see? Dr. Thivan?" He asks, looking up from my paperwork.

I look down. "Oh, no Sir, I haven't been to any doctor in the last few years. I, uh," I clear my throat, "I couldn't really afford it."

"Oh, that's quite alright, Ada, not a problem there." He gets up and moves over to a fridge. "Do you know if you're up to date on your vaccines? Being up here is like a nursery for bacteria. Wouldn't want anything to spread to your peers."

I scrunch my eyebrows. "I'm sorry, I don't think I have had any shots since I was fifteen. My foster parent didn't believe in health care." I trail off. "I couldn't get anything without his sign off. I tried. Will that affect anything? I'm willing to get them. I just didn't get a chance on Earth before I left."

"That's quite alright. We can get you all squared away now, not to worry. Just means you will be here for a few more minutes, that's all." He pulls a few more syringes and labeled vials out of a small fridge in the corner. "Okay, let's start with the easy part. You see that little bar there," he points to the wall where a bar that looks like one you would find in a gym is attached to the wall. "Go hang on that for a few seconds for me. Oh and please take your boots off." I do so before grabbing the bar. To my surprise, it slides up the wall to the ceiling then comes slowly down. A display on the wall flashes 52kg. "Perfect, thank you, Ada." He notates something on his tablet. "Now stand beneath the bar with your back and heels against the wall." I press my body flat against the wall. A small LED light shoots from the bar above my head and slides down until it comes in contact with the top of my head.

The display beside me flashes 1.6 meters. "Now just stay there for a moment; there is one more measurement we need to do." When he taps the tablet screen, the light continues to scan down my body and takes in data for my fat, muscle, and bone weight and percentages. "Thank you, Ada. Every two weeks, when you get your benchmark test facilitated, you will also get a similar test to the one we just ran done; this is to make sure your body is acclimating well to life in space. Please sit. Let's get these shots done."

I sit on the bed and quickly get eight shots in my right arm, and a few vials of blood taken for testing.

"Is that all?" I ask, holding a bit of cotton to my elbow crease.

"Almost—" he turns and puts the used items in a biohazard bag before turning back to me with one last syringe "—We just need to implement your tracking chip."

"Wait? A tracking chip?" I glance from him to the syringe.

Karrie never mentioned anything about a tracking chip… Maybe it's new?

He nods. "Yes, it's one way we monitor that all your systems are working correctly here on the station. When you go off base for missions or leave, we can find you in case something goes wrong. Ready? Breath in, and out." The others all felt like minor pinches. This is like being bitten by a massive bug. The chip is inserted in my left arm. He gives me a small smile. "I apologize, your arms will be sore the next few days. Let me know if the discomfort lasts for more than seventy-two hours." He turns off the screen of his tablet. "You're all set. You are free to go to your barracks and get settled in. Welcome to the Galactic Garrison, Agent Gomez."

SENT EMAIL 8/12/2228 17:46:16

Hey Sark,

I made it. I'm off-world! If the training is anything like what these tests have been like, then I might not be able to send these messages often. But I made it. It's wild up here. Don't worry, I will try to make a few friends I think I already found some. Good luck today with the move. I love you. I want to hear all about the new place when you get there. I found a link to a program; it shows where the base is in the sky. It's hard to navigate, but it should help you see where I am. Sounds sorta lame, but I thought it might help.

I love you, Sarkus.

A

Chapter 13

"Oh my gosh, I heard what you did. You are crazy!" Dita says the moment I walk into the barracks. Dita jumps up from a couch and runs over to me. "The guy came back, and he was pissed."

I look around the space. I expected to see rows of bunk beds like in Houston, but this room is full of small tables and couches, while the walls are lined with about a dozen doors. "Oh, right, you haven't been here yet. This is a common area. I already checked cause I thought most of the other rooms were full, and I was right; they assigned you with me. Come on, I'll show you." She leads me down to one of several doors. Our room has two bunks stacked on top of the other, a small table, an armchair, and a bathroom. Cabinets line one wall next to a small fridge. Dita jumps up onto the bottom bed and rolls over to look at me.

"So why did you tell off Edonne?" She asks, playing with one of her many tentacles—It wraps and unwraps itself around her fingers.

"Honestly," I sink into the armchair. "I don't know. He was acting like a prick, and he was doing it on purpose. People like that really, really piss me off."

Dita rolls back off the bed and pulls a glass bottle filled with deep green liquid out of the fridge. "Want one? It's a smoothie."

"Sure," I take the bottle from her. "What's in it?" I ask, taking a sip. I immediately spit out the contents.

"It's a kelp juice, saltwater, and what you humans call a banana. I have seen quite a few of your people put banana's in smoothies." She watches as I wipe down my tongue with my sleeve.

"Yes," I croak. "But we can't drink saltwater. I mean, we can, but we really, really prefer not to."

She takes the smoothie back from me. "Really? But you require the compounds of salt and water to survive, don't you?"

I laugh, "I mean, you're not wrong, we do need both things, but we can't have them in that concentrated of a form. It'll make us sick."

"Ooooh," she says, putting the smoothie back in the fridge. "Is that why you don't simply drink your oceans when you have a water crisis?"

I sit back down at the table, "I don't think we ever would have been able to. Between the salt and pollution, it probably wasn't ever safe."

"Huh," she says as a tentacle comes down to hold her chin. "You learn something new every day. Especially here, it's been really cool. I'm learning so much!"

I pull at the cuffs of my shirt. "I'm excited to get training, but I feel like I need a break from it all already."

"Tell me about it. I don't want to be an awkward bunkmate. So, what's been going on, how did you get here?" She laughs, "if we're going to be living together for at least the next eight weeks, I don't want to just be the weird person you live with."

So, I tell her. It feels really good, honestly, to tell someone who has no idea who I am, how hard I have worked to get here. To see the excitement and the pride she exudes for me. But it also feels incredibly vulnerable and embarrassing at times. Sarkus, Jaxon, my parents, the issues with past guardians and teachers. I wasn't kidding when I told Kathel that I was one of the few that beat the statistics.

"You're a fucking badass! I can't believe you're my roommate!"

We agree at that moment. Whatever we need, we do. Does this mean we spend our personal time in the gym working through Dita's punches so she can nail it and pass the fight test? Yep. And she programs a series of different jump simulations for me, so I can practice not feeling nauseous and working through that nausea when it comes. Yeah, yeah, it does. We don't get as much rest time as the others but it means we improve. And she thinks Sarkus is great, they chatted a few times about what it was like on Ganymede and school.

I sent him a picture of her, and he thought it was so cool that she's ya know, blue.

The training is intense, and this is just to get us to their baseline. I couldn't be more grateful for Karrie and everything she taught me. I sent her a message in my third week, but as of now, I haven't heard from her. She was never good at checking her messages.

One thing I didn't fully expect to happen, but in a way, I guess I should have, was that I have gained weight since getting here. While most of the other females in our group have lost weight since arriving here and are proud of it, I have gained weight. My muscles have filled out. While other people are so proud of how cut they look, I am happy to feel like my clothes fit more like they are supposed to. These are the results Karrie wanted.

There was a benchmark test every two weeks. We would stand in a line while the Sergeants read off our scores for the week and our averages. Each week the required average would rise. Our names on the screen moved, some getting closer, some falling under the red cutoff line. We didn't see those beneath the line after the next meal. They got shipped off to infantry posts around the galaxy to wait for their next chance. After the second test, the number of people coming back to the mess hall and sitting at our tables slowly fizzled from thirty-two to eighteen of us.

"Edonne called you a bitch again," Dita says, sitting down beside me. "He was telling anyone that would listen. But when I asked why, he wouldn't say. What was it about this time?"

I pick up the last glorious chocolate cupcake and find Edonne at the Male's table. I look him dead in the eye and take a massive bite. "He's jealous," I say around the mouthful. Dita laughs, but I hear a scoff from down the table.

"Ada," a drawn-out, annoying-ass voice says. "Why do you always have to stir up trouble?" I glance over at Miessa. She's the type of pristine race you would never expect to be willing to fight. She has the softest looking lilac skin and perfect frizz-free blonde hair. But that is what you get when you are Owliano. Shifters can make themselves look as pristine as they want. "I feel like someone is always cussing you out. If you didn't have to stick your nose in everything, you wouldn't have issues like this. You're going to get the rest of us in trouble again."

I put down my cupcake. I turn to her, pressing my shoulders down and back and lifting my nose in the air, just like she always does. "I'm sorry. I didn't realize getting *my* food during *my* mealtime was sticking my nose in places I'm not meant to be and inconveniencing everyone around me. I am so, so sorry, my liege." I fake a bow. "Honestly, if anyone should get their beak out of other people's business, it's you."

Her skin turns a ruddy orange. She looks like a Plutonian. "You are such a bitch."

"Thanks. If you want, I can offer you a ticket to join my fan club;

it seems to be growing today," I say, letting my voice drip sickly sweet sarcasm. The Males overhead and snicker.

"Attention agents." All eighteen of us jump to our feet and turn to face the voice. Gunnery Sergeant Callahan has been pushing us for the last few months to be the best and strongest soldiers we can be. "Agents, you all have been working very hard these past few weeks. Now you will demonstrate your skills to our Commander Eugenia Carver." He gestures to the woman beside him. She is a harsh looking Fem. Her icy blonde hair pulled tight into a bun, pulling the skin taught against her cheekbones. "We will go through a series of tests. After it is completed, only sixteen of you will remain. These tests will put you in your teams for your spec ops training. This will be, without a doubt, one of the most important tests you will take here at the Galactic Garrison."

Carver nods as she interlocks her fingers in front of her. "You have already sent in the divisions you would like to be in. However, we will adjust your location based on your scores. These tests will begin at 1500. You are to go back to your rooms and wait until you are called to begin the test." I glance over at Dita, but she looks as confused as I do. "You are dismissed. And good luck. Until all—"

"—the stars are found." We intone, and all give Commander Carver a tight salute before turning to clean up our lunches.

"Come on, let's get back to the room first, make our battle strategy." I say.

Dita nods and hurries to get out the door. She already has her tablet out, pulling up a few different charts with our rankings and notes she has made. But I can see she is a bit more sober than usual. This is the breaking point. There can only be four teams. And they are based on our scores. I stop outside the room for a second when a question catches me off guard. *What if someone ranks lower than the needed score? Does that drop it down to twelve available slots, or does it just mean someone's team will be short?*

"Ada," I turn to see Miessa slithering her way into Kathel's room. "Don't worry, I don't think they have a personality test. You and your piss attitude should do fine." She wiggles past a stern-looking Kathel before closing the door behind her.

"What was that about?" Dita asks.

"I have no idea. She's probably trying to get under my skin. She likely thinks just because Kathel stood up for me during intake, we're best friends or something? I don't know why. We haven't talked in a few weeks. Not since the last set of hand-to-hand training sessions when I kicked him in the balls. He thinks I did it on purpose." I flop down onto my bed. "Honestly, I don't care what half the people here think. They all try to stand out, like they think it will give them some sort of advantage. I don't want attention. I just want to get paid to do something I can do well, protect people, and bring Sarkus somewhere he'll be safe."

Dita sighs, "I know. Okay, well, let's work on what we can do.

We have to figure out these tests. What are they? How do they work? What are they testing for?" Dita writes a few things on her tablet. "What are the sections again?"

"Jumper, Fighter, Espionage, Tech, and Medic," I list off. "Everyone gets two specialties. I want Medic and Fighter, and you want Tech and Espionage?"

She and all her tentacles nod. "Definitely more tech, but I can't really see myself in any other role. Sneaking around seems like it'd be easier. Though by the tests, I can definitely say it's not!" She sighs, "I am kind of worried about that, Ada. What if I pass all the tests needed to be a techie, but I fail the other tests and then have to go do rounds at some space station outside of Jupiter?"

I sit up. "Are you talking negatively about yourself or others?" I say incredulously, mimicking one of the many training videos we watched.

"I know, I know. Very funny. I just don't want to be stuck for a long time on some planet I don't want to be on. I left the Jupiter Sector on purpose. And that is where everyone is being sent." her tentacles twisting. "I don't want to be back up."

Silence falls as we contemplate the possibilities. Her tablet makes a soft chirp, bringing us back. "Okay, well, for the Jumper test, unless they are going to send us somewhere, it will be a sim," I say, thinking of our past tests. We stop, and both look at each other. "Do you think they would send us somewhere off base?"

One of her tentacles reaches down to grab the stylus from her fingers rolling it back and forth as she ponders. "They may, that would be a really good twist. It would test how we would react to being tossed somewhere new versus kept on the station or in a sim. It would also directly impact how we would move on with the other sections of the test. Do you think it will be a group process or individual?"

"Honestly, I'm not sure. I feel like parts need to be individual, but some, like Fighters, need another person to effectively show how their skills. Some form of target." I pull out my tablet and review the notes from our last few sessions. "I think we should expect to be sent off base somewhere. At the very least, to go into an environment, one we haven't practiced a lot. Like a spacewalk or something." The idea instantly brings up the fear instilled by several safety videos portraying snapping tethers and spinning off into the deep vacuum of space.

"That would be intense. It would probably be a great advancement test." She taps a few things out on her tablet. "So, I figured out a way to see what was going on with the jump gates. You can see when it is booked for." She scrolls through, "So, today, for 1500, the gate is blocked off for about six hours. So, if we do use the gate, then it must be during those times. Or is it just for supplies?" Dita says. She gets up and grabs one of her weird kelp smoothies. "So, if we go off base and we aren't doing sims, what are we doing? We have to do something with tech, medical, and Espionage. Fighting would be pretty straightforward. We just pick up a gun or swing a fist."

I scroll through my notes, attempting to glean anything from them. "Well, maybe when we get there, we'll need to get something? I don't know..."

"Do you think this test is going to be all in one day?" Dita asks.

"No, it can't be. They would have to spread it out. Right?"

Chapter 14

We spend the next two hours trying to figure out what to do for these tests to no avail. At some point, we just lay down and set the alarm for a little before 1500. When we get up, I change into my cargo pants with the most pockets because no one can ever have too many pockets. I go over my supplies, not knowing what I need for the test I go for the basics. A small pen light, stylus, my tablet, and a knife.

We sit and wait with our tablets out, ready for the notification. We thought it would be the launch bay, but we still had to wait. At five to 1500, Dita gets an encrypted message; mine comes through a few minutes later. My message is encrypted with a series of puzzles. I have to unlock the different pieces to understand the clue. In the top right corner, it says one of five. The first is a maze with a series of moveable parts. It is like a current that needs to make the connection. As I move the pieces, it progresses through. When the current meets the end of the maze, the walls of the maze rearrange and go again. It was sort of fun.

Dita gets up and leaves. I watch her go, but she is so focused on her tablet she doesn't say anything. I glance back down, and the words have reformed to a string of letters. NGIEDLCMIAW. In the bottom corner, similar to my test on Earth, is a hyperlink. I click it, and it says, "Find the place you need to go within the letters."

I stare at the letters on the screen. "What the heck?" I murmur. I select the letters and copy them into a notepad app. I stare at the letters and try putting them in different fonts to see if anything stood out. Nothing does. I start slowly rearranging the letters.

INGEDLCIAMW

WINGMDECIAL

WING MEDICAL

"Medical Wing!" I jump up and type the answer into the little bar. And it moves onto the next puzzle. I head to the medical wing as it does. The next problem seems way too simple: it's a picture that I rearrange into a photo of medical locker 74. I jog; for all I know, everyone is headed for it. I slide the tablet into the pocket of my pants so I have both my hands free. The tablet thumps against my leg as I run. I keep my head on a swivel, looking for anyone in my group, but the halls are oddly empty. The medical wing is only a short way from my room.

Where is everyone? I muse *Surely other people are out here taking the test.* I gasp in surprise as someone bowls me over, shoving me out of the way. I stumble and catch myself on the wall. Edonne shoots me a glare over his shoulder, saliva pooling between his teeth. I hang back a moment and let him continue on to wherever he was in such a hurry. I wait until I see his tail disappear around the corner before I follow. *You definitely should have heard him coming.*

Keep moving, Ada, come on. The medical wing isn't that far away. I turn the corner, and there it is... but so are a bunch of the other cadets. I pull back down the hall and move into one of the side rooms, closing the door quietly behind me. Using my tablet, I search amongst the accessible files for a set of blueprints. Once I have the files up, I look for my location, eventually zeroing in on the hall. I pop my head back out and look for the room number. Closing the door again, I zero in on the room before clicking on the overlay for the air vents.

One plus of being a small woman is that I can get into places other people can't. "Perfect," I whisper and slip the tablet into my back pocket so it doesn't bang against the vents as I move. It barely fits. I move a table under the single vent in the room. The vent is held up by a few pins that I am able to remove with a pinch and good twist. I slowly bring the grate down to the floor. I climb back up and test the distance. I am going to have to jump up at least a foot or so to get enough leverage. I press my hands into the side of the hole and jump, rotating my hands so I can push myself up. My hand slips and I thud to the edge, I scrabble for a grip, but fall back down. The table bobbles and I let myself fall to the floor and roll away, trying to minimize the noise. I can't tell if anyone heard, so I duck out of sight of the door for a few seconds before climbing back up.

"Come on!" I growl. I push up again and this time, I make it up. When I get to the top, I lock my arms. Leaning back, I get a leg up on the edge and push the rest of my way into the air vent. Laying down across the vent, I prop my feet up on the other side. I breathe and roll over as quietly as I can, spreading my limbs out to the outside edge of the rectangular vent in an attempt to keep my weight distributed and to limit any noise.

I move thirty feet down the shoot then hang a right. Light comes from the room below in the medical ward. Through the small slats in the vent, I spot the lockers just off to my left. "Perfect," I whisper to myself. I wait a minute more before I slowly try to remove the pins, pinching my fingers through the grate and pulling down. "Shit," I hiss as the pin falls to the floor below, with a soft ping, ping, ping, as it bounces. I bobble the second pin and drop it beside me, which still makes an unwanted metallic thud, but it doesn't roll across the floor.

Slowly I turn the grate in my hands and rotate it so its diagonal and hopes that it fits back up through the vent so I can store it out of sight. It doesn't. So here I am, dangling from the ceiling, holding a grate that's digging into my fingers, hoping that no one will walk in and see my arms hanging out of the vent. I brace my feet against the sides and try to lean down. *Is there somewhere I can toss this? Not really... Fuck it.* I take a deep breath and drop the grate. I knew it would be loud. But... I didn't expect it to bounce... I didn't expect it to bounce into a cabinet ... I didn't expect a box to fall off the cabinet. I scoot away from the hole and wait, praying that no one comes in at the sound. I wait for what feels like an eternity before I feel confident enough to move.

I drop, rolling as I land to absorb the impact and come face to face with Miessa. We stare at each other for half a second before she shifts, taking the form of one of the higher ranking people on the base. "Nice try, Miessa. But you aren't tricking me with your shifting." I stride past her like I'm not freaking out that she caught me. *If this was the Espionage section of the test, I just fucked up.* I turn away, and as I do, she freezes. I tense, remembering the way Miessa always paused before jumping to attack during our fight training.

The thing about Miessa and the other Owlianos is they are like cats. She focuses on her prey, and nothing else matters. I have watched her go through the entire wiggle-butt process, just like the felines back on Earth. The freeze is her targeting her prey (yay me) before pouncing. She jumps, and I duck to the side. Grabbing a tray from a nearby cart, I swing it at her head. It clips her chin, and she returns to her natural purple form, her tail lashing back and forth.

"You bitch!" She says, holding her chin. "You aren't supposed to attack anyone!"

I drop the pan and move away from her. "Says the one that pounced at me." I snap. "You can't just yell at someone when you're literally doing the same thing. Don't attack me. Cool? Cool." I turn and not caring anymore about her. I move to locker seventy-four and rip it open. At the bottom of it sits a small box. I grab it and stalk past Miessa, shouldering her out of the way. She shrieks and flails. I don't look back.

Once the door is closed, I dash down the hall to the classroom I used before. I clear the room and close the door with a soft snap before opening the box. A small thumb drive sits inside.

"Where are these still used?" I whisper, turning the drive over in my hands. I've seen old USBs before in museums, the kind with the wide square bases that they used to plug into personal computers. Laptops, I think they called them. At some point in the last hundred years, tablets and holograms took over as the primary technology.

"Are you even a USB?" I turn it over, and on the back is a tiny button. "What do you do?" I murmur.

From the tip of the USB erupts a hologram. The soft blue lines are hard to see under the harsh fluorescent lights. I hit the panel for the lights and a three-dimensional blueprint of the Galactic Garrison's station comes into focus. "Something about this must be special," I say, walking around the projection. The lines connect and follow most of the blueprints that I have seen. But near the base, close to the original parts of the International Space Station, is a small orange pulse. I pull out the tablet and attempt to pull up a map of that section. But all I can find are the storage bays, and they don't seem to line up correctly. I flip back to the puzzles. But I must have completed them all for now, as it still shows a photo of locker number 74 in the medical wing. I creep out of the room, but no one is in the hall. *I hope Dita is doing good. We must be sent to different parts of the station?*

Rushing to the closest lift, I punch in level 2. My ride is fast and quiet. When the doors open, I am met with nothing, much like my test on Earth. *What is with the Garrison's love of darkness?* I step out of the bright lift and press myself against the wall. I hold my breath listening closely, but all I can hear is the quiet hum of machinery.

I make my way around the edge of the room, trailing my hand on the wall as a guide. Peering into the dark, I move slowly through the room again.

Moving away from the wall, I put my hands out in front of me. I swing my arm to the left and catch the edge of something, I push against it and it rolls away, and then I slowly pull it to me. Dragging my fingers across the top of the cart, they brush a glass. I slowly reach my hand in but there is nothing inside. Next to the glass, I find a knife. I check the blade on my thumb. The dull serrated edge doesn't do too much, but I put it in my pocket, anyway.

My foot hits something solid as I continue across the floor. It shifts when I make contact. I jump back and freeze, holding my breath. Nothing happens, and I slowly bend to the floor and reach out for the thing I kicked I jump back when my hand bumps the item. My heart rate spikes and I take another deep breath. Slowly I feel up the fabric. *What the fuck? Is that a leg?*

My heart pounds, and sweat beads on my temple. *Focus Ada* I slowly reach into my pocket and pull out a penlight that I swiped a few weeks ago from the Med Center. Covering the tip, I turn on the light. My finger glows a pinky- red, but I slowly let light into a small circle as I slide my finger away from the tip. It illuminates a soldier; his fatigues are torn, and blue blood stains the fabric around a ragged hole. *What the hell? What caused this?*

The sight of the wound makes me want to help him and flee the room. *You want to be a medic? Be a medic.* I step closer and try to find a pulse. The skin feels warm, but strange, rubbery. Like it isn't real. I don't know if this is part of the test, but with the different species on board the Garrison's base, I can't take that risk. I find a pulse and count the beats against my watch.

Too slow.

No matter what race this guy is, unless he is going into hibernation, he shouldn't have that slow of a heartbeat. I tilt his chin and lower my ear to his lips. Faintly I hear him exhale and feel the breath tickle my skin. *Okay so you are alive.* I turn back to his leg. I hold the penlight in my mouth and grip the edges of his pants, pulling the fabric away from the hole. The frayed edges drag across the wound, and a moan comes from my patient. I shriek in surprise and jump away. I have to remind myself several more times that this is a fucking test, and I need to get my shit together. I drop back to my knees and continue to pull the fabric away, slowly tearing to reveal the entire wound.

"I don't know what you did, dude, but I'll try my best to get you fixed up." First step, I need to stop the bleeding so I can try to clean it and close the wound... somehow.

I shine the penlight around the room, searching for something, but the light is too weak to see far. I find a series of cabinets on the wall and wrench them all open until I find towels. I go a few more down and find bottles of water. "Perfect." I carry my stash back to my patient. Then go back to the cabinets. I need something to stop the bleeding. Finding nothing, I turn back to my patient. "Fuck it," I move back to him and pull at my belt, slipping it from the loops. As gently as I can, I slide the belt under my patient's leg and tighten the belt well past the holes. I pull it through the loop and tie it off, pulling it down towards his foot. The patient groans again. "Dude, I know, but we need to stop the bleeding."

I get up and scan the room again, looking for something to clean the wound to stop an infection. I slowly tip a bottle of water onto the wound. Pale blue liquid flows away from the cut, leaving the hole, free of debris. Taking a towel, I gently dab at the wound until it is as clean as I can make it. The makeshift tourniquet has reduced the bleeding significantly but not entirely. I roll one towel into a tight tube and press it into the cut before taking two more towels and wrapping them around the tube to hold it in place.

"Tape? Is there any tape?" I didn't see any the first go but I search the cabinets again and come up empty. I turn back to my patient "What can I…" I drop back to the floor and fumbling at his waist, I try to pull his belt off as gently as I can without moving him too much. I lift his leg a few inches and slide the belt beneath the towels, and loosely wrap it around the triaged leg, securing everything is place. "Okay, Sir, what should you and I do now? Do we need to move you?"

My vision goes white and I bring a hand up to cover my eyes as the florescent lights crash back to life "Agent Gomez. This portion of your test is complete. Please proceed back to the barracks."

I rise and look down at my patient. A lifelike robot dummy, he looks ridiculously real, but the harsh light reveals what I couldn't see with my little pen light. "Okay, well, I hope the next few hours go well for you," I say.

My journey back to the lift is a lot easier now that I can see. When I press the button to take me back up, I leave a smear of blue blood on the wall.

Chapter 15

I move through a series of warm-ups, watching those who do the same. "Morning, Ada," Kathel says, mid-stretch. "What do you think they are going to have up their sleeves for us today?"

"Hey," I stand up and stretch the back of my arm squeezing it to my chest. I glance to where Sergeant Wayne watches all of us like a hawk. "No idea, but if Wayne is involved, it likely has something to do with fighting."

Kathel stands up, "I heard you got into a bit of a tussle yesterday."

I look over at Miessa. She glares in my direction a deep purple bruise marring the perfect skin on her chin. "Well, you know, sometimes people need to get knocked down a peg," I say a bit too loudly.

Kathel bursts out laughing. "Shit! That's going to piss her off."

"What, you gonna go back and tattletale?" I snap.

"No, I just find it funny the fights that Fems get into. They don't seem to have a real purpose."

"As if the fights Males have over Fems make any sense." I scoff.

He nods, "Okay, you got me there." He grins. "You have been doing a pretty good job."

Dita and I share a look. "That was a shift," I say, confused. "You went from commenting on how I got into a fight with your friend to complimenting me on fighting her?"

He laughs, "I meant in training."

"Oh."

He shrugs, "Well, yeah. You're good at what you do. You are going for a Fighter Jumper class, too, right? Gotta pay attention to the people working for the same things as me."

"I mean yeah, I wanna be on the ground. I'd prefer the Medic class. Those haven't been going as well. It's easier to hit things than to fix them."

He opens his mouth to say something when Wayne whistles. "Cadets, line up against that wall!"

We all line up on the wall, and I can feel the cool metal through my thin t-shirt. Wayne grins: whatever he has up his sleeve for us today won't be pleasant. Though most of the training we've done since we got here hasn't been pleasant. But as Commander Carver likes to remind us, 'Not all training has to be fun to be educational.

Not everything has to be nice to have a purpose.'

"Agents, today we will do a fight bracket. Some of you came here to be in the Espionage or Jumper categories. I'm here to prove today that some of you aren't quite ready for that." Some people laugh, but Wayne's face doesn't change. He means business. "Because what happens when you fuck up? When you reveal your location to your target? When your techie gives you the wrong coordinates, and you end up *in* the enemy base? You have to fight. You will have your specialties. My job is to make sure you are well rounded."

He taps a button on the display in front of him and a bracket appears. "You will be fighting each other today. And this isn't a training exercise. This is a test. You will be fighting to incapacitate your opponent." He scrolls over a slide. "Either your partner is hurt to the point they can no longer fight, or they pass out. I, of course, will step in before any maiming or killing. We would like to keep you a bit longer. Well, most of you." This time, no one laughs with him. I glance over at Dita, whose eyes are wide like a cat's. "This will most likely take place over a few hours but know the fights will be closer together as we go down the brackets. We will have a winner and a loser's bracket. So, you will fight twice at the very least." He swipes one more time and reveals the first fights. "You are starting by weight class. After that, all bets are off, and it's up to your skills."

I stare at the brackets. It makes sense. I'm small. I'm tiny, really. But I didn't think I would be in the *first* fight.

"So, unless there are any further questions, are we ready?" we give a weak cheer. "Are you fucking kidding me?" Wayne asks, eyes flashing, it's like a sick summer camp. "Are you ready?" We cheer again, louder this time, though a bit of the enthusiasm has been leached from it. "Good." Wayne turns and presses a button on the wall. A stage raises a few inches from the rest of the floor and a few mats slide out. "Gomez and Monet, are you ready?" Wayne challenges.

I roll my shoulders back and jump up on the block, attempting to take up as much space as I can to look confident. "Yes, Sir!" I relax into a fighting stance, bouncing lightly on my toes, ready to move. *You should feel confident.* I remind myself. *You took out Steele on Earth, and he had a good sixty pounds on you.* The more positive side of me says, but the negatives cut through. *Yes, but that was in the dark, and you were on your own. You had no idea who was attacking you. And you stopped when you were told. You didn't make him pass out.* I shake the thoughts away and move around the circle.

Monet, like me, is slight, but she is tall. She probably has a good five or six inches on me. Her weight is distributed over long arms and legs.

"Remember, we are fighting to incapacitate," Wayne says.

"When you are ready, fight!" He presses a button, and a timer ticks above our heads. "Oh yeah, I forgot to mention, this will be timed. Take too long to finish the fight, and both parties will move to the loser bracket."

Monet locks eyes with me, her small hands curling into fists. She circles the edge, vying for a closer spot, but I move opposite her, keeping her away. Her movements are sharp and jerky, her eyes jumping to each of my limbs as they move. *She's nervous.* I step towards her as a test, and she jumps back three feet before catching herself and glancing around to see if anyone noticed. They laugh and cover their mouths with their hands as they whisper. Our class is brutal. But we need to be. Not everyone is meant to be in the Spec Ops. We need to cut the weakest links.

I move forward again, keeping my knees bent and my weight on my toes. I watch her jerky movements for a sign. The scared goat jumping away. That's when I notice her hands. Monet has her thumbs tucked in under her other fingers. A small part of me wants to correct her, but I doubt she would believe me. I step in a zigzag pattern closing the distance between us. She jumps away, turning her back to me.

"Come on, Monet, have you learned nothing?" Wayne barks as I make my first strike. I reach out quickly as I can and grab her fleeing ponytail, ripping her back toward me. The movement is simple but upsets her equilibrium, and she tumbles to the ground with a grunt. I let her get back up.

"Come on, Gomez, don't play with your food!"

Monet is shaken, but she fixes her hands. She jumps at me, swinging wildly with both hands. I easily block them, pushing her back. A single tear rolls down her face, and I feel bad before I realize it's a ploy. She uses that moment to lunge at me. I jump back, but not fast enough, and she clips my jaw.

I rub at it, using the movement to scan her. "Okay, Monet, come on," I say before launching again at her. She holds her ground this time. I swing at her shoulder with my right hand, which she blocks, but my left hand jabs into the stomach. She bends over, out of breath. I swing both hands down and punch her in the back, knocking her to the floor. She grabs at my legs, but I kick her away. My foot connects with her face, and she slumps unconscious.

"This round goes to Agent Gomez."

The surrounding agents cheer as I step off the platform, I glance over my shoulder, stunned as a few medics carry Monet off the mat. I look up as my name shifts forward to the next section of the bracket, and they place a timestamp between mine and Monet's names.

1:26.12.

That's all it took. I watch as they carry away her to the infirmary for her short break. *Hopefully, her later fight goes better, and she can stay.* But part of me thinks she won't. She was too skittish; I don't believe the Galactic Garrison would allow anyone to be in Spec Ops with that mentality. Everyone has to be able to fight. As Wayne said, you never know what could happen. You always have to be prepared.

I look back up at the board. The next fight is between Elara, a Plutonian, and a guy named Vespar. He is small, maybe a meter and a half tall, and built like a barrel. Their fight goes longer. Vespar is very steady on his feet and takes Elara's blows like a champ. He lands a damn good punch that sends her flying, but she pushes through, even with blood running into her eye from her split eyebrow. Their fight ends around the eight-minute mark when Elara finally got Vespar off his feet. He catches his shoulder mid roll on the edge of the stage, and even across the room I can hear the pop of it dislocating. Wayne calls it there.

Elara nods in my direction as she passes me on the way to the infirmary. The nod says, *Good luck. I'll see you soon*. A fighter to a fellow fighter. No malice, just respect.

I don't deserve it; my first fight was too easy. I should have squared off with someone like Elara or Vespar. But because I'm smaller, I had what I'm sure will be known as the easy fight.

Even Dita has a harder fight than I do. She squares up against Miessa. Dita does her best, but Miessa doesn't play fair. She almost instantly gets told off for shifting.

Miessa tried to argue that shifting was one of her skills, but

Wayne didn't like that. "You have to know how to fight as yourself before you can fight as anyone else." And he had a point there. But this just fuels Miessa. She uses it as a way to prove him wrong, knocking Dita out three minutes later.

I follow Dita out to the medical wing, hoping to be there when she wakes up.

Her nose is swollen and a blotchy purple from the blow Miessa landed. As the nurse wipes away the crusted blood from her nose, Dita's eyes fly open and she tries to jump from the bed.

"Dits, Dits, it's me. Relax, you're okay," I grab her hand, and her eyes lock on mine.

She slumps back on the bed. She lifts a hand to her face, covering her eyes. She bumps her nose. "Oh, ow. Oh no. She knocked me out, didn't she?" Her voice is already thick and slightly nasally from the swelling.

"Yeah, she did." I sit down next to her. "You did a good job though."

The nurse passes me a cup with medication. "It's an anti-inflammatory to help the swelling go down."

I nod and take the meds from her. "How bad was it?" Dita asks.

"Here, take these," I say, passing her the cup with the three green tablets and a small cup of water. "It really wasn't that bad. Just Miessa is crafty and didn't fight fair."

"So, she walked all over me?" Dita says, sitting up and taking the meds, chasing them with a bit of water.

"Not quite, I think you'll do pretty well with your next fight," I say, trying to sound encouraging.

"Great, I'll do a good job in the loser's bracket. Who will that be against?" She asks, slumping back down against the bed.

"Oh, come on, gotta think more positively than that. I think you may be up against either Vespar or Monet. I'm not sure which exactly. I don't know when the second bracket will start their fights."

She sighs, "I guess that's not too bad. I think I can do that." She touches her nose gently and winces. "As long as no one punches my nose."

I give her a wan smile. "You know they'll try to target that."

"Yeah, I know." She sighs, "I don't want them to use it against me, but I'd rather not get knocked in the head again."

The PA system pings. "Agent Gomez, your next fight will start in five minutes. Please make your way back to the ring."

My adrenaline instantly spikes in preparation. "Who do you have to fight now?" Dita asks as I head for the door.

"If I looked at it right, it's my turn to knock out Miessa."

The fighting ring is much quieter now. The winners are the only ones left. Kathel and Edonne sit against the wall, watching each other from a distance. I glance up at the bracket as the current fight finishes up. Both of the Males won their respective matches, as I figured they would. But based on the next few fights, it seems likely they'll be up against each other.

Miessa watches me from the other side of the ring like a predator watching her prey. *Don't let her intimidate you before you've even started. Take up space, have a presence. You are small but fierce.*

There is a crunching thud as the fight in front of us ends with a knockout punch to the face. I wince at the brutal sound. Agent Ackley cheers over her opponent before stepping off the mat, wiping a drop of blood from her split lip. She claps Miessa on the shoulder and says something that makes the two of them laugh. There is a sharp spike of adrenaline in my chest, and it's like my veins are singing with energy. I don't like the way it makes me feel. I am on edge, but not quite to the point where I am jumpy like Monet was. A few soldiers jump up on the mat, cleaning and drying it before the next match.

"Alright, would Agents Gomez and Guamianna please take to the mat?" Sargent Wayne barks. Miessa swishes her tail back and forth. Even without shifting, she has an advantage over me with that extra appendage. "When you are ready, fight!" Sergeant Wayne calls out, and the bell tolls, signaling the start of the timer.

Miessa lunges forward with a few quick punches. I block them easily but her quick attack rattles me. I roll away and up to my feet. "What's the matter, little Earthling? Scared to fight?" She asks, rolling her shoulders back.

She's trying to play the intimidation game. She stands tall; knees barely bent, hands loose. Cool, casual, like she doesn't need to be ready to fight me. But she's ready. When I move around the circle, each new movement makes her hands jerk into fists. How her eyes are wide, calculating, taking in every movement. They have been described as cat-like, but seeing her move now is like watching the lizards that would run around our vacation home. Quick, darting, moving before you could react.

"Nah, I'm not scared. Just waiting for you to get over yourself." I jump in toward her like I am going to swing but hop back. The movement sends her skittering.

"Ada, what have we said about playing with your opponent? Attack her!" Wayne barks. I glance over at him. His arms are crossed. And he looks pissed. These fight must not be at the level he wants.

Sure, I get yelled at for lunging, but not her? Okay. I roll my eyes and do the same movement again, this time swinging one arm up in an attempt at an uppercut. The movement looks weak, she easily bats my hand away and steps closer to me. I jump at her, driving my shoulder into her stomach, plowing her to the floor. She cries out in shock and beats at me with her tail. I roll away from the thick wall of muscle.

She takes another moment to rise to her feet, puffing for air. She glances over at Wayne, "What, not going to yell at her for that?"

It's too easy. I plow into her again; my fist connects with her

145

jaw. She goes spinning, but not before she knocks me aside with her tail. I land on my hands and knees, a sharp pang lancing up my wrist.

Your hands are delicate, never land on your wrists; we humans are prone to breaking our wrists when we do that, Karrie's voice chimes in my ears. Miessa has her back turned to me. I need to incapacitate that tail. I grab it, the rough, scaly texture cutting into my hands as she whips me back and forth. I plant my feet and pull backward, hoping to use it to topple her over again. But she pulls too. My hand slips, and she wraps part of the tail around my wrist. She backs me up, holding my wrist uncomfortably high above my head, forcing me to dance on my tiptoes. The crowd laughs as I struggle to reach the ground. My free hands trying to get free. I am out of range to hit anything but her tail

"Really? You think you can beat me by grabbing my tail?" she hisses in my faces, her nose mere inches from mine. She slams my arm back down against the wall, wrapping her tail around my arm tighter.

I pretend to fluster, letting a stream of unintelligible syllables pour from my mouth, like I can't think of anything to say, and give a feeble attempt at a wiggle to become free. She throws her head back, laughing and tightening her tail around me. I scrabble weakly letting her think she has won. As brings her head back down, I jab my fingers directly into her eye. She shrieks in pain, dropping me instantly. *Always be aware of everything your opponent is doing.*

146

Karrie had drilled that into me, giving me black eye after black eye. You can't let your opponent create a diversion. I let myself fall to the ground and swing my legs, knocking her to the ground beside me. I thought like in the tunnels in New Seattle I would have a moment, an advantage but Miessa launches herself on top of me. She latches her hands around my neck and squeezes. She sits on my legs, and her tail comes around and pins one of my hands to the floor. I blindly flail with the other, desperate to get a hold on her. I try peeling her fingers away from my throat, but the pressure is already building. I gasp for air and black spots block out my vision.

Come on, damn it. I try desperately to make my body cooperate with what I want my hands to do. But they feel weak and floppy, like they aren't entirely mine. Like a wire has come loose, and the connection is misfiring.

I punch at her again and again, but she easily knocks aside the blows. I can't see her anymore. Past the ringing in my ears the buzzer sounds calling the end of the fight, and then she is off me. I lay there coughing for a minute as air, blissful air, flows back into my lungs. Someone lifts me and plops me on a chair on the sidelines. I lean forward, resting my head in my hands and breathing deeply. Slowly the world comes back into focus.

"Agent Gomez can you look up for me?" Someone shines a light in my eyes and I blink away even more spots. A buzzer sounds and the next fight takes off. When my vision clears I look to the board.

My name has dropped to the loser's bracket. I cover my face. "Shit."

Chapter 16

After a long night, and a futile attempt at sleep, the breakfast bell finally rings. I woke up with a splitting headache from lack of sleep and several beautiful purple bruises around my throat. I stumble into my clothes and follow Dita down to breakfast. Our minds roll, going over every detail of the last few tests, trying to calculate how they would score us. It's silent at our tables. The rest of the hall is a buzz of noise, well-rested after their night spent off base or getting some extra sleep. Some of us, like me, just push our food around our plates, too uneasy to eat.

"You have to eat something. I'm sure we're going to have more things to do after they assign the teams." Dita says pushing a cup of coffee toward me.

I nibble a piece of toast. I can't kick the stone out of my stomach. I feel like the tests went okay. They weren't what I expected, and I don't think I did as well as I could have. I just hope that it's enough to be above the cutoff point. *Will they cut a team if some of us score poorly? Curve the scores down to get the best people?*

A tone plays across the speakers. Everyone freezes and looks up toward them. "Good morning everyone in our potential Spec Ops class. Please come to the jump deck immediately." I glance around, and we all stand as one; we are a trail of grim reapers, each one of us harboring that little seed of doubt. Dita looks cautiously optimistic. As she should. She won her second fight easily. She did a great job. She's trying to keep her head up, and not look worried, but her tentacles hang low. Miessa's tail drags across the floor, as out of it as I am. Part of me wants to stomp on it. Though she still has a small, satisfying bruise on her chin from the pan I smacked her with in the medical wing.

We have to make three trips in the lift to get down to the jump level. Dita and I take the second lift down. When we get there, everyone is standing around. There are no superiors to be found. Dita and I move to the side, further away from the jump gate. "That was Commander Carver's voice over comms, wasn't it?" I whisper as the eighteen of us press in together.

"I thought so," she whispers back. "But last night I looked at the log, and she didn't have a return jump scheduled after everyone else got back." Her face turns purple from a flush under her skin, "I got booted off the server not long after that. I think they finally tracked my IP and shut down my access." The last lift arrives and we end up smushed against the wall. This low in the station, everything is cramped. Thank the expanse we made modifications to the levels above.

"Agents, please acquire a jumpsuit. You will meet us off base," Commander Carver's voice says echoing slightly in the space. "Programmed into the data log of your suits are the coordinates for a location. Please enter that code into the gate. Each one of you has a different code. If you arrive at the station at Jupiter Prime, you have not passed your training to be in the Special Operations Division. If you arrive on the Moon, congratulations you have made. Upon arriving you will find a colored flag. Match flags to find your official squad. You and your team must find myself and Sergeant Callahan to receive your insignia." Dita and I glance at each other. Commander Carver continues, "I will award the team that comes in first a break from duty for forty-eight hours. The three other teams will rotate patrols in eight-hour shifts." I sigh, what I wouldn't give for a few nights of unbroken sleep.

"This will be interesting." Edonne hisses.

"I hope he and Miessa get on a team." I say, nudging Dita, "They're perfect for each other." Dita snickers.

"Good luck, cadets. I hope to see you soon on the Moon." The voice of the commander cuts out with a crackle.

Someone shouts out, "Well, let's go," and the crowd of us moves like a wave for the locker rooms, banging open doors as we look for our suits.

"Where the hell is my suit?" Someone shouts out.

I open my locker and when I grab my suit I don't see Gomez on the patch but someone who's name is Spero.

"You didn't really think they would make it easy for us, did you?"

People put aside their competitiveness for a moment and start shouting out surnames, trying to help each other find their suit. I eventually find my copper-colored suit and yank it over my clothes. I latch the helmet closed and boot up the internal computer. On the visor of my suit, my vitals pop up, and a code. It's a string of numbers that I can only hope places me somewhere on the surface of the Moon. The line to the command station of the jump gate is already long. The water-like surface of the gate roils, waiting for a command. People around me are trying to compare numbers, but from what they are saying, they don't seem to have any correlations. They must have encoded the numbers so they don't match up. But none of us are going to take the time right now to hack it.

The first person steps through, and there is a bit of jostling as people try to claim the next available spot up front. My heart rate monitor spikes a bit. I want to go; I wanna get this ball rolling. Each person in front of me gets a little more time to figure out if they have made it or not, and to find their teammates. After seven people, I am next in line. The person in front of me steps through, and I tap in the coordinates when I suddenly fly back. Those waiting behind me gasp. I look up, and Edonne is standing over top of me. "You were taking way too long. Move over."

"Look, dude," I say, climbing to my feet and shoving him back and off the jump gate's ramp. I feel my little ear piece come loose and pause to make sure it is solidly in my ear. The last thing I need is for it to come out right before a mission. I lock my helmet into place and hope to the expanse I don't need to fix it again. "At some point, you are going to have to get over yourself. Yes, right now, we are in a competition. But, once we walk through that gate, we are in the same force. At some point, you need to get the stick out of your ass as realize we are on the same fucking side." I turn and enter the last bit of the coordinates, and the surface of the jump gate smooths out, waiting for my passage. "I am done with this shit, okay? Just let people do what they need to do. No one here thinks you should get your way because you're an ass."

Someone grumbles behind me "been saying that since day one." There is grumble of agreement from those behind him. Edonne turns to them, hissing, but no one falters. He stalks back into line, and I turn back to the gate. I step up to the surface, take a deep breath, and step through. Once I am in, I close my eyes. I can't look where I'll land. The dizzy feeling is amplified, but I only crack them slightly when I feel like I should be close. In the distance through the shimmering surface of the gate is my exit. I step through, pressing my eyes closed. I hear nothing. I can't see any bright lights through my eyelids, either. Slowly, I flutter my eyes open. And sigh in relief and awe. I am on the Moon.

Chapter 17

I turn around in time to see the gate ripple closed. This point is just a receiving end as there is no console, and the water like surface dissolves, into the vacuum of space. *Okay, guess I won't be going back that way.* I take a few deep breaths, taking in everything so I can tell Sark later. The surface of the Moon is a muted grayish color. And just like the photos I've seen, the surface is riddled with holes. My feet float a bit as I walk. I take one little hopping step, and my heart rate spikes again as I fly off the ground about six feet. "Okay, whoa, let's not do that again," I say, bouncing back down onto the Moon's surface. Each time my boot comes down, I leave a distinct footprint on the soft surface.

I survey the surrounding area. *I need to find a flag.* I squint against the darkness. About one hundred feet to my left, a pole with a blue pennant is stabbed into the ground. I move toward it, looking as I do for other flags or people. I need to find three other teammates and Commander Carver. I hit my headlamp and attempt to illuminate the surrounding area. I reach out and grab the pole and use it as a walking stick, stabbing the end into the surface of the Moon with every step to keep me rooted in place.

Remembering the comm unit in my ear, I pause and tap into it, cycling through different frequencies. "Hello, this is Agent Gomez, can you read me?" I ask the darkness, continuing my slow trek across the surface of the Moon, scanning the horizon for any other movement.

"This is Agent Odyssa. Over." A clipped voice answers one of my calls.

I freeze, "Hello, Agent Odyssa," I say, pausing for a second, trying to figure out what to say. "Have you found your flag? Over."

The sound of static crackles over the comms "Affirmative. I have a purple flag. What color do you have?"

I sigh, "I have a blue flag, over."

"Thank you, Agent Gomez, please keep this frequency open for purple flags. Over." The Agent says, and the comm returns to static.

Well, screw you too. I continue checking and come across a yellow and a green team. Both only have one or two people.

"This is Agent Torrac calling for any members of the blue team." I freeze.

"Seriously?" I scoff. Of course, they put Kath on my team. I accept the call. "This is Agent Gomez answering the call for the blue team. Over."

There is a good twenty-second pause before he answers. "Ada?"

"Hey, Kath." I reply. "Where are you? Have you found anyone else?" I pause, waiting to see what direction to go in.

"I think I can send you a ping. I haven't found anyone else yet. Over."

I wait a moment, and a message comes across, the notification popping up in the top right of my HUD display. I switch comms to my computer. "Open message." It takes me a few moments to program in the string of numbers he sends me, and a little light at the top of my HUD display flashes. I turn away, and it disappears. "I think I figured it out," I say over comms. "I have a ping; I will send mine in a second. Over." I pause then speak to the system, "Send Agent Torrac my location."

There is a small beep, and I hope I send the correct information. I start my hike across the Moon. "How far am I from Agent Torrac's location?" I ask the AI in my HUD.

A distance appears next to Kathel's flashing light. 400M, 398M, 390M, the number of meters drops as the two of us make our way to each other.

"I'm going to keep scanning comms," I say to Kathel. "Can you stay on this frequency?"

"Will do." There is a pause. I'm about to start rotating channels again when he comes back on. "Ada, you still there?"

"Yeah, what's up?"

"On your flag, there should be a number on it. What is it?" He asks.

"On my flag?" I pause and examine the pennant before the pole. Right near the top of the pole, there's a number, "one hundred three," I relay over to him. "Why? What do you think it is?"

"I think it may be the location of where we need to go to find Commander Carver."

"What number do you have?" I ask.

"Thirty-seven. I have already tried to input our two numbers; we need the others."

"Hmm, alright, I'm going to go see if I can find them. I ran across some other the other teams earlier, so they may block off my calls to those frequencies if they have all their people. Do you know how big the Moon is?"

"Roughly thirty-two thousand kilometers in diameter, give or take." Kathel replies, "I, for one, would rather not have to blanket this entire rock for two other people."

"Same. Okay, I'll call back in a few minutes, or see you. Whatever comes first." I scan again and, as predicted, they have blocked some frequencies off. "We need to pick up the pace," I grumble to myself, looking for Torrac. My HUD says that I should be able to see him. I should be right on top of him. "Kath, where are you?" I ask.

"I am above you." He says. I look up, and sure enough, he has on a jet pack and is expertly negotiating it through the air.

"How come you got a jet pack?"

"How come you got a headlamp? I didn't get one. I could see you for a while now. I mainly used the HUD in case it wasn't actually you."

We think for a second, then both say at the same time. "Carver."

"Hel-hello?" A new voice breaks in over our comms, and Kathel and I both jump. Luckily, my flag keeps me planted.

"Hello?" I ask, "Who is this? Over."

"Great expanse, you can hear me? Finally, yes! Right, uh, it's Miessa. My comms were down, I had to rework them. I just found my flag. What color are you? Uh, over?"

I glance at Kathel, but he isn't looking at me. "We have a blue flag, Miessa. This is Agent Torrac and Gomez."

"Are you fucking kidding me?"

I sigh. I was afraid of this. "Hi, Miessa, welcome to the blue team. What is your location? Over."

"No, you bitch, I am not on your fucking team. There must be some mistake. Fuck off." There is a hiss and a snap as she goes offline.

Until All the Stars are Found

Chapter 18

"Well, that is just great." Kathel sighs. "Miessa, Miessa, do you read me? Miessa come on." we are met with empty static. "Fucking A—she is so stubborn." He growls.

"That is one way to put it," I retort.

"She—you know she isn't that bad." He sighs. "I—nope, I won't defend her." He stabs the ground a few times with the butt of his flagstaff.

"Right. Okay." I turn to the horizon when I see a little yellow icon flashing in the corner of my screen. "Hey, how much oxygen do you have? Because even if we can't find the others, we'll need to find a jump gate soon." I say, glancing at my HUD display. "I am down to like half a tank already."

He turns to look at me, and his face is pinched in concern. "You are only at half a tank? Did you check it before you jumped?"

I flush in embarrassment. "No, I assumed we would all have full tanks. I mean, last time I handled my suit, I hooked it up to the oxygen supply. I was kinda busy dealing with Edonne. Rookie mistake."

"I swear he is going to get himself kicked out. What did he do this time?" Kathel asks.

I roll my shoulders. "Well, he was impatient, and apparently me going before him was too much to handle, so he tried to smack me out of the way as I was putting my coordinates in. I mean, he *did* smack me out of the way, but I was flustered, so I didn't go through all my checks." I think of his bonus of a jet pack, but lack of a flashlight. "Do you think this was on purpose?"

"What do you mean?" He keeps squinting and staring into the darkness.

I shift my grip on my flag. "Well, you didn't have a flashlight, but you have a jet pack. I have the flashlight but am low on oxygen. And it seems like Miessa had to fix her comms? Maybe this is part of it. Maybe we have to overcome whatever obstacle we have on top of trying to find our teammates and the commander before we get a jump back." We pick a direction and start walking; I glance down at my HUD. I freeze.

"What? Is your oxygen lower?"

"No, I have a message, but I don't know who it's from, it's just a location."

He glances down at his screen too. "I have it too. Maybe Miessa's comms went down again, but she could get our suit codes to send a message?"

I program it in, and we move for the dot. The person stands in place, shifting slightly. "Hello?" I try to get our suits to connect to see what channel they may be reading on. Nothing.

Kathel motions and we slowly circle the person until we can see their face. We freeze, our visors are tinted, giving us some protection from the sun's glare or lights in a firefight. But this visor is blacked out, I can't even see the shape of the person's face underneath.

"Go in slow," Kathel advises "we don't know if this is a person or part of the test."

I nod and move in slowly, matching my pace to Kathel's. The person doesn't react as we get closer. "Computer can you zoom in on the person?" I ask squinting to see the letters on their chest.

"Affirmative Agent Gomez." My visuals zoom in I see a familiar line of letters.

"Dita! Dita are you okay?" I keep trying to ping her comms but nothing happens. I say, giving her an awkward hug. She jumps back in fright. "Shit, Kath, what do we do?" And I'm guessing it blocks out sounds too. But like us, she has a blue flag. I turn the volume way up on my output speakers. "Dita," I shout into the mic inside my helmet. "Dita, it's me, it's Ada."

A hand comes up and taps on my helmet. Three taps for three

letters.

"Yes, Ada. A-D-A. Is it you, Dita? Give me a thumbs up if it's you." She gives me a thumbs up.

Kathel mimics me and turns his comms all the way up. "Dita, I'm also here. It's Kathel." She reaches out, and he grabs her hands as she taps six on his helmet. "Yes, Kathel." He turns to me. "What should we do? I can't tell where the seal is on this. But all of this must have happened once we walk through the gate somehow? There's no way she put her helmet on and didn't notice that the glass was blacked out."

I grab her flag from where it floated away. "Well, we have the third coordinate. Should we just start moving as close as we can?"

He programs in the numbers and sighs. "I don't think we need the last number, but we need to hurry."

"Why is that?" I ask as he grabs my arm, hurrying me across the ground.

"Because it wants us to go toward the original landing site, on the other side of the Moon, and you only have half a tank, and who knows how much oxygen she has?" He says. "Hang on." He powers on the jet pack and I squeal as Dita clings to my arm. "I can use the three coordinates we have for a general area, but we need that last point to know exactly where to go."

"So we need to find Miessa soon."

"Yeah." We zip across the surface of the Moon, and I pray that he stays close to the surface because the galaxy is huge and his fuel tank is not. "Be careful. You're going to use up all the fuel in your tank! We may need that." I scold him as my feet lift off the floor again.

He carries us another twenty feet before taking a few awkward running strides and doing it again. "We have to hurry. You only have half a tank of air left, and we still need to go another three kilometers before we reach that point." We break onto the side of the Moon that can be seen from the Earth's surface. Bright white light reflecting from the sun makes everything blur together. Edges aren't as harsh, but distances don't look as far.

I glance at my HUD. And my heart rate picks up. "Shit."

"What is it?"

"It's nothing."

"What is it, Ada?" He asks again.

"Oh no, it's nothing," I say as I watch another pixel of air disappear. *This shouldn't be happening. I must have a leak. The air shouldn't be depleting that quickly.* I mute Kathel for a moment. "Computer," It pings in response, "Do a quality scan on my air tank."

"Expanse damn it, Ada, what's going on? Answer me." My legs jolt as he brings us back down to the surface.

"Hang on, Dad. Didn't realize we put you in charge."

The answer comes back. A minor leak. The valve of my air

pump is on crooked, not something I would have noticed when I put it on. *My computer should have picked up on that. Why didn't it give me a notice before I left the base? When Edonne knocked me over, did it knock it loose? It shouldn't have.*

"Ada!" He grabs my shoulders, "Ada, what is going on." He shifts catching Dita as she loses her balance on the uneven ground.

"I'm running a scan. My tank is leaking." I see his face blanch. "The valve is screwed on crookedly. It's slowly leaking air, probably on top of not having enough to begin with." I pause and look over the readout. I gulp, and all I want to do is take a deep breath, and I hold it, focusing on slowing down my heart rate. "I have about twenty minutes of oxygen left."

"Shit, shit, shit. Miessa!" Kathel gets back on comms. He scoops up Dita, and I and tries to fly again, but he is running dangerously low on juice. The engine sputters a bit, "come on!" he growls and smacks the tank. It coughs in response before kicking back to full powers. We fly for another ten minutes, sometimes touching down for a moment before pushing back off before he says. "Miessa. You better fucking answer me. You only have so much air in that tank, and you need all three of us to get your rank badge."

The comms cracking in response and much to my relief, she answers. "Fine, where are you? I'll meet you there. Did you at least find the last person on our team? Is it someone I like?"

Kathel glances down at Dita and me, I shake my head. *Do not answer that.*

"I'll let you decide that for yourself when you get here. How does that sound?" He asks, I don't like the way his voice sounds. It is annoyingly sweet. Like he is softly begging her to do his bidding. It's gross, but it works.

"Fine. I will meet you there. I wasn't dropped off far from there. How long until you get here? My suit is so heavy. Whoever gave me this suit was dumb, they gave me an extra tank of air. I'm tempted to drop it somewhere."

"No!" Kathel and I shout at the same time.

"What?"

I start to move faster, my body lifting a few feet off the ground with each step. "Miessa, please start moving to the northwest quadrant. I need that tank."

"Why?"

"Would you stop asking so many expanse damned questions and just move?" Kathel asks, the sickly sweet voice gone. "We are a freaking team. We need that tank, which means you need to move that stupid tail of yours!"

"Jeez, fine, I'm coming. I'll see you in a few minutes."

"Computer," I ask my suit. "Is there a way to shut down or seal off my air valve from my suit so I can attach the tank without the air escaping?"

"Affirmative Ada, I can seal off the air now?"

"How much air is currently left in the body of my suit?" I ask, glancing at the marker Kathel's shared. We have about another kilometer before we reach the site.

"You have enough air for about three minutes in the suit without access to the tank of air."

"And how much air do I have left total?" I ask, looking at the very low bar on the screen.

"About seven minutes of reserve air is in the tank."

"So, I have about ten minutes of the total left?"

"Affirmative Agent Gomez. You have roughly ten minutes of air left before you experience oxygen depletion." The computer replies.

"Kath!" I call over comms.

"Yeah, what is it?" He replies, his voice strained. He has resorted to carrying Dita, who couldn't keep up with the pace.

"I only have ten minutes of air left. Three fresh, seven reserved in my suit. How far until we find the lunar landing point?"

"Shit, shit, shit, shit." He glances down then up, "I see the point," he says, releasing one hand and pointing in the distance. I can just see the reflective light of the Apollo Lunar Module, now dented by several meteors. "But I don't see Miessa, maybe she can't see us? Flash your light around?"

I do, and that's when I see the movement, "There!"

We break off into a sprint, and that's when I fuck up. I push too hard and my feet float, frantically I reach "Kath!" I shriek, and he grabs my hand. Pulling me down, though, my momentum lifts us both for a moment. His jet pack flares to life for a moment and we touch down, and I stab my flagstaff into the ground hard. "Shit, okay, I won't do that again," I say, trying to control my breathing.

"Please," Kathel says, stabbing his own flag into the ground. "Miessa, hurry," Kathel calls. He puts Dita down and starts scanning. "I don't know where we need to go, but the coordinates should put us around here."

Miessa bounds over, "Why have you been yelling at me so much?" She sees me and scowls before rounding on Kathel. "Who is that?" She asks, pointing at Dita's covered visor. She leans in, reading the nameplate on Dita's chest. "Are you kidding me? Dita is on our team too? What the hell? I don't want to be on a team with them." She whines.

I don't wait for Kathel to make some civil, friendly response. "Look, Miessa," desperate for air, and for her to just fucking shut up. "I know this isn't your ideal team. This isn't exactly how I thought it would go either. But it is. And now we need to work together. Or we won't survive. We think we were each given one pro and one con for this test. One to help each of us when we get together, but also something that can fuck us up. You have an extra air tank for me. The one they gave me was half full. I am almost out of air. Please, I need it, I only have a few minutes of air left." I don't even give any thought to the fact that I am begging her for help. The little air tank symbol in the corner of my HUD screen is flashing red.

She just stares at me for a moment, seeming to process the information. Sweat prickles on the back of my neck. *She's going to deny you. She isn't going to give you the air. You're going to die on this rock.*

"Are you freaking serious? That is fucked up. What the fuck?" She shrieks, flailing to grab the tank. "Take it! Seriously! I'm so glad you guys called me when you did, I was about to drop it. It was heavy." She tosses it through the air at me. It rotates, but I grab it easily.

I immediately move. "Thank you, seriously, thank you. I owe you a huge one." I mute my external comms. "Computer, how much air do I have left in my suit?"

"You have two minutes of oxygen left. I highly suggest you find a reserve oxygen supply."

"No, shit. Please cut off my air to the current tank."

A little notification pops up on the screen. "Are you sure you want to turn off your access to your air supply? Please say yes if this is what you want. Say no if this is not what you want."

"Yes! Yes! Yes!"

It plays a low error tone. "I am sorry I wasn't able to understand you. Are you sure you want to turn off your access to your air supply? Please say yes if this is what you want. Say no if this is not what you want."

"Yes!" I scream into the comm.

"Thank you. I will now turn off access to your air." Chirps in a happy bright tone, and with a hiss the air supply is off.

I turn my outgoing comms back on. "Okay, can one of you take the old tank out and snap this one in?"

Miessa immediately moves back to my side and does what I ask, twisting the new tank and all the valves into place. "You should be good now. Run a scan." I do, and this time there are no issues.

"Okay, Miessa, thank you. I need the number on your flag," Kathel says.

Miessa turns the flag over, looking for a number. "There isn't a number on it."

I grab it and look over it again, checking the actual flag, the staff, and both ends. Nothing. "She's right, there is nothing there."

"Why, what do we need the number for?" She asks as Kathel hits the tablet screen more frantically, attempting to compute all of our options.

"So we can get off this rock, you know, find Carver." He spins in a circle, trying to find an answer.

Dita waves her hands, and I move over and take her hand, "hey," I shift my audio to my outbound speakers, hoping it would penetrate her suit. "Are you okay?"

She nods heavily, she releases my hand and kneels onto the

Moon's surface. She drags a hand across the surface, disrupting the dirt with a thin line. She moves her hand over and writes what looks like a letter c, and a lopsided number sign.

"I see number?" I repeat. "You see the number? Where is it?" I ask, grabbing her hand again. She pulls away and taps her helmet.

"They must have put it on the inside of her visor when they blocked it out," Miessa says.

Kathel moves to stand next to Dita, "What is the number, Dita?"

She drags her hand over the ground, disrupting the previously written letters, it's hard to mark out exactly in all the lines. "Fifty-six?" Miessa reads off. "It looks like fifty-six?"

"Looks like it!" Kathel says, punching the number in. "Yes! It worked, and the location isn't far from here. Come on!" He grabs Dita and pulls her to her feet. He tosses her up on his back and takes off in slow bounds across the rock. Miessa and I follow not far behind.

I catch Miessa at one point and pull her back down to me. She squeezes my hand in thanks and keeps moving. After about ten minutes of slow running, Kathel moves to a walk. The little cursor tracking our progress flashes more as we get closer to the end of our journey. It's a deep pit, probably from several large meteors hitting the same point.

"How will we get down there?" I ask. About thirty feet below looks like a landing pad of some sort, the perfect place out of sight to hide from us cadets.

"Carefully," Kathel jokes. He taps out another sequence on the tablet, and another cursor flashes to life, "Come on, this seems to have a path. Let's see if it works." At the top rim of the hole, there is a small gap with a path leading down. It spirals slowly around the corner.

We make the careful step down to the next level, Dita clinging to Kathel's suit like a large, awkward balloon. Both Miessa and I slip on weak parts of the trail, but surprisingly Carver doesn't seem to have anything up her sleeve for us here.

When we get down to the bottom of the basin, the four of us clump together. "Now what?" Miessa hisses, "we need to think of something quick. We are way exposed over here. And it isn't like we have anything to defend ourselves."

"We can't really fight with Dita," I say.

"Maybe there is no fight, maybe just getting down here was the fight," Kathel suggests. Miessa and I share a look and burst out laughing. "Okay, yeah, it is probably not that easy, but you never know, it could be."

"Let's start moving toward the hanger and see what happens. I think that is the best we can do."

The other two shrug and nod, and we slowly make our way across the flat, open terrain. All three of us keep our heads on a swivel scanning for whatever may be out there. We make our way a hundred feet from the wall with no issues. "This is going too well." Kathel whispers. I nod. I hate how paranoid this training has made me already.

"I know." Miessa whispers. "What could it be?"

"This is where the coordinates lead us. And putting the numbers in a different order didn't give us any other options. We had to come here."

We press up against the wall of the hanger. I stick my head around the corner. The front part of the hanger is empty. But at the back, a bunch of officers sit around waiting. "We may be the first ones here. They're just hanging out back there. They really don't seem to be paying any attention."

"So, should we just go?" Miessa asks.

I look around the corner again. "Honestly, we might as well. They don't seem to have weapons on them."

"It's on you then," Miessa says, walking past me and into the hanger. Kathel and I hurry behind her. We make it about ten feet into the hanger when the group rounds on us. A force field keeping the atmosphere inside the hanger blocks our entrance.

"Ah, our first team is in," Carver says, a wide, unsettling grin spreading across her face.

Chapter 19

"That's not good." Kathel whispers. "That smile is not good."

"No shit," I hiss back through teeth gritted in a smile.

"Hello, Commander. Our team would like to check back in." Miessa says.

I hold back a step, waiting for the commander's response to see if we are truly done with this test. From my time here, I have quickly determined a few things about Commander Eugenia Carver. She likes initiative. She likes leadership and power. She thinks weakness must be squashed, fear is the devil, and hesitation is worse than death.

"Agent Guamianna, good. Please proceed to the airlock to your left, then you can join us here in the hangar while we await the other teams." The three of us that can see give her a tight salute and guide Dita to the airlock so we can get this dang helmet off of her.

We step into the airlock and close the door behind us. The

mechanisms lock into place and hiss as they push air in and adjust the pressure. A buzzer sounds, and we can finally remove our helmets.

I sigh as I pull mine off, and I lift the sticky layer of hair from my back. The suits are temperature regulated, but that doesn't mean they are comfortable to be in for hours at a time. I turn to Dita and help her out of hers. I laugh as her tentacles burst from the helmet and stretch as long as they can before retracting into a curly mess and relaxing. Dita blinks against the harsh light inside the airlock. "Great expanse. You have no idea how scary all of that was!" She squeaks. "I'm so glad you guys are on my team." She turns to Kathel. "Thank you for carrying me. Seriously, I owe you one."

I glance around at my teammates, "I think we can call it even. We all owe each other something. But that happens when you're on a team."

"Agreed," Kathel says. "To our team."

Miessa gags, "Oh no, this is way too sappy for me. No." Usually, I would have wanted to deck her. But I just laugh, tucking my helmet under my arm and punch the button, releasing us into the hangar. All four of us tense at the sight of Commander Eugenia, waiting for us on the other side of the door.

"Our first team of agents are back. How does it feel soldiers?" She asks, spreading her arms wide to present us to the rest of the people in the hanger.

"It feels very good, Ma'am. We thought we were taking too long through most of the challenges." Kathel glances at my pack and the replaced air tank. "But as a team, we worked together, and well here we are." Out of the corner of my eye, I see Miessa roll her eyes.

"Yes," Carver smiles sweetly, the muscles in her face stretching to accommodate the foreign movement. "You are here. Please, step forward to receive your next class ranking." The four of us do. "When I say your name, please step forward. Agent Adorari." Dita steps forward, her movements tight. "Thank you for your service." The commander lays the badge across Dita's palm, as she does I see the lines of a motherboard in the back. "Agent Guamianna." Miessa steps forward. "Agent Gomez," I step forward, and finally, "Agent Torrac." We stand in a line admiring the bits of hardware. "If you would proceed behind me, you will change into your fatigues; these new fatigues have a place in the arm where you will attach your badge. It will sync up with the tracking chip embedded in your arm. This, helps our medical facilities. On the far side of the hall, opposite the locker rooms, you will also find a galley. Go fuel up, then please join me back here in the hanger to welcome your fellow cadets as they finish their tasks."

"Yes, Ma'am!" The four of us salute, "Thank you, Ma'am." I slip my badge into my pocket and make for the locker rooms.

One blissfully hot shower later, and I am sitting in the galley with a new set of long sleeve fatigues on. A gap sits on the sleeve, level with my heart, the perfect size to snap the chip in. And a place below it for two smaller patches, which I have to assume is for our specialties. While I wait for the others, I examine the piece. It is hexagon that's about two inches by three inches Threaded across the badge side is a border, the image of the Intergalactic Garrison Earth Station insignia within. I flip it over. The back is covered with the fine lines of a motherboard. The ends have little grooves that must attach to a conductor, and which must be how it syncs up with our tracking chips.

"It's a cool piece of tech, isn't it?" Dita asks, plopping down beside me on the bench.

"You want to hack it, don't you?" I ask.

"I mean, yeah. I won't, though. At least not right away. That would be too obvious." She taps her badge on her arm "I love it. I just hope I don't have to do any more tests like that soon. I felt useless through most of it. Almost like I don't deserve this badge. All I could do was run scans and attempt to hack your suits." She laughs at the shock on my face. "What? It didn't work."

Kathel sits down across from us. "Nah. See that right there? That's why you do deserve it. At any point during that, you could have freaked the fuck out. You would have had every right to. But you didn't. You have that mental toughness. That's very important. Gotta stay cool under pressure."

"Yeah, sure," Dita says, her cheeks turning purple. "So, uh, where's Miessa?" She asks, changing the subject.

Out of the corner of my eye I see Miessa cutting between tables and coming around behind Kathel. "If she isn't already out here, she is probably shifting, trying to find the most attractive form to show off to the other cadets as they come back through," He says around a mouth of food.

Dita put a hand up to cover a grin. Miessa walks over. Her eyes turning to narrow slits of annoyance. She pounces on him, smacking him upside the chin. "What was that, Torrac?" She purrs. "You want to say that again?"

"Say what again?" Kathel grumbles, rubbing his chin. "I didn't say anything."

She nods, coming to sit on my other side across the table. We fist bump. "Oh, come on. This is not what I need. We already have to go against everyone out there. I don't need to have you three Fems against me too." Kathel whines, rubbing his face. "I was never told this would be something I would have to deal with when I signed up."

"Hey, just admit you have the best Fems of any team, and maybe," Dita glances at Miessa and I, "maybe we can cut you some slack, occasionally."

He sighs and mutters something under his breath.

"What was that?" I coo, leaning forward, "I'm sorry, I don't think I quite caught that."

"I have some pretty badass Fems on my team." He grumbles a bit louder.

"I am sorry, I didn't quite hear that either," Miessa says, growing a larger ear.

"The Fems on my team are badass." He shouts.

"Damn, they already got you whipped into shape?" An officer laughs, walking by our table.

I haven't known Kathel that long, but I know for sure that this comment made him blush more than I have ever seen. It crosses his cheeks, tops his ears, and goes down the back of his neck. Which, of course, makes all of us, including the officer, laugh even harder. We get up and grab heaping plates of food and quickly devour them.

"So, what are our specialties? Or what do you want to focus on?" Miessa asks around a bit of what looks like some hybrid chicken-rabbit thing. "I wanted to do Espionage and Tech but would also be down for Espionage Medic or Jumper." She says.

Dita raises a tentacle to indicate that she wants to speak next. "Yeah, I wanted to do Espionage and Tech too. So, they will probably have one of us divert. I just know I don't want to be a Fighter. I can do it but I'm not good at it." Dita says, and one of her tentacles slashes the air to emphasize her point. Not for the first time, I wonder if she realizes it's happening or if they move on their own accord.

"Fighter and Jumper. That was what my dad was when he was

in before he—he used to tell me stories about all the amazing places he used to jump, too." Kathel stabs a potato-like thing. "I just wanna make him proud. Keep his legacy going." He swallows hard. "What about you, Ada?"

"I wanna be a Medic Fighter. Someone always needs a hand. Sometimes the hand they need is just one upside the head."

We all laugh again and after clearing our plates head into the hanger bay to wait—the four of us taking a seat on the risers off to the right of the airlock doors. We start off talking amongst ourselves but quickly fizzle out when one of the officers shoot us a look. This leads into a tense, fidgety half an hour before the next team comes in. I share a look with my team, all of us thinking the same thing. Why did it take them so long? Eugenia meets them by the airlock and congratulates them for being the second of the four teams in. They walk past us on the way to the showers; they look how we probably did, shaken and tired. But I wonder what went wrong for them.

It takes another two hours for the other two teams to come in. The last team carrying two people, one with the blacked-out visor and the other I can only assume is unconscious from lack of air.

"Come, let's join everyone back in the Galley," Carver says, and everyone stands with her like a wave. It's more like she's a dignitary than a commander.

I share a look with Dita. I don't want to spend any more time with Carver than I have to. Something about her that is too much. There's disciplined and rigid, and then there's Commander Carver. I think back to what she said before we started this: "The first team that comes in will get the first break from duty, while the others will have to do an eight-hour patrol shift. Do you think they have to do a patrol on the Moon or back on base?" I whisper to the others.

"It will probably be a mixture," Miessa says. "The Garrison controls both, but I someone said they've had some threats by the Federation as of recently." She whispers this last part in case Carver hears. People usually have to do some punishment if they mention the Federation.

The Federation has come up a few times since we got to the station. I make a mental note to ask her about it later and to see if she has heard anything about the kids getting taken. The Federation when a Spec Ops class left the Garrison. They would rather leave the Galactic Garrison and all its strength and protection rather than be under her command. Some say it was because they thought Carver was too corrupt. They split off around six years ago. While they don't have the same backing that the Galactic Garrison does, the Federation has held their own, blocking the Galactic Garrison from doing specific missions. With their growing strength, it wouldn't surprise me that they would want to have a good base location like the Moon. But I wonder if the proximity to the Galactic Garrison's base on the ISS would be worth it. And again, if they are the one's taking kids, why? Are they having trouble recruiting people?

We enter the galley and mingle for an awkward thirty minutes while the last team recuperates and gets some food. I try not to watch them, so they don't feel too rushed, but I can't help it. They look awful, like something terrible happened when they were out there.

"Do you think there will be consequences for them being so late?" I ask Kathel.

He looks to the team, then to Commander Caver, who watches them like a hawk. "Possibly. She didn't seem pleased. But they did ultimately pass the test, and they sent two people away. Speaking of which, who was it?"

I examine the faces of everyone around me. "I think Vespar. Not sure about the last one. Possibly Vannier," I say. "I didn't think Vespar was going to last long, honestly. He did his best in most of the tests, but he seemed to keep ranking low."

"Yeah, he was a good guy, a good soldier, but not the best candidate for spec ops." Kathel makes a face, then hurries on. "Not that I'm the best candidate. None of us is the perfect soldier. We would need to be robots to fit that prerogative."

"I heard the Thesians are using robots now. At least in trial runs." Dita says. "They published the results of the first few runs. They had an eighty-five percent success rate compared to an eighty percent rate, but the casualty count was significantly higher. The robots weren't able to take, or just didn't take, the time to differentiate between an enemy and a friend. So, they aren't implementing it quite yet. They wouldn't want to take someone out in friendly fire."

Kathel laughs humorously. "Yes, I think that's generally frowned upon."

Miessa pokes the three of us. "Hush, Carver is standing up."

The three of us snap our heads to the commander. She rises to stand at the end of the tables. The light above her head makes her cheekbones stand out even more. Her skin is so pale that the veins in her hands stand out like bruises.

"Specialists," she says, addressing the sixteen of us. There is a ripple of pride as it settles in that we have made the rank we have been working towards for months. "Your class has worked very hard to be here today. You all deserve it. After today, you will begin your individual trainings in your classes, building your repertoire and your skill set to represent the best that is created and protected by the Garrison." There is applause, and she waits, a fake smile plastered on her lips. "You have each worked hard to earn your place here. And I expect you will continue to work hard. If you do, you will go very far."

"Is this just going to be a vague inspirational speech?" Miessa whispers out of the corner of her mouth, "Because I know quite a few things that I would rather be doing right now."

Carver turns to the four of us and Miessa snaps up, back rigid. "As promised, our first team in will have eight blissful hours to do as they will, free of all responsibility, starting at 1000 tomorrow morning. If you wish, you have permission to go off base. Please be back for 1800." She turns to the other teams. "You will each be on patrols starting when we get back in eight-hour shifts. However, your downtime will either be spent with lights out or doing as the Sergeants require." She places her hands behind her back. "When you are ready, you can head back to base. My first team, if you would proceed, you may report to your barracks for lights out as it is past curfew. Three other teams, when you arrive on base, please report to Sergeant Wayne to receive your patrol schedule."

Our team rises and quickly heads toward the door, with the other teams' eyes piercing our backs.

Chapter 20

"We have moved your barracks to the fourth level." Dita reads the message on her tablet. "So, do we have to move all of our stuff?"

We hurry to where our rooms used to be, but find the door locked. "Strange, okay, maybe we don't need to move anything?" We head down to level four and find Miessa and Kathel standing outside a door.

"Finally! Where did you go?" Miessa whines from where she leans against the door.

"We went to our old room to make sure we didn't have to move our stuff. Are we all living in the same room now?" Dita asks,

"So, what are we waiting for?"

"All four of us had to be here to get in. We have to register our biomarkers." Kathel says, pressing a button next to the door. "We tried doing it with just the two of us, but it would just restart."

Miessa punches a few buttons and quickly imputes her name

then presses her palm to the scanner. The rest of us do the same and quickly file into the room. I don't know what exactly I was expecting, but it wasn't a tiny apartment for the four of us. As soon as we enter the room, it opens up into a common area with four doors.

"I want this room," Dita says. She puts a hand on the scanner at the door, and it buzzes, the sensor turning red. "Oh?"

I move to another door and it buzzes red too. I move to the door she stands in front of. This time it buzzes green. "Guess they already assigned our rooms." I shrug.

The four of us each move into our rooms, checking that our stuff is all there.

"Come on, let's go off base. And not like to the Moon." Miessa says, "I don't know about you, but the idea that I can get off base has me going stir crazy." Now that we aren't around any Commanding Officers, she has shifted to look more human with long blonde hair pooling down her shoulders. "I just want to pretend that I'm a civilian for a bit."

"I'm down, where do you want to go?" Kathel asks.

Kathel and Dita sit at the table in the middle, pulling up locations on their tablets. "I'd like to go back down to Earth, but I don't think I could see my brother, which is the only reason I'd want to go." I shrug. "He's still in foster care."

"How often did you get to see him?" Kathel asks.

"Legally or not? I saw him as often as I could, but a lot of the time, it was me sneaking over to his foster parent's house. It was about once a week or every other week. But his foster parents weren't too fond of me being around. It wasn't that they didn't like me, they just thought me coming and going would make things worse for Sarkus. But he always told me it made him sad to see me leave, but he would rather see me than not."

Miessa leaned forward. "So, what's the foster system? I don't think we have a foster system on my planet. It doesn't sound nice."

I laugh uncomfortably, "Yeah, I mean, it's not that nice. It's a— the foster system is a thing in place by our government to support children under the age of eighteen if their parents die. It places them in homes of people who will raise them so we don't have to sit in an orphanage." I open my tablet and check to see if I have any new messages. Nothing.

"That sounds great, much better than the homes full of sad children we had. You had people to take care of you!" Miessa says.

I shrug, "Sort of, but people sometimes do it with bad intentions or for the wrong reasons. My last foster parent did it mainly to get money from the government. He was kind of an asshole." Nobody responds. Miessa shifts her tail swishing quietly against the floor. "Okay, well. On that bright note, where do we want to go in the morning?" I ask, quickly changing the subject. "The only time I've been off-world is doing stuff here, so I'm up for anything."

"Well, there's this market I used to go to sometimes with my family. It is huge and full of all different vendors from all over the galaxy. Even if we don't buy anything, it could be cool to look around and see what we could find. Just hang out." Dita suggests.

Miessa sits up, excited, "I love a good market! My father is still sending me credits—I'd love to burn through it. Where is this one?"

"It's on Titan, so it was never far from my home. If we use the jump gate, it shouldn't be that long, either."

"Wait, why shouldn't it be instant? Isn't that like the whole point of the jump gates? They help us jump quickly, so we don't have to attempt ship travel since it isn't reliable?" I ask.

"Well, yes. Over shorter ranges, jumps are almost instantaneous. The jumps we do are a fraction of the time that it would take to travel by ship, but there is still a slight increase in time relative to the distance. I think if you were to jump from Earth to Pluto, it would take roughly four hours, but you wouldn't feel the full four hours," Kathel explains. "So, if we are jumping to Titan, we would need to factor in, I would say around forty-five minutes on either end for travel to make it back on time." He laughs. "The last thing we need is for Carver to get pissed off at us for being late right after we impressed her."

"So, do we want to go for it?" Dita asks. "I'm putting our jump request in now, so we don't get blocked."

"I'm so glad you're the organized one." I yawn, stretching my arms above my head.

Dita turning her tablet off. "We'll take off from Bay 3, by the way." She heads to her room. "Well, goodnight. I, for one, want to get as much sleep as I can knowing I won't be woken up for a patrol tonight and I don't have to listen to Ada snore anymore!"

November 2nd, 2228 11:48:37

Hey Sark,

I miss you. Tonight was a big night. I ranked up! After today, I will start individual training with my team. I have a team now! Today was also my first day off the station. We went to the Moon! It was intense, but it was really cool at the same time. I'm going off base tomorrow to Titan, one of Saturn's moons, with my team. There are four of us. Dita is on my team!

I'm glad your classes are going well. Find a good teacher to be your person? Have things gotten better at your new house? I'm sure some of that awkwardness was just getting used to a new space. Did you get all settled into your room? I know you said you were having some issues with their son. Max, right? It'll get better in time.

Just so you know, Tortie sent me a message. There has been some action in your area from whoever has been taking kids. He says you should be fine, but I wanted to make sure you know. Just be aware of your surroundings.

I have to get to bed, but I love you. Hope to hear from you soon.

A

Chapter 21

Miessa is ready and lounging on the couch by quarter after nine the next morning. I don't know if it is some of that shifter bullshit of hers or if she really looks that pristine every morning. She daintily sips at a cup of coffee while I rip my hair out of my head, attempting to brush the knots from it. "You know your hair won't stay healthy if you attack it like that. And you have such nice hair. I wouldn't want you to ruin it." She comes over and plucks the hairbrush from my hand.

"Hey!" I snap swinging for the brush.

She steps back, "let me just show you something."

"I swear to the stars if you try to show me that whole start at the ends and working your way up bullshit, I will leave your ass here. That shit has not and probably never will work for me." I hiss. *It's too damn early for this beauty nonsense.*

She laughs lightly. "Come on, it works. They have proven it to work."

"Nuh uh. Not my hair. It looks at everyone's little pretty excuses for trying to make things easier, and it laughs and then gets into a bigger knot." The door pings as Kathel comes into the room. I try to run my fingers through a two-inch section and get tangled up instantly. "See, I just brushed that part through. It didn't have knots a few seconds ago."

"You know I am sure Wayne has some scissors," he says.

"No!" Miessa and I shriek at him.

I walk up to him, threatening him with the tip of my hairbrush in a way that would have made my mother proud. "You touch my hair, and I swear I will take those scissors and make a few cuts in places you won't like." He glances down, and I grin wickedly.

He puts up his hands, "okay, okay, I know when to admit defeat." He looks over my wild hair. "So, uh, how long does it usually take to tame that thing? We need to get going if we want to make our jump gate."

I rip the brush through my hair a few more times, much to the chagrin of Miessa, who winces every and force it into a bun. "Okay, let's go."

I grab my bag, and Dita is one step behind me. "You know I always wondered what it would be like to have hair. But after seeing your relationship with your hair, I don't know if I really want hair." Dita laughs.

I flip her the bird, and both she and Kathel laugh. "Come on, we don't want to miss our jump time," I growl.

The jump deck is just starting to get busy. Most days, they have jumps scheduled in fifteen-minute blocks, for people coming and going from the base on different missions, going on leave, or traveling to different stations. We arrive with a few minutes before our jump. We get our suits situated, doing an extra check to make sure there is no funny business laced into the tightly woven fabric this time.

"Next jump in ninety seconds!" The jump gate operator shouts, and people move away from the gate in a flurry of activity as people move away from the gate.

"Come on, let's go!" Dita says excitedly, "it's such a fun market!"

"Okay, I have four jumpers for Titan," The jump gate operator reads off. He counts us, "Okay, to make this easier and faster, I would like all four of you to link arms and jump through," his words so close together they nearly blur into the noise of the surrounding machinery. The four of us do as we are told, Dita leading the chain through sideways. "When you are ready, you may proceed."

"Ready?" Dita asks over the comms, eyes dancing in delight, "Oh, this is going to be so much fun!" she squeals, before pulling the three of us in after her.

The guy said that having four of us go through at once would be easier. He must have meant that it would be easier for *him*. Kathel had said that the trip would feel longer but that we wouldn't feel the full forty-five minutes it would take. *Liar.* The moment Dita steps through the portal, a magnetic pull rips at my shoulder. With our linked arms connecting us, it's like it's trying to stretch us out over the entire distance of the galaxy. And it isn't as smooth as any of our other jumps either. It's turbulent, throwing Miessa and me all over the place.

The landing is a blessing. I stumble through the gate and immediately hit the button for my helmet as soon as I knew we're in a pressurized environment. I hold my head between my knees and take several large gulps of air, attempting to get my stomach out of my throat.

"What the fuck was that bullshit?" Miessa asks, bent over beside me.

A pair of boots appear in front of our noses, and we snap to attention, trying to keep our balance as the world shifts beneath our feet. A Male with the deepest skin, and most gray colorless eyes I have ever seen, scans the four of us. "Did Loft send the four of you through connected?" He asks in a lilting voice much gentler than I expected from him.

"Yes, he did, Sir," Kathel says, glancing at the three of us. "Some of us also haven't experienced longer jumps. I think the combination didn't sit well. Sir."

The man grumbles. "Well, I apologize for that. I have informed him before that this is not acceptable behavior. Is there anything I can do for you folks today?" the soldier asks.

"No, Sir," I say, "just a bumpy start to our leave, but we will survive. Sir." I say, adding the formality.

"Good, on your way then. I hope you can enjoy all that Titan offers today."

The four of us leave the space quickly, Miessa and I leading the pack to escape the hot, stuffy gate room. "I hope that operator has to do so many patrols." She groans, holding her stomach. "I shouldn't have eaten so many of Cook's scrambled eggs."

"You can eat those?" Kathel laughs, "no wonder your stomach hurts—those things are as hard as a rock. Eggs aren't meant to be hard."

"I usually feel fine. I eat them every day." She groans, bending over to grab her stomach. "Okay," She says, straightening up. She pushes her blonde hair back over her shoulders, but she still has a greenish tint to her complexion, "I want to have a good time. I won't let some weird stomachache, and bad jump experience ruin my day off." She turns to Dita. "Okay, so you've been here before. Where should we start?"

I pipe in, "I for one need somewhere to convert my money unless many places out here take Earth credits."

"Negatory, my good friend. You will need to convert those. No

Earth credits here." Kathel says, he surprises me when he loops his arm through mine, "come on, I know a place where we can get that money exchanged."

"Have you been here before?" I ask as leads the way the other two a few steps behind.

"Once or twice. I didn't want to say it when we were back on base," he says over his shoulder so the other two can hear. "But I snuck off the base on Europa to do some under the table sales from time to time. Just to make some extra credits from time to time." He says slyly. "That may have been the start of my troubles. I got caught up in a bad gig once and they told me to suit up or got to prison. Simple choice."

"Do you still do that?" Dita asks wide-eyed.

"Oh, hell no. If I tried to do that under Carver's thumb, she'd have me court-martialed before we even began. It would not be worth it. No matter how many extra credits I would get." He pulls me out of the building. Above the door is the symbol of the Galactic Garrison, letting everyone know that the people inside mean business. At least that is what we can pretend they mean. That is what Carver and the rest of the Garrison over on the Earth base would want.

The building opens up to a sea of peoples mingling around various vendors' carts, some leading into buildings with more specific wares or restaurants.

"Come on," he grabs Miessa, and motions for Dita to link up too so we can all stay together. He relaxes his grip as we come up to a small hut on the far side of the marketplace. It has a register and a lever. "You put in however much money you want, turn this dial to select the currency, and it will spit out the money." he pulls out an Earth twenty-credit bill to demonstrate, selecting Ganymede stones, it spits out a pile of the little copper stones.

"Oh, okay, that is cool. I thought it would be a much bigger pain in the ass than that," I say, pulling some credits from my pocket. "What would be the best thing to convert it to?" I ask the three of them.

"I think it would be best just to do Cerian Units. Most places accept them, and if they don't, then honestly, you probably shouldn't be doing business with them." Miessa says. Her skin is flushed, and she scrapes her hair back into a ponytail.

"I gotta agree with Miessa on this one," Dita says, "though I appreciate the use of Ganymede stones." She says, swiping for the money. "I could always use more of those."

"Fuck off," Kathel laughs, turning away from her.

While the two of them fight, I process the money, selecting the Cerian units. The money comes out in flat sheets of metal, not unlike memory cards. I slip the little cards into my pocket and turn to the other two. "Really?" I laugh. Kathel has Dita in a headlock, who wriggles her little tentacles swinging at his face and tugging on his ears.

"Hey!" he says, batting her away. He lets go of her but keeps a hold of the stones, shoving it into his pockets. He waves his hands in front of him to keep Dita at bay.

"Hey, you two!" I say, and the two of them freeze and slowly turn to look at me. "Let's go find something to do!" They jump up from the ground and I grin. We're a bunch of idiots. I turn and lean into the crowd, letting it wash me away. This market is like a nicer, brighter version of The Market where I would meet with Tortie back on Earth.

Miessa catches my shoulder. "Wait up, you can't just jump into the crowd like that. We should stay together. If we lose you, we may not have time to do anything." She says.

"Okay, mother of mine." I laugh, "You forget, I have spent the last three years of my life in the black markets on Earth acting as a scrapper. I can hold my own in the middle of a crowd."

She makes a face, "Okay, well, you can, but that doesn't mean other people can," I cock an eyebrow at her. "Okay, me. I am not comfortable in crowds like this, okay? Don't leave me alone."

"Are you scared of crowds?" Dita asks, coming up on her other side.

Miessa flushes maroon, drawing the eye of others around us. "I sort of am, okay?" she says, trying to move us along so people can't just stare at us. "Let's go get food or something." She looks away, her hair shifting as she walks, the blonde hair retreating into her scalp and transforming into black hair with tight curls that frame and hide her face.

"She good?" Kathel asks quietly, catching up to me.

I nod, "Yeah, she just got nervous that I jumped into the crowd to get going. I guess she doesn't like crowds, so she got uncomfortable." I whisper. "I think we should find a quiet part."

He nods and trots up to catch Miessa. He puts an arm across her shoulders feeling the slight pang in my chest, like I did a few weeks ago when I saw Miessa going into his room. *Why do you care?* I think. But I don't like the feeling. Kathel bends to whisper something in Miessa's ear, and she shakes her head. I wonder what he's saying to her. He grins down at her and then squeezes her to his side with an awkward hug. She laughs, tossing her head. As she does her hair shifts again; it stays a dark brown, but the curls fall into loose waves down her back.

"That is so weird," Dita says.

"What?" I say, jumping. *Was she watching me stare?*

"This!" She says, stopping. She lifts a jar with a green goo inside that moves away from her hands. "What is this?" She muses, but she quickly puts it down at the sight of the shop owner staring at her with beady eyes.

"No touching unless you're buying, you grubby Ganymede!" He snaps.

Dita quickly steps away from the jar, grabs my arm, and drags me away, her skin flushing violet.

"What the hell?" I ask, twisting away from her to turn back to the shop owner, but Dita digs her nails into my arm, forcing me away. "What the hell did he mean by that? He realizes that's ridiculous. You were just looking at it."

She nods, but her tentacle wriggles in sharp agitated twists. "He knew that I'm a Ganymede. That is all he needed to know. That's how it is for most people. My people have a habit of being thieves. So, most people don't like us hanging around. They always assume we're pilfering something. Which is false, but you can't change people's minds once they've decided something about you." She shrugs, "I'm used to it by now. I kinda hope that over time, if more of us join the Garrison and reputable organizations like that, people will trust us."

"I'm really sorry, Dita," I squeeze her hand. "I sorta understand what that's like. Some people would assume because my name is Gomez, that I was someone that would push drugs back on Earth. I guess my ancestors, three hundred something years ago, were really good at it, or at least had access to a lot. Utter bullshit."

She smiles at me, and her eyes dance. "Thanks for understanding. And just to put it out there, I definitely think you could have beaten the shit out of him." She laughs.

"Who is beating the shit out of who?" Kathel asks, pausing his walk with Miessa so we can catch up.

"Some assholes back there. Just some people who needed to be put in their place and not be rude to my friends." I declare.

Dita grins down at me and turns to the others. "So, who wants to go get some lunch?"

Chapter 22

"Are you sure you don't want to try anything new?" Miessa asks.

"No, I'm one hundred percent sure. I need to get some of my food," I insist.

"Alright, your loss. See you soon." She and Dita head around the corner to a little pub that serves food more up their alley.

I hurry, nearly skipping to the Latin vendor. I sigh at the spicy smell of cumin, paprika, and chili powder. Kathel and I order several empanadas to share, which are quickly cooked up fresh, and deposited in my hand hot, with oil still popping on the beautiful golden-brown pastry.

Kathel and I lean against a wall, devouring the last few bites. "How did someone get authentic empanadas this far across the galaxy?" I ask around a mouthful of food. "This is amazing. I didn't realize I missed it this much. Cook is okay, but oh great expanse. I haven't had food like this since Mama died." I laugh, "One time, Jaxon, my foster parent, tried to y'know, help me feel more at home by getting me a can of black beans and tortillas."

He laughs, "That's… wow."

"That pretty much describes Jaxon in a nutshell. Effort level? Zero."

"Yeah, I will say, your food on Earth is pretty great."

"What do you mean, my food on Earth?"

"Well, I grew up on the Kuiper belt, but I spent a bit of time on Earth. Dad took me once before he got shipped to the Titan wars in 2215. It was one of the last times I saw him." He says. He looked up at the flash of stars above our heads through the thin atmosphere and the pressurized shield.

"I love being under the stars. It's been cool to see them all the time, instead of only at night on Earth."

"Ada," Kathel says, looking down at me. He turned to me, his food gone for who knows how long. "You're babbling again."

"Right," I flush and look up at the stars. I nearly jump as Kathel reaches over and weaves his fingers between mine. I flush even deeper, suddenly very aware of the grease still coating my fingers. "What are you doing?" I ask.

"I don't know," he grins down at me then looks back up at the stars. "It just felt right. You know pretty stars, pretty girl."

I slide my hand away and rub it on my pant leg, scrubbing the grease from it. "You're just messing with me."

"No, I'm not." He says, catching my hand again. "Ada, you're a fucking badass. And you're gorgeous. Do you not realize that?" He asks, searching my face. "You have continuously proven that you belong here. And..." he runs his free hand through his hair. "You just amaze me constantly. Starting from that first fight with Edonne, I haven't met anyone like you before."

I scoff. "You haven't met anyone like me before? You realize how douchey that sounds?"

His face scrunches up in annoyance. "How? Douchey? Ada, what are you talking about?"

"'You're such a fucking bad ass. I've never met anyone like you.'" I mimic. "I just-you can't be serious." I step away from him.

He closes the gap, and my shirt catches on the course texture of the brick at my back. He grabs my hands and pulls me close. With my back to the wall, I don't really have anywhere to go. But if I am honest, I don't think I want to go anywhere. "Ada, I'm one hundred percent serious right now. I didn't really want to be in the Garrison. I've felt sort of lost. Like I didn't have a purpose. And then I met you. This hotshot girl, who's so sure of what she wants. We ended up on the same team." He runs the pad of his thumb over my knuckles. The movement is small, but it sends shivers up my spine. "But as I got to know you, I realized how genuine and complex of a person you are. Sure, you can be harsh at times, but it's real. And your determination has honestly been so motivating. It made me feel like maybe this is where I'm meant to be."

"I…" his touch is soft; it coaxes a feeling from me I didn't expect to feel when in the military. "I just… I just want to help my—"

"I know," he says, his voice husky, low and gravelly. "You just want to create a space for your brother. And that!" His fingers float just above my hips—hovering above them like a question. I shift into his hands and he grabs my hips and pulls me closer, even through the fabric I can feel the warmth of his hands. "That is amazing. You are so much of a better person than I am."

His lips are inches from mine. I never really looked at his lips. They're thin and they look so soft, like they hold all the warmth and joy that he has kept hidden for so long.

"You're serious? This is a bit much," I laugh breathily. He steps forward, and I am wrapped up in the clean smell of his aftershave, like ivory soap we had back on Earth, and the smell of oil and machinery that clings to his shirt. His arms wrap around me and they feel strong, sturdy. I had been so focused on my own strength and what I need that I never anticipated someone else's touch would feel so supportive. Men have been tools, ways to get what I want, or walls blocking me from the things I need to do. But Kath is different.

His arms wrap around my back, and his fingers brush my skin under the hem of my shirt. He doesn't press himself against me, but I almost wish he would.

"Of course I'm serious. I was trying to make a move, but apparently, I'm not as smooth as I think I am." He grins, the city lights catching in his eyes turning them liquid gold.

"Kath?" I whisper, and he bends his head down closer to me.

"Hmm?" he asks.

The stubble on his chin is definitely against code, it scratches the inside of my palm as I cup his cheek, inching my fingers into his snow white hair. Being this close to him is intoxicating. "Shut the hell up." I flush at the sound of my voice cracking slightly.

His lips quirk up in a grin. "Yes, Ma'am." I scoff as he lowers his head, and our eyes flutter closed as his lips meet mine.

Now I've kissed the occasional boy on Earth. So it isn't like I am entirely new to this. However, Kathel is confident. He's slow but sure of his actions, letting me move how I want. His hands tighten on my back, and I step into him. I trace my fingers up his arm and the feeling is electric.

He pulls back first and looks down at me, eyes dancing with something I can't place. "Ada," he growls and kisses me again more fiercely.

I bring my hands up to his chest, ready to stop him, but at the same time, I don't want to. My heart feels like it is going to beat out of my chest. "Kath, I think this is a bad idea," I say against his lips, but even as I do, I kiss his chin and then the side of his neck, his stubble scratching my skin.

"It's a fucking awful idea." He breathes, "But—"

"Hey! Get a fucking room! Get out of my alley!" Kathel and I jump apart as a short Male in a dirty apron waves a towel at us.

I push Kathel back, my skin flushing an even deeper red. "I'm so sorry, we were just leaving." I grab Kathel's arm and drag him away.

We walk down the road away from the food district for a few minutes before we speak again.

Kathel finds a corner and leans back, scanning the area.

I try to avoid looking at him but my eyes are drawn to him, to his lips, like a magnet. He catches me looking at and grins, but keeps an eye on the crowd. I'm sure I'm as red as a tomato by how hot my skin feels and it's not just from embarrassment. "Look, I am flattered. And I think you're really great but—"

"But you don't think we should do it again?" He grabs my hand, sliding his fingers between mine.

I shake my head, moving his hand away. "No, not right now, at least." I smile, "I'm not gonna deny you. It'd be fun. That was fun. But we're on the same team, we've gotta keep it professional. And what about Miessa?"

He steps back, genuine confusion plastering his face. "Miessa? What about her?"

"Weren't you, you know, all buddy-buddy?"

He covers his faces and laughs, "oh great expanse, you thought

208

Miessa and I were a thing?" He shakes his head, "No, no, Miessa and I are not, and were not ever a thing."

I cross my arms across my chest. "I mean, what about all the times she went to your room? Or that weird cutesy voice you used on the Moon to get her to do what you wanted?"

He sputters for a moment, and I feel a pang in my chest. *This was a bad idea, Ada. Go, you need to find the others.* I don't need to be wasting my time worrying about a Male.

I turn away, but Kathel catches my arm, "Ada, wait, I'm sorry. I don't know what you thought. Though it is sorta flattering that you've noticed. But, uh—" He rubs the back of his neck. "I actually knew Miessa before training. I may have sold her some things over the years. Don't tell her I told you. She doesn't like people knowing."

"Know what?"

"I… you know what I mean." he hedges. Though when I don't respond, he continues. "Okay, so you were a scrapper on Earth. I'm sure you had some connections that would have been frowned upon by others?" I think of Tortie and nod. "Well, as I said, I got into a bit of trouble. Her family is very wealthy. And her father, well, he likes to indulge himself from time to time. I was his source for a while. Sometimes she was sent to pick it up. One day she got caught with it. She had a few other strikes on her record. To help appease people, she signed up. We didn't know we were going to be in the

209

same unit until we showed up on the base." He pauses and looks up to the curved dome overhead. "I don't regret any of what I did, but I will say it was nice to have someone I knew when I got here."

I nod, "that makes sense. It would make it easier. She doesn't hold it over your head that you made her get in the force?"

He laughs, "I mean, yeah, when she saw me when we got here, she wanted to beat the shit outta me. But I think it's been good for her? Gives her something to do." He clears his throat. "You know I'm sorry about earlier." He rubs his jaw where my lips had found his skin. "You're probably right."

"Oh, yeah, no, it's fine." I want to kiss him again. I want to grab his shirt and pull him back to me. So I take a big step away. "So, uh, do you want to go find the others? They are probably done eating now too." I lick my lips and try to tell myself they are tingling from the spice of the food, not from the pressure of his lips on mine.

"Right. Yeah," He presses his hands deep in his pockets, avoiding my gaze. He pushes off from the wall and I follow a few steps behind. *What did you just do, Ada?*

Chapter 23

"He did what now?" Dita shrieks, her tentacles standing on end.

"Hush!" I say, jumping to my feet to make sure the door is closed. "Shhh, don't let him hear you!" I hiss. I come back to the bed. "I know! I was… I don't know." I pace the floor.

"Did you like it? I don't know, was it good?" She asks, hugging a pillow to her chest. "Do you like him?"

I make a sound that that can be best compared to a squeak and blush. "I mean… You would think so, yeah, it was nice. But it isn't like we can do anything about it. We are on the same team. We can't be in a relationship."

"But, you want to!" Dita says, wiggling her eyebrows at me. "Who said you have to be in a relationship?"

"Dita!" I squeal, punching at her pillow, and she bursts out laughing, dodging my blows.

"You like him. You *like* him *like* him!"

"Shut up! I do not!"

"Yes, you do! What are you gonna do?"

My cheeks go crimson, betraying me yet again. "I don't know. Probably nothing." I flop on the bed beside her.

"Wait, did you try to stop him?" She asks her tone shifting from prodding to protective. "If he—"

"No! No, no! He-I wanted it, I did. I kissed him back. Like I said, it was fun." I flush a deeper shade of red at the memory of my fingers through his hair, his hands on my waist.

I cover my face as she squeals. "Ada, what are you going to do?" We both jump as there is a ping on the door, "Open." Dita calls her voice cracking slightly.

Kathel stands on the other side of the door. He looks a bit sheepish. "Uh, we just got a ping, not sure if you saw. We have to report to room 504."

"Right, thanks," I say, jumping off Dita's bed. Kathel holds my gaze for a second before ducking back out the door. Dita giggles behind me, and I flash her a grin and flip her off before following him out the door.

* * *

The room is lined with officers. More than I have ever seen in one place since our orientation. "What do you think is going on?" Miessa whispers from the corner of her mouth. No one answers. We stand in formation, waiting for orders. From what I can tell, they are on edge—some more than others. I can't tell if it's apprehension or uncertainty.

A door at the far end opens and in walks a line of soldiers. "They're from another base." I hear Edonne whisper down the line to his team. "Look at the patch." And he is right. When we stand at ease as we do now, right hand over left, you can see a patch on our bicep. It has a small, embroidered picture of the Earth over the milky way. The newcomers have a few different patches, one I remember seeing yesterday on Titan's base and another I don't recognize.

"Kuiper." Kathel supplies. "It's from the Kuiper base. I have one from my infantry training."

"What do you think they are doing here?" Dita whispers.

We stop whispering when I notice Wayne staring me down. I shift and poke Dita nudging my chin towards Wayne before looking forward again. Best not to step out of line right now.

Commander Carver stands on a small platform. That emotionless grin back on her face. "Welcome! For the next few weeks, we will be honored with the presence of every single member of the spec ops class for this year. This is a new attempt at training— a little competition. My recruits here on the ISS have moved to new lodging to make room for our wonderful new soldiers. After today, all trainings will be held together. There will be two tests leading to graduation. And we," she indicates two officers below her, who I have to assume are from Titan and Kuiper. "Have made it a little more fun by adding this competition aspect. Make it a bit more real." She nods to someone and a projection behind her head, displays our team members, team names, and roles. It appears the officers have gone with a terrain theme for us on the Earth station, and spatial objects for the other eight teams.

My team is Arctic, and we all have the roles we applied for. Kathel will be our Fighter-Jumper, our tank. Miessa will be an Espionage-Jumper, our stealth. Dita will be Tech-Espionage, our hacker. And I will be our Medic-Fighter. My team grins at each other, hopeful, excited to get started. The other teams are a mixture of grumbles and excitement. It seems not everyone was placed where they wanted. Team Jungle is a bunch of glares and rolling eyes. Desert is quiet, stone-faced. And Monet looks pissed, despite the rest of Ocean's smiling faces.

"In the boxes before you are your new uniforms. You will wear these from now on. You will each be given two suits. Your training will start up again tonight at 1400. Don't be late. You will get a message with your respective orders. Good luck."

We hurry and grab our boxes and form a tight circle opening them together. The material is light and stretchy, but thick. There are places on the arms to snap in our insignia. Our specialty patches have already been placed inside the two smaller points. I have a human heart with a small crescent moon representing Medic, and a blaster representing Fighter. The fabric is white, with pale blue accents, like the arctic our team is named for.

"Why do you think they're doing this?" Dita asks, looking over at the teams from the other bases who are getting a rainbow of uniforms.

"Carver." Kathel and Miessa say in unison.

"She's written all over this. I don't know why. But she wants to monitor or control all of us." Miessa lowers her voice and waves for the three of us to come closer. "My guess is it is something to do with the Federation."

We move back to our rooms. "Yeah?"

"Oh yeah, they have been making some major moves. I heard they cut off a major supply line. Something about getting people to switch carriers: I don't know specifics. My dad wasn't sure."

Dita pulls out her tablet, and I put a hand on it, "Wait. Do it later when we are in a more secure area."

She nods, "You're right."

Chapter 24

Miessa stood in the middle of the living space, looking at her reflection in the mirror. "I can't decide if I want to hug the person who designed these suits or not." She says, turning to look at the back. "Look how amazing it fits. Look at my ass. It looks great but is it really all that practical? If we do a spacewalk, is this going to protect us? It looks like we just snap our helmet into place here." She says, pointing to a point on the neckline on the suit.

"The material is interesting. Maybe that would help to deal with all the environmental systems we may experience?" Dita says. She has the suit on her lap and is examining all the panels of the suit. "It looks like it has a similar structure to our jumpsuits, so they probably move the oxygen as needed similarly."

"It's too tight," Kathel says from his doorway. "This can't be right." He peeks his head around the door. "Are we sure we all have the right suits?"

"Why? Is it too short on you?" I ask. Dita and I are small in frame, and maybe the suits got mixed up.

"Uh, no, that is not the issue." He says, and I look at the girls. Something in his tone makes us smile.

"Are you having some issues there, buddy?" Miessa says, barely holding back a laugh. "Little squeezed?" She goes to his door and bursts out laughing. "Yeah, you are! The person who designed these suits made them for Males like you!"

"Fuck you!" He says, laughing himself.

Dita and I snicker. "It's going to be an interesting few weeks, isn't it?"

An alarm goes off in the corner. "Okay, we've got to go! Come on, Kath, we have training." I call, knocking on the door.

"I'm not going." He says.

I roll my eyes. "Come on, drama queen, we need to go. We have the first fight training in fifteen." The door opens, and he comes out, hands in front of himself. "Ready?"

"Yes. Let's get this over with." He says, brushing past me. And I must say, the suit is rather tight. Miessa's right her ass looked good in her suit. But Kathel's is in the running too. *You are not really ranking people's ass right now, are you?* I scold myself, making it a point to not look below his chest as we walk to training.

"So, uh, what do you think we'll go over today?" I ask, "I mean, we already had to pass some fighting training already."

"I don't know. I feel like they're going to go more into strats. That's what I want more of, at least." He says.

"Yeah, that would be good. Maybe more sim training?" We enter the room and stand amongst the other Fighters. Most are bigger in stature like Kathel, with broad shoulders and enough muscles to earn the title of the teams lead Fighter. But there are a few smaller Fighters like me.

"Soldiers!" Wayne says. "Welcome to day one of your advanced fighting training. We are going to touch on a few things today, so I hope you are ready." We move forward, gathering around him in a loose circle. "We will meet every other day to accommodate the time you'll need to spend with your other division. Our training sessions will average between three to six hours a day, depending on the training. Some rules. You better all eat. I don't want to hear some dumbass excuses about you being tired because you didn't eat Cook's eggs. Just eat the fucking eggs and deal with the stomachache like the rest of us do, okay?"

There is a collective laugh at this, and Wayne moves on. "You all have a basic level of training. I say basic compared to what you will do from here on out. I expect you to kick any random infantryman's ass. That is your job. You take people out; you are the Fighters. We don't have time to be pandering and figuring out a negotiation. You hit, and you hit hard." Everyone cheers, Kathel and I glance at each other and grin; it is hard not to get swept up in the speech.

"Good, now that you're all excited to be here, go take a lap of the station. Levels 7-10. Jump to it."

So we do. During Wayne's little motivational speech, someone transformed the halls of the station into a massive obstacle course of ropes to weave through, piles to climb over, and gaps to jump over. I grin at the burn in my lungs and the ache in my chest as I pound up the stairs to the tenth level. It's been a few weeks since I have run hard like this. I probably should hold back a bit, save some more energy for the other training Wayne has up his sleeve for us today, but I don't. It's exhilarating, the feeling of my boots pounding on the deck, and how smooth I feel running in this suit. I wipe a bead of sweat away and turn to see Kathel panting beside me, trying to keep up.

"What's the matter? This pace a little tough for you?" I ask.

"Your legs are so short. How do you move them so fast?"

I give a breathy laugh, "Your legs are so long. How come you don't take longer strides?" he snorts.

"We should probably—" he pauses as we climb over a short wall, hang off the side, and jump across a small gap, launching over it in the open air. "We should probably stick together." He says when we both have landed on the other side and are running again.

"You know, being on the same team and all?"

"Makes sense. You gonna be able to keep up with me?" I ask, even as I slow down a bit to accommodate him.

He barks out a laugh a bit louder than he means to. "I don't think I have a choice, do I?"

We run in for a few more minutes, the only sounds our breathing and our shoes hitting the floor. I was a bit worried after what happened on Titan that things would be awkward between Kathel and I. But maybe I was wrong.

After the laps, Wayne puts us through a series of bodyweight exercises until our limbs are jelly. "When I am done with you, I want it to physically hurt to punch you. I could cuddle some of you and pass the fuck out like a comfy little baby." He barks over us as we struggle through our third circuit.

By the time we get to the shooting range, I am dripping with sweat and I can barely lift my arms to chest height. One thing to say about these suits: while they keep me cool, it does nothing for the sweat that coats my skin beneath the tight fabric.

"Moving targets. Should be easy enough, right?" Kathel asks as he swings his arm around like a baseball pitcher, trying to stretch out his shoulder.

The shooting range has twenty aisles that look sort of like the bowling alleys I saw as a kid. A series of targets line the far end of a long alley. But these multi-colored targets are sitting on individual raised platforms that whiz around in different directions. Kathel takes place at an alley and punches the button on the console, starting up the sequence. An LED light above the range flashes a different color over each alleyway, letting us know what color our targets are for this round. We are aiming for orange.

He squares off with the pins and fires. His arms shake ever so slightly from the weight of the gun. But his shots are nearly on. Of the five pins he was meant to hit, three are down. "Your turn." He says, stepping back.

The gun feels heavy in my hands as I raise it to eye level. I lock on to the pins as they reset, trying to focus solely on them and to convince my brain that the ache in my shoulders is a totally manageable thing that we don't need to worry about. I thought I had figured out the pattern the first time when I watched Kathel, but now the pins move in a different pattern.

A buzzer sounds, and a blue light flashes above the pins. I fire and wince as I hit not only a blue target but one of the green ones as well. Distantly I hear Wayne making some comment about making sure my shots are accurate unless I want to spend more time working as a Medic to clean up my messes. My next few shots are better, but I miss the last one.

We rotate like this for a few more minutes, alternating colors. Then we change blaster types to some that are more suited to long-range. I enjoy this, and not just because I finally get to rest my shoulders. Laying down against the cool metal of the floor, I feel grounded. I am better able to steady my breath and take careful aim. I'm in the middle of these careful aiming sessions focusing down the scope, about to shoot, when Wayne is back in my ear. "Gomez, do you think you really will have time to make each shot so pretty every time?" He barks at me.

"No, Sir."

"Then why do you insist on taking at least thirty seconds between each expanse damned shot?"

"I don't know, Sir," I reply, choosing to go for the safer option. If I said that I was trying to make sure that the shot would hit based on the patterns I had deciphered over the last few rounds—two intervening figure eights—and that I was waiting until the target pin came to the front of that larger figure eight to make sure I had the ultimate chance of hitting, he probably would have said that I was making up some bullshit excuse because I was afraid of taking the shot. And you know what. He wouldn't be fully wrong. I'm always afraid of messing up. I'm just good at ignoring that and pushing through it so I can get the job done. Fake it 'til you make it, right?

"You better figure it out, Gomez. I want to see you hit the next shots in the next minute." He hits the button, resetting the board. "Go, I want you to hit the white pins."

I focus on the sight, aiming for the outside edge of the circuit, waiting until the pin is moving into the space and fire, taking out the first pin before shifting my aim to the other side of the circuit to repeat. "Good, now hit the blue pin with the green sticker on the base."

"Wh—" I start to say before I see it. One blue pin spins, revealing a small circular green sticker on the base. BAMPH. I take the shot and sigh as the pink pin beside it is obliterated.

"We will work on that." He groans, rubbing a hand over his face. "The last thing I need is to get a report that you've killed a target because you failed to incapacitate them. Fix it, Gomez."

"Yes, Sir," What else can I say? I should have been able to hit those shots.

Kathel waits until Wayne walks away before saying, "You're doing a good job. I think you're just tense."

I roll my eyes, "Thanks. Wouldn't you be tense if your instructor was hovering over you barking orders?" I eject the dead power cell from the gun and exchange it for a new one.

"No, I definitely would be. He was picking targets from afar. He had been watching you for the last few rounds." Kathel says, passing me a bottle of water. "But what I was trying to say is that you're physically tense; it's causing you to hit high. When you shoot, the recoil is kicking up a bit higher with each shot because you aren't relaxed enough to absorb the impact."

I nod, "Okay, I follow you. And how can you tell that?"

He smirks, "cause even right now your shoulders are to your

ears." He reaches over and taps the top of my shoulder.

I press my shoulders down, the muscles groaning at the release. "Guess I was a bit tense," I say, pulling against the muscle in my neck, trying to work out the knots.

"Wayne is just giving you a hard time. You're doing a really good job. Especially compared to some of the others." I glance down the line and watch a few take their shots. We all had to have ranked a certain way to get here, but some of the new Fighters definitely have strengths other than firing a blaster.

Wayne releases us not long after that, and we trudge down the hall to the mess. "I can't even lift a fork without my body yelling at me." I groan over a plate of food.

"You guys look rough. What did Wayne have you do?" Miessa asks.

"The better question would be, what did Wayne *not* have us do? We touched on almost everything. I think he wanted to get a baseline before we dive into more advanced topics, you know, to see where everyone is." Kathel says. "What did you ladies do?"

"Oh, we went over a lot of different things. It was really cool. It was a lot of the politics of everything, especially right now." Dita says excitedly; she leans forward, keeping her voice down. "We even spent a good fifteen minutes talking about the Federation and what they've been doing. They are definitely making the officers uneasy. That may be why everyone else is here."

Miessa nods, cutting into a very, very red steak. "It was a lot of information. I think it will take a bit to fully understand all of it. But it was necessary, like you said, to get a good foundation going. When we get back to the room, we can show you the notes we took, make sure everyone has the same general level of knowledge. Never know when they're going to throw something into a test."

We hurry back to the rooms. After a quick shower, we all sit in the living area, ready to go over the day. "Well, what did they tell you about the Federation?" I ask.

"What, you don't want to hear about how we were first tested on naming different diplomats from different sectors, and we had to get them all right with no help?" Miessa asks, twirling a piece of the blue hair she had given herself tonight.

"Did you really have to name them?" Kathel asks, "that very unproductive."

"We didn't actually do that. Miessa is messing with you." Diva says, wrapping a blanket around her shoulders.

"Called it," I say from my spot on the floor.

"You did not." Miessa rolls her eyes. "But no, we didn't have to do that. But someone is overly eager about the Federation. Do we need to report you to Carver?" She asks, pointing at me with a perfectly manicured claw.

"No, look, I'm just curious. I've never heard so much about a group and known so little. It's like everyone wants to talk about them but doesn't have anything to say."

Miessa and Dita glance at each other and shrug. "Yeah, that about sums it up." Dita says, "like they didn't give us any current information about them. Just that they exist, and they were originally part of the Garrison. Something we learned that I didn't know, was that they were started when an entire spec class deserted. We learned some names of people, some dates. It was like a big threat to not do it again."

Kathel leans forward at that. "An entire class? Not just a team, but the entire class?"

Miessa nods, "All sixteen of them." Even though we are alone, and it's our own rooms, she drops her voice, and we all lean in. "Now, what I want to know is how so you fuck up so bad an entire class disbands? I mean, what if any of them are ever caught? They're done, they're all court-martialed."

I sit back, thinking, "do we know when that happened?"

"Almost eight years ago," Dita says.

"I'm still stuck on everyone leaving part, though. Like what would have to happen for me to feel a kinship with someone like Edonne and be cool deserting with him?" Kathel says. "Something doesn't add up."

"So, what does that have to do with the kids?" When no one knows what I am talking about, I explain what has been happening on Earth when kids go missing. "People keep saying it has something to do with the Federation, and it's their way of recruiting? Most of the kids who get taken are under ten. I haven't been able to figure out why?"

Everyone thinks for a minute or two, "I don't think it's them. I mean, I know we're meant to hate them with all our being to please our great protector, the commander, but I can't picture people in my class wanting to steal kids." Kathel rubs his hands over his face.

"What else did they say?" I ask.

Dita shrugs, "nothing actually worth anything. It was twisted. Like you said, people like to talk about it but don't actually say anything, and I think we were all too scared to ask questions in case it got back to the commander."

EMAIL SENT 09:35:22 November 4th, 2228

Hey Bud,

Try using the link below to send me a message. Dita said that the Garrison has been upgrading their security lately. Maybe that's why I haven't heard from you, she said messages might bounce. I'm sorry if you've tried to send me a message, and I've missed it.

Love ya,

Ada

Chapter 25

"Alright, let's take a fifteen-minute break. Refresh your brain so when we come back, we can move on." Doctor Skovnia says. All the other Medics around me stand up and stretch, reaching toward the ceiling and walking into the hall to stretch their legs. I look at my tablet screen filled with notes and start highlighting various bits that could be important. "It's Ada, right?" Skovnia says. "You were the one who got into a fight with a Corsican as soon as you got here? I treated your face."

I stand up and press my hands to the small of my back. My spine pops a few times. "Yeah, that was me." I sigh. "Edonne is a character."

"Ah, Edonne, yes. That name is familiar. Which is a lot to say since your class has only been here for a short while."

"What does it say if you remember me too?" I ask wryly.

"Oh, well. Edonne is a much clearer memory." She explains,

"but it was also easy to remember you since I did help you with that when you came aboard the station, and you are on my list." She says, holding up her tablet.

"Right," I say, looking down at my screen full of notes. All the bits I'll need to remember to keep my team safe, to help anyone we may come into contact with, or the bits of information that may make me a better Fighter because I'll know where the enemy will be weakest. I knew going into this that there would be a lot of information to learn and absorb. I mean, there's a reason people back on Earth would go to college for years to specialize in one section of the body. And here I am, learning it over a few months with different species.

"It's a lot of information," Skovnia says with a small smile. "You'll get it. Are you planning to stay on base?"

I glance up from my notes, "uh, no, not exactly. I want to be in the field."

Her grin grows wider. "That's what I thought. So why are you worried about being trained in every capacity of every race?"

"I-I don't know," I say, twirling my stylus to hide my embarrassment. "How did you know I was worried about that?"

"Because everyone that comes through those doors to my class worries about that at some point." She sits down at the desk beside me. "You are going to be a combat Medic. You will be going into emergency medicine. You don't need to know how to do brain surgery on a Corcian while on the Moon. What you will need to know is how the brain works and how space affects it. Most of the species we employ in the Garrison have a relatively similar bodily function. You need to know what to do when shit hits the fan and how to keep your team together until you get to safety. If you choose to go farther in a few years, that's a problem for future you."

I look over the bits I highlighted and my scribbles in the margins and take a deep breath. "You're right," I say, tapping a side button and letting the screen go dark. "I'm going to go take that walk now."

She nods and heads over to the panel on the wall. "Alright, we'll gather again in about five minutes."

I leave my tablet on my desk and head out of the room. I do a lap of the floor, letting my mind wander. I sometimes wonder what my life would have been like if my parents hadn't died. Would I be here now, thousands of kilometers from home? I don't know what I would've done with my life. It feels like a lifetime ago, and yesterday. I know at the time I had no real plans. I never had to think about it before.

I wonder what would have happened if my parents weren't scrappers? Would Dad have worked? Maybe for Tortie? I don't think he was ever an informant for him, but someone must have thought so. Sometimes I wonder what would have happened if the car bomb hadn't instantly killed them—would a Medic have been able to keep them alive long enough to get to a hospital?

"Hey, Ada, you done with class?"

"What?" I jump, nearly running into Kathel, "Oh, hey, sorry. No, we're on a break. Are you done?"

He leans against the wall with his arms crossed. I look down at my nails, picking at the rough edge of one. The light above him makes his eyes look even brighter, the gold hues stark against the white of his eyes. "They have to program some sims; the tech wasn't working. I'm excited. I don't know how I missed the announcement, but they reintroduced flight to the Jumper class."

"Wait, really? I thought we moved away from ships a long time ago. Wasn't the tech too difficult to maintain?" I ask, wishing I hadn't left my tablet back in the room so I could look it up.

"I know, right? I think most people thought that, but I guess they're bringing it back. Maybe that's part of bringing all our classes together from the different bases? They said they wanted to incorporate it back into the training plan so we could go back to some locations where our jump gates have broken down. It will be nice to fly again. I haven't since I left home, and that was a few years ago." He explains. "Like Hygeia and Phoebe? The Garrison hasn't been there in at least half a century. It's so cool. Until all the stars are found... Really makes you wonder when we shifted from the technology and research to military power. What happened to going to different planets to learn? I just want to explore everywhere."

"I think your Kuiper is showing." I laugh.

232

He grins, "Yeah, yeah, it is."

"So I know the people who live in the Kuiper belt are considered nomadic people, but how does that work? It isn't like you could just walk to a new place. You had to migrate to a whole different object in space."

"When you put it that way, it sounds complicated. It didn't feel like that. We just sorta lived out of our ships. And we moved in packs. There was always someone who could fix something that was broken. Nothing was ever new, but it didn't need to be as long as it still worked." He shrugs, "It was easy. Just move when you felt like it or stay as long as you needed to."

I nod, "I guess that sounds simple enough," I glance past Kathel down the hall and see some other Medic class soldiers heading back into the room. "I have more questions, but I have to get back."

Kathel looks at the people passing us, "Okay, cool, I'm not sure if the sims will cause us to be late to dinner or not, but if they do, I'll catch you back at the rooms."

I hurry back, keeping my head ducked to avoid eye contact. Skovnia is already back in the lesson, explaining what will be in our Garrison issued Med Packs. She holds up a small pouch—it's about the size of my tablet—and a small backpack. "You will have most everything that you need between these two bags. Some of you may feel you need more supplies; I just want to remind you that you are an emergency medic. You need to be able to move quickly and unencumbered. You do not want to be the reason that your team takes too long to exit a situation."

She goes through each item in the bag from gauze to IV sets, fluids, tourniquets, a stethoscope, some meds, and shears, amongst other things. I try to write each item and a little descriptor that I can go over again later on. "You'll each find your own way to organize your kits. And you'll find different things that you want to carry that aren't part of the primary kit you'll be getting today. Check with the med team if there is anything you want specific for your team. We may be able to give them to you. If we cannot, you'll need to purchase those items yourself."

The sheer amount of stuff that came out of the bags is ridiculous but also completely necessary. I almost can't process how someone could feel under prepared. I scroll through my list to see if there is anything I want to add or grab more of.

"Okay, on the back wall there's a set for each of you."

We each get up and grab the bags. Mine feels huge on my back but not quite heavy, just bulky. Where for others the bottom of the bag hits the small of their back, for me it sits a few inches low, forcing it to just out. I adjust the straps, feeling better when it is tight to my back. I bounce on the balls of my feet a few times, getting a sense for the weight of it. With the tightened straps it stays flush to my back and doesn't bounce around as much.

"Who thought it would be a good idea to make the smallest

person on your team the medic," Elara mutters under her breath. She isn't looking at me, so I can't tell if she meant for me to hear it or not.

"Command seemed to see something in me." I snap back. "Sure, I might not be able to carry someone for as long a distance as you, but I won't be as easy of a target."

Skovnia crosses her arms and raises an eyebrow looking between the two of us. "Is there something you would like to share with everyone else?"

"No ma'am," I say. Elara ducks her head slightly, avoiding Skovnia's glare.

"Right, now that you have your packs, I want you to go through them tonight, get acquainted with them, learn the contents, find what goes where. And I want you to talk to your teammates. Learn some of their medical histories. Make sure you know anything that could come up as an issue going into our first mission. You need to take care of your team no matter what." Slovenia powers down the projector. "Okay, that's it for the day. I'll see you in a few days."

Chapter 26

"You've got homework?" Miessa laughs, playing catch with one of my many bandages.

"Sort of. More gathering information for the future. To make sure I know all I need to know to support the team." I say, moving some items around and trying to get the bag to zip shut. Miessa tosses the bandages back to me, and I shove it into a pocket. "You know, make sure that none of you have some allergy or something, so I don't give you meds that immediately kill you? That sort of thing."

"So, you have to play doctor when you first go see someone?" Dita asks.

"Yeah, like when you first go somewhere and have to go through all your medical history. I don't think I need a full medical history, just anything that would come up that you think I should know." I pull open a new notes tab. "We can do it in your rooms if you would prefer, so you have your privacy. You know, for HIPPA and stuff." I say.

"Hippo? Wasn't that some big animal on Earth at one point?" Kathel asks, jumping over the back of the couch.

I burst out laughing, "Not a hippo! And we do still have them! Only a few, though. But no, I said HIPPA. Like the medical law? You don't have any laws like that?" I ask. All three of them just look confused. "Okay, I will take that as a no, you don't have HIPPA. Well, until I am told otherwise, I'll practice as if it were the case, so if you want to, we can go to your rooms, or we can stay out here. It's a privacy measure. So, think of anything you would only want a medical professional to know."

"I can go first," Dita says, bouncing over to her room. "I will help you practice the HIPPA." I grin and shaking my head follow her into her room. She is already sitting on her bed, hugging her pillow to her chest when I get through the door. "Okay, Doctor Ada, what do you need to know?"

"I'm not a doctor," I scoff. "I don't know, did you ever fall down as a kid break any bones that still hurt sometimes? Or have any medication you take regularly? Things like that."

Dita thinks, twirling a few of her tentacles around her fingers. "I don't think I have anything for you. I haven't broken a bone. And I don't take any special medications. I don't take anything. My mother used to, but I don't."

"Do you know what your mother took medication for? Is it a disease or something that Ganymede's normally have that you may develop later in age?"

"I don't think so. Wouldn't the med center have all this

information in their records on the teams?"

I nod and minimize the screen. "Yeah, they do. I think they're just trying to encourage a good dynamic between the teams. Medics are often left out to dry. And it is good to get the trust and communication going between us rather than by docs."

"That makes sense. If I think of anything, I'll let you know." She says, beaming. "Did I do good? Was I helpful?"

"I-yes, yes, you were Dits." I grin. "I'm going to go talk to the others now."

"Wait!" she grabs my hand. "Before you go, how are things with Kathel?" she asks, wiggling her eyebrows at me.

I growl out a response and lightly swing at her, which sends her reeling back laughing. I move back out to the living room, shaking my head, the sound of Dita's laughter following me out.

"What's that about?" Miessa scowls. "I don't know if I can trust the treatment of a Medic who makes her patient lose it laughing."

"She's just being ridiculous," I shout over my shoulder. "And I'm not treating you. Not yet, at least. Just asking questions." I open a note tab dedicated to Miessa. "So yeah, do you want to go to your room, or stay out here?"

She glances at Kathel and shrugs. "I don't have much. Anything I have is normal for an Owliano." She lifts her shirt to reveal a small pump attached to her lilac skin. "So, I can shift, right? Well, my body likes to just do it randomly. My hormones get out of whack,

238

so I have this little pump. It makes sure that everything stays on track that I don't shift when I don't mean to. It was a real issue when I was little. But like I said, a lot of Owliano have this. I have to go get a refill of the meds the pump uses once a month. I have about three weeks until my next refill."

I scribble down the notes, my pen going on the fritz a bit at the end. "Okay, and just so I know, what happens if you don't get the medication? Do you just constantly shift without meaning to? Are there other issues you have?"

She taps her chin, thinking, "I don't think so? Not constantly, but I wouldn't be able to stop it. It has been years."

"Right," I make a note to myself in the margins to look up what I can about it and glance up at her. "Anything else? Broken bones, childhood traumas, anything?"

"Nope, that should be it." She gets up and goes to the fridge and pulls out a smoothie. "You would think you want there to be something wrong with us. You know, so you have something."

Like for the other two, I open a new tab dedicated to Kathel. "I do not! Sure, it would be interesting, but I would gladly take a boring team with no medical needs than a team with a ton of medications to manage and things to keep aware of. I'm cool with a nice neutral team." I turn to Kathel, tablet ready. "What would you like to do, Sir?" But he isn't on the couch where he was a moment before. I look around and find him by the door to his room.

"Come on. We'll do the HIPPA thing. I think it's a good idea."
He waves me over.

I hurry over to the door *this will be the first time the two of us
have been alone since we were on Titan.* His room is like the rest of
ours, but he has a window looking out to the galaxy. "Whoa." I
whisper moving to the glass.

"Miessa has one too. I don't know why we were assigned these
rooms, and the rest of you don't get one."

"I'll never get over it. It's both so beautiful and terrifying to
think there are only a few inches between safety and instant death."

He presses a button on the wall and a thick piece of metal slides
out to cover the window; he presses it again, and it slides open again.
"I can do this whenever it gets to be too much. Helps to ease that
feeling of dread. Sometimes."

"That's nice. So, it this your view all the time?" I ask, peering
out the edge of the window.

"I mean, it changes from time to time. But normally it's just the
black. I saw Earth once, and the Moon another time. It just depends
on how the rotations line up." He sits on the edge of his bed, fingers
interlaced, circling his thumbs one way then the other.

"Sorry, I got distracted," I say.

"All good," He says, "I just figured it would be easier. I have a
bit I wanted to tell you."

"Oh, okay, cool," I say. I put my tablet down on the edge of the bed and reach up to fix my hair. "Mind if I sit down?" I ask, pointing to the side of the bed.

"Oh yeah, you can sit." He blurts, scooching over to make room for me. "They should give us some extra chairs for our rooms."

"Yeah, that would be nice. Though they probably don't expect us to do much outside of training and sleeping. I feel like that's all I do anymore." I laugh.

"Yeah," He runs a hand through his hair, his fingers snagging on a knot. "Earlier I said I'd tell you more about what it was like living in a nomadic society in space. And my health history is intertwined with it."

"Okay," I say, stylus hovering over the screen.

"So, I said earlier that it was pretty simple to live in the Kuiper Belt. That wasn't true. It was simple for a while. We moved from place to place and kept to ourselves. I lived like that for most of my life." He looks down at his hands. "My mother taught me to read and to write on an ancient blocky tablet." He grins, "Mom had to make a case for me out of bits of rubber because I kept dropping it and almost cracking the screen. She used to joke that I did it on purpose, so I didn't have to do my classes. She may have been right." He glances up at me and then back down at his hands, spinning his thumbs around each other.

"Like I said, it was easy for a while. Then someone got into some trouble. Something about someone owing someone money. We tried to move on from it, but it just kept coming. Trouble will follow a caravan like a plague." "They came looking for the son of a Garrison officer. They decided to shoot first and ask questions later." He looks away. Slowly he twists and lifts his shirt. Underneath is a large, puckered scar, the skin discolored and surprisingly smooth, almost like someone smeared bits of wax on his side.

"Great expanse," I say, putting my tablet aside. "How old were you?" I want to reach out and touch the skin, even as a part of me recoils at the sight.

"I was fourteen. It damaged part of my obliques and my back muscles. They wanted to take the person out. I'm strong enough to pass the tests and stuff, mask it, but sometimes it just…" He drops his shirt. "I guess the muscles just spasm. I can't do anything about it. It happens once every few months. So yeah, just so you know I, uh, I'm on a medication to help make sure I can still lift stuff, but I have this." He points to his stomach.

"Kath, I am so sorry. That's awful." I whisper.

He shrugs, tugging at the hem of his shirt again. "It's okay. I would do it again if I could."

"Really? Why?" I ask.

"It stopped my brother from getting shot." He says. "I never got to ask him what he did. He ran away the day before. But if it means that Mycall got away, and he's safe, then it was worth it."

I look out the window again and the edge of the Earth swing into

242

view as station turns. I get up and move to it, looking down at my former home. "Yeah, I understand that. I'd probably do that too." The bed creaks slightly as he moves to stand next to me at the window. I glance up at him, light shining gently through his white hair. His amber eyes bounce around take in the stars beyond. "Do you think he is okay?" I ask, not entirely sure if I mean Kathel's brother or mine.

"I think so. At least I hope so." We pause as the North American continent comes into view. "I haven't heard or seen him since then. But if anything my mother taught us stuck with him, he should be okay."

"Yeah, you're probably right."

Chapter 27

The week leading up to the first test is a welcome reprieve. Unlike the times Wayne had us fight until we were practically incapacitated because of fatigue, Wayne has made sure we are well-versed in offensive and defensive maneuvers and strategy. The sims Wayne programs for us are incredibly complicated more so than any mission we should ever find ourselves in. But I guess you can't be *too* prepared.

I shift my goggles and wipe the sweat from my forehead. I crouch down as my eyes adjust to the Simulated world. We're in the hanger of a shipyard, cargo boxes like the one I am hiding behind litter the floor. The point of this sim, according to Wayne, is to get to the far side of the hanger to an informant.

"Can you see the target?" I ask over comms. There is a crackling squawk, but then silence. "Kath, what is your status?" I move forward, trying to make out his form to my left. I shift my position from behind the crates and quickly pull back when a patrol goes by.

I wait a few moments before I hiss, "Kath, where are you? We need to push forward." I look over my shoulder and freeze. "Fuck me," I growl a moment before the enemy behind me fires their blaster. The vest I have on buzzes, lighting up where I am hit. I don't wait for the end screen to load before ripping the goggles off my face and tossing the controls to the side.

"Gomez, what happened? That is the third sim you failed this week." Wayne snaps, coming up to me. "And why the fuck are you throwing my tech around?"

I sigh. "I don't know, Sir." I bend and pick up the hand controls and move to the rack.

"How far was Torrac?" He asks, arms crossed over his chest.

"I don't know. I lost communication with him. That was part of why I failed. We lost contact, and I stopped being aware of my surroundings. I'm hoping he made it through." I say, looking to where Kathel is crouched, controls up in front of his face, moving slowly around the designated area.

Wayne scoffs, "I'm sensing a theme of you not knowing."

I nod, "I will work on it, Sir."

A sharp moment catches my eye, and I see Kathel stand up abruptly, his hands up before they fall to his side. He pulls the goggles off and wipes his brow. "Almost made it."

Wayne shakes his head and walks away. "You two need to figure it out. The test is tomorrow. I hope you're better in real life than you are at these sims."

I smack my thigh and turn away. "Fuck. That isn't good. Expanse damned it."

"Hey, it's okay. We can work on it some more," Kathel says, jogging to catch up with me.

"We don't exactly have time to do that. The test is tomorrow, remember? In less than twelve hours?" I snap.

"Hey," He puts a hand on my shoulder, "We aren't doing that bad. We'll get there. We can come back after dinner during our free block."

"Kath, the test is *tomorrow*, and I flunked out of every sim this week."

He brings his tablet up, showing me the team rankings. "He wants us to fail the sims this week. They were pushing us to use every aspect of the tests. Remember what Dita said?"

I take the tablet and scroll through the data. "They will do everything they can to test us, and break us, to make us the best agents they can."

"Right," he smiles, taking back the tablet. "And if you look at this, you're doing just fine."

"Just fine?" I ask, glancing at the stats. The Garrison likes to test you on every little thing. From how many sit-ups you can do, to how long you take to apply a bandage, to how far you get in sims.

Looking at the scores, I find the Fighters. "I'm in the top five Fems?" I scroll, looking at the various stats.

He plucks the tablet from my fingers and slips it into his pocket. "You're really surprised by that?" I shrug and follow him. He lightly bumps my shoulder. "Ada, you're a good agent."

We move into the hallway, following the other Fighters. "I don't know, I don't like to assume that I'm better than anyone."

He laughs, "Well, do it more. I do, and it feels pretty good." He laughs harder at my face; my mouth falls open as I try to find something to say. "I'm kidding. Sorta."

I punch his arm, "You can be so full of it sometimes."

"Eh, it is what it is." He shrugs. "So, if you want, we can come back here after dinner go through a few more sims?" He asks again.

I shake my head. "I can't tonight. I'm going to call Sarkus. I want to make sure he is okay."

"Didn't you try to call him yesterday too?" Kathel asks, his eyebrows crinkling.

I sigh, "yeah, I did. I can't get a hold of him." I shrug, "I just need to hear from him."

Kathel nods, "I get that," He pauses, "Now, don't take this the wrong way, okay?"

I roll my eyes, "you know when people say that it usually is followed by something bad, right?" I think of Shaelin, and the many times I yelled at her.

He pulls at the back of his neck. "I know, but I don't mean to be an ass." He pauses, and I wave him on. "Okay… Did you ever think maybe he doesn't want to talk to you?"

I stop in the middle of the hall. "What did you just say?" My face flushes in anger. *What if he doesn't want to talk to you? Fuck Kathel. Fuck this station. Fuck it all. Of course, I have thought of that.* It's a thought I have been avoiding like the plague. Because if I'm doing all of this, putting myself through all these tests, and at the end, he doesn't want to come to me, I don't know what the fuck I will do.

Someone curses at me for stopping, and Kathel reaches out to move me. "Ada, you can't just—"

"What the fuck did you just say?" I ask, stepping back from him.

His face drops, "Ada, I didn't mean—"

"Stop. Don't say anything." I spin on my heel, trying to put as much distance between the two of us as I can.

He catches up with me and grabs my arm. "Ada, I didn't mean to hurt your feelings. I just wanted to make you think—what if there's a reason?"

I pull my arm away. "Don't touch me."

"Ada, I'm sorry. I—" He runs a hand over his face. "It fucking sucks, I know. I've been there!"

I dart around a corner, trying to get away from him. But his long legs keep an even pace with me. I turn to an empty classroom and

248

dart inside. "Will you fucking just leave me alone?"

He slams the lock into place. "No, because clearly you're fucking pissed and need to talk."

I grind my teeth together. "I'm fine. I just… It's been a bad week, okay? Just leave me be." He searches my face and sits down on the edge of one of the tables, crossing his arms. "What?" I snap.

"You aren't okay, Ada. And that is fine, but you can't keep shoving it down." He says. It isn't said pityingly, but I almost wish it was. It's understanding. It says, 'I see your pain, and I understand where it comes from. I have been there too.'

"Don't. Please don't compare me."

He shakes his head. "I'm not. I just don't want you to get hurt by it."

"Too late," I mutter quietly under my breath. I step away and start pacing the room. "So, what do you want me to do about it? I got hurt. I keep failing tests no matter how hard I try. And I don't know what the fuck is going on with my baby brother. So what exactly would you have me do?"

He shrugs, and the movement makes me want to punch him. "I don't know. That's something I can't do for you. But you need to talk to someone about it."

"I have been to enough shrinks. I don't need help." I think of Sarkus' face when I left. The way he had to walk away from me. The flash of fear I felt thinking he didn't want to talk to me anymore.

That he needed to remove himself. He can remove himself if he needs to.

"You need to be careful. Keep things separate."

"What do you mean?"

He waves his hand vaguely around the room. "You know," I cock and eyebrow at him. "Look—" He runs a hand over his face. "You need to just be careful. I know a good portion of you being here is so you can get him back. But right now you need to focus. You need to keep the two things separate. We need you focused."

I open my mouth to snap a reply. But he isn't wrong. And it hurts. "I just need to hear it from him," I whisper, Kathel stands up and moves away. I grab his arm. "Wait, look if he is in trouble, I can help him. If he doesn't want me, I'll just… I need—he wouldn't just leave me." I let the words falter. "He isn't Mycall."

"Okay." Kathel sighs, running a hand over his hair. "Just know, I warned you. This cycle of wanting to hear, of reaching out over and over… it gets harder. At some point, it won't be worth it anymore." He watches me for a few more moments, but I don't respond. I don't know what I would say to him. He pulls his arm away, and I feel my eyes start to burn. "I am going to get dinner. You should get something too."

I keep my emotions at bay until he has left the room. But as soon as the door slides shut, the first tear falls.

* * *

I settle in on the couch with my tablet, flipping to Sarkus' contact card. I stare at the little picture of his face and the dread and doubt that has been slowly building over the last few weeks settles over me again, just like it has every time I try to reach out to him lately. I blink away the burn of more tears threatening to fall. *What if I am hurting him by trying to contact him? What if he is doing better without me and the time comes, and he doesn't want to leave? I should leave him alone and let him try to grow up with a family that loves him. He needs the space.*

I power off the screen and press the cool glass to my forehead. I get stuck in this loop, punctuated by the sadness on his face when I said I was leaving. *I never should have left.* But where would I be if I had stayed on Earth? I power the screen on again and tap the call button next to his name. It rings, the sound echoing around our living room. After about a minute, the ringing stops, and the room falls quiet again.

"It's fine. It is a school night. He was probably just busy." I remind myself, just like I did last night and last week.

"Hey, what are you up to?" Dita asks, flopping onto the couch beside me.

"Hey," I say, scooching over, so she has more room. "I was just trying to call Sark. He didn't answer."

"Again?" Her tentacles go flat. "I am sorry. He must be

251

swamped. Did he say he had joined any clubs or anything? That may keep him busy."

I shrug and put the tablet on the table. "Not sure. I'm sure he is fine. He might have broken his tablet or something. I'm not too worried." I lie. I get up and pull open a cabinet, hoping a few crackers will soothe the pit of dread making my stomach turn.

"Do you ever wonder if Carver made our training the way it is because of what happened with the Federation?" Dita asks.

I pause at that, turning to her. "Go on?"

"Well, I mean, since the beginning, I feel like there wasn't a real sense of comradery between our class. It was all a huge competition to get to the top of the charts, and now pitting all the teams against each other, and bringing in another set of teams from different bases. It seems like she doesn't want us to form any alliances."

I nod, thinking of the way Edonne and his team would throw insults across the room, and the other medics would do whatever they could to not ask each other for help in our lessons. "It makes sense. If we don't work together, we can't stand up to her. But in the long term, how does that help her? We are a military group; we have to work together, right? We won't always be in these groups of four squads. If we go to a different division, we need to be able to work together."

"I know! That is the bit that I keep getting stuck on. It's just a theory. But it really makes you think, doesn't it? Should we be trying to make nice with the other teams or just focus on making our team be the strongest it can be?" she shrugs. "I don't know."

The door to our room slides open. Dita and I turn to see Kathel. He pauses for a moment, taking in the room. "You know you can't just sit on your tablet all day hoping for a response," Kathel says, walking past us.

I glance down at my tablet on the table. "Yeah, I tried to call him, but he didn't answer," I say.

"Whatever." He says and goes to his room.

"What was that about?" Dita asks.

"It's nothing," The door slides closed behind him. "Well, I think that's enough conspiracy theories about training for tonight. I'm going to go to bed, try to get lots of rest before the test tomorrow." I say, checking my tablet for a message from Sarkus one more time. "You probably should get some sleep, too," I get up and moving to my bedroom, placing a hand on the door. "We are going to have a long day tomorrow."

Chapter 28

I tug at the neckline of my white suit. The flight deck feels humid today, and my suit is working double-time to keep me cool. Dita pulls up the stats. "Based on how we have been doing in the individual training, our team is averaging higher than most of the teams. There are three teams that we should monitor though. In particular, their spies. They rank high." She relays over our comms. "I'm going to run a few tests, make sure our comms can't get hacked."

Miessa goes over each of our supplies again, double-checking that when we leave, we shouldn't have any issues. Not like we did on the Moon. "Everything looks good." She says, "I don't like that we are only allowed one power cell per gun."

"Just gotta make sure your shots count," Kathel says. He seems a lot more tense than usual, his shoulders locked and his gaze darting around.

I switch to a private system with him for a moment, "Kath, you good?" He glances in my direction and shuts down the link. *Okay, that isn't good. Something is up.*

"Arctic. When you are ready, the jump is yours."

"Are we all supposed to jump? Or is it just you two?" I ask, turning to Miessa and Kathel.

"Don't be stupid; this is a team mission. We don't need to split up." Kathel says, I snap my jaw shut and don't respond.

Miessa raises an eyebrow at him. "What Kathel means to say is, probably not. We haven't been given clear instructions, so it seems best that we all go together." She says to me, but she looks pointedly at him, arms crossed, like a mother scolding her child for talking out of line at church. "We can decide how to move forward when we know for sure what the test is."

The jump isn't bad. At least it doesn't leave me wanting to throw up. Which is good because I would have been stuck with the smell for a while. We land on red dirt and immediately raise our guns, locking in back to back. "Clear," Kathel calls, and we all echo him. "We have a countdown on our HUD." Sure enough, in the bottom right corner of my screen, a red timer ticks down from three minutes.

"Looks like it is nearly showtime." I ask, going into my messages. "Okay, this should be fun." I read off. "First, we have to head east to a maze. At the entrance of the maze, we'll find a flag. We need to protect our flag while navigating the maze and trying to get as many enemy flags as we can. Blasters are in play. Levels are turned down, which is why we only have one cartridge, but they will deal damage." I pause, "So don't get hit. After an hour, the team with the most flags wins. Sounds simple enough."

We move east quickly, kicking up bits of red dust as we move. "There, I see the door," Dita calls.

"One minute until we are in play," Miessa says, trying the door. "Shit. Locked."

She and Dita turn to the door, whipping out their tablets. "Is it encrypted?" I ask.

"Doesn't seem like it." The lock on the door flashes a few different colors as they work through unlocking it.

"Thirty seconds," Kathel says.

"We are almost through," Dita says, I try to look over her shoulder, but the numbers on her screen move too quick for me to pick up what they say.

"Ten."

"Just hang on."

BAMPH.

Dita, Miessa, and I jump back, raising our blasters, looking for the source, but it's Kathel. He shot the lock; he reaches out, grabs the door, and turns the handle, the door squealing open. "We were running out of time."

"What? We were almost there! You didn't need to do that." Dita says as we file in. Kathel tries to close the door behind us, but now the door is warped from the heat of his blast and won't close correctly.

I punch the button for the airlock and get an error tone. I try it again. Same sound. Kathel throws his weight against the door, trying to slam it into place. He nods at me, and I push the button again, but I know it won't work, a gap at the top of the door revealing the clear issue. "Are you fucking kidding me? They're going to get our flag before we even get in there." He says.

"Just hang on a minute." Miessa says, "Sometimes airlocks like these will have a second system of closure, so if things like this happen, the pressure system can still function."

"What do you mean if things like this happen?" Kathel snaps.

"Like if people get in a firefight and a door gets hit, or some other impact. Relax." I say as the secondary door slides out of the ceiling, locking over the original. I reach over and press the button. This time the dinging sound is much more pleasant, and we can hear air being pumped in. My suit chirps and a reading in the corner says asks if I want to switch my air supply to external air, vs using my tank. "Yes, switch away from tank air." It pings again and the tank light fades.

We file out the door, blasters at the ready. "Okay, I see the flag at four o'clock. Let's grab it and then figure out our next move." Kathel says, making a break for the flag.

Miessa snaps something over comms, but it gets drowned out by Kathel's scream of surprise as a team comes around the corner.

Dita rolls behind a wall and brings up a map, passing the message to all of us, so it shows up on the top left side of our screens.

"We have team Jungle here now," She says, "and looks like Comet is coming up behind them."

I peek out from my crouch position and do a series of three quick shots where I saw their team's heads poking out. "Okay, Kathel, I'll cover you. Grab the flag and then come back to us. And then we can move them out."

"Roger." He says.

Finally, he's gonna listen. "Okay, remember we only have so many shots. When you're ready," I step out, directing the fire to me and lay a series of shots above the heads of the other team sending them back to cover. Kathel darts out, rolls, grabs the flag, and sprints to the opposite side of the hallway. A few seconds later, he moves back towards us.

A shot hits a little too close to me on the wall, and I duck back. They rain a series of shots at Kathel. "What happened to cover me?" he snaps.

"I didn't want to get my head blasted off. Thanks, so do a little thing called bobbing, we learned about it on our first day as you may recall?" I respond.

Miessa sends me a private message, "I'm sorry I don't know what crawled up his ass today."

"I don't care. He just needs to stop until we get through this."

"He told me what happened on Titan." She says sheepishly.

I look over at her, "Okay, do we need to talk about this now?

We're kinda in the middle of a firefight here."

"Right," She moves to team comms. "Kathel, what is our plan?"

"Hang on!" Dita shouts a little too loud for the mic. "Sorry, I just... Kathel if you can get back to us, do that! Ada to your left is a panel. It looks like if you pull the right lever, a wall will slide between us and Jungle as long as we keep them far enough away. That way, we can get out of the way and let Jungle and Comet take care of each other."

"Okay, sounds good," Kathel says.

He jumps behind me, squatting to cover as I step out from behind the wall, reaching up to a panel box. If Dita hadn't found it on a map, I wouldn't have known it was there. It was high enough on the wall that it wasn't in my line of sight, and the designer did a good job camouflaging it. "Any idea which lever it is?" I ask, glancing towards Team Jungle, who moves closer and closer by the moment.

"Does it matter?" Kathel snaps.

"Well, it might! I'd like to have some intel. For all we know lever one could eject us, so how about you chill for a moment?" I snap.

"Lever three." She says before he can answer. "I think it's going to be lever three."

I reach up and pull the lever in the center. The wall slides closed, but it is painfully slow. I am sure the entire squad is going to make it through the wall before it slides into place, but we hold them off.

We regroup, checking our blaster's power levels. "Everyone good?" I ask, visually checking each of them for damage, but their suits are still pristine and white.

"Yeah, we're good. No hits." Miessa says. "Okay. Game plan? I personally don't want to be on the defensive the entire time."

I turn to the new hallway that opened to us when we moved the wall. "Well, can we all see each other on the map?" I ask. I peek at the HUD but don't dare to manipulate it in case someone comes up the hall.

"Yeah, and you can see who has the flag. There's a little icon." Dita reaches out to Kathel, and he passes her the flag. "Okay, yeah, and you can see which team member has the flag." She quickly passes it back to him. "So, we can see who to target, but also who may target us since we have a flag."

"How much time is left? Of the hour, I mean." I could have sworn I saw a flicker of movement down the hall, but so far, no dots appear on the map. "Dita, or Miessa, can you get us a target? Preferably a nice easy one to start?"

"Forty minutes."

"If we head down this hall, and then take a right, looks like team Nebula is there, I think it is them by the color. They're about four hundred meters away and it looks like they have two flags. They're the closest I see on the map." Miessa says.

"Yeah, I agree, they seem like the best option," Dita says.

"Hey, Miessa, can you shift the color of your suit?" I ask.

Behind the visor, I see a wicked grin cross her face. "I like the way you think." She closes her eyes, and there is a rippling motion as her suit changes before us. But it quickly shifts back to white. "Fuck," She growls. "Normally, I can, but I can't seem to hold it today."

"Worth a try." I turn to Kathel, "Ready then? Stealth doesn't seem to be working today."

"Oh, now you want my opinion." He snaps.

"I'm sorry, what?" I sputter.

"Are the three of you done? Can I talk now?" He snaps.

"What crawled up your ass and died?" Miessa asks. "No one ever told you to stop talking, you're just doing whatever you can to be rash today. Stop acting like Edonne. What do you want to say?"

Through the tinted visor of his helmet, Kathel's face turns a deep red. "Fuck off, Miessa." He turns and starts stalking toward the enemy team.

The rest of us share a look and keep moving. What else are we gonna do? We have forty minutes to defend our flag and capture the others.

Dita monitors the map as we move, watching Nebula, but they seem to have set up camp in this corner. "I'm sure they have eyes on all angles." She says, "just be ready."

We keep our blasters up, ready to fire at a moment's notice.

Kathel holds up a fist, and we freeze, waiting for his move. He pulls around the corner and calls quietly over comms, "Clear." We follow him around the corner, Miessa swiveling to watch our back in case anyone else had figured out the wall trick.

"Okay, our target is up ahead on the left. But there is a right turn first. We need to pass that, but it looks like there may be a few teams moving in that hallway in the opposite direction. We need to sneak by them." Dita advises.

I line my back up with the wall and peer around. I can see at least eight people—they seem to have made a pact and are working together. I can't help but wonder if they will be rewarded or docked for that. No one looks in our direction. "Okay, we are good to move." I say, "cross the gap." Dita and Miessa do, holding their blasters close to their chests. And Kathel seems like he is about to, but then he turns and makes a break for it toward the enemy team and the three flags they hold. "Kath, what the fuck are you doing?"

"Going for the target." He barks.

"That isn't them." I follow him, torn between the safety of the wall and the fact that my teammate is running hellbent towards eight enemies. "Fucking A," I growl and run after him, ducking behind any protrusion I can.

I don't know what the actual fuck he thought he was doing, but it doesn't last long. Someone must hear him coming and spins, blaster up. They get one good shot off as Kathel ducks behind a piece of wall. "They hit me!" He barks, "fuck that stings," and it takes every bit of self-control to bite my tongue. The teams turn to make their way down the hall toward us, and I stick my arm out and just start blasting, hoping to make them think there are more than the four of us. A few shots come from behind, telling me Dita and Miessa are giving me some cover. I crouch and run over to Kathel. He is holding his arm. "Ada, right, so they shot me."

"I saw," I growl, ripping open the medical pouch attached to my thigh. "What the fuck do you think you were doing? You can't take out two teams by yourself. I shouldn't heal you for that." He must find an ounce of sense somehow because he doesn't say anything. "You have our flag. If you go down with it, we lose." I grab a wad of gauze and shove it into the black hole in his suit where the blaster hit. I pull it out a second later, "You aren't bleeding." I say, wrapping bandages around his arm and tying it off. "Once we get to a better spot, I will check it more, this is just to keep anything from getting into it. We need to keep moving." I look back down the hall towards the rest of our squad. "Are we good to move back to you?"

"Yeah, hurry," Miessa says. "They decided you weren't worth it."

I want to ask why but decide not to clutter comms. I offer Kathel a hand up, but he ignores it, choosing instead to shoulder past me. The moment I get back to our rooms I'm going to give him a piece of my mind. But for now, I need to focus on the mission. No matter what is going on between us, we need to get through this and rank high.

Chapter 29

"Has Nebula moved?" I ask when we get back to the girls.

"No, we should be good. If we can get past them, we can use a panel box to shift the wall again. Then we won't be as exposed, and you can check out Kathel's arm." Dita says, pointing to the location of the panel on the wall.

"Sounds good. How do we want to move in?" Miessa asks.

The three of us turn to Kathel. As our lead Fighter, he's the one that's good at strategic moves; I'm still working on it. "A 'V' formation should work as long as we move fast. Break through and spin, one person grabs the flag while the other grabs the box. Other two cover."

"I'll go for the box." Miessa says, "I would say you would be best for the flag, but with your arm…"

"I'm fine. I'll get the flag." He snaps.

"And Ada and I will keep them pinned," Dita says.

"Okay, we ready?" I ask as we step into the 'V' formation that Kathel had suggested.

Kathel nods and starts the advance. We creep around the corner, moving at a fairly steady clip. Nebula is facing in the other direction, preoccupied with something else.

"Dita, is there anything on the scanner?" Kathel asks. His voice is tight, and I can tell the shot to his arm is really starting to affect him. *Just get through this section, then I will work on you.* I hope it won't take long to get through this section. I look at the timer. Thirty minutes. If we can at least get one more flag, we should rank okay.

"Something is showing up on the radar, but it isn't another team. At least it isn't any color I remember. But I'm sure Carver would throw something in here that isn't just teams." Dita says, glancing into the distance.

"Right."

We keep moving. "Maybe we shouldn't strike until we're closer. And we can see what they're facing?" I ask.

"It doesn't seem like they're fighting. We should be okay." Kathel says dismissively.

"Ada may be right," Miessa says, "They look like they're really focused on the other side. That must mean something, right?" Kathel shoots her a look and keeps walking.

Dita shifts to a private comm with me. "So, what's going on with Kathel today? Why is he being so bossy? In all of our other training, our communication has been amazing. I mean, there's a reason we have been ranking so high."

"I think I know, but I'll talk to him. I just want to get through this."

Dita nods. "Yeah, okay, focus here. And then we can go from there. Right."

Nebula is still focused on the opposite side; they don't seem to be shooting at anything, but they aren't relaxed. They keep turning back and forth, actively discussing something. When we are about twenty meters away, Kathel gives the nod, and we push forward. Our first shots are wild, letting them know we are incoming since we aren't trying to actively take anyone out. The team spins with wild eyes. They start shooting, but their shots are all over the place. They shoot at us, but also behind at the drones.

"Something has their attention. Go, now, go!" I shout as we charge.

I jump out and rain a stream of cover fire for Miessa and Kathel to dive in. Kathel rolls forward, but the movement is cut short when he rolls over his arm. He reaches out for the flag hanging from one of the Nebula member's hips. He misses. The member moves down quick as a shot and snatches the white flag from Kathel's waist. He rolls away and looks down at his empty hand. I aim and hit the person's leg. It isn't much, but it slows down their escape. "Kath, our flag!" I shout over comms. He spins and dives for the person, hitting them in legs and tackling them. He grabs the two flags, white, and a muted purple. He spins and starts to make his way back to us when he is grabbed by one of the other team. They go down in a flurry of fists as Miessa takes off for the panel box.

Dita and I keep firing, but our shots are fewer and fewer, as the other members of their squad close in. "Fuck, I don't want to hit him." I say lowering my blaster. *You need to get in there Gomez.* Kathel kicks the legs out of the person who has his arm and falls, half crawls half running away. And I shoot the person who was on him, but, as I do, one of their other teammates hits Kathel in the back of his leg, and he goes down again. "Cover me." I run to him and help him up. "Come on," I say, throwing his arm over my shoulder. I do the best I can, moving with him while Miessa and Dita provide cover for us to move behind the wall. The white and blue of his suit is stained black with the shot, and his skin is red and angry beneath.

"What's the point of these suits if they don't even hold up in a firefight when the blasters aren't at max power?" He winces, and I wish I had an answer.

I switch over to a private comm. "I've got you. Just hang on, okay." I can't help but think of our conversation in his room weeks ago when he told me he took a shot for his brother. He glances over at me but doesn't answer.

Miessa stands at the wall aiming shot after shot. "There are drones or something on the other side. They aren't deterred by shots." The wall thuds shut, and Kathel and I stop.

"Okay, let's drop slowly," I say, and with a grunt of agreement from him, we slowly lower to the ground.

Kathel passes me the flags, and I stick them in my belt. "At least I got these."

"Right," I say, undoing the hack job work I had done to his arm. "This doesn't look bad. It obviously hurts, but it looks like your suit absorbed most of the damage."

"Sure, as hell doesn't feel like it." He growls. I pack the place under the suit with more gauze and wrap a bandage around it.

"Okay, I need you to roll over so I can take a look at your leg."

Miessa moves past us, gun raised in case anyone else comes through. "It would be a real shame if that ass doesn't come through this." She comments, and Kathel flips her the bird.

"Okay," I pull the scraps of the suit away from the wound. The thing about blaster wounds is that at their core, they are deep burns. To start the healing process, you have to stop the burn, because it continues long after the hit. As expected part of the wound is already beginning to blister, the angry red skin forming uneven bubbles. A few of the blisters popped in the short move behind the wall exposing even more irritated skin. I pull on a pair of gloves and grab some clean gauze, and a small bottle of water. I pull a knife out and, as gently as I can, cut away the ragged edges of the suit, trying not to pull at his shin. I dab at the cut, drying it out and cleaning it as best as I can. "This will probably sting a lot," slowly I trickle the water down his leg. I pour it higher than the wound, so it runs into it rather than hitting it directly. It won't be enough to cool the internal damage but it's a start.

He winces and his leg tenses, shifting the wound, "Okay, I need you to relax your leg. I am going to wrap it now. I need to you to relax the muscle." He nods. I loosely wrap the bandage around his leg, protecting it from any outside damage. "You doing okay?" I ask noting the beads of sweat dripping onto the visor of his helmet.

"Yeah, I am okay." His voice is tight with the pain, "let's just keep moving."

"Hang on I want to check your arm first." I unwrap the bandage on his arm, but it isn't nearly as bad as the burn on his leg. "I think this one was just a graze."

"Remind me not to get shot when these are on full power," Dita says. I share a look with Kathel, thinking of the scar that lays under his suit.

"How much time is left?" Kathel asks as I finish tying off the wrap. He rolls over and tries to stand up.

"Hang on. Give it a second." I say, grabbing his shoulder and forcing him back down. "If you move around too much, you're going to aggravate it more."

"We can't just stop. We have to keep doing the test." He says incredulously.

"Kathel, we need to move to defense. You can barely walk." Miessa says. "We just need to hold out until we can get you to the infirmary."

"No, I'm fine!" He says, trying to get to his feet again. But the moment he tries to take a step, his leg buckles under his own weight.

"You just took a severe burn to a major muscle in your leg. You need to sit down." I say, catching him. He glares at me but listens, sliding down the wall. "Move into the corner." He does as I ask with a sullen look on his face, and Miessa, Dita, and I form a half-circle around him, waiting for the rest of the time to fizzle out.

After a few minutes, we move through the maze. I offer a hand to Kathel, but he shoulders past me, choosing instead to lean on Miessa. My cheeks flush and want to tell him he is being an asshole again. That I am just trying to do what is best, but we don't have time. *When we get back, I am going to give him a piece of my mind.* turn to move through the maze, gun up and ready. Most of the teams have all but cleared the maze by now, and we advance slowly with no more trouble. "We are going to get points docked if we don't make it to the end of the maze," Kathel grumbles for the third time since I finished working on his leg.

"We might," Miessa says. "But we have two flags."

"Yeah, Storm just crossed with no flags. We can't do much worse than that." Dita says.

When we round the last corner to the exit, a line of drones blocks our path. "This is what Nebula was facing when we stole their flag," Miessa says. She tries to shoot, but her shots are off target under the weight of Kathel's arm slung across her shoulders.

Dita and I step forward, shoulder to shoulder. "It takes three shots to take them out!" Dita calls.

Four drones advance slowly shutting down as we move forward.

"I'm out!" I call as my blaster powers down. Miessa presses her gun into my hand, and I tuck mine in my belt.

"One minute!" Kathel calls as we take out the last drone.

We stumble across the line with five seconds left. The other teams stand at attention, waiting for us. We fall into line, waiting for our next orders. Moments after we cross the line, the walls of the maze fall, sinking into unseen grooves. I hold in a small sigh of relief when I see we are not the last ones. One other team didn't make it over the threshold.

"Squad. Please come join the others." Carver's voice is amplified. She doesn't sound happy.

The squad walks across the clear floor toward us. They walk with their shoulders are slumped, clearly disappointed in their performance.

A projection glows on the top of the dome, slowly Commander Carver's face comes into focus. "Cadets. This was your first test as an established team. Some of you did exceedingly well. Others did not." A second projection glows next to the first, showing the names of each of our teams in the ranked order we went into this test. I wince at the sight of our third-place seed, knowing we're going to fall. "Let's start the scoring. If you held on to your own team flag, you received two thousand points." A glowing +2000 appears next to our name, along with four other teams. "For every additional team flag, you captured, you received an additional one thousand points."

The team names shift, and we are one of two other teams to get at least one additional flag. "If your team took any damage to a member of your team, you lost eight hundred points." We drop a bit again, but we aren't in last. We still have a chance in this. "Finally, for every minute you were faster than the last team in, you get 100 points." I close my eyes at the sight. 8th. We tied for 8th place. The closest team had come in five minutes faster than us. "I hope this is a wake up for some of you. The Garrison will cut teams if, on our second test, you cannot meet expectations. Some of you are in jeopardy of that now." There is an awkward shuffle, and everyone avoids eye contact. "I will see you all back on base. You are dismissed."

Chapter 30

Back on base all is quiet. Dita took Kathel to the infirmary to get his leg worked on. I offered, but he just ignored me, and Miessa already left to take a shower. So, he begrudgingly took her offer. I took a quick shower as well and wait in the living room for Miessa. We need to talk about what was going on. Miessa sighs when she sees me. "Really, you want to do this now? Can't we just take some time to lick our wounds from that test?"

I scrunch my face up in disgust. "I never liked that saying." I shake my head. "Anyway, you said the two of you talked about Titan. Do you want to deal with him being a prick for the next month? Because I don't."

She sighs and flops down on the couch next to me, wrapping her tail around herself.

"I know he is going to be pissy when he gets back, but I'd honestly rather get it done and out of the way as soon as I can," I say.

Miessa plays with the end of her tail, running her hands over the smooth scales. "Okay, well. He's gone, Ada. Like gone, gone."

"Okay… what do you mean?" Tucking my knees up to my chest.

"The two of you need to figure out if you are into each other or not. Well, you do. Cause he is long gone." Miessa says with a laugh. "I knew Kathel briefly before all this, and I have never seen him treat any Fems the way he treats you."

"Yeah? You mean when he's a right pain in the ass?" I scoff, but I think back to what he said on Titan. It was such a lame move. It was some of the worst flirting I have seen. I keep thinking about it though. *Damn it.*

Miessa laughs again, "that would be the floundering Male brain unable to explain emotion again. But seriously, he said that you thought it would be fun to be together?"

My cheeks flush. "I-I mean yeah, he, yeah. I just—"

The door to our room slides open, and I clamp my mouth shut. "It's just me," Dita calls. "Kathel had to stay longer." She shimmies her way between the two of us. "So, what are we talking about?"

"We were just discussing Ada and Kathel." Miessa hedges, glancing between the two of us. "You know what is going on?"

Dita jumps a bit. "Oh, good, yes. Please, just kiss him or something already. You know you want to." I open my mouth to reply, and she cuts me off. "Adaline Sierra Gomez, if you tell me you don't like him, I swear to the galaxy I will tell him myself."

Miessa burst out laughing, and I scowl at the two of them. "So, you're gonna be like that, huh?"

"Yeah, yeah, I am." Dita grins. "But seriously. If you talking to him makes whatever happened today stop, that would be golden. Because golden boy? He's looking like pyrite right about now." Dita says.

"I mean, what do I even say?" I ask, crossing my arms. The door hisses open, and Kathel limps in a pair of crutches under his arms. "How is your leg?" I ask, hoping for a moment he might have come back in a better mood. "Anything they say I should do in the future?" I ask. *I'm the team's medic. It is information I would need to know.*

"Yeah. Don't let me get shot." He says and heads for his room.

Both Miessa and Dita give me major eyebrow wiggles and nudges. I open my eyes wide to say *he doesn't want to talk. What do I do?*

Dita points to the door when it hisses shut. "You literally just said you wanted to get this over with! *Go!* Follow him now. That is an order." She whispers.

"What, he doesn't want to talk?" I hedge.

"Go!" Miessa and Dita say in unison.

"You said you were gonna talk to him when we got back. Don't chicken out!" Miessa gets up and waves me over. "Here, I'll tell him I want to talk, and you go in."

"I don't know, Miessa. I think I should just let him rest."

"Ada." She says, her tone shifting, "you need to talk to him. You know why? Wanna know how I knew before you told me tonight and before he told me what happened on Titan?"

"How?" I ask, sure she is going to have some dumb reason.

"Because you call him Kath. Not Kathel. Not Torrac. You're the only one who does that on this base."

"No, I—" I pause. *Am I?* I rack my brain trying to think of another person. But I can't.

She nods and turns to the door pressing the intercom button. "Hey, it's me. Can we talk?"

"Why?" Kathel's voice snaps.

"Because of that tone right there, Sir. Open up." She steps away, letting me take her place by the door. "Just walk in. Don't let him stop you." She says before walking away.

Kathel's door opens, and I walk in, the door hissing closed behind me. "Miessa, what the hell? What are you doing? Are you trying to be an asshole?"

"I'm not Miessa."

He rolls his eyes and flops on his bunk. "Okay, cool, fine, whatever, Mies." He covers his hands with his eyes. "Go ahead, give me a lecture on how I was an ass to her, and that 'isn't the way to process my emotions'… Shit." He drops the crutches beside his bed with a loud clatter. Sighing, he lays down on the bed rubbing his face., "I fucked up, Miessa. I messed up, and now it reflects on everyone. On me."

I lean against the wall next to his bed. "Well, I'm glad you register the error of your ways, Kath."

Kath slowly uncovers his face and peers up at me. "You really aren't Miessa?"

"I did tell you that." I smirk, "but it's okay. You're having a bad habit of not listening today."

He sits on the side of the bed and winces a bit, shifting his position. Kathel sighs. He puts his head in his hands for a second and then runs his fingers through his hair. "Shit," he mutters under his breath. "I-shit."

I move to sit in the chair and turn to him. "How is your leg?"

"You shouldn't be in here."

"Really? You're going to go from saying that you are an ass to telling me to leave?" I scoff. "We need to talk this out. Whatever it is. Because this," I point between myself and him, "can't affect the rest of the team. First, we are going to start with my job. Then we can move on." I say firmly. "How is your leg?" He sighs again, and I roll my eyes, "Do you have a breathing problem I don't know about?"

He glances up, his eyebrows knitting together in confusion. "What?"

"You keep huffing and puffing like you're having a hard time breathing."

He rolls his eyes and, grabbing for the crutches on the floor, stands up. "I can walk, sort of. I can sit. It's fine."

"But?" I ask.

"But," he allows, "I'm on these for at least two weeks, and I'm not allowed to run or do any hard training for at least a month. And my recovery is all up in the air."

I nod, "that makes sense. It was a large burn. I tried to stop the internal damage, but it was extensive." I uncross my arms, watching as he slowly paces around the room. "Does it affect your position on the team?"

He looks at me as he passes and then away. "No one else had damage like me."

"No one's suit was that compromised. I'm sorry, Kath. I should have been a better shot."

He tries to shrug. But it doesn't work with the crutches. "Yeah, I mean, it's fine. It's whatever."

He moves toward the door, and I get up and move to the door. "What are you doing?"

"Leaving."

I sputter, "Why? We were just talking fine."

"I don't want to talk anymore." He says simply.

"This isn't like you, Kath," I say, looking into his eyes. But he looks away. Deep shadows cling under his eyes, and dark stubble covers his face. "Are you okay? How's shot to your leg? And your arm?"

"Ada, please go." He whispers, turning away from me.

"No," I say firmly. He growls something under his breath, but I push on. "Because, you know what? I'm not done doing my job." I point to the bed, "Go sit."

"Ada, really, please just go."

"No, I'm not leaving until we figure this out."

"Ada, leave now." He yells.

"Oh, now you are ordering me? Well, I am sorry, Sir, but no one voted you the captain of this team. I don't answer to you." I yell back.

"Fucking hell! I never said I was!" He snaps, throwing his arms in the air. "I never said I was the fucking leader!"

"Kath!" I snap, pointing, "I swear to the expanse, go sit down. And stop pacing." he curses again and turns away from me. "You are a right ass. And you know it. And I'm not leaving until we figure this out." I shout.

"You clearly don't want my advice, I got the point yesterday. What happened today won't happen again."

"How do you know? Tell me what is going on?"

He sighs and the muscles in his jaw tick. "I was mad at you. But not *at* you. That you get the chance to get a hold of your brother—"

I freeze. "Oh. Kath when I said he was—"

"—You were right. He isn't Mycall. I was mad at you for having the chance. Him for leaving without explaining. The whole thing was fucked."

"I'm sorry I hadn't thought of that."

"Yeah so, you got your answer. You can leave now. I was honest, I was an ass and it won't happen again. I'm sorry." He presses the button on the wall and the door slides open.

I take a deep breath because I need to bite the bullet. I can't stall anymore. I reach over and press the button allowing the door to slide closed again. "Do you know what it was like on Titan for me?"

He turns back to me at that. "I don't know, Ada. What was it like?" There is a hint of anger at the question that I want to bite.

"Fucking confusing," I say, crossing my arms. Heat creeps into my cheeks again, and I look away from him. "I-fuck it. I never do anything for myself. I don't. I haven't had the chance to in years. I couldn't for Sarkus. I had to do everything perfectly. Anything for me was a secret anything I wanted was 'wrong' or dangerous. Scrapping got us separated, but it was the only way I could take care of him, and it ruined everything. But I need to do things for myself. And you, you made me want to."

"Ada, you don't need to explain yourself. You made it really clear on Titan," Kathel says, turning away from me. "You didn't want anything.

He finally sits back down on the bed. "Just go, Ada. I don't need an excuse, really. I am not going to bring it up again. Just—It won't happen again."

"No, I just… I lied," I say. "Well, sort of. I-I don't know, okay? Let me try to talk this out."

"Ada, this isn't a debrief you don't need to tell me everything that happened in your life right now."

"Kath, shut up. Please." I move across the room to him as he speaks. And he jumps back a bit in confusion as I grab the front of his suit, and I pull him up to me. His lips are hot, and our noses crash together in the most unromantic kiss I have ever had. But his arm is around me, and I grip his suit tighter. "Just shut the fuck up, okay?" I breathe. I pull away a bit, just enough so I can talk, and slowly let go of his suit. I run a hand over his chest smoothing out the wrinkles. "Sorry, you were babbling again."

He gives a breathy laugh, "I guess I was, huh?"

"Now, are you going to fucking listen?" He looks like he wants to say something but changes his mind and nods. I sit beside him on the bed, our knees brushing. "I haven't had the chance to do something just for me that I *have* wanted in a really, really long time. And then this weird guy with silver hair," I reach up and gently tug on a bit of his hair, "came along and agreed with me and tried to help when I thought it was a smart idea to stand up to a giant lizard." I laugh, searching his amber eyes. I take another deep breath. "When you… On Titan, I was scared because I was afraid if I did something

282

for me, it would backfire, and things would get a thousand times worse. I used to say that going into the military was a chance for me to escape, but that ultimately it was for Sarkus. But this." I kiss him again. It is softer, his hands on my back are loose and warm and inviting. "This is for me. I'm still fucking terrified of what would happen if any officers found out. Or if it's the smart thing to do as team members, but I don't know if I care."

"Ada—" he searches my eyes, his golden eyes glassy in the overhead lights "—are you sure? You don't have to just say this to make me to feel better."

I pull far enough away to flick him in the forehead. "Asshole, I literally just poured my fucking heart out for you. Do you think that was easy? That I would just say those things to make *you* feel better?" I ask.

"There you are. That sounds more like you." He grins, rubbing the spot. "You're serious?" I grab his shirt again, pulling his mouth to mine. "Okay, yes, you are serious." He pulls me closer, it doesn't take long for his hands to get tangled in my hair, and for me to fall on the bed beside him. He pulls me close trailing kisses down my jaw to the collar of my suit. As I shift my position and my knee slips off the edge of the bed, I laugh as he clamps his strong arms around me stopping me from falling. Our lips meet again as he slowly tilts back lying on the bed with me above him, my hair creating a curtain around us. "I'm so sorry I was a dick." He says, a bit out of breath.

"But then again," he says, taking in our current arrangement, "maybe I'm not."

"Asshole." I growl, "don't pull this shit again or I will leave your ass on the Moon."

"Speaking of my ass," He winces. "Can, uh, we shift a bit?"

"Oh, right, your leg." I quickly slide off him and the bed.

He rolls onto his side and props his head up with his arm, watching me. "So, are you going to stop yelling at me now?" He asks.

"Oh, fuck no." I laugh. "This just means I won't yell at you as much." I pause. "Or it means I'll yell at you more. I haven't decided yet." I move to the bed and push him back down. I pull up the blanket, and he grins like a fool, tugging me back to him. I lean in like I'm going to kiss him again but pause about an inch from his lips. "But now you need to rest. And I swear to the galaxy if you pull some bullshit like you did today, I will end you." I tuck the blanket around him. He groans and rolls around, undoing the blankets as I head for the door. "Doctor's orders."

Chapter 31

Training has been interesting with Kathel's leg injury. He does everything he can to keep training but has to modify a lot. Even now, two weeks after the test, he has to go back to the med center every day to get new bandages—something I have to remind him of constantly.

"So, Ada, you going to make sure your team makes it through training in one piece? I've seen Kathel in the med center a lot. Did you fuck up that badly during the test?" Edonne sneers as he walks away, making sure Wayne is out of earshot.

"Don't listen to him, I'm fine," Kathel says. "Though I wish I didn't have to go every single day."

"You sweat a lot," I say as we leave class. "Like I remind you every day, you need new wraps to keep it clean."

"It just seems like sure a waste of supplies."

"Do you want it to get infected? Besides that's what we make medical supplies for. How is it a waste?" I sigh.

Some other teams jog past us, using the extra time they have to get in some additional training. "Do you think we should do that?" He asks, watching their backs.

"What extra training? No, I don't." I say resolutely.

"Are you saying that just because you don't want me doing anything more than I need to be?" He asks.

"Partially. But also, I think some are over training. Resting is just as important as training is." I pull up the stats on my tablet. "We didn't rank high in the test, but we have been ranking high individually and have been averaging okay. If we do well on the second test, then we should be fine. I don't think we are in jeopardy of being kicked." I say, scrolling through to see where we stand. "Yeah, we started third and dropped to sixth. We have moved back to fourth place, tied with team Desert." I show him the stats, and he shrugs.

"We should be in first. I feel like someone from this base needs to be at least second place before the officers have a fit. Have you noticed how much pressure they've been putting on our teams?

I scoff, "You think I haven't noticed as the only person actually from Earth on our team on Earth's station? Oh yeah, I've noticed." I roll my shoulders. "You would think by now our muscles would have adapted to everything that Wayne puts us through. But it seems like each week is a new level of hell."

We turn down the hall for the medical wing in time to catch Miessa coming out, her skin burnt orange like a Plutonian. "Hey, you okay?" Kathel asks cautiously.

"No! I'm pissed." She snaps.

I glance at Kathel. "we can tell. What's going on?"

"What is going on?" She snaps, rounding on me. "Someone conveniently left my meds out of the latest shipment. And they won't be able to get more for at least another two weeks, possibly three."

"But you need—"

"I swear on the sun if you are about to say I need my meds, I will smack you." She swears, "No shit, I need my medication. Do you really think I want to be shifting randomly once this thing fully runs out?" She says, pointing to where the little pump resides under her shirt.

"What happened? Like, how did it get forgotten?"

She runs a hand through her hair, yanking furiously at a knot. "I don't know. Some blockhead seemed to think I put down that I didn't want it refilled anymore. But when I asked him why the hell he would think that, or where he could have gotten that information from, he didn't have an answer for me."

"Do you want Ada to go back to the room with you?" Kathel suggests, "I can go to the med center on my own."

"No. *No*. I just need some time to decompress. I have a meeting with Skovnia later to figure out what we can do. I'm just so pissed." She fumes. "I need to find Dita. I got called out of the end of class, so I have no idea what's going on. I'll see you guys later." She says before stomping off.

I watch her go, "do you think we should warn Dita?" I ask.

"Oh, hell no. She's much safer if she doesn't know. The last thing we need is to tell her and have her say something stupid when she's trying to be comforting. Miessa will bite her head off." Kathel says, turning back to the med center. "Come on, let's get this over with."

He heads to the desk to check-in, and I grab us two seats in the corner like we do every day. "How much longer do you think I'm going to need to do this?" He asks, sitting down.

"I think you should be good by the end of the week," I say, struggling to find a comfortable position on the hard chair. "You probably won't be allowed to go back to full work, but you won't need to come by every day to get new bandages."

He sighs. "I hope so. I am getting really tired of my personal time getting cut into by trips to the med center."

A nurse comes up to the counter with a clipboard in hand. "Kathel? Someone will be with you to change your bandages in a few minutes. You can head to your normal room."

Kathel stands and heads toward the door. "You gonna hang out? I can get back to the room fine on my own."

"Yeah, I would rather not deal with Miessa right now. It'll give her more time to cool off." I say. He nods and heads through the door. I settle back in my chair to wait. A few other people come in to grab medication, or to go see a doctor. I watch one soldier go up to the county, looking quite annoyed. After a bit of back and forth they leave in a huff. *Maybe their medication is delayed as well?* I get up and moved to the counter. "Is Skovnia in?" I ask.

A soldier looks up, "I believe so. You can head back to her office."

I head through the set of doors back where Kathel had gone. Skovnia's office is the third on the left. I knock on the door. "Skovnia, it's Agent Gomez. Can I come in?"

There is a shuffling sound inside, and then the door slides open. "Ada, yes, come in. I was just reading over some reports." She settles back in behind her desk. I wait until she looks up at me. "Thank you for waiting. What can I do for you?"

"I was just waiting for Kathel to get his bandages changed, but when we came in, one of our team members, Miessa Guamianna, was leaving. She didn't say much, but she was really upset. Something about her medication hadn't been ordered correctly, and now she won't have her next refill for a few weeks?" I ask. I hope Skovnia can give me some more information. Something I can tell Miessa, a solution to the issues or to ease some anger.

She sighs, "that was actually what I was just reading the report on. Agent Guamianna is not the only one facing that issue. Though she may be affected the most right away. The person in charge of filling the orders dropped the ball, and the order was not put through before the necessary window. The earliest they will be able to get us the order is next week, which may be better than what Miessa told you? I believe she was told three weeks?" I nod. She sighs, "At this point, that's the best that I can do. I have ordered someone to go through all of our inventory to try to see if we have any extra medication for those that need it. This has highlighted an issue in our system that will be resolved."

I nod, "is there anything I can do for Miessa, until we get the medication for her?"

"It's good of you to ask. I hope the other medics follow your lead. As far as Miessa, try to keep her as calm as you can. Double-check when her meds will run out. The next week her body will go through a lot as it tries to compensate for the missing hormones that her medication provided. Remind your other teammates of the side effects that she will have so they don't react too adversely. But you would do well to remind Miessa that even if things aren't going well, it's not an excuse for her actions." She stands. "When I have more information, I'll make sure it is passed on to Miessa and yourself." She walks me to the door. "Thank you for stopping by Ada. I hope you have a good rest of your day."

Kathel meets me in the hall. "I'm all set, you?" He asks, glancing from me to Skovnia and nodding. "Good evening, Ma'am."

"Good evening. How is your leg, Agent Torrac?"

"Never been better. Ada and the rest of our team have been doing a good job making sure I rest it whenever I can." Skovnia smiles and nods before retreating into her office again. "What were you doing?" Kathel asks, making a break for the door like he can't wait to get out of the med center.

"I was trying to get an update on what exactly is going on, you know, from someone other than a heated Miessa."

"How did that go?"

"Well, her meds are coming sooner than she was told. But not soon enough. Come on, let's get back before she bites off Dita's head."

December 23rd, 2228 20:43:07

Hey Tortie,

I hope business is going well. Can you have some guys check in on Sark? I haven't heard from him in a few weeks. We keep upping security lately, I'm not sure if his messages just aren't getting through or what. Attached is an encrypted link that my squadmate set up for me.

Let me know if you hear anything.

Ada

PS: Merry almost Christmas. Do Plutonian's celebrate Christmas?

Chapter 32

My tablet chirps, the notification that I have an incoming email. I grab the tablet and quickly swipe up to look at the message. It's another email from Karrie; I smile and tap open the message, scanning through before replying. I see another one from Emma updating me on the weekly drama of our bus route since she can't tell me in person now.

"You okay?" Miessa asks from the other side of the couch.

"Hmm? Yeah, I'm okay, why?" I ask, glancing up from the tablet as I type, telling Karrie about training and how we are getting ready for our second test, which will be in about a week.

Miessa sits up from where she has laid down and pulls out her earbuds. "You got all excited about the notification, and then you looked sort of sad." She says, "sort of like you expected it to be something that it wasn't."

I sigh, "I haven't heard from Sark in a while. I sort of figured that I would be the person taking too long to reply. I just want to make sure he is okay, you know?" I shrug. I scroll through the emails and see a reply from Tortie.

Hey baby girl,

When you get a chance, call me. If you use this link, it will lead to an encrypted call. I have some info.

T

I glance up at Miessa, "Hey, do you mind if I make a call really quick? The signal can be stronger out here."

She pulls a nail file—yes, a nail file—out of her bag and files her long lilac nails down a bit. Though I should say, they still seem very talon-like to me. "Sure, no problem."

"Thanks, it's just, you know, a family friend. He sent me a message yesterday. May have an update on Sarkus." I tap the link Tortie sent and wait for the connection to pass across the space between us. My screen makes a happy chirp, and Tortie's face appears on the screen, orange skin, and all. "Ada, baby! How are you doing? I'm glad you got my message!" He coos.

Miessa's head whips around out of the corner of my eye, and I glance up at her and sheepishly. "Hey, Sir." I say, "I'm doing well. Training has been going smoothly, mostly. Had a few hiccups here and there but nothing I couldn't handle."

He grins, "that's my girl. Gotta go around kicking ass, right?" he laughs. "How is your team? You got your teams, right?"

"Yeah, we did. I like my team. We work together well." I look at Miessa and smile, but she is staring hard at the back of my tablet like at any moment it might burst into flame. "Just one second."

"No problem," Tortie chirps as I mute myself on the tablet so he won't hear me.

"Hey, you okay?"

"Your old family friend is Tortintelli!" She hisses.

"Tortie? I mean, yeah. My dad would sell scraps to him, and I did too after he passed. Over the years, we got to know each other more. He's been there for me when I needed help."

"He is an awful Male. You know what he's done, right?" she waves the nail file at me. "He has ordered civilians to be murdered!"

"I never said he was a good person." I snap. "But my life would be drastically different without him."

I rub at the scar that runs through my eyebrow. It was stupid how I got it. Looking back, I could think of so many better excuses. Maybe if I had gotten into a fight with someone and took a good hit, or if I had at least like banged my head off something. But no. I got into one of the first of many arguments with Jaxon, but I hadn't learned his angry mannerisms yet. It was, of course, a beer can. Now hundreds of fights later, I don't know what it was about anymore. I'm sure it is written somewhere in the docs Shaelin kept.

I stumbled out of the apartment across the road to my stash and wiped one of the dust-covered glass panes. My face was rough. My right eye was swollen, and a deep cut crossed vertically on my browbone about an inch long. Blood dripped down my face, smeared on my cheek, where I had pressed against my face to stop it from dripping into my eyes.

I didn't know where to go at that point, so I just found a dirty rag from my stash, used the cleanest part to dab at the cut. I probably needed to get couple stitches, but it wasn't like I could go to the hospital. I needed an adult with me, and Jaxon sure as hell wouldn't take me. That was when I ran into some of Tortie's men. Well, they found me. I was supposed to meet Tortie that afternoon. I promised him I would sell him some metal from a ship I found. But then everything happened with Jaxon, so I missed the drop.

They picked me up and took me back to Tortie's place. I thought I was going to get in trouble. Instead, Tortie asked how things were. It was the first time I got to talk honestly about what was going on with someone who wasn't Shaelin. He didn't promise to take a hit out on Jaxon or that he would do anything I wanted. But he made sure I was cleaned up, and he listened. And that was what I needed. He offered more help if I wanted it, but I didn't. He gave me a place to stay for a few days and let me move on my way. I've seen Tortie's cruelty. I've been there when his guys brought in people that wronged him; I knew what happened when people didn't follow up with what they promised him. He never turned that on me. But he never hid it from me either.

Miessa just shook her head. "I can't believe it. He has no

kindness in his body."

"I know he isn't a good person which is why for years I let nothing transpire that wasn't business-related. He has been a parent when I have needed it." I look down and see a Tortie waving up at me. I didn't realize I tilted the tablet down. Tortie can see Miessa. I quickly lift the tablet up, so the camera is back on me. "Do you have a history with him?" I ask, holding my hand over the camera.

"He put a hit on my dad. We figured it out, and we fixed it, so he stopped it, but he tried to have my dad killed!" She fumed.

"Oh," I mumble. "I'm sorry." I look down at the tablet.

"It's fine. I'm just going to go." She says, her voice is tight, and her eyes stay locked on the tablet.

We aren't done with this conversation. I nod and tap the mute button again. "Hey, sorry."

"Is Miessa still there?" Tortie asks. And Miessa freezes as her door slides open.

I purposefully keep my eyes down on the screen. "No, she had to go to training." Out of the corner of my eye, I see her flinch at the acknowledgment.

"I see." He says, and I can tell he doesn't quite believe me, but he doesn't question it. "Can you do something for me then?"

I push my hair back behind my ear, making it easier for me to see her out of my peripheral. "Yeah, sure, what's up?"

He sits up straighter "I would like you to tell her I'm sorry. Her father is a good Male, and what happened between the two of us was a series of rash emotional decisions that went a bit too far. She'll know what I am talking about." He says formally.

"When she gets back later, I'll tell her," I say. Miessa looks at me and nods. She heard the message. It doesn't mean she has to accept it, but she heard it. "So, you sent me a message to call you?" I say, shifting the conversation back to me.

"Yes, right, well, have you heard from him since you sent me that message?" He asks, he glances off-screen at someone. And they say something to him in Plutonian. "Okay, it looks like I have to speed this up. Someone is trying to shut down our connection."

I glance at the notification bar on my screen, wondering if it's the Garrison and the higher security Dita found. "Okay! Yeah, no, I haven't heard from him yet. I don't know, I might be overreacting. I just want to make sure he's okay."

He nods, "right, so there is a reason for that. And I only want to say so much with this line being shut down. I am working on it. And I will send you any information I have." He says vaguely.

"Okay, but what do you have? You said you had something." I blurt. My chest feels tight, breathing doesn't feel sufficient, and I my heart starts to pound.

"So, like I said, we are actively working on it. But the address you gave us, there was no one there. The house was empty. It was condemned."

I open my mouth. And close it, swallowing a few times to relieve the sandpaper feeling. "What do you mean?"

He takes a deep breath, and I mimic the movement, my heart stuttering for a second as it tries to decide whether it wants to race at a million kilometers a minute or slow to a less panicky pace. "I mean, it's desolate. The windows were shattered. And the door hung off the hinges. We scoured the building, but there was no sign of a fight. It seemed more like it was just old. They found Sarkus' tablet." Tortie says, holding up the tech. "It isn't broken, just powered off." He turns it on and holds the screen up to the camera, showing me his messages. My last two messages are there, unopened. The signal lags, and I lose connection for a moment.

"Tortie! Tortie!" I say, tapping the screen. "I still have questions!"

"I will—Sarkus—men searching. Garrison—" The connection cuts him off, and the call ends with a sad bleep.

I stare at the screen for a moment. I open my contacts and scroll down. I take a deep breath and stab a contact. I wait for the call to go through, rubbing my hands on my pants, trying to stop my hands from shaking.

"Ada, how are you doing, Hun? I'm sorry I haven't talked to you in a while!" Shaelin says brightly.

"I've been better," I say through clenched teeth. I am pissed. I am so pissed. Tears prick at my eyes. "Shaelin. When was the last time you did a well visit for Sarkus?" I ask.

"For Sarkus? Oh, I haven't gone on one since he moved in with his new family. He falls out of my jurisdiction now. I have another social worker who keeps me updated on how things are going." She says, surprised. "I got a message last week saying things were going well."

I nod, but I want to scream at her about a million things. "Did they say anything about the issues he was having with the siblings?"

"Siblings? The family we sent him to didn't have any kids." She says. She swipes her hand around the screen and the keyboard I know she has off screen is clacking away as she tries to figure out what is going on.

"Last time I heard from Sarkus, he told me things weren't going well with the family. The son was really mean to him, but over time it was getting better. But he found a teacher in the school he really liked." I say paraphrasing one of his emails to me.

Her face goes pale. "What—what school? The family that applied said that they wanted to home school. The wife had been a teacher at one point." The words fall out of her mouth and hang between us.

"Shaelin. I know you told me to separate myself a while ago, and I'm not getting into that now. But I asked Tortie to keep an eye on him." I see her face scrunch up in disgust, but I run over it. She doesn't get to judge me right now when she has lost my brother. "He said he would check in on Sark now and then. I haven't heard from Sarkus in weeks. So, they went to check on him. That address you gave me? Apparently, that house is garbage. No one has lived there for a long time. But they found his tablet. My last few messages were still there unopened."

"They said they talked to him two days ago, and it was fine. School—good grades—" She says, the message lagging and breaking up.

"Our call is being shut down. Shaelin. I swear to the expanse. Find him! Find him now!" I scream even though the screen has already transitioned back to my home screen, the picture of Sarkus and I hugging mocking me. The tears filling my eyes fall, splashing on to the screen, distorting the image. "I'm sorry." I sniffle at my baby brother's smiling face.

"Ada, are you okay?" Kathel asks, resting a hand on my shoulder.

I jump away, "I didn't hear you come in." I say, quickly scrubbing the tears from my eyes.

"Were you crying?" Kathel says, dumbfounded. "What's wrong? Are you okay?"

The words are a gut punch, and a whimper escapes from my lips. And I can't help thinking since coming to this station, I keep doing things that aren't like me. I shake my head. "No, no, I am not okay," I mumble.

"Okay. What is going on?" He asks. He sits on the side of the couch.

"Sarkus," I say, my voice cracking harshly on his name. "Sarkus is missing." I try it again. I whisper the words. And part of me doesn't believe it, even as I say them. It can't be real. "No one knows where he is."

Chapter 33

My eyes still feel raw as we line up in the center of the gymnasium—all the teams, including those ranking above us. I clench and unclench the fists at my sides. The order to come to the hall came eight minutes after my call with Shaelin was shut down. It took another ten for everyone to get here. We have been waiting in formation another twenty at least. My thoughts are reeling, but the two things that I keep settling on are: Sarkus is missing, and Carver knows that I was on the call. She had someone shut it down. It seems paranoid to think like that, but I know it must be true. Why else would everyone be gathering together like this? What is she going to do when she traces the call back to me?

"You okay?" Dita whispers from beside me. I look at her and glance away. The concern on her face is something the old me, the me on Earth, would have hated. I would have cussed her out and said something awful. But now I look at the little blue alien who doesn't have the same social standards as me but has become the best friend I've had in a long time. "I am sure if you talked to one of the officers, they would let you try to make a few more calls." She says. "They can't have shut down your calls on purpose."

I just shake my head and keep my eyes forward. I know they won't let me make any calls. And even if they did, who would I reach out to? Shaelin had no idea, I don't have the contact for the social worker closer to Sarkus, and the Garrison sure as hell isn't going to let me call Tortie. I press my eyes closed and take a deep breath, fighting off another wave of angry tears.

I hear a shift in the crowd and open my eyes to see Carver taking the stage with a few other officers. Her pressed white business suit's sharp edges are beautifully striking and completely out of place for a military base. It still has her rank and insignia on the sleeves, but the color is strange in the sea of black and green training fatigues.

She moves to the podium in the center of the stage and grips it. Her jaw is set in a hard line as she scans us. "I won't fuss about. Recently, as many of your Tech may have noticed, the collective bases of the Garrison have had to increase our security systems. We have been under a deluge of cyber-attacks from the outside. Someone is trying to hack our information. To know our movements. To see how our recruits are doing." Her sentences are short, clipped. Perfectly enunciated. She clearly has practiced this speech, reworked it countless times to find the words that strike the hardest. She purses her lips. "Now, it doesn't take a genius to know that these actions are from the Federation." There is a ripple in the crowd as she acknowledges her enemy number one.

The muscle in her jaw ticks in anger. "The Federation has been a thorn in our side for years. But we will not allow it any longer." She pounds a fist on the podium, and a cheer goes up. I glance at my squadmates, feeling uneasy. "We will crush them where they stand. We have known for months where they are, and now? Now they will see that we know." Her eyes are ablaze with anger, and it makes me want to take back every moment that I questioned my gut. "We will see how the information they have stolen serves them. In order to do this, we will have to make a few sacrifices. But it won't be for long." She readjusts her posture back to her usual calm demeanor. All the while, soldiers around us cheer and shout their outrage at the Federation. Carver raises a hand and all fall silent. "We may have a spy in our midst, someone who has been getting information in and out through an encrypted link."

My face goes pale and I glance at Dita; she doesn't look good either. "Shit, Dita, what do I do?"

"I… you will just have to tell them the truth about Sarkus. They have to believe you! If they want, I can show them the software I used to make it. I won't let them get you in trouble for a link I created." She says resolutely.

"In order to ensure that this will not continue, we will require all of you to download an app that will closely monitor the security of your device." I glance again at Dita, and she does not look happy about this information. "We will get to the bottom of this. And with your help, we will rid our solar system of these worthless rebels. Until all!" She shouts.

"The stars are found!" The surrounding soldiers cheer.

Carver grins. "You are dismissed, soldiers. See you in the mess."

And I freeze the phrase I have heard over and over four months makes goosebumps rise over my skin. "Until all the stars are found. She isn't going to stop. She is going to hunt them to the edges of the galaxy." I murmur. Kathel nods, his face blank, more neutral than Dita or I's, but the set of his shoulders is higher, tensed up towards his eyes. Just like how I was in training. "What do we do?"

"We get back to our rooms, and we download that app," Kathel says like it should be obvious, but he glances around like he wants someone to hear him say it.

"Right," Miessa says, leading the way back to our rooms.

We make it part of the way across the room when I am stopped. "Gomez. You need to come with me." Callahan says, his voice clipped.

I look at my team and nod for them to go on to the rooms. They slowly turn, eyeing up Callahan like I want to, trying to figure what exactly he could be up to. "Yes, Sir. What can I do for you?" I ask, trying to keep my voice even and not let on that my heart rate just spiked into the stratosphere.

"I need to speak with you privately. If you will just follow me to my office." He says, gesturing for me to follow him. I walk after him, keeping my eyes down and away from the judgment of all those around me who likely assume the worst. He holds the door to his office and lets me in. I glance around quickly, half expecting Carver to be waiting for me in the far corner or something else just as sinister. "Do you know why I called you in here?" He asks. He sits on the edge of his desk, his arms folded over his chest.

I question for a moment if I should stall or not, but just give in. It isn't worth the run around. They clearly know something, or at least think they do. "I believe I do, Sir. If I can just explain my case first, I would appreciate that."

He nods, "okay. Go for it." He opens his tablet to a recorder and presses play. I watch the little line bounce for a second, catching and recording the ebbing noise of the engines.

I take a deep breath and pull my tablet out of my pocket to show him my call history. "My brother is on Earth, in the foster system. I have been keeping in contact with him through emails and video calls when I have free time. A few weeks ago, he stopped replying. Tonight, I received information and called one of my contacts, who told me he was missing. I then called our social worker. Both calls were shut down; these calls were on encrypted links to get past the security wall." I say, showing him the links. "I went around the security of the base, but for non-malicious reasons. The members of my squad will attest to this."

"You are putting words in their mouths?" He asks, cocking an eyebrow.

But I don't jump at the accusation. "No, Sir. Some have said they would speak if required." I try to keep my voice even, but the fear I have repressed for the last hour makes my throat close up again.

"Okay. I'm going to take this." He says, reaching out for the tablet. "Someone will follow up with you in the morning. This shouldn't affect your record, but take this as a warning."

"Yes, Sir."

He watches me for a moment as if trying to read me. "Alright. You are dismissed."

I hurry back to our rooms. Some people linger in the halls, talking, but I move past them, eyes down, leaving no space for anyone to ask questions.

"Ada, are you okay? What did they ask? Are you being punished?" Dita asks, rushing me as soon as I walk in the door.

I nod, feeling my throat get thick again. "Yeah, yeah, I'm okay," I say, pushing her back so I can have some space. "They are going through my tablet. I told them what happened. I am going to get more questions again tomorrow. But I was upfront. I explained what was going on and showed them my history."

Miessa's jaw drops. "Did you tell them you talked to Tor—your friend on Earth?"

I shake my head. "Hell no, the call log just shows the encryption. So, I just said that I talked to my contacts on Earth. If it comes up, then I'll tell them. I didn't go out of my way to lie. Just you know, omitting information until they require it of me."

"Well, what can we do for you now?" Kathel asks. "I'm sure they are going to want more information from you tomorrow like you said. So, like what can we do?"

"I don't know—I said that if there were more questions, they could ask you. Dita said she would talk." I say sheepishly. "I should have checked with you too. I hope it's okay that I said that?"

"Oh yeah, no, that's fine." Miessa says, "If you said that when we first got here? Bitch, I would have hung you out to dry, but now? You're pretty cool, even if I don't agree with everything you do. I'll answer any questions they have."

I nod. "Thanks. Really. You aren't as big a bitch as I thought you were."

"Are you sure you can't think of anything you need?" Dita asks, reaching out to grab my hand.

"Nah, I'm good," I say, squeezing her hand back. "Go get some sleep. We all need it. Things are about to get interesting up in here, if Carver is accepting that the Federation is an issue."

"Yeah, what do you think is going to happen with that?" She asks.

"I don't really know. I'm sure something will, but I can't really process that right now." I say honestly. I yawn. "I probably should get some sleep too." My yawn sets the others off. "let's all turn in early." I say. I head to our little kitchenette to get a glass of ice water; The pressure behind my eyes telling me stress headache coming on.

When I close the freezer door, I come face to face with Kathel. I jump and throw the door back open. He catches it before it hits him in the face. "Whoa there!" He laughs closing the door.

"Kath! great expanse! I am sorry!" "How are you really doing?"

I grab a towel and clean the water from the floor. "I'm fine." He crosses his arms, looking down at me. "Seriously, I'm fine."

"No, you aren't. And we all know it." He says, taking the towel from me. "You don't have to play tough guy." He lowers his voice. "The others are already in their rooms. You don't need to hide." He says. "Especially not with me. I understand what it's like losing a brother."

"Kath, I'm sorry, I—"

"You're okay."

My eyes burn at the words, and I turn away quickly before he can see. "I know I just—" He catches my hands and pulls me close into a tight hug I didn't know I needed. I take a few deep shuddering breaths, trying to keep myself under control.

"Come on," he says, pulling me to his door. When I hesitate, he says, "Just to talk. Not to do anything else. Unless you want to?" He asks, waggling his eyebrows at me. I punch his arm, right below where he was shot. "Okay, okay. Just talking."

I sit on the edge of the bed and put my head in my hands, taking a few deep breaths. "Computer, turn room lights to thirty percent." When I come up, I blink a few times my eyes adjusting to the dimmer room. "It sometimes helps me to relax." He says, shrugging, and I nod numbly. "So, what's going on in your head?" He gently asks, his voice low and gravelly. His warm hand runs over the thin fabric on my back, gently massaging some tension from my muscles.

"I just—" I try, but my voice cracks. I clear my throat and try again. "After what happened to my Mom and Dad? I never really thought I would get over it. And I haven't, more you know, just processed it, and accepted it. And now, Sarkus..." I stop to take a moment. "I don't know. It's just a lot. I just feel completely overwhelmed."

He nods, "I wouldn't expect anything else. You've been through a lot in the last few years. And you've been working hard to fix it."

I sniffle and nod. He puts a hand around my shoulders, and I lean into his chest, listening to the sound of his even breaths and his heart. "Can I stay here for a bit?" I ask quietly, taking comfort in his warmth and the stillness.

"Stay as long as you need."

Chapter 34

My eyes creaky open this morning, puffy and swollen from crying, and it sort of feels like someone stuffed my head full of scratchy cotton. The room is dark, which is weird since I have a light programmed to come on slowly to wake me up. I haven't gotten used to the fact that there is no sunrise or sunset in space yet.

"Morning. How are you feeling?" Kathel asks.

I let out the most superior, unattractive screech I can and fall out of bed. "Holy shit." My foot hangs in the air, caught in the tangle of blankets. "You let me sleep here?" I ask, eyes wide. *What were the others going to think? If I leave now and go back to my room, maybe they won't know!*

He rolls over, peering down at me. "I mean, I thought it might be nice. Should I not have done that? I swear I didn't—we didn't... You just went to sleep." My cheeks burn and I duck my head. "I'm sorry. I thought it might be nice for you to have some company. You fell asleep, and I didn't want to make you move."

"No, no, it's okay," I say, slowly untangling myself. Everything that happened the night before hits me like a wave. The fear and uncertainty twisting my stomach in knots. "I just—I didn't mean to..." I take a deep breath. "Thanks." A knock at the door makes us both turn, "What time is it?"

"A little after 0800. I figured the four of us would head down to breakfast soon?" Kathel says, running a hand over his hair. "Uh, who is it?"

"Hey! It's Dita. Can I come in?" Her voice sounds a bit off from her normal chipper morning self.

I hurry away from the bed to a wall where I can't be seen right away. "Remember, I said they wanted to talk to me this morning. What if it's an officer?"

His face blanches for a second. "Right. Well, just say you came to talk to me this morning. At least you're dressed?" He offers, pointing out that I am still wearing the same clothes as yesterday. "Hey, Dita, yeah, you can come in."

Dita enters the room and quickly slams her hand on the button to close the door behind her. She spins, searching the room until her eyes lock on me. "Oh, thank goodness. I couldn't stall for you much longer." She glances from me to Kathel and back. "Your hair is an absolute mess! You need to fix it before you go out there. Did you sleep here last night?" She gasps, pointing between the Kathel and I. "Did you? Is that why they call it bedhead?" She says a bit too loudly.

My already flushed face goes beat red, "Dita, no. I... *no.*"

He glances at me. "We slept together." Dita's eyes grow wide. "No, I mean sleep like, you know, snore, snore." He presses his hands together like a pillow, laying his head on top, "you know, snore sleep. We slept together. Not like *slept* together." He says frantically.

Dita giggles behind her hand, "it's funny watching you scramble."

"Dits! This is not the time," I say. "You said you wouldn't be able to stall any longer? Who were you stalling?" I ask, wrenching my hands through my mane, trying to tame it back into an acceptable bun.

"Oh, right! So, um, Callahan is outside. He's waiting for you. They went through your tablet, and they want to talk to you and give it back," She says. "I thought at first you might have been in Miessa's room talking to her about her meds. But you weren't in there, or your room, so I came here."

"What did you say about my room?" Kathel asks.

"What do you mean?" Dita asks, a tentacle coming to sit on her chin like she is the alien version of The Thinker.

"Like what was the excuse, why I was in here?" I ask.

"Oh!" Her tentacles stick straight out. "Oh, I didn't think of one. I wasn't sure what you were doing."

"Nothing." Kathel and I say in unison.

"Okay, well, I guess I better go talk to them. The faster we get them out of here, the better, right?" I say, tugging at my clothes, wishing I had a change of clothes so I wouldn't look so rumpled. Dita and Kathel nod, and I follow Dita back out the door. "Good morning, Sir." I give Callahan a tight salute. "I'm sorry to keep you waiting. I didn't realize you were here."

Callahan looks from me to the door to Kathel's room. "Gomez, what were you doing in Torrac's room alone?" he asks.

And I want to roll my eyes because even in space, a woman can't walk around without her morals being in question, and it's too damn early for this. "Sir, Torrac and I are Fighters together. The second test is coming up. We have set up a routine weekly to go over any weak points we felt we had during the week of training to keep up with the pace and learn the best we can. Sir." I reply tightly, leaving no room for questions. At least I can hope.

"And just what strats were you going over this morning?" He asks.

"Well, I was reviewing the notes Torrac had taken on his tablet. Since you had mine, it made it a bit more difficult, but we made do. It was just a review for now. We go over the more detailed list in the afternoon since it's the weekend and we have more free time to do that." I reply.

Kathel comes out of his room as I'm saying this and heads for our little kitchenette. I can only pray he heard enough of what I said when Callahan turns to him.

"Torrac, what part of Wayne's training have you been struggling with of late?" The officer asks.

"Good morning, Sir. I wouldn't say I've been struggling. But it's good to make sure one is always reviewing, as Ada said. We wouldn't want to think we knew everything one hundred percent and then forget it. I forget different types of blasters that I don't work with regularly. That could be an issue in the field." Kathel says, quickly spinning a perfect web of lies. I could kiss him for that. I might have to later.

Callahan nods. "That's a good point. An important lesson to always remember." He turns back to me, proffering my Garrison issued tablet. "Here you are, Gomez. You may have this back. You will find we already installed the app that was spoken of yesterday. And as of this point onward, you will not be allowed to have any outside communication. If you attempt to reach out to anyone outside the station using this tablet or one of your squadmate's while you are on this station, we will be aware. Is that clear?" I nod, refraining from pointing out the fact that, as I told him last night, my brother is missing, and he is the main one I want to talk to. "Good. We may follow up if we have any further questions."

"Yes, Sir," I reply, quickly slipping the tablet into my pocket. Something about it feels tainted now. The feeling of unease from the rally with Carver oozes out of me, spurred on by the introduction of the tablet. I want to shove it in the back of a drawer and bury it under some clothing so it can't monitor me. That is all this new app is going to do. Monitor our every movement and make sure we aren't a mole for the Federation. I want to ask Callahan if they found anything or what sort of questions they may ask me. But I don't want to open that can of worms. Callahan nods and backs out of the room, and I quickly shove the tablet as far away from me as I can.

"You don't like it either?" Miessa asks, sitting up from where she laid on the couch, out of sight.

"Were you there the whole time?" I ask.

"Oh yeah, I love doing that to people." She grins, but it fades quickly as she goes on. "But I know how you feel. I put my tablet in a box last night as soon as I downloaded the app. I'm only going to be taking it out when we have lessons or for the test."

I nod, I don't know what to do. Part of me wants to play the part of the good soldier. The part of me that's worked on getting where I am for years now. The part of me I was proud of. But since being here, I've changed. I see differently, and I don't like how Carver is running things. The officers are jumpy around her. They do a good job of hiding it, but I know what it's like to be around someone who abuses their power over others. "So, what do we make of last night?"

I ask. "Cause I have some thoughts."

"Personally, I don't like it at all," Miessa whispers, we all lean in to catch her next words. "I haven't been a huge fan of Carver since we got here. But lately, things seem really off. It's like, I don't know, the balance is off."

Kathel laughs, "the balance is off? You mean she's off her fucking rocker. Look, the Garrison is a vast organization. It's the fucking Galactic Garrison. There are much bigger fish to fry that a couple of kids who ran away." He shakes his head. "I don't understand how someone hasn't taken her out yet. She's clearly abusing her power in a self-serving manner."

"You may be on to something there." I murmur.

"I am?"

"Yeah," I snap my fingers "when did the Federation split off again?"

"It was about six years ago," Dita says. "Why?"

"Is there a way to look up what Carver's rank was at the time?" I ask.

Miessa sucks in a breath like she understands where I am going with this. "But why would that work?"

I grin, "that's what I want to find out."

Kathel waves his hand in front of us. "Uh, hello, you want to clue the rest of us in on what your thought is?"

The sound of Dita furiously typing into her tablet cuts him off.

"I already know what Ada is looking for. The confused one here is you." She says, not looking up.

He slams his hand down on his thigh. "Fine, I'm the confused one. Sorry I don't have feminine telepathy like the rest of you. What are we looking up?"

"Aha!" Dita shouts. "Sorry, I've got it," Dita says excitedly. "Eugenia Carver, Command Sergeant Major of the Galactic Garrison."

"You found her record? Dita, you can't keep hacking into things right now!" Miessa hisses, reaching for the device.

Dita smacks her away, "I didn't! I am not stupid! It's a Wikipedia page!" She says, turning the screen to show us the white page of text. "I just looked up her name."

"Oh," Miessa says. "well, what does it say?" she asks again, reaching for the tablet.

"You know, for someone in intelligence program, you are incredibly impatient," Dita says, holding the tablet above her head and out of reach.

"Ladies!" Kathel barks, and the two of them freeze. "Will someone please explain to me what exactly you think you found?"

Dita gets up and begins digging around in a cupboard. "about six, nearly seven, years ago, Commander Carver was work working closely with the Specialist class of the time, class of 2222. She had to have been working closely with them to feel burned." Dita pulls her head out of the cupboard and quickly hooks up a small projector and displays the information on the Wikipedia page. "If we compare who we have close relationships with, it would have to people like Wayne, Skovnia, Callahan, or Minerva," Dita says, listing off our current staff sergeants. "So the question is. How did Carver go from a staff sergeant to a command sergeant major in seven years?"

Kathel squints at the days next to the positions. "I mean, it makes sense. It isn't the weirdest number I have ever seen."

"What if I said she's only been in the military eight earth years?" Dita counters scrolling up to the first ranks.

"How the hell?" Kathel sputters. "We have been in for years already. If she has only in for eight years, how does she have that position? I mean, I could understand a rank or two below, but..."

"Who's above Carver?" Miessa asks. "I know they have told us a few times, but I can't remember."

"That would be the sergeant major of the Garrison, Lootgam. He's on the Martian colonies. What do you think his relationship is to Carver? It must be close if she was instated so soon." I turn back to Dita, "what else does that page say?"

She scans the page quickly "it gives a very brief description saying that she was the one teaching the Fighter branch at the time of the Federation's disbandment. So, she would be our Wayne. It doesn't say why, and this article doesn't put the blame on her like other people have."

"So, do we think the Federation is producing these cyber-attacks?" Kathel asks, reading over what Dita left up on the projector. I skim it, but nothing sticks out to me.

"I haven't seen anything flare up out of the ordinary." Dita says, "though I won't be able to track it anymore."

Kathel reaches up and taps one link on the wiki page. "I thought so," He murmurs, reading over the description. "I don't know if this really gives us any information, or if it is just an interesting tidbit of information. But my caravan and Carver's used to trade together when I was little, but I don't remember ever seeing her. There aren't many Rogues left."

"Wait, your people are called Rogues? How did I miss that?" I ask. "Way back when Edonne called you a Rogue, I thought he was implying that I was this damsel in distress."

Kathel shakes his head. "Nope. I'm a Rogue." He takes the tablet from Dita and pulls up a map. "My people came from Pluto. Sort of like with the Federation, a group of them broke off about fifty years ago to go exploring. When they tried to return, they were shunned. They so creatively called us Rogues." Kathel says, pointing out a few points on the map. "The groups broke up, and my people mainly live on these four large asteroids. But really, they go wherever they want."

I think of what Kathel told me about his brother Mycall, and how he had been hunted. He was right; it was an interesting tidbit if they had run into each other before joining the military, but it doesn't really help us figure out what could be going on with the Federation.

"Um, guys," Kathel says, looking up from the tablet screen to the projector. "We are going to have to cut this short." A message has popped up on Dita's tablet.

Chapter 35

We all stare dumbfounded at the screen and the message flashing across it. "You have to be fucking kidding me!" Miessa says. "We still have another week of training!" She stomps her feet like a child, something I'm tempted to do as well.

I read the message and sigh, but the sound comes out more like an angry growl. "You know, I think at this point, I should just ignore any dates they give us because none of the tests will ever be when they say they are."

Dita powers down the projector and puts it away. "Do you think this is on purpose?"

"Oh yeah, this is one hundred percent on purpose." Kathel says, "Carver wants us to graduate out so she can get boots on the ground." He laughs humorlessly. "I love that the test gets moved up days before we were going to be briefed on what the test actually is."

"That is pretty convenient," I say. "So, we have…" I glance at the notification over Dita's shoulder again. "How long do we have? Was there any more information given?" I ask, turning to our blaster rack by the door and checking to ensure that the power cells are charging. The last thing I want is to go into this with a half-charged blaster.

"It says that we are to meet in room 434 at 1300." Dita reads off.

I glance at my watch. "Cool, so we have six hours until this test. Great. Fantastic."

"I mean, I think it'll be better this time, right?" Dita asks, glancing between our squadmates.

"Yes," Kathel says. "Today will be better."

We head down to the mess for a quick breakfast, then hurry back to the room. We break off and start preparing our respective gear. We gather again around 1230 adorned in our white suits. Kathel's suit was fixed within a few days. You can't even see where he was shot anymore. Though he does still have a slight lump on his leg where the bandage covers the burn.

"How do you feel?" I ask Dita, dropping my med pack by the door. I grab a pouch and use the straps to attach it to my thigh.

"I think I'm good. I'm definitely getting more nervous now." Dita pulls at the edges of her suit, trying to get it to fit just right.

"You'll do great. I wouldn't want any other Techie with me."

Kathel says, clapping a hand on her shoulder. "Really, you're brilliant."

Dita's cheeks flush purple, and her tentacles draw in, spiraling in on themselves. "Thanks, Kathel."

Miessa comes around the corner, her hair styled in a short black pixie cut. "We ready to head down?"

"Yeah, I think so," I say, swinging my bag onto my back. I adjust all the straps so the pack sits flush against my suit and won't bump around when I run.

The walk down to the room is silent. All four of us are in our heads, trying to figure out the best way to proceed through all of this. Whatever this will be.

"Do we knock?" I ask as we stand outside the door.

"I mean, maybe?" Miessa says. "Or maybe it will open right at 1300. We still have a minute." We stand in a half-circle around the door.

Kathel steps forward and knocks on the door. "I'd rather say we tried. Show initiative, ya know?" The three of us nod. A few seconds pass, and then the door slides open. "See?" He says before stepping through. I roll my eyes, following close behind him.

We move into a large conference room. A projector on the wall displays a slide that reads 'TEAM ARCTIC' in big letters. On the table are four memory cards. An officer I've never seen before sits at the end of the table. "Good timing, Arctic. Please take your seats."

She says.

My fingers itch to plug the card into my tablet, but I wait until I'm told I can.

"Welcome, Arctic. As you may have gathered, some things have changed over the last few days regarding your testing. Even with these changes, Commander Carver has every bit of faith that you will complete your mission."

That's because she will kick our asses if we don't meet her standard.

"Where your first test was a way to see how you worked together as a team, this one will test how you use the skills you have been training for the past few months and incorporate them in a mission setting." She presses a button, and the presentation shifts to the next slide, showing a map of the solar system. "If you would please open the flash drive in front of you, we will start your mission objectives."

I insert the card into my tablet and wait for the file to open. There is a photo, a map, and a few other documents. I click the photo. There are a few people in the photo. Kathel tenses slightly and I glance over. He has the map pulled up and the list of objectives. I do the same. It's a map of the outer regions, with a few red X's and a circle. The circle is on Pluto. Based on his reaction and what I remember of the map he showed me, I guess this mission will take us a bit too close to where his family travels.

"You will engage in a reconnaissance mission to find a subject and, if possible, attach a tracking device. For this mission, you will be sent to Pluto's moon, Nix. You will go via jump gate to Pluto; there will be a ship for you to fly to a colony on Nix. Once you are there, you need to find and locate two targets. You will find their photo also in the file."

"As you can see, they should be fairly easy to distinguish based on their appearance. But you are not to directly engage with them." The people she references are a young man and woman with sickly looking pale skin and bright green and blue hair, respectively.

"These people are agents of the Federation. You are not to engage with them." She repeats, "You are to find their ship and put a tracker on it if you can. Your primary objective is to confirm that they are on Nix."

"What do we do once we have confirmed their location?" Kathel asks.

I click over to the document and read up on our targets.

Name: Blaithin "Roxie" Roxinate

Sex: Female

Race: Rogue

Age: 25

Height: 5' 6"

Weight: Approximately 140lb

Known Features: blue hair

Affiliation: Federation

Roxinate is a defected Garrison soldier. While she didn't defect with the class of

'22, she is a known associate. Roxinate failed specialist training and was sent to the Martian colonies. She fled her post in her third month with her brother. Roxinate was training to be in the Jumper class.

Roxinate is now known to assist with the recruitment for the Federation. As of this time, she has no known connections within the Garrison.

She was last seen on Nix with her brother, Vielcent.

Nix is not a known recruitment location for the Federation.

I read through the file, trying to glean more information from what little data they have given us. I flip back to the Male's file. The officer nods, "that is an excellent question, Torrac. The answer is simple. You need to find a way out."

"That is sort of vague, isn't it, ma'am?"

"All part of the test."

Name: Vielcent Roxinate

Sex: Male

Race: Rogue

Age: 27

Height: 6' 4"

Weight: Approximately 200 lb.

Known Features: green hair

Affiliation: Federation

Roxinate is a defected Garrison soldier. Class of '21. Roxinate is considered highly dangerous. Do not engage. Roxinate was a fighter class. Highly skilled in all blasters. Roxinate is in charge of training new recruits brought in by Blaithin. He was last seen on Nix with his sister, Blaithin.

Nix is not a known recruitment location for the Federation.

"You are sending us to get information on Federation operatives as the test for our graduation? With limited information?" Miessa asks incredulously. "I know that's what we'll do after we graduate, but is that really how we should be tested?"

"Do you not think your team can handle it?" The soldier asks.

"No, that isn't what I am saying." Miessa backtracks. But I know what she means. There will be no undoing this. If something goes wrong, we'll have to figure it the fuck out on our own.

"You will have seventy hours to complete your mission; credits have been added to your account to cover the cost of any required supplies for discrete housing and supplies upon your arrival. There is an open jump scheduled for you to return to this base until the seventieth hour. If you do not make that window, you will be transferred to one of our other bases, and your team will be demoted to infantry soldiers. Do you have any other questions?"

On paper it seems simple enough, but that's how it always is. "What advice would you give us?" I ask, "not as the person who has to explain the test, but a soldier yourself who has worked missions before."

She clicks through the remaining tabs to the end of the projection, where a timer is already ticking down the time. "Be aware, at all times. Of your surroundings, your team, your enemy, the time left. Be aware. You have no extraction plan." We nod solemnly.

"Ma'am, are all the teams looking for operatives?" Dita asks.

The woman pauses at that, and I can tell she's mentally going through the script given to her. "Each team has been given a mission with the same basic framework. Some have already started their seventy hours; some will start a bit after you. If you have no further questions, I suggest that you get moving. You will leave from jump gate seven."

"Thank you, ma'am," Kathel says as we all rise.

"Until all," She says, saluting us.

"The stars are found." We intone, mimicking her salute.

Chapter 36

We file out of the room, and Kathel takes off down the hall. "Kath, where are you going? We need to get moving." I call.

He hits button after button on the wall as we pass until he finds an open room. Miessa, Dita, and I file in behind him, bewildered. "What is going on?" Dita asks when the door shuts behind us.

Kathel paces up and down the room, helmet tucked under his arm. "Nix, why would they send us to Nix? Nothing has been going on there." He mutters.

"Kathel?" Miessa asks, snapping her fingers in his direction. "Hello? Wanna fill us in?"

He whips around to face us. "Have any of you ever been to the Kuiper belt?" He asks, pulling at the shadow of a beard he didn't shave this morning.

"I haven't," I say.

"I've been to Pluto, but not any of the moons," Dita replies.

332

"Why?"

"I haven't either. I suppose you're probably the reason we got this specific mission." Miessa says. "I mean, you grew up around there. You know what it's like."

He nods. "Yeah, I do. And that's the problem. I know how difficult it is to move through there undetected." He opens up the file they had given us, swiping to the photos of Blaithin and Vielcent Roxinate. "If we are meant to track them and see if they have a base on Nix, they're known to be there. They'll have allies. There will be people that will recognize us on sight as Garrison soldiers who will notify them. This easy in-out mission won't be that easy."

"Okay, so what should we do? You grew up there, how do we blend in?" I ask, "And what did you mean by 'nothing has been going on there'?"

He sighs, "I've been a part of the Garrison for three years now. Rumors of the Federation came long before that. We always thought they had some settlement in Kuiper, but no one ever found it. Last I heard, it was thought to be on the far side of Pluto. But no one has ever said anything about Nix." He pauses, running a hand over his hair. "We need disguises. Something to wear in the colonies. We can't be walking around with our suits and our insignias." He says, gesturing to the badges on our sleeves.

"I mean, I figured we would need something," Dita says.

He nods, "Once we get to the colony, we will be under a dome.

So, we can put civvy clothes on top of our suits. But we will still have to be aware."

I glance around at what we have on us. "Okay, so let's go back to our rooms, grab some of our regular clothing, and we can pack it. Then we won't have to spend credits on that. Kath, you can tell us what will pass as a disguise." He nods, "And Miessa, as much as I like the dark hair, I think we need you to look like a Rogue?" I ask Kathel, and again he nods.

"So straight up like Carver?" She asks, her skin shifting to palest white.

"Yeah, it'll look better if there are 'two' of us."

"Any style I should adopt?" She asks, fussing with the way the hair lays over her eyes.

"Not that I remember. I never paid attention to how Fems did their hair." He closes his eyes for a moment, scrunching his face up in concentration, "My mom, and I think one of my teachers in school, had short hair. But it always was longer in the back. It kind of tapered out. They couldn't really ever style it but," He watches as Miessa's hair grows longer, "yeah like that, I always thought it was a weird style, but Mom never changed it."

"It's pretty simple." She shrugs, running her fingers through it. "Okay, let's go grab some other clothes."

We hurry back to the rooms and grab our clothes. I haven't worn my jeans since the night we went to Titan. It feels like a lifetime ago.

Just as we thought, with our suits being as skintight as they are, it is easy to slip our clothes over them. I swap out my v- neck shirt for a dark blue turtleneck.

"So, guys," Miessa says in the living room. "One thing we haven't thought of. Our helmets. We still have to attach them to the suits." She pulls her own on with a laugh.

Kathel laughs. "If anyone asks, just say it's a new fashion statement. That might deter any questions."

"Might?" she asks, pulling her helmet back off.

Leading us out of our suite. "I mean, yeah, it might work. But you might also get a few more questions about fashion around the galaxy. Remember, it is a remote settlement on the edge of the solar system. They don't get to hear a lot about fashion."

Edonne and the rest of the Desert team stalk down the hall. "Where do you think you are going in that?" Their medic, a spritely Capming, asks with a sneer, his pointed little teeth hanging over his lips.

"Wouldn't you like to know," Miessa mutters.

Edonne steps forward, blocking the hall with his large frame. "I think you should tell us."

"And I think you should move your saggy tail out of the way," Kathel says.

I pull my helmet on and step right into Edonne's face. "We're on orders. Now you can shove it up yours and move, or deal with officers later."

Edonne sneers. "What's with the helmet, little human?" He hisses in anger, and droplets of his acidic venom splashes across the visor.

I don't flinch or make a move to wipe it away. "That's why. Now. We have places to be. So, if you and the rest of your little troupe can move out of the way, we would appreciate it." Their techie waves them over, trying to show them something, probably the notification of their mission.

"You know, you like to act really tough. But I've never seen you do anything about it." Edonne says. "If you were actually as tough as you pretend to be, you would take a swing here and there."

"You realize how dumb you sound right now?" Dita asks from behind me. "Ada is one of our Fighters. She can clearly hold her own when she needs to. She is just smart enough to not go looking for trouble every chance she can. Anyone with a bit of muscle can fight. But it takes someone with a real brain to know when it's smarter to stand down. Something you're clearly lacking." She saunters past him, nodding at Desert's techie, who is still frantically trying to get the rest of his team's attention. "Good luck," she says, nodding to them.

Edonne hisses something under his breath but lets us pass, shooting us death glares all the way down the hall. When we're a bit of the way around the corner, I rip my helmet off and turn to Dita.

"You can be a badass when you want to!"

She looks down at her hands, which are shaking slightly. "I just get so pissed off at him. Herc, that's their techie, and I have talked in class. I feel really bad for him. Edonne is just such an asshole. I figured if I said something, it might throw him off guard, since I've never stood up to him like that." She stares at her hands, opening and closing them a few times before looking up. "It felt really good to do that. Sorry if I stole your thunder." She says to Kathel and me.

"Please, steal it." I laugh. "You give me too much credit, all I wanted to do was deck him. If I had done that, we would still be in that hall instead of heading down to the jump gates."

We hurry the rest of the way down to the jump sector and make it without running into any more teams. "Arctic reporting for our jump," Miessa says, grabbing the first attendant she can find.

"Team Arctic," he murmurs, running down a list. "Right, you are at jump gate seven." He taps out a message, "I just let them know you're here. They'll be ready for launch within five minutes."

He turns to walk away, but Kathel stops him, "By chance, do you know how long our jump will be?"

"Your jump is to Pluto? Max, it should take three or four hours. Hope that helps."

"It does, thanks." Kathel turns to Dita. "Can you—"

She waves him away. "Already on it. Setting a timer for six and five hours before our deadline as a warning and four hours out, so we know when we need to be getting on the jump to get back if we haven't already."

Kathel grins, "I love you sometimes."

"Just sometimes?" She grins. "I also sent it to all of you. You should have the countdown, and the alarms listed in your HUD notifications. If you want to put the counter in your HUD, it should be easy."

"How do you do this stuff so fast?" Miessa asks. "I feel like I wouldn't have even processed the thought yet, and you've already completed it."

"And that." Dita laughs. "Is why I'm your techie. Come on, time isn't going to stop."

"A three-hour jump?" I mutter. "Please be better than our jump to Titan."

"It should be."

"That makes me feel so much better." I huff.

We find gate seven, and thankfully we don't have the same tech that told us to link arms this time. "Team Arctic for Pluto?" He asks and we nod. He runs through each of us, making sure we are the people assigned to the jump and then through some rules. "There are a few cosmic storms brewing out there. You should make it to Pluto with no issues. But I wanted to let you know you might experience some turbulence."

I mutter a curse under my breath. We all step up to the gate and, on the tech's mark, step through to Pluto.

Chapter 37

I haven't done many jumps. The jump to Titan was by far the worst. Attached to everyone, it felt like I was being torn apart from within. This jump is strange. The turbulence that the tech described was almost like I was walking across a treadmill that went over a series of hills, the floor undulating below me.

"How is everyone feeling?" Kathel asks when I step through the gate. His cheeks are flushed pink, but aside from that, he shows no signs of having just traveled over three billion kilometers in a few hours.

Dita wipes her face a few times before answering. "I don't feel awful, but I don't feel like I just woke up from a nap either."

"Because naps are the best thing ever?" I ask from my bent-over position as I attempt to get my body used to being still again.

"Obviously."

"Okay, well, when you two are ready, we have to get going,"

Miessa says. Her fingers stray near her blaster but she never pulls it from her side.

I stand up, scanning the area. We thought we would be sent to either a base owned by the Garrison or one of its allies. But looking around, this looks like a commercial jump gate. "Good thing we wore our clothes," I say over comms.

"Looks like it," Kathel replies. "Come on, Dits, we have to keep moving. Another jump will be through in a minute." He takes her arm and pulls her away from the ramp.

"I'm okay, really." She says, pulling her arm away. But she takes three steps in a straight line and the next four in a zig-zag. "Whoa," she says, grabbing her head. "That was weird."

"You okay?" I ask, grabbing her arm. I pull her to a bench and carefully remove her helmet. Her eyes are dilated much more than they should be in the bright lights. "It looks like you got a little jump sick. You should be okay in the next ten minutes or so," I reach into my bag and pull out a few mints. "Eat these; they should help settle your body. Give you something to focus on and ground yourself here."

Miessa sits next to Dita on the bench. "It feels weird, but it should pass really soon. Then we can get moving to the ship. I should warn you, that can be worse than jumping. You'll feel all the turns." She glances around the large area we are in. "Any idea where we need to go?" She asks.

The jump sector is large, with hallways branching away on each of the four walls. Above each door, written in bright lights, are the words casino, hotel, parking, and shopping center. "My guess is parking. Does the info they gave us say where the ship is?"

Dita raises a hand to answer. "I looked at that back on base. It was ship number 053015. She has the name Nuka."

"Okay, Nuka," Kathel repeats.

"Just as a precaution," Miessa whispers. "When referencing the place, we came from, it is home. Cool?" She says vaguely.

"Cool," I reply. She's right. Anyone could be listening now. We're in the field, we have a set of targets, and we don't want anyone to let those targets know that we'll move in soon.

Kathel taps out a few commands and turns to us. "So, I found our ship in the public logs. It is sleek, but not too fancy. Should be a good ride." He says to Miessa, "I used to fly one when I... before I moved. It should help us keep a low profile."

"What is it?" I ask, eager to see a picture of the first spaceship I will ever ride in.

He glances down at the diagnostics and back up at me. "I, uh, I'll let you wait and see. Wouldn't want to spoil the surprise."

Dita stands up, wavering for a moment before finding her balance. "I'm okay. I can try to get my bearings more once we're on the ship." She says defiantly when I try to pull her back down beside me.

"Okay, if you're sure. We can stop at any time." But that turns out to be a lie. Making our way across the room to the hallway labeled parking proves to be almost as tricky as it would be to get a spot at New City Hall back on Earth on election day. Flocks of people move in front of us, barely giving an inch of room. And when we get to the hallway, we're met with the fastest people walker I have ever been on.

Dita grips the handrail until her knuckles are a pale blue. "Why do people need to move so fast here? I thought Pluto wasn't a very popular settlement." She groans, holding the side of her head.

"It isn't. Or at least it wasn't," Kathel grumbles. He keeps scanning the area all around him. *It's changed.* He knew it would be hard to come back here after a few years away. But he never expected things to have changed so much from what he knew.

"Well, hopefully, our next stop won't be so bad," I say. He catches my eye and nods. We pull our helmets on and pass through the air lock, forced into a corner by a family that crammed in behind us. I nod at the mother as she adjusts her little one's gear before hitting the button and letting the air cycle out.

The best way I can think to describe the parking area is interesting. On Earth, you park cars in nice even rows. But apparently, on Pluto, they like to throw any sense of order out the window. I have never seen so many vehicles parked so haphazardly. They are nose to nose, some under another's wing like a mother bird protecting her chick, in rings where the owners have formed a little tent city in the center... You name it and we walk past the configuration.

"So, did the paperwork say anywhere in it where our ship would be parked?" I ask.

"Not that I can tell." Miessa sighs. "Why would they give us a ship but then not tell us where it is?"

"Hello, my name is Moke. Can I help you with anything today?" A tiny Plutonian pops up beside me. Moke wears a suit and bow tie.

"Uh, hi, Moke. My name is-is Brookes. My friends and I are renting a ship. But they didn't tell us where the ship would be." I give a trilling laugh. "Which isn't very helpful, as you can imagine. We are having a bit of trouble finding it."

He beams. "Of course, Miss Brookes, I can definitely help you with that. Do you have the serial number for the vehicle you are looking for?"

Miessa steps forward. As one of our spies, she would be better at reading the field than me. "Hello, Mr. Moke, the vehicle we are looking for is number 053015. Do you know where it might be?" She says sweetly. She moves her body in a way that makes her seem light and carefree. Like this is just a casual jaunt around the galaxy, and we have all the time in the world.

The Plutonian pulls up a chart that just looks like a bunch of squiggly lines to me. But he poked purposefully at a few different points where a chat bubble comes up. "Hmm, I seem to be having some troubling finding that number." He says, closing the third bubble and shifting the view on the screen. "Do you know the name of the ship?"

"Yes, Sir," Miessa says brightly. "It's the Nuka, that's spelled N-U-K-A."

"Right," he zooms in on another point on the map before inputting the name in a search bar. "Here we are. Your ship will be in the northwest quadrant." He zooms out, showing us the location on the map. "For fifty credits, I can schedule you a ride over there whenever it would be most convenient."

"Well, we were hoping to get to the ship now. Would we be able to walk there?" Miessa asks sweetly, but she cranes her neck at an odd angle, trying to see the map again and how far it would be.

Mr. Moke shakes his head. "Oh no, that won't do. I can't have you walking that far. Not with how pilots have been lately, there are too many chances of you getting hit."

I raise my hand slightly. "I'm sorry, Sir, I've never been here before, so I'm a bit naïve. How far exactly would it be to get to our ship?"

Mr. Moke looks at me for a moment and then turns back to Miessa. "I will order a ride for you."

"Sir, will that really be necessary?" Kathel asks.

"Yes. Now, if you will sign here, it will wire your sixty-five-credit payment. Your ride will be here in ten minutes." He says, holding out his tablet and a stylus for Miessa to sign.

I dealt with a few hustlers like this back on Earth. And by dealing with them, I mean the interactions usually ended with us cursing at each other. Miessa has more restraint than I do and glares down at the little man, her arms crossed. "I am not signing that."

"You have to. I gave you a service." He insists pushing the tablet toward her again.

She cocks an eyebrow at him, not moving to take it. "And when did we agree to partake in your services?"

"Well, I got you a ride."

She smiles, but there is scorn behind it, and I can't help but grin. Because as much as Miessa can be an utter bitch, it is fun to watch when you aren't on the receiving end of it. And unfortunately, any sympathy that I had for the Plutonian is running down the drain. "But when did we ask for a ride?" He starts to stutter out a reply, but Miessa holds up a single finger. "Ah, that's right, we didn't ask for a ride. You said you could get us a ride. When we asked how far of a walk it was, you, Sir, deflected."

"I told you where your ship was." He snaps.

"You used public records." Dita pipes up from the back, holding up a map, with a pinpoint hovering over our ship's location.

"Exactly. You used public records that we also have access to and asked us if there is anything you could help us with today." She scans him from head to toe again. "Now, my friend here, as she said, is naïve. She didn't take the time to see that you, Sir, have no affiliation with this establishment. You," she points at him, stepping closer, "are a scam artist looking to make a few bucks off of unlikely travelers. We owe you no money and will not be discussing anything with you further." She walks off, nearly brushing him with her shoulder, in a way only Fems from rich families can. Kathel, Dita, and I hurry after her, attempting to look just as refined as the Plutonian screams insults at us, threatening to let the authorities know that we now owe him two hundred credits.

"So much for keeping a low profile," I grumble. "Sorry, guys."

"It's quite alright. Keep your head up." She orders. All three of us improve our posture. "We do not slouch when we flounce."

"Uh, Miessa, our ship is in the other direction." Dita chimes in. "And he may have been right. It might have been better to get a ride."

"Not for fifty credits!" Kathel laughs. "That was just his fee for ordering the ride. We would have to pay the driver once we arrived."

"Well, it's a twenty-kilometer walk to the ship," Dita says, looking off to where our ride should be.

I consider our situation and what I can do. "Well, let me make a quick call. I might be able to get us a ride." I say.

"You have got to be kidding me." Miessa snaps. "No, we are not doing that right now."

I shrug, "You have a better plan?"

She scowls at me. "Not yet, but I'll think of one."

Kathel crosses his arms, "okay, is this some Fem mind-reading thing again?"

"I don't think so. I don't know what they're talking about this time." Dita says. "I'm sure whatever Ada is thinking is a good idea, though."

"Thanks—"

"—It is not a good idea."

"—wait come on, what other choice do we have?"

We stare at each other for a moment before she blurts out. "She wants to call in a favor with the Plutonian."

Kathel looks from Miessa to me and back again. "*The* Plutonian? No, Ada never left earth. You can't be right. How would she have connected with him?"

"Well, that is where you're wrong." He spins towards me, confusion written all over his face. "I mean, you're right. I've never left Earth, but uh, Tortie has a pretty good foothold in New Seattle."

"To-Tortie?" He asks, his voice cracking slightly. "You are on a first-name basis with him?"

Something about the way he is looking at me with horror tells me I should never mention my last in-person interaction with Tortie. "I… yes, my dad sold him scraps. I eventually did too. But like I told Miessa, that is all I did. I sold him scraps of metal. That's it."

"Bits of metal." He murmurs. "Like the hunks of metal that came looking for my family?"

"What? What are you talking about? You said you—" I clamp my mouth shut, not wanting to say more than I should. "I'm sorry," I say to him. I turn to Miessa. "I'm sorry." I turn to Dita. "I'm sorry. Okay? I'm sorry that my association with this Male hurts you. I know he is not good. Believe me, I do. I've seen it in person. But I owe him a piece of me. Not because of some deal I made or any shit like that. But because without him, I wouldn't be here today." I turn back to Kathel. "I—he saved me in more ways than I want to go into right now. But believe me when I say every choice I have ever made has been my own. He doesn't dictate my life."

"But you're close enough to call in a favor?" He asks flatly.

I hang my head, "okay. Forget it." I walk back in the direction we came.

"Ada, wait," Dita says. She runs up and catches my arm. "We need to stick together." She searches my face. "I accept your apology. I've never had any interaction with him. I can tell you're sincere."

I sigh and look at the other two who are furiously discussing what Miessa knew and what this could mean for the team. "I didn't know it would be an issue. I'm not working for him."

"I know. And they know that. They do. They know they can't hold you accountable for his actions against them. But they are hurting. It reminds them of their hurt." She squeezes my hand. "Some of us have to do things that when we get older, we aren't proud of, but it was the only thing we could think to do at the time."

I nod. Miessa and Kathel walk back to us. "Okay, you can make the call. But when we get somewhere less open, we need to talk." Miessa says harshly.

"Okay," I reply simply.

"Okay?" She asks, like she expected me to put up more of a fight.

I nod. "Yeah, okay. We can do that. Once we get somewhere quiet, you can ask me anything." She looks at Kathel, and he nods. That slight movement represents his distrust of me, of my past actions. I can't say it doesn't hurt. "Well, we can't make the call from my tablet. The Garrison is tracking it. We might have a better chance from one of you. But they'll probably watch it too through that dumb app. They said they would know if I did it from anyone's device."

Dita grins quietly to herself, "well, how much would you love me if I told you I set up a shadow network on my tablet that they can't see with that 'dumb app'?"

Her grin grows as disbelief spreads across my face. "You little hacker. I could kiss you." She laughs, "will you install that on my tablet when we get back?"

"Absolutely." She says, passing me her piece of tech. I copy the link Tortie gave me a few days ago into her tablet, hoping it's still active.

They reject the call the first time, which I expect; it's coming from a different IP than the first time I called him. It rings again, and one of his men is on the screen. "Who's calling me?"

"It's Ada Gomez. I need to speak to him." I whisper as a group of tourists walk by. I hold the tablet closer to my face, and my squad and I move under the wing of a ship out of sight.

"He? Who is this? This is my number. I don't know who you are."

I scoff, putting on my scrapper persona, I can feel the eyes of my team boring into my back as I slip back into this character. "He gave me this link. You know who I am. Put him on. It's urgent."

The henchman squints his goat-like eyes at me. "Not yet."

"I already know this." I roll my eyes. "You're going to ask me a question about him. And I'll answer it, and you'll say it was too easy, and I'll answer the next question, and we'll go back and forth, and honestly, I don't have time for this. I need to speak to him." The man scowls. "The last thing I sold him was a sheet of copper for 190 credits. He gave me a tablet so I could talk to my brother when I was off-world. He hasn't celebrated a birthday on Earth in the last ten years because even though his birthday would be in January on Earth, he wants to stick to the Plutonian calendar." I rattle off dryly, hoping it's enough to cover my ass and get us through.

The eyes of my team bore into me while I wait for this Male to respond. "Okay. You can talk to him."

The screen goes dark for a second, and I think the call has dropped when Tortie's face appears on the screen. "Ada, baby, what's going on? Ya said it was urgent? I don't have any new word on Sark yet. But I promise ya, I'm working on it."

My throat squeezes at the mention of Sarkus, I haven't been able to do anything to help look for him. "I know you are. And I appreciate that." Kathel clears his throat, but when I glance up, he won't meet my eyes. "But, uh, that's not why I'm calling. I was wondering if you or your guys could help me out with a little something."

The Plutonian takes a sip of a drink, nearly the same shade as his skin. "Depends. Whatcha need, Ada?"

His tone is tight. *He's busy. I interrupted him, and if I don't get this train rolling, I will have wasted his time.* "What did Dad always say? One day we would meet in your neck in the woods, right? Well, here I am. I'm on Pluto," at that, his eyes light up, but I don't let him cut in. "You see, I have a ship; me and a few friends are out here doing a little exploring on some time off," I say, and both Miessa and Dita nod. *Good, I am on the right track with someone.* I think. "We got a ship, but it is on the far side of the parking area. Why didn't you ever tell me the settlement was so big? I would've come sooner! Anyway, our ride is several kilometers away, and I was wondering if anyone is in the area that could give us a lift?" I coo, and Kathel scrunches his face in disgust. *Well, I can't win them all right now.*

Tortie barks and orders off-screen. "Sure, baby girl. We can get that done for you. Just send me your location, and we will get someone there in the next few minutes. Look for a black car. It'll have my mark on the door handles. I have to go, but I'll talk to you soon. As soon as I have something on Sark. Okay? Okay. I gotta go," And with that, the screen goes dark.

"Humph," Kathel crosses his arms. "Well, 'baby girl', I guess you do know him pretty well, don't ya?"

Chapter 38

Our ride pulls up a few minutes later, as Tortie promised. A tiny orange gem, cut through with a bit of black onyx decorates the door—Tortie's symbol. The doors of the car lift and the four of us crawl in. The interior is lush, and clearly, a car that Tortie himself rides in when he comes back to his planet. My jeans don't want to slide across the white velvet seats. I want to wipe my hands on the seat but fear I might leave a streak of dirt and sweat that Tortie might hold over my head later.

"So, uh, where we headed?" The driver asks once we're seated. Dita reads off the coordinates of our ship, and it slowly ascends above the others flying to the next location. Miessa and Kathel both sit forward on the edge of their seat like they can't let their bodies touch anything Tortie created. It makes me feel wrong. Like I shouldn't take a moment to enjoy the feeling of the plush seats after the hard metal chairs that the Garrison insists on using.

"So, what's your name, Sir?" Dita asks, settling back into the seat and testing out the armrests.

The driver looks up into the rearview mirror, then back down to where he navigates the flying car above the various ships and vehicles. "I think it would be better if you didn't know."

"Oh, oh, okay," Dita mumbles, retreating into the seat.

I notice Kathel won't look away from one spot. I lean forward, trying to see what it is exactly and tense when I see it. The butt of a blaster sticks out from between the driver's seat and the console. Slowly Kathel turns to look at me but quickly looks back down at it. I scan the rest of the space. There are a few places where the upholstery in the ceiling doesn't quite mesh with the rest of it. Gun ports. Tortie has a fascination with tiny blasters. They are only three inches long but will hurt. A dial controlled by the driver targets the suckers and controls how much juice they get. In other words, you're leaving with a nasty headache or not leaving at all.

"Right, this shouldn't take us more than ten minutes. If you all sit back, we will begin our journey." The driver says. Reluctantly, Miessa and Kathel sit back, with Kathel shifting his gaze to monitor the driver. *If he wants us dead, we won't see him move for that blaster.* Wishing I could tell them this, I reach a hand out and gently squeeze Kathel's leg before pulling away. He jumps but looks up at me. I nod slowly, hoping he will understand that it's okay, at least as far as I can tell.

Dita keeps the map open, tracing the path we take with her fingers. Her tentacles wriggle and spiral around each other.

"You folks staying out here long?" The driver asks, attempting to make small talk.

My squad looks at me. "Just a few days, maybe a week. You know, playing it by feel. Anything good we should check out?" I ask, turning the conversation back on him.

Unlike Tortie or Mr. Moke, this Plutonian is tall and thin. He has the seat pushed back all the way, and still his knees come up to the base of the steering console. He wears a pair of yellow sunglasses that are used to reduce the effects of glare on Plutonian eyes. "Check out the Red Sea Observatory. It is beautiful this time of year."

"The Red Sea is on Chiron, though, not Pluto?" Dita questions. Her face flushes purple when she realizes she has interrupted.

The driver grins, "No worries, little Ganymede, you are right. The Red Sea is on Chiron. But the observatory here on Pluto is the best way to see it. Better than going to it, in my opinion. There isn't much out there worth noting." Kathel tenses at this but says nothing.

"Right," I say slowly. "We'll have to check that out. Any particular time that would be good? Anything good to look at on the other moons from here?" Miessa's ears perk up at that. *I can do a little undercover snooping too. I took some of those classes too.*

The car slows down, lowering amongst a few ships. I peer out the window, trying to see which ship has "Nuka" written on the side of it. I pull back when I see someone outside. I nudge my chin toward the window, and Miessa leans out. "Someone is out there."

"What?" Dita asks. She leans forward, putting her head right next to Miessa's. "Who would be waiting for us?" She whispers.

The driver turns the car and slowly spirals us down landing between a few ships to the ground. "Were you expecting anyone when you got here?" He asks, turning back to face us.

"No, Sir," I say slowly.

The driver nods. "I'll hang out until you get on your ship."

"You really don't need to do that," Kathel says.

I punch him. "Thank you. We would appreciate the support." I turn to him and breathe, "we don't know what we are walking into." He reluctantly nods. I push open the door and exit the ship, I wrap my hand around my back like I need to adjust my jeans, but I am really adjusting the grip of my blaster, so I can grab it quickly if need be.

"Ah, Agent Gomez, how was your trip here to Pluto?" I freeze at my name.

The man stands casually; he's human, wearing a tapered suit like what fancy lawyers would wear around New City Hall in New Seattle. I turn to my squad, who slowly files around me. "I'm sorry I don't know who you're talking about." I hedge.

He turns to Dita, hands folded in front of his chest. "It's fine. I know why you are here. I'm actually here to speak with Agent Adorari." Dita tenses at her name. The man walks up to her. Like Carver, he wears his rank and insignia on his sleeve.

Dita's tentacles move back away from her face. "Me, Sir? What do you need me for? I think you are looking for a different Ganymede?"

He steps uncomfortably close to my team, my heart rate spikes as he moves in. I don't see anything on him, but something about his demeanor makes me want to step in front of Dita. Kathel feels it too and steps up, flanking her other side.

"We need to talk about the decisions you have been making with your technology." He says.

"My technology?" Dita asks, subtly moving the tablet in her hand behind her leg. Miessa motions beside me, and I glance down at her hand, she is making a subtle chopping motion. I glance at Kathel. He saw it too. I place my hands loosely on my hip's inches away from my blaster. "I am sorry, Sir; I don't know what you mean." Dita steps back a few steps. Before Kathel or I can move, the man falls. the echoing sound of a blaster sends us diving away to safety.

"What the fuck?" I shout, turning to see our driver holding a blaster of his own, a single column of smoke drifting away.

"He wasn't an actual officer." He says, placing the blaster back in the car.

"What the hell do you mean? He clearly has a badge!" Miessa says, pulling her blaster on the driver.

He sits down in the car and puts his hands up, "check him out."

My squad nods, and I move forward. The suit of the man is charred black, and the smell of burning flesh washes up my nose. I move forward, feeling for a pulse. The man's dead eyes stare into me. "No pulse," I announce. I roll the man over and pull at his badge. Sure enough, where ours are backed with a motherboard that connects to the circuitry of our suit and our tracking chips, this is backed by plastic. The badge is flimsy and snaps easily. I look up at the driver than my team. "Miessa, drop it. He is right. He was a fake."

Miessa slowly lowers her gun, glancing at the body. "Take it." She tells the driver. "You shot him. You need to take care of it."

Our driver watches her for a second, seeming to size her up. But after a moment, he nods. "Sure. Yeah, I can do that."

I glance around, looking for our ship and hoping no one heard the shot. "We need to get going." I spot our ship to the left and motion for Dita and Kathel to walk towards it. I don't know when they both drew their blasters, but they circle the ship, making sure no one else lies in wait before entering. Miessa and I watch as our driver hauls the body of the fake officer into the back of the car. I wait until the trunk is closed, and the body is out of sight before saying. "Thank you for the ride and your quick actions. Please pass along the message to Tortie. And thank you for the lesson you taught us here." I say, gesturing to the trunk. "I won't forget this."

He nods and climbs into the seat. The window rolls down again. "If you need anything else, give me a call, Ada. I'll be there." He says, passing me a small, square business card. It has Tortie's symbol on one side, and on the other, in small boxy letters, a phone number and the name Mendon.

"Mendon." I catch his eye. "Thank you."

Chapter 39

Miessa and I hurry onto the ship. I keep my blaster out, tucked close to my chest until I hit a button next to the ramp, and the door lifts, locking into place with a pressurized hiss. I see Kathel is already in the driver's seat, and Dita is already buckled up in the seat behind him. Miessa moves to take the copilot's seat.

Miessa spins in a circle in her chair. "So, this is our ship, huh?" she asks, taking in all the flashing lights on the consoles and the screens that show all sorts of data about flying this vehicle.

The ship is simple, a small cargo ship probably used to move freight locally. The hold is lined with empty shelves and straps to lash the cargo down. Miessa and Kathel go through some preflight checks. "Yeah. This is the sort of ship I grew up with." Kathel says, flipping a switch above his head "How is our fuel? They give us enough to get where we need to go?" Kathel inputs the coordinates for the base on Nix and settles his hands around the controls.

Miessa looks to her left at the gauge. "We are at a full tank." she taps a button, and the engines rev a bit. On the center monitor, a map appears with a blinking blue line showing our planned route. "We are ready whenever you are."

I find a seat and strap in. "Alright, let's get out of here."

He pulls the ship up, and we move down the lane, gaining altitude as he does so.

"Ship number 053015, you have reach altitude of ascent. What is your purpose? Over." A voice asks over comms.

Miessa hits the intercom button. "This is 053015. We are leaving Pluto. Are we clear for takeoff? Over."

The comms crackle to life before the reply squawks out, "053015. You are clear to leave the atmo. Please proceed directly to the gate and airlock. Over."

"Copy that." Kathel turns the joystick, and the ship tilts to the left, and we move down the row until we can see a gate. Once we get through the gate, it doesn't take long to be released into space. "Okay, shifting us into cruise control," Kathel says. He taps a few things, and the stars shift around us as we move at a steady clip through space. "And we are at cruising speed." He pulls his headphones off and lays them on the dashboard. He spins his chair to face us, unbuckling his harness, and leans forward, running a hand over his face. "Okay, what the fuck just happened back there?"

Dita opens her mouth, and a small croak comes out. She clears her throat and tries again. "I don't know. I'm sorry." She keeps her eyes down on the tablet on her lap, the thing an extension of her.

Miessa leans forward and taps her leg. "That wasn't your fault. That was a plant. They did that on purpose." Miessa says firmly.

"How do you know?" Kathel asks. "Not saying what happened was your fault." He says, catching himself. "I just want to know where you think this is coming from."

"Because they knew too much, and we found out he was fake. He was put there on purpose to get us off track." Miessa says confidently. "We went through drills like that, remember?" Dita nods her cheeks, flushing purple in embarrassment.

"But who would put him there? How would they know what we would be doing? Is this the Garrison or the Federation? Do they somehow know about our mission already?" Kathel asks, pacing about the cabin.

Dita tugs on her tentacles. "Carver said that the Garrison has been dealing with a lot of cyber-attacks. Maybe they didn't block them out as well as they thought they did."

I nod, "that would make sense. If someone got a plant in the system and the Garrison tried to close the firewall, wouldn't it still transmit data?"

Dita and Miessa share a look. "I know what you are trying to say," Miessa smirks, "but that made absolutely no sense."

"Yeah, no. Firewalls aren't prisons, but yes. Someone could

have created a bug that is embedded deep enough into the system that the Garrison might have missed it." Dita says. "There are data bugs, and there is tech that can be implanted in the mechanics of a system. Unless there is one on the base, it must be a data one, something where they got in and reprogramed it to do something, but masked it from our servers. I don't foresee a Federation soldier infiltrating that far into the Garrison."

Kathel leans against a wall and crosses his arms. "Okay, so if they have planted a bug, what do we do? Do we move forward as planned? Just on high alert, or do we report it in? If it's on base, we can't be the only team dealing with this."

I shake my head. "I think we should move forward. Carver may have a plan and know exactly what we are walking into, but we are still being tested. This could all be part of the test."

The console sets off with a series of beeping alarms that bring Miessa and Kathel back to their seats. "You see anything on the scanners?" Kathel asks, throwing on a pair of headphones to listen to comms.

Miessa turns a dial, adjusting the parameters. "I don't see any ships on the scanner, but something set it off. Maybe it was just some debris?"

Kathel nods slowly, but he closes his eyes, a hand pressed to the headphones. "I feel like I can hear something, but I can't make out exactly what it is." We pass the headphones around, but none of us can figure out the source. It sounds like a combination of the quiet whooshing sound you hear when you hold a shell to your ear and the soft whir of machinery. "Okay, well, I'll monitor it." He presses a few buttons, and an audio track pops up on one of the monitors, the sound bars shifting with the noise. "We're nearly halfway to Nix now."

I rub my hands together in apprehension. I don't really want to have this conversation. But we won't have time once we get to Nix, and I don't think it should wait. "Okay, well, since we still have some time. What do you want to know?"

My squad looks at each other. Kathel sighs, "I was angry, but I don't know if I want to know anything. I think I was frustrated. Why didn't you tell us?"

I nod, "I didn't keep anything from you on purpose. It never really came up. He was a helpful person who my Dad used to work with. Not for. Not that I knew of, at least. After my parents died and I was trying to make money as a scrapper, Tortie was one of my regular customers." I shrug. "It didn't come up until when Sarkus went missing." I pause. "That was just yesterday." The phone call with Tortie feels like a lifetime ago, not less than twenty-four hours ago.

The questions bounce back and forth for another fifteen minutes. They range from have I ever been there when he puts a hit on someone—*yes*—to what sort of support did he give me; food, medicine, and on the very rare occasion, credits so I could replace things like shoes. By the end, Kathel and Miessa are silent. They don't look happy, but they are content with the answers I have given.

"Okay." Miessa nods, "Okay." She rubs her hands on her thighs. "I guess that's it. Just don't get in any deeper than you are." I nod, "I know you want to say you know, and I'm sure you do, but I just feel like I need to tell you to be careful."

I swallow hard and nod. I know she means well. She holds my gaze for a few more moments before moving back to the console to monitor things. Dita follows her over, asking a few questions about the various notifications on the screens.

I turn to Kathel, but he is looking down at his hands. I want to ask him if we are okay. Whatever this thing between us is. I know I care about him, and I value his opinion. But he also pisses me off to no end. But he and I have shared some things that we have never told anyone else, like the situation with his brother, Mycall. I want to ask him if we are okay, but I can't change the things I had to do to get here in my life.

"Okay," He whispers, mimicking Miessa's response.

"Okay?" My voice cracks slightly in the quiet, and I try again. "Okay." He nods, rubbing his hands up and down his thighs. He has more questions; he isn't fully okay. But for now, it will be. I clear my throat again and lower my voice, so the others won't hear. "Can I ask a question?" He tenses like he already knows what the question is and wants to avoid it, but eventually, he nods, meeting my eye for a moment. "You don't have to answer," I blurt, "but why did you… why did you react so much to hearing Tortie's name? You said the hunks of metal…"

Almost instantly, his jaw tightens, like it's some animal instinct to gnash his teeth and prepare to fight. I wait quietly, watching the muscle in his jaw tick as he decides whether to answer the question. "We weren't sure. But my mother thought—"

Dita bounces to the back of the cabin. "So Miessa says we are nearly there, but I figured out what the noise was. At least I think I did." She pauses, taking in the way the two of us are leaning into each other. "Oh, am I interrupting something?"

Kathel stands up and moves back toward his pilot's seat. "Not at all, Dita, what's up?"

"It's a bug." She whispers, her voice nearly inaudible.

"A bug? Like a microphone? A transmitter?" I blanch, thinking of all the private information I just divulged, thinking I was saying it to my squad.

She nods, "I'm running a scan now to find it. It's the disturbance that came through, and that sound we were hearing? That's the frequency it uses to mask, and echoes as the recording is sent back to its hub."

Kathel nods tightly. "How long will the scan take?"

"At least an hour." She says, tapping the program on her tablet, showing us how it sends out pings to the ship. "It should be done in time for us to reach Ni—to reach our location. Once I deactivate it, we can plan our next steps."

She turns to go back to the flight deck, and I catch her arm. "Is there any way the person who planted that could use it to track us?"

She nods gravely. "Oh yeah, easily. If it's the tech I think it is, definitely. So, for now…" She makes a motion of zipping her lips and throwing away the key.

Chapter 40

Dita's scan found the plant a few minutes before we landed. She pulls out a small tool case and pulls the panel off of the wall, "this shouldn't affect the mechanics." She says, disconnecting a few wires from the panel.

"What mechanics?" I take the sheet of metal from her.

"The door. That button controls the door." She says, glancing up, her words are slightly garbled by the screws she holds between her teeth.

"Oh," I say, placing the panel gently against the wall.

She holds her tablet up in front of the panel, and the program she has scans the box with a few pulses, lighting up the planted tech with a white box. She slips the tablet back into her pocket and moves the wire around tracing their sources. "I think this is all additional cabling." She murmurs. Following one cable to the edge of the panel. "Okay that connects to—" After a few minutes she extracts the small box with a few deft cuts of the cables holding it in place.

In the distance, the glass dome around small clusters of buildings and a ring of ships around it. "Make sure anything that would mark you as a member of the Garrison is hidden. Some people will not take kindly to it." Kathel says.

I want to ask him what he means by this, if the Garrison did anything to the people out here, or if the Federation has that much of a hold. *He said when he left, nothing was happening, not that nothing had ever happened,* I remind myself. I glance down at the timer on my HUD: sixty-four hours left.

Miessa makes sure the ship is powered down and hits a button. The ramp opens with a whoosh, and a cloud of dust puffs out as the gate lands. If my helmet wasn't intact, I would be dead, but I still reach up to touch the point where my helmet joins my suit to make sure it is connected correctly. "Come on, we have to get off. It's going to shut and lock up. The only way it will open is our biosignatures." She says, pointing at the panel as she walks by.

We make our way across Nix's surface slowly, leaving our blasters holstered in case we draw attention to ourselves. My fingers itch to wrap around the butt of my blaster for that bit of comfort and protection.

"We won't have much time to find a place to crash for the night. Unless rules have changed, there is a curfew." Kathel says, keeping his eyes locked on the gate into the dome.

I glance at him, "why would there be a curfew? You said nothing was happening when you left?"

He keeps his eyes trained forward. "I have gotten a few messages from my mother lately. Things haven't been going well. I didn't want to face it." He stops, and we turn to him. "She thinks the Garrison is up to something. If the Federation is here, that might explain it, but there have been lockdowns, searches of the caravans, threats to cancel the festivals we celebrate. The Garrison is fighting tooth and claw to have a foothold here, but no one knows why. Most caravans aren't allowed to move anymore, so the Garrison can keep an eye on them."

I don't know what to say to this. The Garrison is an organization that helps to maintain peace in the galaxy. But if what Kathel says is happening, then the Garrison is overstepping its limits.

"Right, let's hurry and get in then," Dita says, leading the way.

I watch Kathel as he walks. His movements are tight, very purposeful. I switch to a private channel. "Kath?"

"Yeah, Ada, what's up?" He replies, not looking toward me. He kicks a stone, and it skitters over the surface before ricocheting off the surface and floating away.

I hurry to catch up with his longer stride, "when did you last take pain killers?"

He speeds up his pace, his limp even more pronounced. "I am fine, Ada."

"That limp says otherwise."

"I'm fine." He repeats.

"You okay, Kathel?" Dita asks, glancing over her shoulder. "You are walking funny."

I smile wryly. "I just want it to be known that I didn't ask in the public channel, and thus I am not the one putting you on blast right now."

Through the tinted glass of his visor, I see him roll his eyes. "Thanks, Dita. I'm okay. Just a bit stiff." He says, looking at me. "I'll be okay once we get to the settlement. Changes in pressure, ya know."

She nods, satisfied with the answer.

I am not. "You need to take something once we get there. I don't want that leg to get worse over the next few days."

Miessa's voice over comms interrupts any further complaints on his part. "Incoming vehicle, two o'clock."

I look up. It's a small transport vehicle that looks similar to a heavily armored school bus. It floats above the surface of the planet, sending puffs of dust up into space. "It's a transport ship," Kathel says, moving to an outcrop of rocks, waving us over. "Nix has a really active mining community. That ship is probably taking people home after their shift."

I cycle my HUDs camera and zoom in on the ship. The image shows up in a small panel at the bottom of my visor. Through the windows of the ship, the wide silhouettes of the soldiers are visible. "Do they have any support?"

He nods, "they usually have one to two guards. They're mercenaries."

Dita crouches down lower. "So, we shouldn't catch a ride from them?"

Kathel laughs humorlessly. "Uh, no. That would not go well." He pops up higher to watch as the vehicle goes by. "This settlement isn't the largest on the planet. If we caught a ride, it would be very noticeable. We need to make sure we keep a low profile."

We slowly file out from behind the rocks, watching the bus for any sign that it has spotted us. "So, why are we here?" Miessa asks.

"What do you mean?" Dita says, tripping over a stone. We all stop and watch as the rock floats away in the low gravity.

Miessa clears her throat. "I mean, what is our reason for being here. If anyone asks, we clearly have matching uniforms under our clothing, so we must be some sort of team."

"School?" I suggest turning to Kathel to see if it would make sense to the people living here. "If we say we are some science team doing like research or something?"

Kathel is quiet for a moment, considering. "Yeah, because we will be here for such a short time, we should clarify that this is just a passing stop, make sure our story is consistent. Be honest where you can. Life out here can be brutal; I swear it gives people some knack for seeing through lies. We were on Titan, and we stopped on Pluto before coming here."

We spend the next few minutes fabricating a plan. We are from a school in the Martian colony. We are trying to complete a research project on the minerals collected by the various mining camps to test and see if the quality is consistent from the mines to the markets.

The settlement comes into view as we get closer. The wall around it looks almost militaristic, and the gate, while open, doesn't look inviting. "This should be fun," Miessa whispers, voicing my thoughts.

A little light flashes in the corner of my HUD—a notification. Dita must have gotten it too, "hey, before we go in, looks like the Gar—home just sent us some credentials to use." We pause, looking over the details: new names and clearance to the settlement. "You can edit the reason for being here." Dita says, "So we just need to fill it out to go in line with our plan."

"How do they do this? How do they know we are nearly there?" I ask as I fill in the details.

Kathel shakes his head. "Probably the chips," he gestures to his arm. "Best not to ask too many questions right now."

"Who the fuck knows how the Garrison gets away with half the shit it does," Miessa says. She shifts her pack on her back. "We probably should stow these." She says, shoving her gun into the bag. "They'll probably want to know why students have blasters."

We follow her lead, hiding the weapons we carry in our packs. I leave the blade on the outside of my thigh strapped in place. I catch Kathel eyeing it. "What? You don't think a student would have a knife like this?" He shrugs.

As we approach the gates, a light shoots out and scans the four of us. It flashes up and back down. "Well, they know we're here." We stop, waiting to see what happens next.

The gate opens, and two guards come out. They approach, slow and confident, watching us from a distance. "Who are you? Why are you here?" One calls, the speakers in his helmet echoing strangely across space.

Kathel waves a hand ever so slightly, a movement only the trained eye of our team would see. We pause, and he steps forward, making a show of lifting his hands to show that he has no weapons at hand. "Hi there, we're students. We have badges." Kathel says, shifting his voice so it sounds more nasally and unassuming. "Do you want us to show you?" He makes an eager shift to grab his tablet, and when the guard jumps, he thrusts his arms into the air. "Great expanse, I'm sorry! I was just trying to make sure I was complying."

I bite my tongue so I don't laugh. One only has to look at Kathel to see that he is ripped and could easily take these two guards out, but they also take him in, slowing down their movements as if to appease him and not scare him. "No, no, it is okay." One says. "We just have had some strangers lately that haven't been as helpful." The guard said vaguely. "If you will come with us, we'll get your intake started and get you out before curfew."

One guard leads us while the other waits for us to move, taking up the rear guard. "Remember the story," I mutter, keeping my head down so no one sees my lips move behind my visor. I see Dita nod slightly, her fingers inching toward her tablet.

A light flashes over us again as we move through the gate, and an alarm goes off. The guards freeze, rounding on us. "You are students, huh?" The second guard asks. "Do you know why that alarm would go off?"

Miessa shakes her head, eyes growing wide. "No, Sir. Did we do something wrong?"

The guard rounds on me, taking in the knife strapped to my thigh. "It means you have weapons on you. Why would a bunch of students have weapons on them?" He goes to grab the blade from my leg, and without thinking, I step back. The guard grabs the edge of my suit and slams my back against the wall of the airlock. "Why are you so jumpy there, mate?"

I let my face fall, letting the look surprise flood my face with fear while simultaneously tamping down the urge to flip this Nixian over my shoulder for slamming me like that. "W-we got them from school." I splutter. "I don't really know how to use the weapons I have. They just said that we had to take them so we could try to protect ourselves if we ever got into any danger. We've been collecting samples all over the galaxy." I babble, praying it is enough to get this Male off of me. Now.

"Sir, we can explain everything. You said you were going to take us to intake, right?" Miessa says. She puts a hand toward me like she wants to help me but is afraid of what the guards might do.

The guard stares at me for a minute. And not for the first time, I'm glad that the Garrison tinted the surface of our visors so this Male can't see how red my face is flushing. The heat creeps down the back of my neck. *Let go of me,* I want to scream. Finally, he does, "right." he says stiffly, but he doesn't step away until his buddy has already moved on with the rest of my team through the airlock.

Why me? Why did he choose me? I wonder, trying to think of why stepping back would have set him off so much, so I can make sure *not* to do that again. The light above the doorway turns green, and we all remove our helmets. I take an extra moment, letting the cool air hit the back of my neck before letting the thick pony fall back into place. I swear one of these days, I'm just going to chop it all off. The intake center is a small building with narrow halls that remind me of the testing facility back in New Seattle. The motion for each of us to go into a room. *Here we go.* I take a seat on the bench.

The female in front of me looks like she would rather be

anywhere else than here. "Snuck in just under the wire, huh?" She asks, glancing up at the clock on the wall. "You had better not make me late," she mumbles under her breath, but just loud enough for me to hear.

"Yeah, I guess so." I say, pulling my hair over my shoulder and fidgeting with the ends.

She rolls her eye, scrolling through a few files on her tablet. "So tell me your name, what's your story."

"My story? Everything or...?"

She scoffs under her breath, "No, I don't want your entire life story. Why are you here? Why are you on Nix? How long are you staying? That story."

I shift in my chair, which squeaks awkwardly in the silence. "Right, oh yeah, that makes sense. My name is Brookes, Brookes Stirliens. I'm a student studying planetary market schemes, but some of my squadmates study geology. We are doing a research project to test samples of rocks from the source and then at the market to see if traders are doing anything to depreciate the value of the product..." I trail off, "sorry, that probably isn't very interesting."

She writes the information as I speak. "It doesn't matter if I find it interesting or not. It is going in the file either way. How long will you be on Nix?"

I sit up straighter. "Oh, not long. A few days? This is just a passing stop; we added it last minute before heading back to school. We've been traveling for like two weeks now. Nix was a stop that was one of those where it would be really cool if we could hit it, but we knew we might not be able to."

The woman nods but in a way that says that she couldn't care any less. "So, you are going to need access to the mines as well, I assume?"

I nod vigorously. "Oh yeah, on my card—oh, I need to show that to you, don't I?" I pull my tablet out and show her the hastily filled out info card. "That should give us permission to go to the mines, right? I know it hasn't always been accepted across the board at different locations. But it's all that the school gave us to use."

She took the tablet from me, reading over the file. For a second, I think she's going to deny it, but she nods. "Yeah, this is good, it differs from some others that I have seen, but it is valid." She pulls open a drawer to her desk and pulls out an ID card on a lanyard. "You'll need this to get into the mines. Should anyone question you, show it to them. It proves that we have approved you to be here. That should shut them up."

"Thanks," I say, slipping the lanyard over my head. "Do outsiders get into trouble a lot?"

The woman stands, and I mimic her before moving toward the door. "Not if they can help it. But as you can guess, they don't always get a choice in that matter. Just watch your step, and you'll be fine." She laughs dryly, "really watch your step in the mines. I wouldn't want to worry about shipping your body halfway across the solar system because you tripped. That goes for anyone on your team. They should be waiting for you."

"Thanks!"

"Have a good trip, Brookes." She says, turning back to her desk.

"Who?" I say before I catch myself. She turns back to me, confusion and suspicion flashing across her eyes. Realizing my mistake, I hurry to add something to the end of the sentence. "Who do we go to if we need a place to stay tonight?"

Her face relaxes. "Oh, of course, right. Ask for Maxine. She should give you decent accommodations for a few nights that shouldn't break a student budget."

I nod, "Okay, thank you!" I say and hurry out of the room before I can blow our cover.

Chapter 41

Passing through the door, I find the rest of my squad waiting for me. "What took so long?" Dita asks, "They asked me like two questions."

I grin. "I got a contact, so we have somewhere to go."

Miessa perked up at that, "You did? Where should we go?"

We walk toward the residential district of the colony. "I was told to ask for Maxine. She didn't give me an address..." I trail off, realizing the issue.

Kathel sighs, "luckily, I think I remember where Maxine's is. Possibly." He chuckles, "I might be completely wrong, though." We nod and follow him down the road. I watch how he walks; his steps with his right leg are shorter, and he doesn't lift his leg as high. *I need to get some meds in him.* I watch as his ankle gives out slightly. It's a slight movement, a bobble, and an instant catch. The next few strides he takes are slower, more measured. Like he accepts he's having trouble. He glances over his shoulder and our eyes lock. "We, uh, we should be nearly there. I think it is right here," he says, turning a corner. The buildings here are cramped together. They remind me of a lot of the more impoverished neighborhoods in New Seattle. The ones where the families made too much to get government help, but not enough to take care of any damages.

"One of you should knock," Kathel says, stepping to the back of our group. "I have been away from home long enough that someone might not recognize me, but you never know. I'd rather be safe than have to explain something complex."

Miessa steps up to door. She knocks on the door, waiting for it to open, gently rocking back and forth on her heels.

The door opens, and a short Rogue with a thick white streak stands before us. I'm short, and I have to look down at this Male. His hair is swept back with enough pomade to put my hair up in a mohawk. "Who are you?" He asks, scowling up at Miessa.

"Hi," Miessa says, elongating the word with a long, high-pitch, annoying-ass voice. "My name is Niken and I'm here with my team. Is Maxine in? We were told to ask for her."

He grunts and steps back. "Maxi, they did it again. The intake team sent us more outsiders." He calls.

I hear someone out of sight curse before coming to the door. She is the polar opposite of this man, tall and rail-thin. "I told them to stop fucking doing that. What do you want? Why are you here?"

Miessa grabs her name tag and starts fiddling with it, "I'm sorry, ma'am, we're here for research. We didn't plan to come here, so we didn't make any accommodations. They said that you might be able to help with that. Should we go somewhere else?" She asks, putting the power back in the Fem's hands, while also pulling a hint of guilt trip.

Well played, I think, though I also wonder why we all have stepped back to a timid version of ourselves.

The fem looks over us, before pointing at us with a long finger. "No, you can stay. But you need to figure out what you're doing. I will give you a discount tonight because we are so close to curfew. But I won't be as nice tomorrow." We all sing our praises, but secretly, I think this Maxi likes the attention and will say that she doesn't enjoy helping even though she does, and would help you again and again if she likes you. However, I wouldn't be surprised if she enjoys a good session chewing out the guards.

Maxi brings us to a room and sends a dinner menu for us.

"Don't cross her." I laugh, unhooking one of the many bags from my suit and drop it on one bed.

"Kathel, do you think she knows you?" Dita asks, laying down on the bed, and using my bag is a little pillow.

He shakes his head. "If she did, she didn't say anything. She might not say anything to me, but I wouldn't be surprised if when I get back to base there's a message from my mother, yelling at me for not coming to say hello to her and the rest."

He slowly lowers himself to the bed, rolling onto his stomach with a quiet groan. "Fuck."

"You gonna let me give you some medication now? I ask, unzipping one bag and pulling out a few tubes.

He nods, putting his head in the crook of his elbow. "Yeah, just give me a second," comes the muffled answer.

"We'll go outside to wait," Dita says, rolling back off the bed, giving me a quick wink, and pulling Miessa from the room.

Kathel rolls from the bed and turns away from me as he unzips his suit. The one downside of the suits provided by the Garrison, as Kathel previously discovered, is that they are tight, the purpose of which is obvious regarding space travel, but getting in and out of them isn't nearly as simple. He pulls the fabric down around his waist, tiny noises of pain escaping his lips as he wiggles the fabric past the bandages on his thigh, leaving him standing in his boxers. I try not to be nosy as I gather any materials out of my bag, my neck growing warm under my hair. He flings the suit to the side and quickly lies back down face first on the bed, face tucked away. Though he is lying down, I can see the edges of his scars peeking around the sides of his chest. "Do you want to put your shirt on?" I ask quietly. "The one you packed?"

"I'm okay, feels nice to get out of that thing."

"Okay," I bring my stuff over, laying it around his body so I can grab it quickly. I grimace at the bandage on his leg. The edges of his burn clearly visible from the soft brown outline soaked through the bandage. "What did you do?" I murmur gently, lifting his leg so I can unwind the wrap. "This won't be pleasant, you soaked through."

His back arches as he cranes his neck around to look. "I did? What the fuck? How did I bleed through it?"

"I don't think it is blood," I say, lifting it away. "Yeah, you didn't bleed, just, well, oozy," I grab a sterile cloth and gently dab at the wound.

"Oozy?" He asks, flinching away, "Sorry," he says, "It stings a bit." He grins.

"Now who's the big tough guy?" I smile back, "It's a sort of plasma." I explain, grabbing a gauze pad and laying it across the wound before loosely wrapping the bandage around it. "It means it's healing, it's your body trying to keep it clean. But you don't want that wrap pressed up against your skin all the time." I sit back, "All set. Just be careful when you put your suit on, I wrapped it looser than the last time. If we were home, I think it would be good if you just let it breathe for a day or two, we don't really have that option, do we?" I say, "here are some pain meds." I pass him a few pills and a small water bottle before gathering my stuff and placing it back into the bag.

"Thanks." He pulls the suit back on, though I notice when I look up again that he has left it open slightly, the front of his suit gaping to show skin. "What do you think the other two are doing?"

I glance at the door. "Part of me thinks they may be sitting on the other side listening," I say with a grin, "you know, have to get that fresh gossip. But part of me hopes they went to go get some food."

He comes to sit on the bed beside me, "So, do you think we have time?"

"Time? Time for what?" I ask, zipping closed my bag. I bend to put it under the bed and when I come back up freeze, a grin of surprise spreading across my lips. He is barely a breath away. This close I can see the stubble growing roughly around his jaw, and the point in the corner of his lip where it is slightly swollen from when he bites it while concentrating. "You are lucky I didn't headbutt you there," I say, and to my annoyance, it comes out all breathy. *How is he able to do that without saying a word?*

He pulls me into his arms "It's okay, I have a pretty good doctor," He murmurs, the soft words hot against my jawline.

"You know, on some planets, I am pretty sure there are rules against patient-doctor relationships."

He stops, confusion making his eyes crinkle, "I-what?"

I grin, "you know cause it's bad?"

"Was that an attempt at flirting?" he chuckles.

I wind up to punch him. "I know, I know it was bad. You know what? Just kiss me."

His lips are on my neck when there is a loud rap on the door that sends me flying off of him. "Are you two done yet? Your dinner is getting cold." Miessa laughs. "I'm coming in, ten, nine, eight…" I scramble to fix my hair into a bun, the wild thing having been partially freed at some point, "Fuck it one, you two better be decent." Miessa looks from me, my hands still in my hair and Kathel lying too casually on his bed on the opposite side of the room, and just sighs with a wide grin. "You two are awful. Carver is going to kill you if she ever finds out."

"Well, I'm not going to tell her, are you?" He asks. I respond with a flying pillow, and Dita collapses on her bed in a fit of giggles.

Chapter 42

I roll over in the dark, startled for a moment by the sound of other people breathing. Then I remember. Nix, our mission. I turn over and look at my squaddies passed out on the beds. Sprawled spread eagle, they all breathe deeply, with mostly quiet snores. I grab my tablet, checking the time. It's early, a few hours before our start time. Looking at the countdown timer, we have around fifty-four hours left. I sit up and scroll through a map of the colony; *I am not going to get any more sleep.* I get up quietly and send a message to everyone:

ADA: Out scouting. Might go find us some breakfast. See what we are getting ourselves into. I'll be back in an hour or so.

I creep out the door. Miessa rolls over at the sound of the notifications trilling through each of their devices before the door slides shut.

I make my way through the inn and down to the front door. If I read the specs right, there should be a twenty-four-hour store and café down the road to the left. I figure I can go there, do some people watching for a bit, and get breakfast before the others wake up.

Turns out I was sort of right. The store is to the left, but you have to go about a mile down the road. I get plenty of stares as I walk by miners headed to their shift, young people on walks, dirty kids who roll through the streets without a care in the world. It reminds me of New Seattle, in a nostalgic way that leaves me feeling out of place. Like Kathel said, this is a smaller colony, so most people know each other. As an outsider, I stand out like a sore thumb.

The market is quiet. Through a broken conversation of bits of Gian and Plutonian, we find what I need. Bags in hand, I head over to the coffee bar. The menu again is in three languages, but thankfully the barista helps me pretty quickly. "Can I help you?" she asks in blissfully accented Gian.

I tap my heel against the bottom of my stool. "I wouldn't suppose you get coffee beans out here?"

She shook her head, the fabric of her headscarf swinging. "Sadly, no. It's too far. But I might have something to substitute for it if you'd like to try?"

I nod and slide the fake ID card loaded with credits across to her. She picks it up with delicately gloved fingertips. Her entire body is covered until her shoulders, where the off the shoulder dress she wears reveals spiraling tattoos that disappear under her scarf.

She squeezes different liquids into the cup, stirring together a black coffee. "So, what brings you to Nix, stranger?"

I took the cup and took a slow sip. She was right. It resembles coffee; it does the trick indeed. "What makes you think I'm a stranger?"

She grins, "Really? You don't think a barista would notice someone new? Besides," she starts stacking cups on the shelf behind the counter. "Word travels fast whenever newcomers are here. And the intake ladies are real gossips."

I laugh. "Should've known. Those with the most information always are."

"So?" She asks, cocking an eyebrow.

I take my time as I stir in a bit of cream and sugar into my drink, looking about the room and the patrons within. They are focused on their tablets. "I'm here on a research mission with my team from school." The lie comes easily now, repeated over and over. "We are part of the geology department. Well, I'm more business than science, but we got paired together." I take a sip of my coffee, and she sits on the edge of the counter, waiting for me to continue. *Don't fuck up Ada, you aren't the spy of the team.*

"How does a business major end up with a science team?" She asks, crossing her arms.

"It's a funny story," I say. *That sounds so fake don't use that line.* "I grew up working with my dad in the black market. I learned how people would raise or drop costs," I say, "so I was the ideal candidate for helping to see if minerals and other things being mined were being tampered with or having prices slashed or jacked at market."

We pause the conversation as she helps someone else with their drinks.

"So," she says once the couple sits in a corner booth. "You are here to test our mines and see if someone tampers them with at the markets?" I nod. "Well, I'm sure people would be interested in that. When do you think the study will be out?"

I pause at that. *How long does it take to do a research project?* I take a sip of my drink to avoid answering for a second, burning my tongue as I do. "We are still in the early stages. We may have two to three more research trips before we are ready to write it. So... I'd say at least a year." I say, pulling a time frame out of my ass. "Well, maybe less than a 'year' for you. How long does it take Nix to go around the sun?"

She laughs, "I believe around two hundred Earth years."

I freeze, "I never said I was from Earth."

She laughs again. "You didn't have to. I've met a few of you earth types. You all have the same passion and spark." She laughs harder and winks at me when I don't look convinced. "Okay, okay. The intake ladies told me."

I relax my shoulders slightly "Oh, okay." I take a deep swig of the drink, hoping it will mask my surprise.

She continues to clean her station, wiping down the counters with a wet towel that leaves little beads of water on the surface that she quickly whisks away. "Yes, you would think they would be more reserved with the information that they have. But these ladies could not care less. They love that people come to them for any news and gossip." She makes herself a cup of something hot, the tendrils of steam floating away from the rim, and leans against the counter. "So you release this paper next year; then what? What are your plans, then?"

I make a big show of sighing and running a hand over my head, tucking away some baby hairs. "You don't get a lot of students out here, do you?" She shakes her head. "Then you wouldn't know. Never ask as a student what they are doing after graduation. It's like asking a Fem her age. It just isn't kind." My new barista friend nods very seriously. I sort of feel bad, "Okay, not that bad," I sigh, "But it can be really stressful. Often, we aren't entirely sure ourselves, and it can feel like a lot of pressure. Especially when things aren't exactly going as planned."

She puts her cup down with a quiet thud. "Is that how it is for you? You know how you want things to go, but it doesn't seem like it will go in that direction?"

I shrug. "Pretty much," I push my now empty cup across the bar to her. "Anyway, enough about me. Tell me about Nix. What is it like? Is there anyone I should watch out for? How is everyday life?"

I lean forward, trying to look as interested as I can, even as I try to deflect questions away from myself, my team, and our lives.

"Oh, you know, it's colony life. Everyone knows everyone and feels like they are owed something. Thus the gossiping. It is so easy for people to feel entitled here. It's like a rite of passage. But these are also some of the hardest working and most passionate people I have ever met."

"What is Maxi to everyone?" I ask, pulling the one name I know out of everyone.

She grins. "Oh, Maxi. You're either one of her favorites, and she'll do whatever she can to help you, or you have wronged her, and honestly, you're screwed. So watch yourself while you're here. You want to be sure to stay in her good graces." I nod, making a note of that. "As far as people to avoid?" She paused, thinking for a moment biting her lip. "I would say keep an eye out for the mercs. They are, well, mercs. They're here to do a job, and most don't care what has to happen to get the job done. Isn't that right, Zachariah?" She asks, as a Male walks into the shop.

"What's that?" The man asks in a voice so breathy it's nearly a whisper.

"We were just talking about the Mercenaries and how sometimes you'll run people over to get the job done correctly." the barista says, beginning to make the Male's drink without stopping to ask for his order.

"Thank you, Shireen, you're a doll," Zacharia says. "Yeah, don't mess with our shit, or our job, and we won't mess with you." He looks me up and down, nodding his thanks to Shireen as he takes the cup, which looks tiny in his large hands. I note the blaster on his hip and a row of explosive charges on his arm. "For in the mines. We have had quite a few cave-ins recently. Blasting them out is the fastest way to make sure we get to our people and that they are getting the airflow they need to survive."

I cross my arms. "Wouldn't placing explosives be a danger? If there is a cave in, would you really risk further collapsing?"

Zacharia's face grows dark. "Some risks have to be taken. We have to decide in the moment and choose what will be best for everyone. My employer demands a steady stream of production. And that is what me and my team deliver."

"Who is your employer?" I ask, and quickly add, "This is just for my research. I'm sorry, I should have clarified. I'm going to be doing research in the mines. I have the information written down, but I've been to several locations over the last few weeks, and I forget who your employer here is. We had to get clearance from them to come here. So I'm sure they won't mind if you remind me." I say, praying the lie works. If it does and I have a granule of information to give Miessa and Dita, this whole trip would be worth it.

The man looks me over like I have three heads. "Researcher?

Why would Bogtrotter allow researchers into their mines?" He pushed away from the counter. "Do you believe this shit?"

Shireen shrugged. "The ladies gave the all-clear. She wouldn't be in this shop if she didn't have the credentials."

Zacharia keeps turning, heading for the door. "Well, we weren't notified of no visitors. I can tell you for a fact that you're not getting on my bus."

Shireen smiled ruefully after him. "Yeah, like I said, avoid the mercs. You will probably get a reaction like that from most of them. While to most of the people here you're a thing to gawk at, to them, you're a nuisance."

A group of four or five people comes in, and Shireen turns to them. Using the opportunity, I quickly duck out of the room with a wave. *Thanks for the intel.* I just hope it can be of some sort of use to my team.

Chapter 43

I slide back into the inn quietly with my bags of food. All three of my squaddies round on me when I walk into the room. "Where the fuck were you!" Miessa snaps, making sure the door locks behind me. "We were trying to get a hold of you, and you weren't answering! We thought something was wrong!"

I put the bags down slowly and pull out my tablet. The screen lights up slowly, showing half a dozen messages and video calls from my teammates. "Shit, I'm sorry guys, I didn't know. I wasn't in any danger. I swear."

"Are you sure? Maxi said that the people here can be a real pain in the ass sometimes." Dita says, helping to distribute the food I picked up.

"Yeah, I had everything under control. I got food for us," I say, handing off a parcel to Miessa, "And I just sort of people watched. I got some information about the mines, though." I say lightly, waiting for anyone to ask me about it. When they don't, I lie down on the bed and munch on my muffin.

Kathel sighs, "Fine, since you want us to ask you, what did you find out?" he asks, muttering, "Pain in the ass," so only I can hear him.

I sit up a bit too excitedly and throw muffin crumbs across Dita. "Well, I am no undercover, but!" I say, glancing between our two spies, "I found out what company owns the mine!"

Miessa sighs. "Ada, how does that help us? We aren't actually planning on going down into the mines." When no one agrees with her. "Are we? I thought we weren't."

"Well, maybe not right away," Dita says, "But we might have to. What if the—what if our contacts work in the mines? We need to trace them." She pulls out her tablet and goes to her trusty search bar. "Okay, Ada, hit me. What have you got?"

"Well, I was sitting in a coffee shop speaking with a barista when one mercenary that guards the buses came in. He said he wasn't expecting anyone and that none of the other mercs had been given the information that some new people would need to get into the mines." I trail off, "That may be an issue, but at least we know about it. They definitely like their routines, and the entire town is a gossip. Ninety percent of people know or will know by the end of the day that we are here thanks to those intake ladies we spoke too. The barista knew a lot about me. At least she knew I was a student and from Earth and stuff like that."

"Did she know your name?" Kathel cuts in. "What if she was a Fed?"

I shake my head, "No, I don't think so; she just knew like the bare bones. It was pretty clear that some of the information was missing. But the town knows we are here. So we can't be sneaking around like we're investigating anything other than the mines. The Mercs are very particular about how things are run. We just need to make sure that if we do go down there that we follow all of their rules."

Miessa nods begrudgingly, "Okay, that makes sense. I was just worried. The last thing we need is for you to have said something that can be picked apart to no end. We don't have a lot of time here, and we need to make each minute last."

I nod and turn to Dita, "So the company that the man said, or at least the owner of the company that he said, was named Bogtrotter."

"Bogtrotter?" Kathel asks, peering over Dita's shoulder as she looks up the name, "like boggy water?"

"That's what it sounded like to me," I reply.

Dita screws her face up in thought, typing a few things out then waiting for a page to load. This goes on for a few minutes while Kathel points out different things and shakes his head. "I don't remember ever hearing this name." He says at one point. "But you never know, it could be the arm of a larger cooperation."

Dita's tentacles curl and uncurl in perfect little spirals. "I am not coming up with anything super credible. There are a few people that make enough money that could own a mining company, but nothing is standing out to me."

"So, you think it's fake?" Miessa asks, "I can tell you I don't remember my dad ever mentioning someone named Bogtrotter. I feel like I would have remembered that name."

I deflate a bit; I thought I had found a great nugget of knowledge. "So, now what?"

"Now," Miessa says, nudging Kathel out of the way. "You let the spies do their thing. Let us look into it more. You might be surprised what we can find. There are always loose ends somewhere."

So Kathel and I wait. I even try to take a brief nap while the two of them work, deliberating over the most minute of details. But nearly an hour later they don't seem to make any traction. "Either this company is the most rock-solid secure company I have ever found, no pun intended," She says with a smile, "Or it's a fake."

"You think it's a cover?" Kathel asks, taking apart and putting his weapons back together for the fourth time this morning.

"Yes." Dita says, "We should be able to find something, like manifests or sales. Good thing that you found it, Ada. We need to be careful moving forward. I mean, we would have to anyway."

Miessa nods, "I think we should keep an eye out for any signs.

When you were out, did you happen to get a hold of any schedules, since you have convinced people we will be going into the mines?" She asks pointedly.

I rub my neck. "About that…"

She rolls her eyes and moves to the door. "I am going to see if Maxi has any information on it." She heads out the door calling over her shoulder. "Please don't do anything dumb while I'm gone."

Dita gets up to make sure the door is locked behind Miessa. Kathel, Dita, and I relax while we wait. It doesn't take long for us all to roll onto our beds, snacking on the food I brought. Dita falls back asleep, and I can't help but giggle as I slowly work the cup of seaweed smoothie from her fingers so she doesn't drop it on the floor.

"You should get some sleep too," Kathel says from his perch on his bed. He is lying down with his head propped up on his arm.

"I'm okay. I wouldn't be able to go back to bed now if I wanted to." After another ten minutes or so, I pull up my tablet and switch to the screen that shows everyone's locations. Kathel, Dita, and I are in a tight little clump in our room. But Miessa's is down the road. "Looks like Miessa went down to the intake building. I wonder what Maxi told her to do?" Kathel moves over to sit on the bed beside me.

"Maybe she had to talk to them about getting into the mine?" He asks, leaning down next to me to look at the screen.

We watch as her little cursor moves around inside the building before coming out and back down the road. "Well, whatever she was doing, it looks like she is on her way back here."

I rise and wake up Dita, "Hey, Miessa will be back in a minute."

She groans. "Sorry, I didn't mean to fall asleep." One of her tentacles comes down, rubbing the sleep from her eyes.

"It's okay, we all need rest," Kathel says, moving to unlock the door.

The door opens a moment later, and Miessa strolls in. "Okay, friends, we are good to go." She says, passing each of us a little card to add to our lanyard. Each card has a small photo of us in the corner and the name of our alias. "We need these to get on the bus." She bends down quickly, shoving her personal items into one of the bags. "And that bus is leaving in the next ten minutes, so we've got to go. Move your asses. Chop-chop."

Chapter 44

The passes Miessa got for us work perfectly. We swipe them across the scanners, and the bus doors open with a happy chirp. I climb into the bus and take one of the first seats. Miessa slides in beside me, while Dita and Kathel take the seat behind us. The mercenaries guarding this vehicle stand at the front and rear doors.

The bus is loaded within the colony and the airlocks, but in the mines, there won't be any atmo. Miessa and I shift around slightly.

"You may use the overhead compartments for bags." One guard says, passing us. I nod and quickly stand, stowing our small backpacks above until we get the word that we will need them.

The guards are in head to toe tactical gear. It seems much to me but makes me wonder what sort of things are in the mines or if it is just their way of intimidating the workers. "So, what is it exactly that they are guarding?" I whisper to Miessa, monitoring the guard that walks past us to stand at the doorway. Making sure no one else comes on board.

She glances up at the guard, eyeing him from top to bottom. "He's guarding us, making sure that the workers are here and on time. And probably make sure that we aren't going to take any of the materials. Maxi said when we show them this card we shouldn't have any issues."

The guard tilts his head slightly at that, like he can hear us, and is either confused or not pleased. I can't tell behind the tinted glass of his or her helmet. "You sure?"

She turns to me, eyes narrowed. "It better work. You got us into this situation."

"I did not!" I hiss, "I was going with the plan we all agreed on. I didn't think you would have an issue with it." I say. Miessa can be infuriating. Why does everything have to be about her unless she could be to blame for something? Distantly, I am aware of the miners on the bus with us and lower my voice even more. "Why are you complaining about this now?"

She sits up straighter, and I swear if she had the room in the seat would have brought a hand to her heart like the rich women in the vids. "Complaining? I don't complain, I—"

"Oh, come off it." I roll my eyes hard. "Complaining is a part of your personality."

"Ow!" She and I stop and turn to grab the back of our heads. Kathel stands over the seat, hands primed to tap the top of our helmets again if needed. "Will you two stop bickering? It isn't helpful." He gives a look that says 'get your shit together, or I will do it for you,' before ducking back down into his seat.

Miessa and I look at each other before turning away. I turn my attention to the window. Nix is dark. The light of the sun won't reach this part of the moon for a few more days—by then we will be gone. In the distance, the lights around the mine come into view, a pinprick threatening to be swallowed up. "That's creepy."

"Isn't it?" Dita asks. "I know it is far away from the colony, but it is so dark. Ganymede got like this sometimes."

A soft tone comes through the speaker, and I look up. All around us the miners are standing up, pulling tools and things out of the overhead compartments. "Guess it's time to go," I say as Miessa passes me my bag. I pull it on and activate my HUD it takes a second for it to load up.

"Okay, how are comms?" Kathel asks, his voice coming across like quiet static.

"Not gre—" Dita responds before her voice cuts off abruptly.

I go through the process and try turning up their audio, but the settings don't seem to do anything. I try switching to a private comm. "Hey, does this work? I am trying a private link." I ask, turning to Dita. Her mouth moves through her visor, but no sound comes through my comms. I switch it to an outboard sound. "Looks like we will have to put it through the speakers."

The others nod. The bus slows as we approach, and the miners crowd to the front of the bus. We follow behind, and as we disembark, Lines of lights lead away from the bus down to the entrance to the mine. A small tin building is surrounded by the lights. The miners gather in front of it and enter in small groups.

"It's an elevator." One says, turning to us as we approach. "You can only have three people at a time go in. One of you can ride with me if you want."

Kathel steps forward, "Thanks, that would be great." He shrugs his backpack a little higher on his shoulder.

He steps forward and speaks with the miners, general pleasantries, and small talk that I don't think I would have the energy for right now.

I turn down my outboard speakers, so no one else will hear, "So, what is going on with the comms?" I ask, turning to the rest of the squad.

"I am running a scan now, but it looks like there is some sort of interference cutting into our frequency," Dita says. "I want to say it is something technical. I don't think the mine itself would do that?"

Miessa nods in agreement, "I don't know any minerals that would do that."

We shift forward; Kathel is next up to go down into the mineshaft.

"How long will it take you to complete that scan? Having an

answer may be necessary for whatever we find down there." Miessa asks.

Dita's fingers wiggle at her side as she remotely programs whatever is visible on her HUD screen. "Not sure," she says slowly. The sound comes through her speakers slightly muffled, like she is biting her lip. "The rate keeps spiking and dropping. At least fifteen minutes." We step forward and watch as Kathel disappears behind the sliding door. "The rate will probably drop to zero in the elevator. We'll just have to see what happens when we get down there." She doesn't sound happy about it.

The light of the door turns red, blinking slowly to signal that the elevator is in use. But gradually, the red light grows dim, and the green orb next to it lights up, and the doors slide open to reveal the empty car. "Here goes nothing," I say as Miessa stabs the button that will bring us down into the mine. It isn't hard to figure out which button to hit, there is one for up and one for down. As we descend into the mine, I bring up the photos of Vielcent and Blaithin. I make the images small and put them in the top left corner of my screen where they won't obstruct my view but will be easily accessible. The two don't have any permanent identifying features: no striking cheekbones, or crazy eye colors. The only thing about them that stands out is their hair color, which could easily be changed. "This isn't going to be easy, is it?" I ask aloud.

A light glints off Dita's helmet as she tilts her head, and I look above her. A small domed camera sits watching us. She shifts and brings eyes back to her. "I mean, I just don't want to get in anyone's way. But I think this will be a good spot to add information to our dissertation. It isn't like any of our other stops." She says. I assume: *As long as we are discreet, we should be able to get in and out pretty quickly.*

"Do you think it will be difficult to get the samples?" Miessa asks, catching on to our little code. *Do you think it will be difficult to find our targets?*

The elevator stops and gives a pleasant little ding. Kathel is waiting off to the left. We pile out of the lift a cheery greeting on our lips like we hadn't left him just five minutes ago when we see he isn't watching the elevator for us. His gaze is trained on the far side of the mine where to a glass wall. On the other side must be a pressurized room. The people inside don't wear a helmet. A female stands up to the glass. She wears what looks like a dark green jumpsuit that perfectly complements her deep blue hair that is done in a fabulous updo that defies gravity. Blaithin "Roxie" Roxinate. I turn to my team. "You know what, Miessa? I don't think it will be difficult to find our samples at all."

Chapter 45

While the realization that we have found one of our two targets so easily gives me a thrill of pride, I won't lie and say it doesn't also make me question us being here. *This was too fuckin easy.* If this mine really is their base, either they knew we were coming and wanted us to find it, or they are nowhere near the threat the Garrison makes them out to be. And as much as I would like to give credit to the latter, I don't believe it. And from the way Kathel has tensed, I don't think he believes it should be this easy either.

"Something is wrong." He says by way of greeting when we make our way over to him. His voice is low, even, and perfectly controlled, like a coiled spring ready to strike.

He meets my gaze, and I nod.

"So, where should we look first?" Dita asks brightly, she has her tablet out and is making passes through the air. I recognize the screen, while it looks like it is a simple scanner similar to the ones the miners are carrying, little numbers scroll rapidly across the bottom as she runs her scan, still trying to figure out what happened to our communications. "I think that tunnel over there would be a good place to start." She says, pointing to a tunnel that sits at about four o'clock from our current position.

I mute my outboard speaker as we follow Dita and her tablet across to the tunnel in question. "Are you able to access a map of the mine I am in?" I ask of my suit.

"Hm, I will have to think about that." It replies, and I get flashbacks to when I had to yell at the Garrison issued suits about my air supply. "Here is what I could find." It continues a few moments later, and a map appears over the photos on my HUD with four little arrows representing each of my squad on it. I pinch and expand my fingers, zooming in the picture.

"Ada, watch where you are going!" Kathel says, catching my waist. His hand lingers for a moment as he makes sure I am steady on my feet. "You nearly walked off the edge!" His voice is more concerned than annoyed. His thick white eyebrows crinkled in concern though the tinted visor. "What happened is there a leak in your suit or something? Why weren't you paying attention?"

"No not again, sorry." I step back and glance around, noticing several people have turned towards us, a security detail in the corner has their hand resting on their blasters. "I-sorry," I say sheepishly. "I got a report from Professor Gar, a map. He had some coordinates on it he thought might be helpful when looking for samples. I was trying to compare our location. Look," I order my computer to forward the map to each of my squaddies.

"This is brilliant," Kathel says. "This is exactly what we needed!"

I make a show of brushing off my shoulders. "You know, there's a reason that the professor trusts me to get all the information."

"Yeah, right." Dita and Miessa say at the same time. We all laugh and follow the map.

A hand grabs my wrist, and I freeze, I have to force myself to relax my fist as I turn so I don't deck the person. It's one of the miners, though this one is noticeably cleaner than any of the others. "Where do you think you are going?" She barks. The bits of hair I can see are normal, black.

I pull my hand away, *not her, it isn't Blaithin or Vielcent.* "I, I was just going with my team. We got clearance." I say, quickly grabbing the tag around my neck and shoving it at her. "See? We are just looking; we will ask before taking any samples."

The Fem pulls on the card, and the snap holding the lanyard in place catches against my helmet as it releases. "Really? You got clearance, huh? Because I sure as shit didn't give anyone that isn't working clearance to be down here." Of course, she must be the foreman—forewoman?

"There must have been some miscommunication. We got

permission this morning. My partner, she got these for us today."

Miessa steps forward to say something, clearly catching onto my mental plea to get me out of this one now, but the boss waves her off. "I didn't give anyone clearance. That means you need to get out. Now." She points toward the elevator, now some four hundred feet away.

"Ma'am, there must be something we can do. Can we discuss the project with you? Maybe not today? What about tomorrow? Could we come down here tomorrow?" Miessa asks, sliding in front of me, trying to pull attention.

And that is when shit hit the fan.

They say time slows down when you realize things are going wrong. And I wouldn't say they were entirely wrong, but it isn't quite right either. Everything and nothing happened at the same time. As Miessa stepped in front of me, blocking the forewoman's view of me, a little notification popped up on my screen from Dita:

I AM ALMOST THROUGH

Miessa shudders, and through the visor of her helmet I watch in horror as her pale white skin shifts, rippling to the soft lilac she was born with, to a deep orange like a Plutonian, and back to the white of a Rogue. *Shit her meds are out.* My thoughts flash to the conversation on the base. *Now is not the time.* The forewoman's eye narrow and she reaches for a blaster.

The icon showing whether or not our team could use internal

chat lights up, and Kathel's voice comes screaming over comms "What the fuck are we going to do about this. Ada, they have blasters on our backs at eight o'clock." I start to turn, "I swear to the great expanse if you look at them."

Miessa jumps slightly as the wave of sound hits her.

And then the lights flash, and a klaxon alarm clangs.

"So, uh, guys. I fucked up." Dita says, her voice quiet and guilty.

"Intruders! Technology breech!" A screeching voice says over the loudspeakers embedded to the walls every forty feet.

"You have to be fucking kidding me." Kathel snaps, his hand like mine drifting toward the gun, stowed in the bottom compartment of his bag.

"My scan did what it was supposed to. It found and got rid of the thing blocking our comms. But that thing happened to be their firewall. I tried to stop it, but I couldn't get the override in time."

Kathel mumbles some not quite intelligible curse and nudges Dita closer to Miessa and me.

"You are the only intruders I see here. So why don't the four of you explain yourselves?" the Forewoman says, but now she has a gun, and so do the four people behind her and every one is locked on a member of my team.

"We should go," Miessa says, all but revealing our guilt. "We didn't want to be any trouble to begin with, and that clearly isn't working, so we, uh, we'll just see ourselves out." She says, side stepping back toward the elevator.

"Brilliant. Masterful. I have never seen anything like it." I say my head now on a swivel counting our many enemies.

"Shut the fuck up, Ada." Miessa snaps, looking at me, but she hasn't programmed her comms internally. She says it out loud. "Fuck."

Kathel, Dita, and I groan. I grab Miessa, and we bolt to the door. "The card I have says, Brookes! She called her Ada. It's them, grab them!" The woman screeches.

"Good one," Kathel says, mashing the call button to within an inch of its life. I pull out my blaster and aim at the first person closest to us. I shoot at his hand, aiming to knock the gun out of his hand when he steps forward faster than I expected, the blast nailing him directly in the chest. Air shrieks as it escapes from the hole in his suit into the unpressured air. And he drops. If the blast doesn't kill him, the lack of air and the cold of space will.

I look up; the light above the elevator is dark. "I think they shut down the elevators." I spin, turning back to the surrounding enemies. "How are we going to get out of here?"

Kathel and I lock into each other shoulder to shoulder, blocking Miessa and Dita from the enemy. "Dita, a game plan would be nice!"

I look up to the window where we had seen Blaithin. Steel doors slide into place, protecting the room. "There's a second entrance." Dita says, dropping a pin on the map in the corner of our HUDs. "In the other sector. It looks like it is the refinery."

"Can we get a little less chitchat and a little more action?" Miessa chimes in.

I shoot at another guard who gets a bit too close. "I would gladly take any suggestions you have." Another guard steps up to take his place.

Kathel pushes into me, working to shift our group away from the useless elevator. "We might need a different plan. What if they shut down all the elevators in this facility?" We stick to the wall, moving slowly as Miessa and Dita fall in.

"Just shoot them already!" The forewoman yells, letting a round blast off over our heads, denting the doors behind us.

I glance up. Hanging thirty feet in the air is one of the beams for a catwalk. "Get ready to run." The wires sway as guards run down the bridge.

"When you are." Miessa says.

"Three, two, one." I step back and Kathel and Miessa lock together, blasters raised. Behind the wall of their bodies, I aim high and shoot the wires of the catwalk. Because of the lack of gravity, it hangs in space for a moment before moving upward, following the trajectory of my blaster's hits.

Nobody moves for a moment, watching as the catwalk rises. But then the people scream as it moves away from the walls up toward the hole in the ceiling. "Warning Catwalk 37 has been compromised.

Warning Catwalk 37 has been compromised." The alarm rings out. Between the screeching alarms, there are shouts and clanks as the miners try to unhook from the cables holding them to the beams.

"Go!" I yell and we punch through the line of workers who are frantically trying to figure out how to get their men back down. I fire a few shots in the forewoman's direction, pinning her down behind a few boxes.

We sprint down a side tunnel, "third left is our route!" Dita says, flinching as shots rain down on us from both sides.

I pull Dita into a shallow alcove, using my body to shield her. "Is there any way you can break into the security system?"

"I can take it over it's still down." She says.

"Left side is clear. We need to move." Kathel says, backing down the hallway.

"I need more time."

"We need to move, Dita."

"Just give me a second."

"Dita," I growl under my breath, a blaster hits above our heads. "Time."

"Got it! It's ours!" I pull her out of the alcove and shove her toward Kathel, firing into the incoming enemy.

I quickly backpedal down the hall, giving the others cover fire so they can get in.

The door to the elevator opens, and Kathel hooks my waist,

pulling me in as I send off three more shots before the door slides shut. "We need a bus. We need to steal a bus." Dita says. "We can't run to the ship. We won't make it."

We all have our blasters out, ready to fire. A bead of sweat drips down the side of my face. "So, we steal the bus, then what? We can't go directly to our ship. They'll see us launch."

Kathel nods, "Normally, I would agree with you. But we don't really have another option. We need to get off Nix. If we go back to the colony, we are even more fucked. They will have people everywhere. That was a Federation base. We saw Blaithin."

"We don't know for sure it was her! We didn't get close enough." Miessa counters.

The doors open, and we take off to the nearest bus. My boots shift as we run across the dirt, large spikes growing out the bottom to grip the ground and hold me down so I don't float off into the ether. "Do you want to go back down there and ask to talk to her yourself? It was her." Kathel insists. We run to the closest bus, crouching down next to the exhaust funnels. I look around the corner and blast out one mirror while Dita fires out the other, blocking most of my line of vision. "Okay, two of you take the door, another to the driver's window. I am going to go through this back door."

"Why are you the one to go through the back door?" Miessa pouts.

Instead of answering, Kathel simply disengages his boots from the ground and floats the few feet to the door, deftly grabbing it and pulling his body close to the door. He presses his feet against the metal of the bus, then engages the mag locks, with a faint thud. "On my mark, we move."

Chapter 46

Dita and I creep around one side of the bus, and Miessa takes the far side. We edge forward until we're right at the edge of the doorway. A quick turn and a few shots, and we will be on the bus. We just need to make sure none of us are hit.

Kathel hangs from the back of the door, waiting until we are in position. "I will shoot first, take out the driver, or at least get his attention. I will fire two shots. If he isn't down by then, Dita or Ada, you take him out. Miessa, you get the controls."

"Roger that."

I hold my breath in the silence waiting. *Bamph bamph* Kathel's shots ring through the bus. The front of the bus lights up, and a figure drops. I shoot out the bottom of the door and rip it open, Dita directly behind me.

We didn't account for the fact that there still might be Mercs on the bus, and we round the stairs to see Kathel grappling with two of them. He kicks one, but they grab his leg, trying to unbalance him as the other tries to get him into a headlock. I jump, using the lack of gravity and the seats to propel me forward, like pushing off the side of a swimming pool. My feet collide with the side of the closest Merc's head, sending him reeling away from Kathel and the other opponent. I fly past Kathel and hit the opposite wall absorbing the impact as I come to a crouch on the wall. The merc I hit falls into one seat. I use the moment of confusion to push off again, floating above him before turning my body and shoving off the ceiling. I drive my shoulder into his stomach, wrestling with his waistband to fling the blaster to the front of the bus where Miessa climbs through the window.

Dita hangs out the door, firing at anyone coming out of the elevators. "Um, guys!" She shouts over comms. I glance up and see colorful blast after blast as she keeps firing. "Can you hurry this up? We gotta go. Like yesterday."

I hear a dangerous pop as the visor of the Male grappling with Kathel is blasted away. I drive my elbow into my opponent's chest then haul him up, flinging him toward the back door. Kathel fires two shots that, at this range, take the man out.

"Watch where you aim that thing." I pant.

He holsters his gun and moves to the door, pulling it closed with a snap. "I had a shot. I took it."

There is a roar underfoot, and the floor of the bus vibrates as

Miessa starts the bus. "Let's go!" She presses her foot to the floor. "Hang on!" She says as we all lurch backward.

"Must go faster, must go faster." Dita says, staring down the incoming ships.

Using the backs of the seats, I climb to the front of the bus. "How long will it take to get to the ship? Do we have enough juice on board to make it back to the launch base on Pluto?" I would give anything right now to pull my helmet from my head and wipe away the sweat dripping into my eyes.

"I think we had enough," Kathel says behind me. "Dita, can you plan a course, so as soon as we're on board, we can just input the information?"

"You've got it." She steps away from the open door, switching places with me.

I rest my back against the dashboard, bracing my feet against the staircase. "Company incoming!" I call, "Hey Miessa, this doesn't come with its own protection program, does it?"

"You kicked it off the bus a few minutes ago." She says, swerving around a few different boulders.

My shots go wide as I fire out the door. Does that make them warning shots? "Right, about that."

Kathel kicks open the back door and kneels on one of the back seats. "Ada and I have you covered, Miessa, just get us to the ship." Kathel nods to me, and I send him a tight smile. "How is your blaster's power cell?" He asks, switching to a private channel. His voice is cool, calm, and prepared, like he has trained his entire life for situations like this.

I tilt my gun, looking at the power bar in the grip. "I'm at about seventy percent. But I have a backup in my thigh pouch. Are you good? Do you need another?"

I watch as he fires two perfect shots, hitting the lead vehicle head-on. It slows, the engine block a domed ball of fire. Those on board leap off, quickly grabbing at anything on the surface or engaging the gravity locks on their boots, gripping the ground. "Nah, I'm good."

"Show off." I lean out the door of the bus, trying to get a better view to aim. I quickly duck back inside as a flurry of shots rain down on me. There are three more vehicles following us, all bursting at the seams with what we assume are Federation soldiers, not at all pleased that we found their base. "We need to get these guys off our tail before we make it to the ship. I don't remember seeing any defense systems on board. There is no way we are doing this once we break atmo."

He nods. "Cover me."

Without question, I put my arm out the door and lay down a steady stream of shots. Most of my shots are erratic, and the three vehicles swerve wildly as they try to avoid them. *We really should have taken out the other vehicles when we took our bus.* But hindsight is twenty-twenty. Had we done so, we might not have gotten out of there as quickly as we did, or someone could have gotten hurt in the process.

I glance up in time to see Kathel lay down a thick line of shots. Between the two of us, the vehicles drive erratically, like they never adequately trained to deal with outside intruders. "Trust me?" He calls. I look over, and he has his spare power cell in his hand.

I nod. "Always."

"Good," I hear the evil grin is his voice as he tosses the power cell out the door. "hang on!" Right before it hits the ground in front of the incoming vehicles, he fires at it. The first two shots miss because he isn't as perfect as he likes to think he is. But the third is spectacular. It explodes directly under one vehicle, sending it careening into a second—the two collide in a glorious blue halo of flame that lights the darkness.

"Mind giving more of a warning before you do shit like that?" Miessa snaps as our bus is rocked by the shock wave.

"I could. But where's the fun in that?" Kathel laughs. I fire off a few more shots at the vehicles, but it seems like we have lost them, at least for now. The last functioning bus has stopped to help the others.

"Good job." Dita says, "Everything is programmed. Once we get on board, we should be good for launch."

"Perfect," Miessa says through clenched lips. "We're coming in hot. We lost one tail, but it looks like we're gaining another." I look out the window toward the colony and spot five new vehicles incoming.

"Just can't catch a break, can we?" I ask. I look at my blaster—sixty five percent. The vehicles aren't in range yet. We all know it. Our blasters are only accurate for so far.

"Just get us as close as you can," Kathel says. He has moved back to the front of the bus and leaning over Miessa as she drives. "Just get us on the ship, and we can go from there. Don't worry about the rest."

"You say that, but I know if we don't lose them, we're gonna have issues." She swings the van around like she is going to take it off in another direction.

"No, Mies, just go right for it. We'll figure it out."

Dita moves next to me, and the moment it looks like the two of us are in range, we fire. It's weird how blasters work in space. In the enclosure of the school, we hear everything. Every shot, every body that falls, every echo. But out here in the vacuum of space, we hear very little. The powered charge leaving the end of my blaster is compacted like it is happening in the distance.

The new ships close in, and my already fast pulse grow grows faster. *We need to find an out. We need to find an out*, I think as the enemy ships become closer. But then I realize we're moving closer to them. They sit in a straight line, staring us down.

Miessa pulls up next to the ship, and we disembark quickly. I walk backward towards our ship, waiting until know my squad is safely on board before moving backwards up the ramp. "Why did they stop?" I ask.

"I don't know. Someone called off the charge. But I don't know why." Kathel says slowly. He lowers his gun, "Don't wait. Let's get out of here. We'll just keep an eye on the scanners and make sure they don't follow us."

We board, Miessa and Dita moving directly to the cockpit while Kathel and I flank the ship, keeping our blasters raised until the door has shut.

I hit the pressure button and wait until the light turns green. "Airlock cleared," I call before ripping the helmet from my head. I scrape the sweat-drenched baby hairs from my face, pushing them back. "We made it."

"Not yet. Come on." He grabs my hand and moves me to the front of the ship.

Chapter 47

We get off world with no problem. I watch the sensors the entire way as we move off Nix. But the blinking cursors representing the enemy only move farther and farther away until they are no longer on the map. My back straight as a rod, waiting for what I think will be an immediate attack as soon as we go airborne.

Kathel never lets go of my hand. It's a loose, steadying comfort as I lean over Miessa's seat.

"How long until we reach Pluto?"

"About thirty minutes," Miessa says. "We need to be prepared. This will not be easy."

"They're going to block our entrance," Dita says matter-of-factly.

"If they don't shoot us out of the air, I am sure there will be bodies on the ground ready for us to land."

I grab my blaster out of the holster and slowly peel my hand away from Kathel's. He gives my fingers a little squeeze. I step away, a small grin on my face, I am glad he is on my team, the pain in the ass he is. I wouldn't want anyone else to be my fight partner. I quickly disassemble and put my gun back together in the middle of the floor, making sure that the pieces are clean and won't lock up on me mid-fight. "Anyone need anything? We probably won't have time to do any med stops for a bit."

Kathel comes over and whispers in my ear, "You wouldn't happen to have any quick fix pain meds?"

I glance up, searching his face for the pain I had missed. He isn't grimacing in pain yet, but I can tell from the tightness of his eyes it's there building up again. *That isn't good.* I dig through the bag on my hip and pull out a syringe and a vial. "This should kick in within ten minutes. It isn't a lot, but it should do the trick. I am worried if I give you too much, it will knock you out."

He nods, "just give me whatever you can, don't worry about me. I'll figure out the rest." He tries to roll up the sleeve of his suit to expose a vein, but the fabric is too tight. He sits down in one seat, "how about this one?" he asks, pointing to the vein pumping in his neck. "I'd rather not strip right now."

"That'll do. But it'll hurt like a bitch."

He grins. "Nothing your boy Kath can't take."

He tilts his head to the side, and I get to work, wiping the site down with an alcohol pad. His eyes flutter closed.

425

"You should know," I whisper for only him to hear. "That I will worry about you so many ways."

His eyes open, and my breath catches slightly at the sight of his golden eyes, reflecting the light of the consoles. "Why would you worry about me?"

I pull my eyes away from his and remove the cap from the needle with the corner of my mouth, pulling a small dose of the pain reliever into the syringe. "Just a little pinch," I say around the cap. I pinch the skin, finding the vein. "ready?" His eyes close, and he takes a deep breath. I bring the needle to his neck when the ship rocks with turbulence. I jump, pulling the needle away. "Hey, uh, could you not do that?" I look toward the front gesturing at the needle in my hand.

"What the fuck was that?" Kathel asks, eyes wide in alarm.

Dita leans around the pilot's chair. "Sorry, we have some incoming enemies."

"Okay, well, can you keep us steady for like ten seconds so I can give him a shot?" I ask dryly as Kathel settles back into position.

"Sorry," Miessa calls. All I can see from my position over Kathel are her hands gripping the joystick tightly as she guides the ship through a series of smooth turns.

"Okay, let's get this done, I'd rather not kill you." I brace my elbows against his chest, "Sorry." I say, pressing gently against the skin of his neck feeling for the pulse and vein.

"It's fine," He whispers, his lips barely moving.

I slide the needle into his neck and quickly depress the medication. He squints a bit at the pain but says nothing. "All done," I say, releasing the breath I had been holding. "Here," I press a cotton ball to his neck. "the bleeding should stop in a few minutes."

"Thanks, Ada." He whispers.

I crouch down to his level, forcing him to look me in the eye. "Is there anything else I can do?"

He shakes his head. "Nah, I just need a bit to rest." The ship rocks again, and Miessa curses. "We all do."

He gets up and moves to the cockpit, switching seats with Dita. She moves back to me. "I'm kind of glad he took over." She whispers. "I had no idea what I was doing."

I smile ruefully, "we all have our own skills. You need anything from me?" I ask, my hand hovering over my open bag.

"No, I'm okay. Just feel really wired. That was crazy back there. Miessa thinks it's just going to get worse."

I look where our two pilots sit, pressing a myriad of buttons on the console and quickly relaying information back and forth. "I'd have to agree with her. If these guys they're fighting now aren't direct from Nix, then they're from Pluto, which makes them a bigger issue."

She nods, "there are at least eight ships."

The ship rocks throwing me off balance, I catch myself on the

427

back of Miessa's chair as the lights got out; a moment later, the engines go quiet. "Oh shit." I mutter, "Are we dead? They hit us?"

"Sort of. Shut it." Miessa whispers, turning off every switch around her.

"I'm sorry, what?"

"Shhhhh!" She hits a button, and the ship goes dark, the red emergency lights reflecting strangely off everyone's skin. "We are faking." She whispers, the sound barely audible over the hiss of the air system. "We were waiting until we were just out of range to take a hit. I'm hoping they will think we are down. And leave us alone."

"That won't actually work, will it? They have to have scanners or something to know we're still alive, right?"

Kathel nods, "I can probably see that we are alive, but will they do anything about it? We are hoping they will think our life support system went out. If they were the Federation, and they think we stole information, they aren't going to care if our systems are dead."

Dita and I share a look. "If this works, these people are the worst kind of assholes."

Chapter 48

Turns out, the Federation is, in fact, the worst sort of assholes. They hung around for about fifteen minutes, the ships circling us. They tried a few attempts to contact us, but we ignored each of those hails.

Pluto was right there, waiting for us. But we had to wait, floating there in space until the ships not only left us alone but flew back to Nix before we dared to bring anything back online.

"I don't think we are out of it just yet. We still need to land, and I assume we'll have to without clearance."

"Should we call in help?" Dita says, looking to me.

"No, we need to do this part on our own," I say. "We don't need help, we are more than capable of doing this on our own."

Kathel catches my eye and gives me a small nod. His way of saying thank you. But he doesn't have to. I don't want to owe Tortie anything more. I already know I'll owe him a huge debt when it comes to his work to find Sarkus. I debt I am willing to pay, but I don't need to bring my squad into that. "Besides, this is what they train us for. We've got this." I move to where our blasters line the wall, checking again to make sure each one is charging. The last thing we need is an empty power bank.

Miessa brings us into the planet's atmosphere slowly. We hope that by not coming in hot, our unassuming little ship will fly in under their radar. Which works at first. We make it within the compound with no issues.

We float in a line of other vehicles waiting for a parking spot. It is like when I used to go to events with my parents, and the attendants would wave you to the parking spot farthest away from the event. But now we are on edge, praying to whatever higher power that the name and serial number on the side of our ship doesn't get called into the authorities before we have time to land.

"Just a reminder, we have forty-eight hours to get back to base." Kathel says, "so we have plenty of time to lie low and make a plan." We all nod, but even still, the time doesn't make me feel better.

"Just going in easy," Miessa says.

A patrol car of police floats by, and I glance at the power banks. They are all nearly charged. *Eighty-three percent is going to have to be good enough.* I pull the banks down and start passing out everyone's blasters. A light flashes, scanning our ship.

"Shit," Miessa mutters as the vehicle swings back around toward us. "Be ready. It might be time to make a jump." She stays on the controls while the rest of us load up, grabbing any gear we have. We pull our helmets on and depressurize the cabin, ready to open the door and bolt at the order.

Dita carries Miessa's bag and blaster, ready to pass it to her if we have to make a break for it.

"Ship number 053015, please halt." A stern voice says over our radio.

Miessa does as instructed, "Here we go. You ready to go?" We nod, Kathel's free hand hovering over the button for the door. Miessa turns back to the comms. "This is number 053015. We have halted our engines. Is there a problem, Sir?"

"Ship number 053015, please halt your engines, and prepare for boarding."

Miessa mashes the response button. "I'm sorry, Sir, did you say boarding?"

"number 053015 prepare for boarding."

She swivels to us, "I am going to bring us down hot, use it as a distraction. As soon as we hit, you get out of here."

"But what about you?"

Miessa gets up to grab her stuff as the angry squawk of the officer's voice comes across the comms, with another slew of orders. Miessa reaches over and turns down the volume. "Don't worry about me. I will be right behind you."

Kathel grabs her arm, "Mies, I don't like this. We can do this all together."

She pulls away, laughing, "why are you all being so dramatic. It isn't like I'm going to go make a martyr of myself."

"No, but what if you get captured?" I ask, "we don't exactly have time to be rescuing you, even with forty-eight hours."

She shifts, her skin rippling back to its natural purple hue, her tail elongating behind her. "You know, you aren't the only one on this team with high ranking." She grabs the headset, bringing the mic to her lips. "I am sorry for the delay Sir; I will land now." She ends the conversation by swinging into the chair and jerking the controls, sending us spiraling down.

Knowing you are going in for an on-purpose crash landing is weird. You know it is coming, and you want to try to prepare yourself mentally for the impact. But there really isn't a way to prepare for the feeling of the ship descending, your stomach rising into your throat, losing all power, and slamming into the ground. "Hang on!" Miessa shouts a moment before with a crash that knocks my teeth together, we hit the ground. My knees buckle at the impact, and I make a grab for the wall. Kathel hits the button for the door a moment later and flees down the ramp. I roll to my feet two steps behind Dita.

Running in a crouched position, we make a beeline between

some parked ships, pushing people out of the way as we go. We hear shouting as we run, but don't stop to turn, even when shots rain out around us and score the sides of vehicles nearby.

We run past an older couple, nearly knocking them over. When they make a sound of protest, Dita yells. "Sir, please don't tell them where we are. They are chasing us, and we don't know why." We duck around a corner as our pursuers hit a vehicle, the engine block exploding. "We didn't do anything!"

"Nice thinking." Kathel pants. "Hopefully, they believe us. And don't turn us in."

"Yeah, hopefully they didn't see these," I say, holding up my blaster, only slightly sarcastic. "How far do you think we should go? What about Miessa?" I ask, turning and jogging backward, scanning the area behind us for our purple teammate.

Kathel pauses at an intersection, pulling back when a patrol vehicle roars by lights blazing. "We just need to keep moving. We have the tracking chips; we will find her after, or she'll find us." He waves us forward, and we run across the small road cutting to the right, hidden by the cars. "Are we near where we took off last time? How far are we from the main compound?"

Dita slows slightly as she does the calculations, and Kathel and I flank her, moving close and guiding her along. "It isn't nearly as far, but it is still going to take us a few hours on foot." She zooms in on a section of the map. "If we go this way," she says, looking up to orient herself and pointing behind us, "then it will lead to a junkyard. We can hide there for a bit, reconnect with Miessa and then go as a group."

Kathel and I agree, and we move back in the direction we came, careful to make sure no one is following us. I watch him as we walk, noting the way he favors his leg again. The meds, while giving him a temporary reprieve, weren't enough to cut through the pain. Not when we have to move as fast as we do right now. He catches my eye; he reaches out and catches my hand and squeezes it.

The look of the surrounding ships quickly deteriorates. Fancy new models break down to ships that don't look like anyone has touched them for years, if not decades. We find one such ship with its hatch busted open and quickly climb out of site.

It isn't dusty per se, the tiny particles aren't able to gather in an atmosphere like this, but decay clings to every surface. The screens light up when Kathel taps a few of the buttons, but it's feeble, quickly winking out.

"Hey, you guys read me?" Miessa's voice crackles on the radio, short of breath and tired.

"Yeah, we read you, Miessa. You have company?" Dita asks, "I am pulling up your location now. You don't look to be too far away from us."

"I think I'm clear, I lost them a while ago, but I thought I heard at least one tail. I don't want to go right for you guys just in case."

434

Kathel and I both move for the door. And I put up a hand. "No, you stay here, rest."

He frowns. "I am fine Ada; the meds are working great."

I shake my head. "No, they aren't. You're limping again. Badly."

He tries to move past me, "What are you talking about? No, I'm not. I don't feel anything right now."

I cross my arms, "walk the length of this ship."

He sighs and grumbles something under his breath before doing as I ask. He walks the first part fine, but as he turns to come back to me, his weight shifts, and he limps, dropping the weight of his leg with each step. "Shit, okay. I don't feel that at all. What is it?"

"Like you said, the medication is working. It's taking away the pain, but it isn't enough to support your muscles. I don't have anything strong enough for that. So, you," I poke him in the chest. "Need to stay here and rest before your leg gives out from the pain you can't feel. Clear?"

He pokes at the wound, "yeah, okay, yeah."

"Are you two done?" Miessa pants, "I could use some help. Someone is definitely tailing me. I can't risk stopping to deal with them if they have back up."

"I am on my way."

Chapter 49

I move out of the ship slowly, making sure no one tailed us here before hurrying away, "Okay, Miessa, you keep heading in the same direction. I'll loop around behind you and see if I can't catch them. If I need support, I'll let you know." Using her location on the map, I chart out a path behind her where I should cross paths with her pursuer.

"Roger," she answers, her voice tight, "I might have a second, I can't be sure."

I pick up the pace, running at a steady clip now. "Don't worry. I'll take care of them."

Miessa runs along the edge of the dilapidated ships and turns to head back toward where Dita, Kathel, and I cut back to hide. I speed up, trying to make sure I can catch up with her. I keep my eyes level, scanning for anyone else in the area. "Do you know if they are in a vehicle?"

There is a pause, "I-I don't think so."

"Okay," I move into the aisle where she runs and pivot. *There,* tailing around four hundred meters behind. I duck back in between the vehicles and wait for the enemy to come up. I make sure my blaster is set to a low setting and from my crouched position shoot at them as they come into view. I miss the first shot on purpose, giving the person a chance to stop and turn, while giving Miessa a chance to duck out of sight. I shoot again, hitting the person in the legs. It won't be enough to kill them or even hurt them, but it will be enough to incapacitate them. They won't be following us anytime soon.

"One down. You should be able to come back now. I will meet you in the middle, make sure there isn't anyone else."

"Okay, sounds good." I look at the HUD and see her slow down before swinging back around.

"You okay?" I ask, watching as she slows even more.

"Yeah, I'm okay." She says, her voice tight and controlled. "I just need to work it out. When I jumped out of the way, I twisted my foot a bit, but that's it."

"Okay, well, take it easy. We can take it slow going back."

Static hisses across the comms, "Hey, it sounds like you two are on your way?" Dita asks.

"Yeah, we will be back soon. How are things over there?" I reply. Up ahead Miessa cuts between two ships, her white suit standing out against the dark metals of the ship. The 'little twist' she has is causing a pretty pronounced limp.

"I think we are good. A patrol car went by a bit ago, but they aren't searching the ships. I am wondering if when Kathel hit the button on the controls, it sent out an energy reading? We are avoiding tech right now."

"I'm sorry about that," Kathel says sheepishly.

"It's okay. It probably wasn't strong enough to get a location, and it died fast. But just something to be aware of. Anyway," she says, "just be careful on your way back, okay?"

"Always. We will be back before you know it." I switch to a private channel with Miessa as I approach her. "So, just a little twist?"

She flips me off, walking past me. "I thought medics were kind and endearing, not sarcastic assholes."

Note for file: Miessa is even more snarky when she is in pain. I walk next to her, watching her gait out of the corner of my eye. She tries to speed up a few times before falling back to a steady pace. There isn't much I can do for her here. I can't have her remove the boot without compromising her suit. There are a few points that are permissible for transmitting medication, like her forearm, but without knowing the extent of the sprain, it isn't the best idea. "Well, most of the time, Medics are Techies, not Fighters. Those tend to make, shall we say, more docile medics." I laugh, "Besides, don't you want a Medic who can kick your ass and put you back together after?"

She glances my way, and a small smile dances on her lips, "If I recall correctly, I was the one who kicked your ass."

I scoff. "Only because you played dirty!"

"I don't know what you're talking about." The smirk clear in her voice. "I would never fight dirty. I was raised to be a lady." She preens.

We keep the banter going through the walk back to the ship where Kathel and Dita are hiding without coming into contact with anyone. I, for one, am glad. I don't want to move Kathel or Miessa quickly, but we don't have a choice. We climb aboard the ship and hunker down away from the window. "We didn't have any issues on our way back. But we won't have a lot of time. The guy I took out should wake up soon. But, before we go, you need to sit for a minute." I say, looking pointedly at Miessa.

She shakes her head. "While I know you have the best of intentions, I can't do that. I want to keep moving. I feel like if I stop moving for too long, my ankle will get stiffer."

"What happened—"

"—What did you do?" Dita and Kathel ask, their voices overlapping over the comms.

"I just twisted my ankle. I'll be fine." Miessa shrugs. "But we should keep moving."

I weigh the options we have in my head before nodding. "Okay, but we go at your pace." I point at the two injured members of our team. "It doesn't matter what that pace is. However, it has to be an easy effort. We can't go all out and then have you get hurt more. Got it?" They nod.

Dita makes for the door, "I will make sure the way is clear so we can start moving."

"Okay, I will hold the rear." I say, checking my blaster again. I probably check it more often than I need to, but the last thing I want is to be caught off guard.

"Looks clear, let's move before your guy wakes up."

I look at the timer in the corner of my screen. We have forty-six hours left.

The map Dita pulls says we are around fifteen kilometers from the main section of the colony. We alternate between jogging and walking, going at whatever pace Miessa and Kathel can maintain. It takes a long time; if Wayne were here, he would say it is taking us too damn long. But we have sixteen hours to kill before we can use the gate. I feel better when we are jogging; it helps the passage of time and honestly makes me feel less paranoid. I haven't seen another person, let alone a potential enemy since I went to get Miessa, a fact that leaves me on edge. I would have thought someone would be on the cameras watching our every move. But as we tick past the hour mark without seeing anyone and slow to a walk again,

I want to rest. I want to let my shoulders fall loose; I want to put away this blaster.

Dita taps me on the shoulder. "I fixed it. You can relax now. At least for the next hour."

I spin, walking backward. "Fixed what?"

"You keep looking around. I mean, we all do, but if you were a machine gun, there would be nothing left in this parking lot. I took down their cams. For the next forty-five minutes to an hour, all they'll see is a looped video. Whereas I," She holds up her tablet for me to see all the screens. "We will be able to monitor their cams and know when someone is near us."

Miessa gives her a high five. "Remind me again where you learned to do all this? Because the Garrison sure as hell didn't teach you."

Dita gives an evil little giggle. "Well, you all aren't the only ones who have a troubled past." She saunters past us and leads the way down a ramp to a different level of ships.

"Thank the great expanse for Dita," Kathel says, trudging down the ramp. His leg buckles slightly, but he catches himself. He looks up at me slowly. "I'm good, don't worry about me." He says, leaning on the barrier. I look from him to the barrier and back again and grin when he stands up quickly. "I'm fine." He insists, turning in a way that can only be described as a flounce. "Worry wart." He mutters.

"Thank the expanse you're babysitting him. Males can be such a pain in the ass. That one in particular." Miessa says, groaning slightly as she smacks her lips. "What I wouldn't give for a drink right now."

I pull up the map again. "We're nearly there. It's just about five kilometers to the city."

I am putting my map away when Dita shoos Kathel back up the ramp. "Go back, go back. Now." She orders, and we fall in step behind her. "They have a whole squad now, maybe twelve men. We need a place to hide. Another ship?"

"There," Kathel says, pointing to a ship down the row. Unlike the first ship we hid in, this one is a legitimate piece of scrap. There is no way we could ever get this one to fly again even if we wanted to, and the blackened and burned frame looks like it wouldn't withstand a firefight. Which, if we get caught, makes it an awful candidate, but as far as being sneaky... they won't see this coming.

It looks like it had been some sort of scouting rig, a small thing that probably held a crew of one or two when it flew. The door is propped half-open. I try to open it more, so it is easier for us all to crawl through, but the door has been melted into place. There are too many holes in the ship for us to risk turning on a headlamp, should any light spill out and give us away. We huddle together in between the broken consoles, in a tangle of arms and legs. Dita slides the door to the hold closed blocking one line of site to our group. A light passes over our ship, and we scrunch together even closer together, my helmet clinking against someone else's. Another light passes over, and I wedge myself deeper in.

"We need to get out of here," Miessa complains over comms from the bottom of the pile.

"Ada, would you mind not digging your knee into my stomach?" Dita asks with a groan. I shift my weight slightly, and she grunts. "Okay, maybe go back to what you were doing."

"How did I end up on top of this pile to begin with?" I whisper.

Kathel cranes his neck to look up at me. "I really feel like this is the last thing we need to be worrying about." We all fall silent for a few minutes, watching through the gaps in the hull as a squad walks by.

My arm begins to tingle with little pin pricks of pain as my arm loses circulation. "So, are we going to just hide here in a pile until they find us, or…?" No one entertains the thought.

The lights scan over the ship two more times as the group heads back the way they came. We stayed put for another twenty minutes before slowly opening the door and disentangling our bodies a bit cramped space.

"What do you want to do?" Dita asks as Kathel walks around this ship, making sure we're clear to move. "We have fifteen hours until the jump gate will be available to us."

Kathel pops his head back in, "Come on, we're good." I follow Dita out, wedging myself sideways through the hole and jumping down. "And let's just take it one step at a time."

Chapter 50

It doesn't take long for us to realize that this one step at a time thing looks more like one step forward two steps back. We move through the ships to a point, then scurry backward, or over four rows to hide in the most dilapidated ship we can find. It happens three more times. Each time, Dita attempts to reset her hack on the camera software. But after the second round, they throw up a more secure firewall. One that would take too long for her to breakthrough. "Sorry, guys."

"It's okay, Dita, it got us this far. We just have to use whatever leverage it gave us." Kathel says, he gives her shoulder a squeeze. "It's enough."

She nods and slips the tablet back into her pocket. "We aren't far now anyway, only another mile or so."

"Well then, let's get a move on. I, for one, don't want to be here anymore." Miessa says, stepping out, and immediately jumping back into Kathel. "Shit!" The spot where she stepped is obliterated by blaster fire.

"I think it is safe to say we have company," Kathel says a little too happily.

I switch to a private comm. "You're having way too much fun with this right now."

He laughs, "Come on, Ada, we have to find the fun in all this somewhere, right? No point in feeling miserable the whole time."

I step up to the spot and peek around the corner. "Looks like we've got six, maybe seven guys on us." I say as the wall behind me heats up with their shots. "And their aim is pretty damn good."

He checks over his blaster and reloads a fresh cartridge. "I think this might be a good time to divide and conquer."

"Flank them?" Dita asks, "If we climb up on a ship, it will also give us a height advantage they probably wouldn't have thought of."

"I like the way you think. Come on, let's go find that height advantage. You and Ada got this?" He asks Miessa.

"Yeah, we've got this." She waits until he walks away. "We have this down, right?"

I laugh, "Yeah, we just need to wait until those two get into position, then we can split the attacker's focus. So—" I pull a small stun grenade out of my bag, pull the pin, and launch it over the corner "—for right now, we need to act on the point of surprise, keep their attention over here. So, the others can get ready." The explosive goes off with a loud bang and flash of blinding white light. The enemy squad on the other side shriek in pain.

"Hey, we are nearly in position. Do you have another stunner?" Kathel asks.

"Yeah, I do," I pull it out. "You want me to draw attention and then you two rain shots?"

"Exactly."

"Tell me when." Miessa and I wait for another thirty seconds while the others get into position. I stick my head out for a second and pull back immediately.

"You are going to get pegged one of these times." Miessa scowls.

"I might, then you'll just have to fix me," I say.

She opens her mouth to respond, but Dita cuts in over comms. "Okay, we're ready. Chuck it."

"Chucking away," I reply, pulling the pin and launching it.

On the other side of the ship there is a warning shout as they recognize another stunner, but they don't know about Kath and Dita, and their screams quickly turn to anger, echoed by the sound of shots firing.

"Okay, let's go," I step out from behind the wall, quickly taking aim at the enemies. In the sims Wayne made us do, when you hit an enemy and incapacitated them, they went down and would dematerialize. These soldiers drop and scream in pain before the sound of their voices is abruptly cut off by the lack of oxygen.

"Fuck, that sounds awful," Miessa says as the last man goes down.

"What? You did the sims," Kathel asks, jumping down from the ship.

"I mean yeah, we did the sims, but I'm not completely heartless. These aren't pixels." She scoffs.

Dita and I search the bodies, looking for anything that might help us. "I have an employee ID card for the market. Must have been an employee with a few jobs. It should be closed by now—" Dita glances at the time "—yeah, it's eight o'clock. If they aren't closed yet, they will be soon. Maybe we could use this card to hole up there since we can't use the gate yet?"

We all nod and start heading back in. After the squad, we don't run into anyone else along the way; it's eerie. We slow to a walk, letting Kathel and Miessa rest a bit. "As soon as we stop, I'll give you some pain meds," I tell Miessa.

We move back through the gate into the market. I fully expect to run into another squad ready to take us out. She turns the corner and shoots off a round.

"Dita, what are you doing?" Kathel asks, gently grabbing her arm and bringing it down. "Careful, I like the enthusiasm, but you gotta watch it."

Through the tinted visor of her helmet, Dita's cheeks flush

purple. "Sorry," She mumbles quietly. "I was just really expecting there to be someone there, and then I thought I saw movement."

I jog over, "It's all good, just gotta have your brain catch up to your hands sometimes." I grin, "I am not going to lie. It was pretty damn impressive. Your reflexes are getting better. Just gotta work on making sure it is an enemy first."

She ducks her head and pulls away, a bit embarrassed. "Right, so, uh, let's get to the market before someone else comes. Okay?"

"Yeah, let's go." Miessa says impatiently, waving the key card, "We don't know if there are any limits on this thing, so be prepared—we might be asking for more trouble" We hurry after her and into the airlock. I sigh in relief when the light above the door flashes yellow then green. Taking my helmet off for a moment and relishing in the feeling of the cool air on the back of my neck. I slip it back on but don't lock it down. As much as I want to get this thing off of me, I need to have my hands free.

"We should be at the door in a minute; the key card is for stall number eighty-seven," Dita says, scanning each of the doors we walk past. "Eighty-three, eighty-five, eighty-seven! Here we are!" She says triumphantly, sliding the card into the lock. The LED light around the slot shines red, "Oh no." Dita goes to pull it out, but the card slides fully into the slot and out of her fingers. "Oh, No!" But the lights turn green, and the door swings inward. We walk in slowly, afraid of what might be on the other side.

The key card sits on the other side in a little basket. The window leading to the market is shut, a small, hooked lock keeping it closed. Soft twinkle lights ring the ceiling with rich fabrics scattered hanging off shelves. We quickly and quietly move through the store, looking in every corner to make sure we're alone. "I guess this is good. Just don't ruin any of the fabric. The vendor didn't do anything."

"Oh, I'm going to be taking this," Miessa says, grabbing a long floral sundress off a hanger. "I need to get out of this suit. And I am the only one of us who can attempt to move without being identified." She says, moving behind a curtain to change.

"Hang on, whoever said you were going out? Why do you need to go roam? We have to wait for the gate to open." Kathel says shifting the curtain.

"Well, I'm going to see if I can move up the jump. Maybe I can override the schedule?" Dita says, scrolling the schedule. "It doesn't look like it should be that difficult. There isn't much on the schedule."

"Right, and in the meantime, I can go see who's waiting for us by the gate," Miessa says, coming out from behind the curtain. With her burnt orange skin and spiky black hair, she should be able to walk among the people of Pluto unimpeded. "And we need information. It's already decided."

I put a hand up, stopping her as she heads for the door, "Hang on, we need to make a plan, and I need to check out your ankle. We have hours before the jump unless Dita moves anything up. The information you get will be shit in an hour. And when was this decided?"

"On the way back. I looked when we took the ID card."

"Were you going to fill us in?" I ask. Her eyes flash in annoyance, but she nods flopping back down onto one of the rickety folding chairs. "Fine. I just want to get back to base." She grumbles, leaning forward to undo the laces of her boot.

Kathel lays a hand on her shoulder, "Look, we all do. This is tough. But this is what we have been trained to do; we can't keep jumping to conclusions. We need to consider every step as we make it. This isn't a training mission on base. We don't have an out; we need to make one." He looks up, meeting each member of our team's eyes before saying, "No more spontaneous jumps to action, okay? Plans."

Miessa pulls her shoulder away and plops her boot on the ground. "Okay. Let's figure this out then." And we try, but we keep hitting walls. We don't know the rotation of the guards, if there's a curfew, what would be the best route, what the process is for this jump gate to travel, or if they have reported to the operators to not pass us through. Miessa props her foot up on the back of a chair. "So, we are back to square one, we need more information."

I nod. "Yeah, okay." I check her foot over, gently poking at the swelling before giving her an anti-inflammatory pain reliever.

She grins, but her voice is bitter. "Don't ya hate when I'm right?" She pulls her boot back on. She taps her earpiece, growing her hair longer, so it covers her ears.

"I will never get used to that," Dita says. "Watching the hair just appear out of your skull... too weird."

Miessa laughs, "Get used to it, baby, won't be the last time. Okay, I'm going to head out. I'll check in every fifteen minutes."

Kathel nods. "We'll set up a series of watches. That way some of us can rest, but still stay in contact with you."

"I will be back before you even know I'm gone."

Chapter 51

We divide the watch into hour-long segments. Dita takes the first watch so she can poke around in the security system. "You both have done a lot more than me. I mean, Ada, you have literally run all over the place getting our team back together. My turn to play doctor. Go to sleep."

I try to make an objection, but when Kathel agrees with her, I give in. Kathel grabs stacks of fabric off the shelves and arranges them into a makeshift bed while I change out of my suit and into my civilian clothes. While these clothes may make us stand out, the suits are even stranger, especially in this section of the colony. "Did you see a tablet or anything while you were pulling this stuff down?" I ask as he moves to change.

"No, why?" He answers from the other side of the dressing room door.

I lay down on the lumpy pile of clothes, poking, and shift around to find a comfortable position. "I just feel bad for the shop owner. I sorta want to leave a message or something, letting them know that we only took the one sundress." I say and he comes out, dropping his suit on the floor next to his bag. "I know it's sorta stupid, but it doesn't feel right just to do all this," I gesture at the mess all over the storeroom floor, "and not leave some explanation."

He lays down, folding his arms behind his head, propping his hurt leg up, relieving pressure from the site. "Nah, that makes sense. I feel bad, but I don't think there is anything we can really do. Not without compromising our position."

I hunker down deeper into the pile, curling up into a little ball. "Yeah, you are probably right." I let my eyelids drift closed. I grab my tablet and look at the timer. We have twelve hours until the gate should open for us. Dita should wake me up in about forty-five minutes.

* * *

I groan and roll over onto Kathel's arm. I jump back as he snores loudly in my ear. "Fuck," I whisper, rubbing sleep from my eyes. "Good morning to you too." I feel incredibly groggy, like a cloud has settled over my brain. *Was I that tired?* I roll to the edge of the pile and scoop up my tablet, squinting at the light, trying to make out the time as my eyes adjust. I spring wide awake and sprint out of the room, grabbing my blaster along the way to the front room.

I sweep the room, but Dita is sitting alone on her tablet, tapping away, "Oh, hey, I was going to wake you up in a few minutes. It's been quiet."

"Dits, you were supposed to wake me up four hours ago!" I say, sitting on the ground beside her. "Why didn't you wake me up?"

"I had this covered." She shrugs, not looking up from her tapping blue nails. "Besides, I didn't get very far in the first hour, and I would have probably stayed up working on it, anyway. No point in all of us being up. And," she looks up at me with a grin. "By the sound of your snoring, you really needed it."

"I don't snore!" I insist.

She laughs, loud before whispering, "Oh yeah? What do you call this then?" She taps around in her files to a video. It is a short fifteen-second clip of Kathel and I sleeping, alternating snores. "You two were going to get us caught."

I wave her away, "Nah, you just stayed up so you could edit the sound of us snoring over that clip." The real Kathel lets out a hearty snore in response.

"Anyway," Dita laughs, "I think I'm close to figuring out their system. It was behind some pretty dense firewalls. It looked easy from the outside, but I wanted to make sure I took it slow. Didn't want to set off any alarms along the way." She stops, "Hey, Mies, how's it going?"

"Wait, what happened to 'I will be back before you know it'?" I cut in.

Dita turns away from me, pressing a finger to her earpiece. "Okay, cool, I'm almost in. If this doesn't work, we'll go with Plan B."

"Hang on, what is Plan B?"

"Okay, I will talk to you soon." She turns back to me, "rude, filling comms with chatter."

"What's going on?"

She sighs, "Well, Miessa can shift, and she got really close to the gate. But they closed it. Shut it down, because of us. So," she holds up a video feed. "She came back here, and I gave her a chip that transmits data to me, kinda like what I did with the stuff in the garage, so we could track when the shift changes are. We are coming up on one in about seven minutes. If I can't get in and change the orders, we made a plan. It looks like they plan to keep the gate shut down until they find us. They shut down the whole residential district."

"Dita, what the fuck? You should have woken us up!"

"There wasn't anything you could do; it's all been recon. But now we need to move. The market district is next on their list to search. So," she taps a few things on the tablet, "If I don't get through, Miessa is going to take out a guard, get his stuff and break into security and override the lockdown. We'll need to book it."

I have ten thousand questions but just nod. "Okay, should I get Kath up? Get our stuff together?"

"Yeah, even if I don't get through, we'll need to be out of here in fifteen." She blurts, her focus back on her tablet. I watch her for a moment as she refocuses. She taps something, and the tablet gives an angry beep. "I know, I'm sorry." She whispers, biting her lip and tapping furiously, "Is that better?" It gives a happy chirp in reply.

I shake my head and turn back to the makeshift bedroom. "Kath," I say quietly, shaking his foot. "Hey, Kath, you have to wake up."

"What?" He groans, rolling over onto his stomach. He scoops the blankets closer to him and buries his head in deeper.

I shake his foot again, a little harder. "Kath, you have to wake up," He pulls his foot back, tucking it close before lashing out and rolling over again. I sit back hard as I jump away. "Okay," I grumble, crawling around to the head of the 'bed', making sure I stay well out of range. "Kath! Get up. We have to go." I say firmly.

He blinks slowly, "Whatchu say?" he mumbles, burying his head into the blankets for a moment before sitting up.

"We have to get ready to go. Dita and Miessa have a plan to get back to base. But it involves us leaving in the next few minutes. We need to get ready." I still don't think he has fully processed what I said, but he gets up and starts shoving his suit into his bag.

"What time is it?" He asks, scratching a hand through his unkempt hair.

I glance down at my tablet. "We have seven hours until the

planned jump."

He spins around, "Hang on seven hours? I was meant to be up—
"

I put a hand up, "Yeah, I know, so was I. Dita let us sleep while she figured all this out. She didn't want to wake us. I already had this conversation with her. We just need to get ready to go now."

He growls something under his breath that sounds vaguely like, "Fems never can stick to any plan," but just continues shoving things into bags.

I work on moving the supplies back into the front room. "How is it coming?" I ask, and she nods. "That good?" She nods again. I settle down by the door to wait for our techie's next move.

"Okay, here goes nothing." She stops the consistent tapping before punching a pop-up on the screen. For a moment, nothing happens. I get up and move to her shoulder, watching as the little loading bar fills with blue. "If this works, we will have twenty minutes to get to the gate before they cancel our jump. If not, Miessa has eyes on her target to swap places with."

"You say swap places like the other person has a choice in the matter." Kathel yawns, dropping his bags by the door.

"Shit." An error message flashes across the screen, and Dita quickly moves to shut down her tablet. "Mies, I didn't get in. Shutting down my tablet so it will take longer to track back the IP. It's all you now." She looks up at Kathel and me, "You two ready to run? Once she gets in, we won't have long to get there. We're figuring on ten, maybe fifteen minutes."

"Should we start moving now then?" I ask, strapping my bags onto my body.

"Probably." She swings a bag over her shoulder. "Just play it cool. We are just a few travelers. We don't know the rules. We don't know there is a curfew. And we definitely aren't going for the jump gates if anyone asks. We just learned they shut the residential district down and have been looking for a place to stay." We nod and follow her to the door, scooping up bags as we go. "I feel bad. They're probably going to trace the signal back to here." She says a hand on the door. "I hope if we didn't take out the actual owner of this shop when we were in the garage and this guy has a good alibi."

"Hey, guys, this is your fancy new captain speaking," Miessa says through the comms. "I'm on my way to the security hut now. I made sure to, uh, say 'goodnight' to my partner there for the night. I should have us up and running in no time. You on the way?"

"Yes, ma'am," Dita says, hand on the door. "We'll see you soon."

We take off at a quick jog, the sound of zippers jingling and bags thumping against our backs echoing in the empty atrium. "It should take us about ten minutes to get there at this pace as long as no one else shows up," I say, looking at the info on my tablet.

"When I checked, it looked like they were in the northeast sector.

So as long as we keep moving in this direction, and there isn't another group, we should be good." Dita says.

"So, what exactly is happening right now? No one has explained it to me." Kathel says, keeping stride with me.

Dita swerves around a pile of boxes. "Right, so I tried to hack into the security software around the jump gates to either move our scheduled jump up so we could get out of here sooner, or remotely open the gate and program a new one. It took a few hours since I didn't want to set off any alarms. That plan didn't work; I couldn't break through. I almost did, but not quite." She affirms.

"I'm sure if we weren't on a time crunch, you could have gotten through," I say.

She beams. "Yes, well, we will have to wait until the next mission to know for sure—anyway. Miessa did a bunch of scouting in the area and figured out their rotation schedule and all that and where the security station is. We figured if I couldn't get in, she could, then she can open the gate from there and get us through. It's right there, so she won't need to go far. Then we can all jump through the gate."

He nods along. "Okay, yeah, that should work."

A scratch of static makes us all jump, "Hey, guys?"

"Yeah, Miessa, what is up?" I wince.

I wince as I hear a slight clatter in the background, thud and then she comes back. "I fucked up. I shifted again. In front of the other guards. So, if you can, you should pick up the pace. Security just flooded in here. They are trying to shut it down."

"Wait, you already opened it?" Dita takes off at a sprint, "We are still at least seven minutes out."

"Well," Another clatter and thud. "You better hurry the fuck up cause this gate is closing whether we want it to or not in less than five. I saw an opening, and I took it. It was before the head honcho came in, who is currently stunned. So, hurry up."

"Fucking hell," Kathel grunts, pulling out his blaster and taking off.

We don't talk for the next few minutes. We just run; at some point, we sprint around a corner directly into a crowd of citizens.

"Shit, guess it's morning," I say, jumping around a small child. The mother shouts something at me, but I don't take the time to apologize.

"Company incoming at seven o'clock," Dita says before darting straight through the center of the crowd using it for cover. There are screams as people get bumped into or see our blasters, but we don't stop. Kathel shoulders someone, sending them sprawling across the floor.

"Three minutes!" Miessa shouts over comms. "Come on, guys, I can't keep this thing open that much longer."

"We are around the corner, meet us there. Get out of there." I pant as the first of the shots rains down on us. "Shit, they would really shoot with civvies around?" I don't know who it is that is chasing us, maybe they are members of the Federation, or maybe just some crazy guards from this colony, but their shots are wild. Everyone on this street runs around like crazy, screaming, crying, and diving to the ground.

"Come on!" Kathel says, slipping down a side alley. Somehow, we move through unnoticed, leaving the screams of the scared Plutonians behind us.

"I can't believe they would just start shooting like that!" Dita pants. "They must be crazy."

"Forget them!" I cry triumphantly, "There's Miessa! And the gate!"

I stop, Kathel has lagged behind, limping. "Go!" He shouts as I turn. "Ada, go, I am right behind you!"

Dita takes off for the terminal next to the gate, "I'm closing it, get through in the next thirty, let's move!" I turn back and move to Kathel's side, slipping an arm around his waist.

"I told you to go!" He grunts even as he leans into me and starts hopping faster.

A shot of bright green blaster fire lances past us, "Yeah, and they're right there, so move your ass."

Miessa comes flying out of the guardhouse. "Thank the expanse, let's go!" She grabs Dita's hand and yanks her away from the console. "It should close behind us; you shouldn't need to program it." A second later, the console erupts in flames as at least three shots hit it.

Shots rain down around us as Kathel and I jump through, Dita and Miessa three steps behind us.

Chapter 52

Kathel and I stumble through the jump gate, falling to the floor.
We made it. I roll over onto my back, fighting to catch my breath.
Sims can't prepare you for the turbulence of a closing gate.

Kathel groans a bit as he climbs to his feet and blows out his
cheeks. "Fuck, that was close." He says, helping me to my feet.
"Miessa and Dita were right behind us, right? They should come
through in a second; we should get out of the way."

He walks down the ramp, heavily favoring his leg. "You need to
get to the med center." I insist.

He waves me off. "I'm fine, we have to go do the debrief."

Miessa and Dita stumble through, arms linked. I catch Miessa
right as she falls. "I've got you, we made it."

She looks down, breathing heavily. I wait until she feels steady
to let go. She nods and stands up, pulling her helmet off, her short
black hair sticking to her face. "That was ridiculous." She shifts, on

purpose this time, returning to her soft lilac skin.

An officer stands at the end of the ramp, waiting for us all to get our bearings. "It seemed like you had an interesting ride back." He stands tall, hands behind his back. "And you are three hours before your scheduled jump."

"Yes, Sir. We had a change of plan, but it is good to be back." I say as we exit the ramp.

He nods, "We will hold your debriefing in the same room as before. Afterward, go back to your rooms and get cleaned up. As of now you have," he looks at his tablet, "Thirty hours left in your mission. You have that long to rest before the gathering. Please report to the Hall once the timer runs out."

"So, we have free time until that meeting?" Kathel asks. He tries to stand up straight but has to lean sideways to balance. Miessa, being the next tallest member of the team, slides under his arm to support him.

The officer nods. "Once you have completed your debrief, you may do what you wish with the time remaining."

We all give the officer a salute and move to the hall. "We better get this debrief done fast," Kathel says through clenched teeth.

"Kath, you don't need to go to the debrief. We can take care of it," I say. "Miessa, take him to the med center."

Kathel comes to a painful shuffling stop. "You know as well as I do that isn't really an option. The only thing that would allow my absence would be if I were dead, and last I checked..." He puts a finger to his throat, looking for a pulse—in the wrong place, I might add. "Yeah, no, I am not dead." He says before beginning to walk again.

"He sure is grumpy when he's in pain, isn't he?" Dita says.

Kathel gives her the bird.

It takes us roughly another fifteen minutes to get there. Kathel stops to get a drink at one point, his face coated in a sheen of sweat. "Don't, just don't," he says when I notice. "It won't do anything. As soon as we are done, I will go." He promises.

The person doing our debrief is the same that gave us the mission. "Ah, team Arctic, I trust your mission went well?" She says, noting Kathel's pale, clammy skin. "I won't keep you long. Just explain to me what happened." So, we do, leaving out the bits about calling Tortie because who knows how that would go over. But everything else seemed to go over well until we got to our escape from Nix. "Were you able to confirm whether or not it was actually Blaithine?"

My team looks at each other. "No, Ma'am," Miessa admits. "We were only able to see her from a distance. However, we were not able to approach and confirm. While we were not able to make that ultimate confirmation, we are more than certain it was her."

"Right." The officer makes a note, and my stomach tightens. Part of me wants to be sure it won't affect us. This mission was meant to be difficult; there had to be people that didn't find their contact at all. "What sort of damage did you cause, if any?"

Dita reiterates that several ships were destroyed as we escaped and that individuals were hurt on Pluto. And of course, the broken jump gate. "Ma'am, was the location on Nix a confirmed base?" She asks.

The woman doesn't even look up. "That information is classified."

"Classified?" Kathel repeats.

"Yes, classified. Was your hearing damaged on your mission Agent Torrac?"

"No, Ma'am."

"Good. You and your team are dismissed."

"You don't have any other questions? On how we got back or what happened?" Dita asks, gesturing to Kathel.

"Your mission was to find and identify two targets. You found who you believe to be one of those targets, and you potentially damaged members of their team. Thus, a portion of your mission has been completed. Congrats." She says dryly. "You are dismissed."

Kathel quickly pushes away from the chair, taking advantage of the brief conversation. "Thank you, ma'am."

We salute the officer before heading for the door and splitting in the hall. Kathel stumbles a bit, but Miessa catches him. "We will see you two back in the room." She calls over her shoulder I watch the two of them as they slowly shuffle down the hall. She looks better, the limp less pronounced, but she still needs to get her ankle checked. Kathel looks like he is getting worse by the second.

When they are partway down the hall, I hear him say to Miessa, "If I pass out, you make them force-feed me enough pain meds for this entire squad." She tells him to shut up.

"Come on, let's get to the room. He'll be okay." Dita says, gently tugging on my elbow. Her tentacles are limp with exhaustion; not a single one gives more than a feeble wiggle every so often.

When we get back to our room, we find it to be clean. Too clean. "Someone searched our rooms," I say dryly. I can't be mad. I don't have the energy. We knew there was always a chance for our rooms to be searched. Heck, they probably searched our stuff when they moved us after the first test.

"They weren't going to find anything. Especially with us all needing to take our tablets with us on the test." Dita says, heading to the kitchen for a drink.

I sink down onto the couch. "You really think that would stop them? They will use any information they can. Whether we think it would be of any use to them."

Dita groans, rolling her head slowly around, her neck popping. "I am going to go take a shower. Do you think they are doing meals like normal?"

"I would assume as much. Unless they sent every single person off of the base, they still have to serve someone."

"That's true." She gets up and heads to her room.

I told myself I would not spend my downtime wallowing in self-pity. But it took approximately thirty seconds for me to get there. I reread Sarkus' messages. I found myself going line by line, searching for when he could have told me he was in danger. I tried to read between the lines. To see when he lived in an abandoned home, where he worried about the fact that he missed so much school. But I couldn't find it. I tried to find the lies, but it was my brother's voice. I don't know if that made it better or worse. *I failed him so hard.*

* * *

I jump when I hear the door slide open. I blink a few times trying to place my surroundings as I wake up. "What the—" I grunt as a bag is flung over the side of the couch and lands on my chest.

"Oh shit, sorry, Ada. Why didn't you go to sleep in your room?" Miessa says, quickly pulling the bag off of me.

"I was trying to stay up. How is your ankle? How is Kath?" I ask blearily before sitting up, rubbing my eyes. It takes a second for my eyes to focus, but when they do, I can't help it I gasp. They have cut away the leg of his jeans, revealing the skin directly under his butt.

"It's a new style, okay." He says, limping to his room

unsupported.

"At least you're walking better," I say, eyeing the bandages.

"You are doing it again." He says, turning at the door.

"Doing what?" I ask, crossing my arms. "I'm your medic. What could I possibly be doing wrong?"

He grins wickedly and winks. "How does my ass look?"

He escapes into his room before the pillow I launch at him can hit him. "You are the one with the terribly placed hit."

"Is it terrible or perfect?" Miessa laughs. "He will be set for a bit. Doc gave him some pain meds to knock him out for a few hours. And they gave him a few injections at the site. Said he should be good by the time we gather for the meeting. He just had extreme muscle fatigue because it's healing. Doc said you were doing a great job keeping it clean and stuff in the Field."

"Okay, cool." I have a moment of pride thinking back to when I told him on the ship. *I knew what it was! I gave a correct diagnosis!* It's cool to be right, but it also makes me wonder how much longer he has to heal. "Anything that I need to do?"

She pinches her nose. "Go shower. While he might have a cute ass, you are a smelly ass."

To my satisfaction, the pillow I throw hits her square in the face.

Chapter 53

The next thirty hours fly by way too fast. Time usually feels like a drag, but when you get to sleep and just relax, of course, it goes by too fast.

"I kinda wish they gave us more than two suits," Kathel says, trying to stretch out the fabric. "You know, rather than replacing one every time we ruin it."

"That sounds like a you problem, Kathel. We haven't needed a new one." Dita says over her seaweed smoothie.

"In other news," Miessa says, fixing her hair. Today she has gone for blue skin a few shades lighter than Dita and long pin-straight black hair. "What do you think this gathering is actually going to be?"

I look up from my tablet, where I may have been rereading my last message to Sarkus for the tenth time in the last two days. "Oh, isn't it obvious? I thought we're ranking up."

"I mean, that is what I thought too, but do you think they would make it that obvious?" She asks, 'accidentally' flicking me with the end of her hair when she turns away from the mirror.

"I mean, what else could it be?" Dita asks, "Unless they are putting off graduations? Everyone knows that graduation from the program is meant to be right after the second test. I feel like unless something happened with the Federation while we were gone?"

We nod, thinking back to our mission. It was intense, and two members of our squad were hurt, but we didn't really face our target. We didn't even see one of them, and we weren't able to confirm if the person we had seen *was* our target. We had heard bits and pieces from the squads that had returned over meals that we all had the same sort of mission. Find one or two targets and determine their location. Some teams had come back in much rougher shape. Jungle team had to carry their tech through the gate. Last we heard, they were in emergency surgery. I look in the mirror again, fixing the badge on my arm.

A quiet tone runs through the speaker system in our room. "Good morning, agents. Please make your way to the hall in ten minutes." The tone plays again, and we all look at each other, letting the excitement and tension hang in the air for a moment.

"Let's go," Miessa says.

* * *

It was weird walking through the halls, knowing now might be the moment we graduate the program. This is what we had been working toward for months now. But for it to finally be here, feels almost anticlimactic. I don't know how to feel. I'm proud of myself for getting this far, especially since so many people on Earth were convinced that I wouldn't make it. *Take that Jaxon.* But my eyes burn a bit too. I wish I could talk to my parents to see what they would say about it. And Sarkus... what am I supposed to do about him? The Garrison had all but cut me off from the people that would help me find him. What would he do if he contacted me and I never answered?

One of the unexplained things within the spec ops program of the Garrison is what happens after graduation. We know we will go on missions and do tasks for the Garrison. We ninety percent of the time we will stay amongst the units that were created, but sometimes teams will be broken up and reconfigured. I look at my team and know I don't want to work with anyone else. I need this team by my side.

"You okay, Ada?" Dita asks.

I shake my head and try to clear my face of any emotion before giving her an encouraging smile. It feels like more of a grimace. "Yeah, I'm okay. Just thinking is all."

"Oh, no, don't do too much of that. You might fry whatever circuits are still firing in there." Kathel says, lightly punching my shoulder.

I am about to spit back a retort when I notice the other soldiers around us. They are all a higher rank than us, some officers, and not a single one talks, or is out of formation in any way. "Oh shit, okay, serious face," I whisper as we fall into line behind them. They are stoic, walking in perfectly straight lines, and all in sync. We see the other squads in our class and give little motions of acknowledgment. A smile here, a nod there. We made it. I try to keep my head up, to take it all in, to focus on the feeling of pride that is making me feel queasy and nervous at the same time. The room is silent; there isn't even the sound of boots squeaking on the too-clean floor.

"This isn't how I thought it would be," Dita whispers.

"Me either. Look," Miessa nudges her chin toward the front of the room.

Commander Eugenia Carver is up on her platform again, and again she doesn't wear anything that looks like a Garrison uniform. Her yellow eyes dance across us as we file into rows. "Will my newest spec ops class please make their way to the front?" We do as instructed, weaving in between the rigid soldiers. When we are at the front, we stand in a line, though each squad stands a little off of the next.

"Something isn't right," Kathel murmurs out of the corner of his mouth.

I glance at him then back front. The last thing I need is for an officer to spot us talking while at attention at our own graduation. "What do you mean?"

Out of the corner of my eye, I see him incline his head slightly. "Look at Wayne."

I let my eyes drift slowly down the line of officers until I see Sergeant Wayne. I almost didn't recognize him at first. "You're right." Wayne is a Garrison Male through and through. But he always had little things about him that were different. He always styled his hair a certain way. Wayne, through all of our training, had a massive beard, one he could put into a little braid. One that the Males in my class were jealous about because they couldn't grow their facial hair that long—some of them couldn't have even if they wanted to—but now Wayne is cleanly shaven, something he always said he wouldn't do, and his hair is combed back. "I mean, maybe he just wanted a change of style?"

"No, look at how he is standing." Wayne has made us stand at attention and mimic him time and time again, but this stance is different. It's like every single joint in his body has been tightened and fused together so they will never move again.

Carver moves forward and smiles down on the row of twelve teams. "Welcome back, agents. You have been working so hard the past few months. I know I speak for all of us here when I say that we are so proud of you." She grips the edges of her podium, leaning down to look over us. "You all completed your tests with ease and gathered valuable information. Information that will help us stop our most fierce enemy. One that has all but been forbidden to mention. Well, I mention them now. The Federation. A group of my former students. Who betrayed me, and everything this organization stands for? They cast it away like it was absolutely nothing." She sneers, and the formerly frozen statues of soldiers jeer in response, making me jump in surprise.

Kathel uses the change to step closer, grabbing my wrist, "whatever you do, don't bring attention to yourself." I glance at Dita and Miessa, and they nod. We look ahead, trying to match the demeanor of the soldiers behind us. Kathel squeezes my wrist lightly before letting go.

"This new class of agents are some of the finest soldiers I have ever met. You are to be commended. We made your testing more difficult than any of the classes before. And you took it in stride. You have proved that you are the strongest and most prepared. You will be the ones that will bring our power across the galaxy, redefining our strength and dominance."

My palms grow clammy as I listen. While as a squad we joked around about how crazy Carver has seemed, and how her rise didn't make sense, I never honestly thought it was real. I thought we were exaggerating. That there was no way that this Fem could be in this high of a position of power, in control of an entire class of recruits, and the whole station, and have this mentality.

I turn to look at Dita, my friend, who has helped to open my eyes and help me understand all the differences across the galaxy, but she looks just ask scared as I feel. Her skin, usually a deep navy blue, is flushed deep indigo, and her tentacles have pulled tight against her head in nubby little spiral knots. "We have to get out of here." She breathes.

Miessa looks just as confused and hurt. "We can't—what do we..." She trails off as Carver shouts something that gains the attention and the cheers of everyone in the room. "This isn't why I joined spec ops."

Kathel watches the other teams. The teams from different stations don't just look mad, or confused, or hurt. They look absolutely livid. Team Nebula looks like they are ready to fight anyone that looks at them. "So, this is what graduation is like?" Kathel says ruefully. "Didn't realize I was joining a militaristic tyranny."

"Now," Carver says, "we will begin the pinning process. Sergeant Wayne." Wayne stands up and moves, and I notice the badge on his arm is different, a new design. "The Sergeant will place the first badge, then each team member will place it on the next, and we will go down the row," Carver gestures down the line until she stops at our team. "Let's begin with Jungle."

At the far end of the line, I watch as the agents of team Jungle stand taller. Wayne approaches with a box, which I assume contains every patch. He hands it to the team member at the end, Agent Odyssa, before selecting one of the badges. Wayne slides it into the patch on her arm. And as she steps up to give the patch to her teammate, it's like she becomes a whole different person. Her usually fluid movements grow stiff and calculated. I watch in growing horror as each member of team Jungle goes through this transformation. Next in line is Desert team. I watch as Edonne is given his new patch, hoping by some miracle it's a fluke. But it happens to them, too.

Kathel turns to me, his eyes serious. "Don't lock it in."

"What?" I whisper back, watching over his shoulder as the line between him and the badges grows shorter and shorter.

"Don't lock in the badge for Dita. Don't press it in all the way." He turns. We are one team away. "You three will have a chance."

"Kath, what the fuck are you talking about?" I hiss.

He turns and takes the box from the member of Nebula as they remove a badge. And it's then I understand, the badge. He thinks the badge is doing it. Kathel stands at attention, his face resolute. Accepting what will happen. The click of the badge locking into place is the loudest thing in the room. The sound of it echoes. He turns to me and quickly passes me the box and takes my arm. He pulls out a badge and presses in the corner. "Trust me." He meets my eyes, and I have to blink away tears. His hand over my arm is firm but gentle. And as he steps back, whatever the fuck Carver has programmed into these badges takes hold. He grows tight, his gaze distant.

I pass the box to Dita and pull the badge out, mimicking the way Kathel laid it over my suit, but don't press it all the way into place. "Don't lock the badge in," I whisper, my lips barely moving.

Dita's eyes lock with me, and her shoulders relax slightly when she sees that I have not changed. She looks past me at Kathel, but I shake my head. She nods and steps to bestow the worst sort of present on to Miessa.

Once I step back into line, I lock my gaze straight ahead and stand as tall as I can, forcing myself not to look at Kathel.

My teammate is now my enemy.

Chapter 54

Miessa waits with the empty box in hand until Wayne takes it from her. She falls back into line beside us. A trickle of sweat drips down my forehead and hangs on my eyebrow for a moment. It drops, hitting the top of my cheek. The movement is small, but it tickles, and it takes a surprising amount of focus not to move and whisk it away.

"Congratulations to every agent. You have truly earned your place in our ranks. Let's give everyone here a round of applause." She says, raising her hands above her head. The reply is a cacophony of noise. I wait to see what the others do. When those of us who were freshly pinned, don't move, neither do I.

"No, we cannot delay. We must immediately make ready. Please proceed to level seven, where you will find tasks waiting for you. For we must work. Until all the stars are found! And every one of our enemies is destroyed!"

Another explosive cheer goes up, the noise reverberating so loud my head pounds. When the sound eventually dies down, the rear line of personnel goes first. Each line does an about-face before folding into two lines leading down the halls. With Miessa, Dita, and I being the last in the line on the right, we can watch every single person in front of us, using them as a guide to mimic. However, it leaves us exposed to Commander Carver as we go. *Don't look at me. Don't look at me. Don't look at me.* I stare hard at the center of Kathel's back, using my peripheral careful to step where he does.

It is one of the fastest and yet longest walks through the halls of the station I have ever taken. The pace makes it fast, and I have to make myself take longer strides than I usually would to keep up with Kathel, surrounded by others to our left that have also been converted. I am afraid that any movement will turn these robotic zombie people against me.

Level seven is a storage level, but it quickly becomes apparent that whatever moves the Garrison will make will be big and fast. We are moved into the storage unit, then divided again. I lose my team. We pass supplies out of the storage bay down the hall to one of the elevator shafts where they are loaded, and an officer rides down with a few individuals to unload it.

I move down the elevator with the third cohort and feel my already tense stomach clench even tighter when I realize we have arrived on the jump gate level. I keep my head down as I work, only ever looking up when I lift a box onto a pile. I can't see where the jump gate has been programmed yet. The agents that have been zombified move at a breakneck pace. Apparently, the ridiculous training we had gone through was for this, so we could move quickly and efficiently without any question of stamina. *Why go through all the trouble of training the different classes?* I try to understand what is going on and why, but there are too many pieces missing in this puzzle.

This goes on for at least two hours—I ride down the elevator another three times.

Eventually, a message must be passed through for all the soldiers to stop what they are doing, drop whatever they are holding, and head back up to the residential levels.

I hesitate for the briefest of moments before following Kathel into our rooms. *We won't be safe here with him.* He walks around the kitchen, grabbing a few bits of salted meat before he goes into his room. Dita and Miessa follow me in.

I wait until the door slides shut behind Kathel before turning to them. "I say go to our rooms. Meet in mine in ten minutes?" They nod and head to their respective rooms. Once my own door slides shut behind me, I relax slightly, before I tear the small space apart looking for anything out of place, any sign that they were here, that they bugged my room. Once I am as sure as I can be that the room is clear, I quickly put it back together.

A very light tap at the door tells me that the girls are on the other side. They slide in quickly, and I activate the lock behind them.

The three of us stare at each other for a moment in silence. What can you really say in a moment like this?

I open my mouth to say something, just to fill the void, when Dita's face lights up, and she puts a hand up. She pulls the badge from her arm, flipping it over. Miessa and I watch in silence for a few minutes while she examines it. I stay close to the door, listening, a small part of me afraid that some sort of alarm was set off when she removed it. After a few minutes, with no sign of any authority coming down on us, Dita puts a hand out, pointing at our badges and her palm. I gladly remove the piece of tech and pass it to her.

She takes the three badges and into the living room when she comes back in, she lets out a deep sigh. "I hid them in the couch. I hope that thing doesn't have a good microphone."

"What the literal fuck is going on?" Miessa snaps, making herself at home on my bed. "What the actual fuck?"

"Keep your voice down," I shush her. "Remember, Kath is our enemy right now."

"I hate this. Is this another test?" Dita asks, "I mean I know it isn't, but I mean, why? Why now?" Her tentacles quivering at the end.

I shake my head. "I don't know. I don't even know if I want to know." I stare at the place where my badge should sit on my sleeve.

"I didn't realize that stupid badge would make me feel like this."

Miessa wraps her tail around her knees. "Right? It feels… I don't know what it feels like."

Dita sits down next to her and leans forward, her head in her hands. She stays there for a minute before coming up. "I think the new badges did something to our tracking chip. The tech isn't the same, like the way that those are programmed, it didn't happen with our old badges. It has some of the same connections, but others don't make sense. It is just an idea; I can't tell for sure unless I run some sort of test on it. And I don't want to do that."

"No!" Miessa and I say a little too loudly. The sound echoes in the small space, and both of us flinch.

"Don't worry. That is why I put it out there. I don't want to touch them." Dita explains, holding up her hands as if to ward off an attack. "You know as well as I do it would be a bad idea. I don't want this being brought down on us any more than you do. We are the last ones left." The last sentence is the final straw I can take.

I clench my hand into a tight fist and punch the bed. The girls jump away but say nothing, even as I walk circles around the space, cursing the thin mattress and shaking out my hand. "We can't be the only ones left. Someone else had to pick up on this. We can't stop this by ourselves." I stop, "And there is no fucking way Carver did this on her own, right? Did any of the other officers look like themselves?"

Dita shakes her head, her tentacles still in nervous knots that refuse to swing. "Not that I saw. Maybe it's an order from the Martian Colony?"

"I doubt it." Miessa says. "Though who the fuck knows at this point. I didn't exactly expect any of this. But I agree with you Ada, I don't understand how she could have gotten away with some scheme this large without support. I mean, it isn't like she programmed each individual badge for every single person on this base. There had to be some techies who were involved in this, right?"

"Maybe not?" We turn to as Dita gasps

"Maybe not? What do you mean, maybe not?" I ask, sitting down on the floor in front of her.

She wrings her hands, "I mean, I—" she glances up at Miessa then me. "Occasionally in lessons we had to code different things. We weren't always told what we were coding, and we had to make sure it was done perfectly. What if some of those exercises were for this in some way?"

"I want to say there is no fucking way," Miessa says.

"But honestly? Now? Who knows?" We sit in silence again. And I don't know if the time should be considered processing or just confusion or what. "So, what should we do now?"

Miessa leans back. "I guess just keep going? Fake it as long as we can? See what we can learn? Maybe we can find a way out from there."

We nod. "Just be careful. No matter what you do. Don't do anything out of line."

* * *

The next two days go the same way. We follow orders we can't hear and move from location to location, trying to learn whatever we can without bringing attention to ourselves. It is surprisingly lonely. We aren't able to talk the next day. For whatever reason converted Kathel, took it upon himself to park himself in the middle of the room, leaving us with no other option but to go to our rooms.

At dinner, I saw Dita; she looked absolutely exhausted, worn through and ready for bed. I figured I probably looked the same. Back in the room that night, Kathel paced like a tiger in a cage. His sight was still unfocused, and he sort of bumped into things from time to time. It was like watching a remote-control car piloted by a child who didn't understand the mechanics of it yet. Dita, Miessa, and I weren't sure what to do, so we mimicked him, walking laps around the room until the arches of my feet ached, and I wanted nothing more than to fall into bed. Eventually, the programing must have sorted itself back out because he slunk back into his room and to bed.

"That was so weird," I whisper as we go to our rooms. "You guys okay today? See anything?"

"I am so tired, I wish I knew what this is all for," Dita says around a massive yawn.

Miessa nods, "Same. Nothing really stood out to me, except that. I wonder if they all had that malfunction?"

Dita shakes her head, "I don't know, but we should get to bed. I don't want them to catch us."

The next day is a carbon copy, minus my breakfast slip up. I pack munitions and medical supplies, and right before lights out, we walk at least twenty laps of our room, bumping into the couch or table every few steps.

I catch Dita's eye at one point, and she smiles. I try to catch her attention again, to ask what she had noticed, but she keeps her head down, her fingers tapping on her leg like she is trying to calculate something. When the cycle is complete, and the robotic Kathel goes to bed, I grab her. "What did you figure out?"

Her eyes gleam, "I thought I saw it last night, but it's a pattern. The way he walked across the floor; it was the same every time. Whatever malfunction is happening is specific. It isn't generating random outputs. So, either someone else is hacking the code somehow, or there is an error built into the programming that is causing them to malfunction that way."

Miessa nods and turns to me. "Do you think it could be damaging in any way?"

I freeze at that, "honestly, I have no idea. I hope not. But I guess anything is possible. If the patch is signaling the chips in our arms then I would assume it is some sort of electronic signal, something that also works at the same frequency as brain waves?" I trail off, trying to piece together how the tech and the medical knowledge would work together. "I have no idea. This is out of my depth."

Miessa nods. "No, I think you're right, that probably is how it works. So, if we disrupt the signal, we should get people back?"

"So, we need to figure out either how to disrupt the signal, or what is causing the malfunction and amplify it?" Dita asks, but like each of our thoughts, it is more of a hypothetical question than anything sure or concrete.

"Tomorrow we work on figuring that out." I say.

Chapter 55

I walk in a loop around Kathel, watching his face, but nothing changes. His eyes remain out of focus. "I have an idea. A sort of plan," I say as Kathel bumps into a couch for the third night in a row. "It might be really dumb," I say, stepping away from him. I stop moving and press my back to the wall, waiting to see if he reacts.

"What are you doing?" Dita asks loosely following the course Kathel takes.

"I'm testing my luck," I say, moving with confidence toward the door. "I want to see if there's any reaction from him or any of the others." I stand in front of the door, waiting.

Miessa stops walking and moves to her bedroom door. "Maybe it's the malfunction? Or maybe they wouldn't have reacted anyway, and we have just been paranoid the whole time.

"That's what I want to test," I say, tapping the door, "I have twenty more minutes until the malfunction is over, right?" I ask Dita. She nods. "Okay, then I'll see you in about twenty minutes. If I take longer getting back, I'll come to your rooms to let you know I am okay. Don't follow me. We don't need all of us to be turned."

Dita jumps forward, freezing as Kathel passes between us, but he doesn't react to the sudden movement. "Are you sure you don't want someone else to come with you?"

I nod, "I would rather it just be me. If something goes wrong, I don't want you two to get caught up in it too."

"Please be safe. And don't take too long." Dita whispers, I squeeze her hand before moving into the hall.

I don't really know what my plan was; I didn't make one, but there was no way that I was going to sit in that room and pace around like a fake little soldier anymore. If our idea of a malfunction was correct, and during that time any or all of the teams affected won't react, that would mean I could walk into any team room without having to worry about any consequences. It is absolutely ridiculous. Stupid, even. But I did it.

Desert had the set of rooms next to ours. I hit the button to get in, but nothing happened. I tried again, then realized that all the rooms are keyed in with our biometric reading. Our handprints. We never had anyone over, so it never came up. *Probably yet another one of Carver's plans. Keep us all divided so we wouldn't turn to each other for help when shit hit the fan.* I move away from the door.

The last thing I need is for some officers to get deprogramed and come looking for the agent who was messing with the bio scanners. Which come to think of it, they should be able to peg directly on me. I pick up the pace, wanting to put as much space as I can between myself and that door.

I freeze when I spot two figures in the distance. They are walking away from me, their gait much too relaxed to be any of the controlled soldiers, but they aren't any officers or soldiers I recognize. *Did someone else not get taken?* But as I get closer, I realize that there is no way that these are Garrison soldiers. The only soldiers in the Garrison that currently wear white are the members of my squad, Team Arctic. We only ever wear our suits when we are going on missions or have a test. I know for a fact my teammates are in my room. I would have seen them leave. And they wouldn't be wearing our suits, it would make us stand out too much. The only people that know about the white suits are members of the Garrison or... *Nix.* We wore them under are civilian clothes on Nix.

I duck out of sight around a corner as they turn toward me. *I have to be crazy.* I take a few slow breaths. But what are two Federation soldiers doing here? How did they get on? Are they the reason for the malfunction? Did they do it on purpose? Did they know about Carver's plan? I peek around the corner, and they are gone. *I have to have gone bat shit crazy.* I move down the hall, hoping to follow the two figures.

I check the hall again, and no one is there. *Where could they have gone?* I move past a door and freeze, slowly bringing my hands up. "Okay, you've got me," I whisper, glancing to either side at the two alcoves they hide in flaking me.

White fabric shrouds their faces. "Go in there." The larger of the two says, pointing his blaster first at me, then at the door behind me. I nod and keep my hands up, doing as they say.

It is an empty classroom, much like the one I hid in during my test when I climbed through the air ducts. I lean against the desk, taking in my two enemies. The suits are pretty good mock-ups of the ones my team wears, they even got the missing badge placement right, though it is on the wrong arm. "Nice try," I point at their suits. "You got a few things off, though," I say, gesturing at the location of the badge on my arm to theirs.

The smaller of the two unclips the front of her shroud, revealing a face that I recognize. "Well, we didn't exactly have a lot of time to examine your suit now, did we?"

I start at her face, my voice taking a second to catch up with my brain, "Shireen? How did you get here? You work on Nix."

She laughs, tucking the end of the shroud under the rest of her headscarf. "The same way you did, though I have to admit I think I did it with a little less of a bang, shall we say? I didn't cause the destruction of a jump gate."

"What?" But then I realize she must be referencing all the guards that had been shooting at the gate when we left, like those that hit the console to program the gate. "Look, we just wanted to get out of there. Your people called ahead to let them know we were coming."

She crosses her arms. "I think that was deserved after you shot down multiple vehicles during your 'escape'."

The way she puts escape in quotes infuriates me. "And what would you have us do? Go willingly with you? Be your prisoner of war?"

She shrugs, "I don't know, it might have been a better gig. Or is the entire of the Garrison fleet usually mindless? Honestly, we've been looking for a way to get in for months now, and this," she gestures vaguely at this station as a whole. "Made it exceedingly easy. Who's bright idea was this?" I don't answer that. I don't know what is going on with the Garrison, but this Fem just practically admitted she's a Federation Operative. "Really? Now you want to be tightlipped?" She sighs, "I thought you were smarter than this."

"What is that supposed to mean?" I snap. I don't want to, but she is suddenly so much more pretentious than she was when I spoke to her the first time on Nix. I know it's probably a ploy and I hate it. Because it works.

"Well, I mean, you seemed a lot more confident when you were on whatever little recon trip they sent you on. But coming here and seeing what state they are in, that isn't surprising. It isn't shocking as a whole. Eugenia Carver is crazy and controlling and will do whatever she can to stop anyone who opposes her. Apparently, to the point where she will turn all her soldiers into mindless things." She watches me for a moment, and I don't know what she is looking for, but she must see something. "Are you the only one she didn't turn?"

I consider it for a second. If I was found speaking to these two, I would be instantly court-martialed and probably sent to die in the vacuum of space. But who knows, that might've happened anyway if I had been caught since I wasn't 'turned', as Shireen put it. "No, I'm not. Two others made it from my team. One did not. We don't know of any others."

The Male nods. "How did it happen?"

I have nothing else to lose, so I tell them. They both nod along, and at one point, I pass over the badge I still wear, only partially pressed into its slot. The Male, who I learn is named Suilius, examines it, but he doesn't make any comments on it before passing it back. "I'm sorry that happened to you and your team."

I shrug. I don't know what to say to it. "So, question for you."

Shireen and Suilius share a look before nodding. "What?" He asks.

"Are you the cause of the malfunction?"

He grins, "Nice, ain't it? When we figured out something was going on, we took a closer look at your security cams. We got those a few months ago."

So, Dita was right!

"We could see what was going on. The first few nights were a test. Tonight, it will last longer, so we can get in and out." He says proudly, "I can control them all from right here. And I can tell you for a fact the bitch upstairs is throwing a *fit* and has no idea what is going on." He holds out what looks like a remote control.

"Can you deprogram individuals?" I ask, wondering if there could be some hope of getting Kathel back. "We had wondered if removing the badge would be all it would take but haven't been able to get close enough to test out the theory."

Suilius shakes his head. "No, it is all or nothing. We didn't have the time to do that sort of programming. We have good people. But not that good. We could do it on our base, but that is too risky."

"Right," I say, nodding.

"What's your actual name?" Shireen asks, "You know my name, and I promise that's my actual name. But I don't think you gave me yours on Nix."

"It was a cover. My name is Ada."

"Ada," she says, nodding, "Much better fit for you. Ada, I want to make an offer to you, and I want you to know I don't make it lightly. I know what would be at stake for you and your team. I've been in your shoes before."

"Shireen, you can't be serious," Suilius says.

She nods, "I am. We've seen firsthand what she can do." She

494

turns back to me. "Do you want to leave with us? We can get you and your team to safety."

Suilius pulls her to the side. "I don't think you realize what you are getting yourself into." He hisses.

She pulls away and gives him a look that says she's the one in charge he, and he needs to find his place. She turns back to me, and her gaze softens slightly. "What do you say, Ada?"

"I have a few questions," I say, thinking of Sarkus and the little boys on earth. "You need to be one hundred percent honest or I won't believe you."

Shireen nods immediately; Suilius is more tentative, but after a nudge from Shireen he nods along. "I will be as honest as I can be," the Fem says, "There are some things I cannot speak on."

"Did your people send the person on Pluto after us? Before we got to Nix?" I ask.

The two Federation operatives look at each other. "I don't believe so. I don't know of anything happening before our interactions on Nix."

"Then who did we shoot?" I muse. "Okay." I slowly exhale, "Do you have, or does the Federation have anything to do with the kids disappearing on Earth?"

The two look genuinely shocked for a moment. "I'm sorry, what?" Suilius asks.

"I don't know. I was told, or at least there was a rumor going around, that it was the Federation. That you were taking kids to train them early." I push a chunk of hair behind my ear.

"You have personal stock in this," Suilius says.

I nod, "My brother. He went missing a few weeks ago. I don't have a way to safely contact him or the people that were looking for him anymore. So, tell me. Does the Federation have anything, anything at all, to do with it?"

Shireen shakes her head. "The only thing we 'have to do with it'," she says with air quotes again, but this time it is kinder somehow, "is that we are looking into it. You aren't the first person to bring it to our attention. I am not personally involved in that investigation, but I know that it's ongoing."

"So, the only thing that the Federation has to do with it is that they are trying to find the source of it?" I press.

"Exactly."

"Would you be able to get the rest of my team off?" I ask.

"We would try, if that's something they want."

I nod, trying to plan the safest route back to my room. "Can you make that malfunction go any longer?"

Chapter 56

"Who the fuck are they?" Miessa hisses, her tail lashing back and forth.

Dita looks just as uncomfortable, her tentacles doing a new sort of shimmy I haven't seen in a long time. Not since she had her first big coding test.

I indicate the two people behind me. "Guys, this is, well, I—" I pull at the back of my neck. "Um, this is Suilius and Shireen. They are Federation operatives. They are the reason for the malfunction, the one that made Kath walk into things."

"He should be fine, by the way." Suilius cuts in. "Ada told me about your concerns. There should be no damage to your teammate."

I nod, "Right, thanks. Um, so guys, they broke in, they wanted to know what was going on. And they want to help us. To get us away from Carver. And whatever hellhole she is creating."

"But the Federation, Ada? You trusted them? You brought them back here?" She hisses, her eyes flash, dancing from brown to green to blue to amber. Her skin ripples growing spines, then flattening to scales. "Shit." She puts her head in her hands, "Stop it, stop it." She tells herself.

I put my hands up, "Mies, relax. It will stop, it seems to happen under stress. Think about it. Do we really have any other options? We are the only three on this entire station that aren't being controlled by Carver. We can't stay hidden forever. I don't want to have to hide anymore."

"I don't either," Dita says, but she still sounds unsure. "What about Kathel?"

"What about him?" Shireen asks. "Isn't he under her control?"

"Yes, but we can't go without him." I insist.

"I don't think one of Carver's drones was part of the deal," Suilius says, crossing his arms.

I blanched at that. "Hang on. You told me you could get my team off. I didn't mean partially; I meant the entire team."

Miessa scoffs, "See Ada, this is what I meant. You can't just trust random people who say they're going to fix everything for you. You're smarter than that!"

"What is that supposed to mean? Why do people keep saying that to me?" I snap.

"You realize how dumb it was to bring them in here? They are our enemy."

"Everyone is our enemy right now. I don't know about you, but I would really prefer not to spend the rest of my life in fear." I snap back.

Dita steps between us, a hand reaching out toward both of us. "Will you two cool it for one second? You both are right. But that isn't going to help us right now. Ada, what you did is really, really risky, but anything we do right now will be. You put your faith in someone you don't know, but it is someone you know isn't in the same circumstances. And if they really can help us..." She looks up at them and gives one of the rare scathing Dita faces that I truly appreciate. "If they can help us, and by us, I do mean all of us—all of team Arctic—I think we should take them up on that."

Miessa growls something under her breath but agrees. "Fine, we go together. But know I'm not happy about it."

"So, how are we going to get Kathel?" Dita asks.

"Might I make a suggestion?" Shireen asks. I nod, "If he has been made into a sort of drone it would be in you and your teammates best interest, if he is unconscious when we get to our base."

"Unconscious," I repeat, trying to think of how the hell I am going to get Kathel unconscious.

"Can you give him a sedative? Or some sort of drug?" Dita asks, already trying to fill in the gaps.

I shake my head, "I'm out. We used everything I had during the mission, and I haven't been able to restock anything for obvious reasons."

"I can blast him for you," Suilius say a bit too eagerly.

I laugh, but it is uncomfortable and high pitched, and I slap a hand over my mouth, "Sorry, I don't know what that was." I say, slowly lowering my hand. "We don't need to shoot Kathel; he already has one injury from someone who shot him that the rest of the medical team here and I have been trying to heal for almost two months now." I turn to my team, "I don't know what to do. We can try to remove the badge, but I don't know how to knock him out."

"Well, let's just go one step at a time. Let's get the badge off him." Miessa says, heading to the door, clearly eager to have something to do.

Dita is quick to follow her, "wait, what happens if removing it sets off some sort of alarm?"

"Then I guess you better be ready to go," Miessa says, turning to the Federation soldiers. "Just how do you intend to get us off this base?"

Shireen passes Miessa her tablet. "We got here by jump gate. You're one of your team's Jumpers, correct?"

Miessa nods, looking over whatever is on the screen. "I can attempt to get to the gate. I don't know what it will be like down there now."

Shireen nods, "It was clear when we got here about an hour ago, but if you can make sure it's ready for when we get there, it would be a great way to ensure we get out smoothly."

Miessa nods and turns to Dita and me, "You two got this?"

"We'll figure it out. We will be there before you even notice." I say, and she grins slightly before she slips out the door. I turn back to Dita. "Okay, but how are we actually going to deal with Kath?"

"Intruder! Intruder!"

I scream in surprise and turn. There stands our Fighter, screaming at the top of his lungs. His gold eyes are hard, focused. He takes two steps across the room and shoulders Dita out of the way, sending her sprawling.

"Oh, fuck." I say, grabbing at his arm. He swings back at me, catching me in the jaw. "Fuck!" I say again, cupping my chin for a moment. My jaw throbs, I turn and see Kathel is making a beeline for the two Federation operatives. "Shit." I run across the living room, jump up on the couch, and launch off it, grappling for Kathel's back. I hook my legs around his waist and wrap my arms around his neck, leaning as far back as I can. He hits at my hands, his fingers scratching at my wrists, trying to get a grip. He starts to topple backward, and I jump off in time for him to slam against the ground.

Catching his balance, he, turns and strikes at me. I roll away from the first set of punches, hitting my side against the chair. The second swing catches me right below the collarbone, sending me staggering back coughing.

Kathel has somewhere in the range of eighty to one hundred pounds and at least a foot of height against me. No matter what I do, his punches, especially now when he isn't holding back, are going to be more powerful. He stands over me, hands raised, so I jump up, driving a knee into his stomach. "I'm sorry, Kath," I say, scrabbling at his arm for the badge. It comes loose, but he hits my arm, and it goes skittering away. I lunge for it but jump back as Kathel shoots a leg out to kick me.

"Got it," Dita says, slamming a boot down over and over on the piece of metal.

Kathel swings at me again, and I duck again. "That's great," I pant feigning left before punching to the right. "When will it reset?"

"Ada, I was a medic, what do you need?" Shireen calls as I weave my way around the room, pushing furniture in front of him.

"I need him to stop. What else do you think I need?" I snap, trying to edge Kathel into a corner.

"We don't know enough about the tech. You need him knocked out." Suilius says.

"Dita, take them to Medical, find some temporary sedative. I'll keep him here." Kathel doesn't respond to the fact that the thing that should be controlling him has been removed. He dives for me but misses, slamming into the corner of our kitchen. He steps back, stunned for a moment, but it doesn't slow him. His eyes swing around the room looking for a new target "I don't have anything."

"Are you sure?" Dita calls, backing toward the door.

Kathel charges them again, and I dive for his legs. "Yes, damn it! Go!" I latch myself around his legs, tasting blood as he kicks out at me again and again. "Kath, Kath, it's me! It's Ada."

He responds by swinging another punch at me. I think I see a flicker of recognition in his eye, and he hesitates, but the blow I thought I could avoid, connects with my chest.

I stumble back, slamming my back into the wall. I hit the back of my head and see stars. He grabs the front of my shirt and pulls his fist back. "Kath! Kath!" I shout, trying to break through to him. He lifts me up, pressing me into the wall. I kick out and catch the side of his knee. He lets out an animalistic shout and drops me to the floor.

I drop to my knees and see the bandage on his leg. "Fuck it." I cough, trying to catch my breath. "I am so sorry." I move to a crouch and launch myself at his knees, wrapping my arms around his leg. I swing at the back of his leg again and again, where I know it will hurt most. He grabs my hair and yanks my head to the side. He rains punches down on my head, neck, and shoulders, I clench my teeth, pushing through the blows. I don't want to hurt him, but I need him to stop.

He cries out in pain, the noise sounding more like the Kathel I know than any other he has made since graduation. He rolls away in pain but doesn't get up, curling to protect his leg. I get on his back and wrap my arm around his neck again, pressing one hand to his pulse, holding him there until he goes. I let him down gently, sliding off his back.

I lay flat on the floor myself trying to catch my breath. I touch my lip, and my fingers come up red. I don't even know which hit did the deed, causing blood to drip from my lip to my chin. "I am so sorry, Kath. I am so sorry." I recheck his pulse; it's strong and steady. I just have to hope when he wakes up, he is mine again.

Chapter 57

I lay on the floor after Kathel passed out, waiting for the others to come back. The points where I will have bruises tomorrow throb. I get up and grab a towel holding it to my split lip, then slide back down to the floor beside Kathel.

Did I just fuck up his leg more? I wonder.

Dita and the Federation soldiers come back to the room ten minutes later. "Holy crap, are you okay?" Dita asks, dropping to the floor beside me.

"Yeah, I'm okay," I say sitting up with a grunt "just resting for a minute". I wipe the partially crusted blood from my chin. "How bad is it?"

"I am impressed you are awake."

I scoff, "that good, huh? Whatcha got for me?" I ask and Dita passes me a few vials.

"Is this okay?"

I look over the labels. "It'll do."

I hear a squawk of a radio and a slur of Plutonian. Shireen is slightly down the hall, speaking into a communicator. "She pulled that out a second ago, I don't know where it came from," Dita says following my gaze to the Federation soldier. "Maybe she's letting them know we are coming." I nod as I administer the drug into Kathel's arm, hoping it will be enough to keep him under.

"We have to go this way," Shireen says, I hear her radio squawk something in Plutonian and lean forward, trying to understand what it said, but she and Suilius move into the hall before a reply is made.

"Can you help me?" I ask, passing my bag to Dita. She nods and helps to shift Kathel up onto my shoulders.

"I can carry him for a bit." Dita says.

I shake my head taking a few careful steps forward. "We need to just get moving. I'll be okay."

"Are you sure? You look like you took a couple hard hits there."

I laugh. "I did. We trained for it though, didn't we?" I start walking to the door.

Dita hits the button for the door, waits until I am through, then jogs up to the two soldiers. "We can't go back to Nix. The Garrison knows about that base." Dita pants.

Shireen and Suilius turn toward us. "No, shit." The Male says. "Thanks for that, by the way. You do realize how difficult it is to evacuate an entire base when it has been compromised, right?"

"Hey!" I snap, "We already said we were sorry. We didn't realize when we enlisted, we were working for madwomen hell-bent on taking you down, okay? You live, you learn. Now can we just get off this fucking base?" I shift Kathel across my shoulders. Kathel is out for now, but I don't know what they will do if he wakes up before we need to leave. *They will make you leave him.*

The Male stares at me hard. "You should learn to better gauge the people you serve earlier on then."

"Look, it isn't like—"

Dita puts a hand on my arm "We need them," she whispers.

When I look up again, the Male is smirking. "Fine. Let's go." I growl.

We continue down the base, snaking our way to the jump gates. At each doorway we pass, we pause, making sure the room is clear before ducking into it and holding there for a few moments.

After thirty agonizing minutes, I drop to one knee and carefully lower Kathel to the ground. I arch my back, it pops several places before pressing a hand to Kathel's throat; his pulse is steady, but faster than before. "He is going to wake up soon. How long will this jump take?" Shireen and Suilius look at each other, trying to decide how much information to give me. "Look, I know you can't tell me where we are going. That is fine. I don't give a fuck. But unless you have some plan to restrict him," I point to Kathel, "I think he is going to wake up in the next hour. I didn't want to risk giving him too much. Who knows what that thing did to him? And I know you can't trust him right now, and the only reason you are is because he's asleep. So, unless you have a plan in place for if he wakes up mid-jump, I am going to need to drug him again. I need to know how long this jump is because I sure as shit don't know what will happen if he wakes up."

Shireen nods, "it's a two-hour jump. You'll need to administer something before we leave."

"Okay, thank you." With Dita's help, I reposition Kathel back up onto my shoulders, instantly feeling the ache in my upper back as his weight settles over me.

"We don't have much further to go to get to the gate. As long as Miessa could get through, she should be ready to program it."

The Male crosses his arms, blocking the door. "And how do we know you aren't leading us into a trap? What if the shifter just joined up with them as soon as she got there?"

"Oh, for fuck's sake! Come on. I know you know next to nothing about us, but you have to see we aren't lying. We want to get off this fucking base. I wouldn't have fought and incapacitated my teammate if I wanted to stay here. I wouldn't willingly carry a man who has at least eighty pounds on me, leaving myself utterly defenseless, unless I wanted out."

Shireen nods, "She is telling the truth, Suilius, come on. The longer we stay here, the more chances they have to find us." She waves him through the door, dropping back to where I walk. "You are going to be questioned when we get there. But I will make it clear you came willingly. You won't be a prisoner. But you should know," She checks her blaster, shifting the power set up. "That there are a shit ton of people that aren't happy with you or any of the teams the Garrison sent our way this week. You will not be welcomed with open arms."

"It's okay, I'm used to that."

She nods, then moves to spearhead the movement with Suilius.

"What do you think they are going to do to us?" Dita asks.

"I don't know," I whisper. "Maybe they will make us pseudo prisoners of war? I am just focusing on getting off this shit show."

"Yeah, I hope Miessa could break through."

Chapter 58

"The door isn't opening." Dita says, trying to open the door for a third time. Suilius steps up blaster in hand. "No, no we don't need you to blast it. Not everything requires blasting." Dita insists covering the pin pad. "It looks like someone changed the code is all. We just need to hope it was Miessa."

After a few more error tones the door to the platform slides open and we are met with the barrel of a blaster. "Get out!" Turns out Miessa did better than just break through. She cleared the entire floor. "Shit, it's you guys," she says, stepping back though she doesn't holster the blaster. "I have the gate opened. You just need to punch in whatever coordinates." pointing to the console next to the gate.

"Right," Suilius moves to it and starts programming.

"You guys okay?"

"Yeah," I grunt, "Help me put him down? I have to give him

something to keep him under."

"Why?" Miessa asks, grabbing Kathel's legs and helping Dita to lift him from my shoulders.

"We have a two-hour jump in front of us. I don't want him waking up." I say, searching my bags for the medication.

Kathel shifts starting to roll over. "Ada? Guys? What is going on?" Kathel asks, his eyes are distant like he can't quite focus on anything.

"Shit, he's waking up. Are those meds not enough?" Miessa says, leaning over the top of Kathel and pressing his shoulders down. "Hey bud, look at me, yes that's it. Just look at me. Nope, don't get up."

"What is going on over here?" Suilius asks, coming back from checking the jump gate. "We need to go. Can you get him up?"

Kathel groans and shifts trying to sit up. Dita slams her hands down on his feet, pinning him down. "Fuck, I feel like I got hit by a train."

I unzip my bag and stuff goes flying; I try to catch a small vial, but my hands are shaking, and I miss it. The sound of it shattering sets off my last fried nerve. *Where are my damn needles?* I frantically search the bag.

"Where are we going?" Kathel groans, "Why are you holding me down? I can walk guys, it's fine."

Suilius is on us in a second, blaster out. "Put him down,

now." He has it trained on the center of Kathel's chest.

"What do you think I'm trying to do?" I ask turning back to Kathel triumphantly, having found a needle. "Now, if you would kindly stop pointing that gun at my team and me, I would appreciate it. We have done, and will do, everything you ask." I drop back down beside Kathel. "Hey Kath, you are going to feel another pinch, okay? Just like back on the ship. This is just to make you feel better." and I jab the needle into the back of his hand. "one, two, three, four, five." I pull the needle out and press the pad of my thumb over the point. "Can you pass me a bandage?" I ask, and Dita does.

"Ada, what is going on?" Kathel mumbles, trying to pull his hand away.

"Trust me?" I whisper, pressing a bandage over the injection sight. I squeeze his hand, "Kath do you trust me?"

His eyes meet mine. "Al—" He falls limp, and I catch his head as the meds, a much stronger dose this time, takes hold.

I check his pulse again and stand up, resisting the urge to gather up my fallen gear. We don't have time. "There, he's out. It should be for at least four hours. I don't know why his system went through the first dose so fast. It could be adrenaline; I could have got it wrong. Is that good enough for you?"

Shireen nods, "Good, now before we jump, the three of you need to know you will be immediately separated and taken for questioning upon arrival. Do not resist. Answer every order and

512

fulfill every question to the best of your ability. You are not going to be prisoners. You're the victims here. Carver is the enemy. I'll clear everything with the higher-ups once we arrive." She turns to her partner. "You better carry him through."

He nods, bending and easily lifting Kathel up and hanging him over his shoulder like a sack of flour.

Asshole could have been doing that the whole time.

An alarm blares, and the lights go dark. "Time's up, they're coming. They will shut down the jump." Miessa says. "I don't know where we are going but I don't want to be here."

Shireen nods, "As long as we're through the gate and they have the other side open, which they should, we'll be good, it will just be a bumpy ride. Come on, let's go. Should be just like your ride from Pluto." She says ruefully, again referencing the broken jump gate.

"After you," Suilius says, beckoning us forward with mock civility. Shireen rolls her eyes before stepping through the gate.

Dita, Miessa, and I link arms before stepping through. It won't be pleasant, but I want my team within reach. The pull is rough, and it makes my already sore shoulder scream, but I need the grounding feeling of them beside me. Shireen wasn't lying when she said the Garrison closing the gate behind us would be rough. And it was worse than Pluto. I felt like I was being sucked in both directions, stretched into a thin ribbon between the two gates, while the turbulence made my stomach roll.

I feel a thrill of excitement, fear, and nausea when I finally see the gate. The moment we pass through, I drop to my knees on the grate, covering my mouth against the wave of bile burning my throat. My vision goes black for a second. Distantly, I hear the sound of blasters powering up. After a few deep breaths, my vision clears, and I am face to face with a dozen blasters.

"I said, stand up." Someone is saying, and I realize they are talking to me.

Fucking jump sickness is going to get me killed. I stagger to my feet. I put my hands on the top of my head, and someone steps forward, ripping my hands down behind my back and cuffing me.

"Didn't the Garrison teach you to follow orders?" They ask.

I don't respond. I am too busy watching Dita and Miessa being led away, hands already in cuffs behind their back. *Shireen said we wouldn't be prisoners.*

Miessa's skin is sickly purple and Dita's little tentacles squirm. I turn my head, trying to get a glimpse of Kathel, but all I can see before I am shoved forward is a single boot splayed out on the ground. *The expanse, I hope we did the right thing.*

Chapter 59

Shireen was wrong about what they were going to do first. They don't take us right to questioning. They take us to a medical wing where they give us a change of clothes. I think at first that they are going to check me out, make sure I'm okay after my fight with Kathel. But they then make me lie down on a bed. I would have been fine, but they insist on strapping me down. They know what happened on the station and presume the same can happen again. The leather straps are a bit too tight for my liking. I can't see Dita or Miessa, but I have to assume they are going through the same thing as me. A large light on over my head blinds me, turning most of the room into shadows when I try to look away. But I think I am in an examination room of some kind.

Someone, a nurse? She wears plain blue scrubs, extends my arm cleans it and uses some sort of numbing cream on my arm. "What are you doing?" I asked the nurse.

She glanced up at me, then back down at my arm. "You are going to feel a little pinch." I looked over to see her cut into my arm.

"What? What are you doing?" I asked again, confusion making my heart race.

She glanced up at the EKG next to my bed. "Lie down dear and take deep breaths. This will be over soon."

When she grabbed a pair of thin forceps, I put the pieces together. *My chip.* It was a quick procedure, practically as painless as inserting the device in the first place. Looking at the tiny chip sitting on the surgical tray, I feel sort of sad. Yet another part of my life that I had worked for was being taken away. Once the chip was removed, the nurse dropped it on the floor and handed me a small hammer.

"What do you want me to do with this?" They didn't elaborate. "Okay, if this helps to prove to you, I am not a robot. Or want to go back." It only takes three strikes. The tiny filigree and mica didn't stand a chance. My ties to the Garrison obliterated.

After they cleaned up some of my minor injuries from my fight with Kathel, they sent me off for the next step of my intake. The interview. It isn't an interrogation. Oh no, this is an *interview.*

Shireen wasn't kidding when she said they were going to question us. The interview is exhausting. The room is small, with clearly this being its sole purpose. Somehow, it makes the interrogation rooms on earth look pleasant. Every wall is a mirror, the table glass, so the interviewer can see my every movement and expression. She is a shrewd Fem, a Capming; she makes careful notes on her tablet and hardly looks anywhere besides my face and her screen. The focus is unnerving.

It goes on for hours, cycling back on questions to see if I trip up, twisting my words and throwing them back at me. I try to answer each one as honestly as I can. But I'm confused. Am I going to be recruited by this company? Are they simply going to rinse us of any information they can use and then dump us? Where should, and does, my loyalty lie? Does my loyalty lie solely with my squad? I chose them. The friends that have stood at my side, even when they didn't necessarily want to. Like way back, when Miessa told Kathel and me to fuck off on the moon.

"You have a brother named Sarkus?"

"I don't think this is pertinent information."

"Do you have a brother named Sarkus Gomez?" I nod. "Is it true that your brother went missing a few weeks ago?"

I swallow down the hard lump of emotion that threatens to make my voice thick. I don't know how they got this information, but I can't let them use him against me. "What does this have to do with the Garrison? I thought you wanted information on them"

"Your brother went missing a few weeks ago?" She repeats.

"Look I just don't know what this has to do with you."

"Miss Gomez. Answer the question." She says firmly.

"Yes, my brother went missing. I don't know exactly when. But I was told he wasn't where he was meant to be about five days ago, but I lost contact with him over a month ago. I didn't really get a chance to investigate the situation."

"And you were under the impression that the Federation had something to do with the disappearance of children on earth?" The Fem asks, looking up at me from her notes rather skeptically.

Another nervous trickle of sweat drips down my back. *What is the right answer to these questions?* "I didn't know what to think. I wasn't really able to track and source where the information was coming from, but yes, I had been told that there was a rumor the Federation was the one stealing kids. I believe people thought that they were being taken to become very early recruits. But I didn't know what to believe."

She scribbled down another note, flipping to what had to be the seventh or eighth page. "And you have now been made aware that we do not engage in that disgusting behavior?"

I nod, "Yeah, Shireen told me."

She nods and looks up at the camera in the corner of the room. The little earpiece that she must have been using to communicate with whoever was on the other side of the lens, is visible glinting dully under the bright lights. "Okay, you are done for now. Someone will come by momentarily to escort you to your room." I look down at the cuffs on my wrists expectantly. "Yes, that person will remove you from your restraints. You are not a prisoner here, Ada. However, you and your team shall remain separated for the time being to ensure that the system used to hack the implants that were in your arm no longer has an effect over your body."

I nod, and wait in silence, knowing whoever is on the other side of the camera lens is watching my every move. It isn't the first time I've been observed and questioned. This time though, my team, unlike my parents hadn't been killed by a car bomb. This time I am suspect. A Male agent comes in a few minutes later. "Gomez, if you would follow me." I stand and do as I am told. In the hall, three men stand with blasters pointed at me.

For all this talk of not being a prisoner, these people sure are on edge.

My room, as it turns out, is a glass cube. To my left I see the distorted images of Dita and Miessa are already in their respective boxes. At the door, the agent escorting me unlocks the cuffs and gestures for me to go into the room. I do so, sitting on the edge of the bed. It squeals in distress and sags in the middle. I sigh and drop my head to my hands. *I am right back where I started*. A tiny room, a bed, a lamp, a dresser, and nothing of value to my name. When I look up, I see Shireen a few doors down, speaking with Dita. She looks tired, but through the several walls of glass I can't see much. The conversation doesn't last long. After a minute or two, Shireen leaves and goes to talk with Miessa. She looks like she is doing okay; like me, she has a bandage around her arm, and she looks stressed. Her cheeks drawn, and the bags under her eyes are deep. She replies to Shireen in short, clipped sentences, her mouth a harsh line. But eventually, they must come to some sort of conclusion because she nods and shakes the Fem's hand.

I turn to watch her come to my room when I see Kathel being wheeled into the room next to mine. He is pale skin has an uneven flush to his cheeks and, like us, he has a bandage on his arm. *I hope someone checked on his leg.*

Shireen clears her throat, and I turn to her, but my eyes quickly drift back to Kathel. "As you saw, I have been speaking to each member of your crew. I want to first thank you for your cooperation thus far."

She stops, and I glance over at her. "Sorry, I'm listening, I... just... is he going to be okay?"

"The Federation has something I need to ask of you first." She says firmly, and I look back to her. "I have posed this question to each of your teammates. You all have the chance to answer this question independently of the other. You are all in a difficult situation." She pauses, waiting to make sure I am paying attention to her. I have to admit that I am drifting. "We are a group of individuals that all want the same thing. To make sure we are here to counter and hold the Garrison accountable for every action they take in this sector. They have ruled unchecked for too long.

However, each of us is vital because of what we can provide for each other. We all want to be here and support each other's ventures. We are individuals. This is why we are asking each of your team members separately what you want to do. And in turn, what we can do for you."

I turn to her, fully focusing on her words. "You want to know if I will join up with you." She nods. "What did Miessa and Dita say?"

"I am not at liberty to tell you that. You have to make this decision on your own without their influence."

"But they are my squad, we have to stick together."

"Is that your decision?" She asks.

"I… Can I ask a few questions first? Before I decide anything?"

She nods, "I will answer what I can."

"What is your role in the Federation?"

She smiles, "you will find in the Federation we wear many hats. As I said on the station, I trained as a medic. But here I go out on different independent reconnaissance missions, while also handling more diplomatic situations, like these." She says gesturing to myself and my teammates.

"Do you have a title?"

She nods, "Yes, but I cannot tell you that at this time."

I nod and pick at the edge of my nail, unsure if I should try my luck or not. "My brother, would you help me look for him? Find out what happened to him? I don't have a way to reach him anymore."

She nods. "We currently have a division that is already looking into that situation. Your brother can easily be added to the list of missing children if he's not already on it."

I nod slowly. I look up to Miessa and Dita, who watch me, their faces distorted by the refraction of the glass. "What about Kath? Are you going to ask him?"

Shireen nods again. "Once Agent Torrac wakes and is strong enough, he will go through the same process you did. He will not know the rest of the team's decision until you have all chosen. You will not meet your team until you all have answered the question."

"What happens if we say we don't want to join you?" I ask slowly, trying to read the expressions of my team members, but their faces are too distorted by the glass.

"I am not at liberty to discuss that."

I scoff and look down. "Well, isn't that nice? You can't tell us what happens if we join up, but you are even vaguer if we decide not to join you." I get up and start pacing the room. "You know, I never would have thought you were a Federation agent." She doesn't respond to this. "How bad was I on, Nix?"

She smiles a bit at that. "Well, it was pretty clear you weren't a spy. But you still did pretty well."

I look up, trying to collect my scattered thoughts and feelings. "What happens if I walk out that door right now?"

"I have told you, Ada, you and your team are not prisoners here."

"All the agents with guns walking us around in here says otherwise." I snap.

She plays with a tassel at the edge of her headscarf. "That is for all of our safety. You would be able to walk around, with limitations, but the only time someone would stop you would be if you were trying to enter a restricted area."

I stop in front of the door, considering it. What would I learn by walking out that door? I'm sure I would be followed. Would I get any information I wouldn't get here? I sit back down on the bed. "You said you want to try to stop the Garrison and hold them accountable. Does that mean it is bigger than our station, and Carver?"

She hesitates at first, but then nods. "Yes, it is bigger than her. But I can't elaborate farther than that."

I chew on my lip, tasting a bit of metallic blood again as it splits open. I don't know what the right choice is in this scenario. "If I do this. What happens to me? You'll help me get Sarkus back, or at least find him, but what else?"

"You can choose to work with us on missions. A skill set like yours would be very beneficial. But you could also expect support. You would be able to try to make a life for yourself, get an education if, after a time, you don't want to work with us. That's fine, but there will be a containment period where you will need to stay with us before you can be released. We would help make any accommodations for you to leave."

I get up and go to the glass wall, looking down at Kathel, wondering what he and the other members of my squad will or have chosen. *They may be your only chance for Sark.* I watch the heart rate monitor on Kathel's nightstand, imagining the rhythmic beep. I can't go back to the Garrison.

I turn back to Shireen and put out a hand, "Okay."

Katelyn Costello

Katelyn Costello, a lifelong reader, started writing when she was twelve out of spite. Her best friend was going to a writing workshop, and her class wasn't. So she begged her way in and showed up with a twenty-eight-page short story to what turned out to be a poetry workshop. Several NaNoWriMo's later Costello knew she wanted to tell stories for the rest of her life. Costello graduated from Wells College in 2018 with a BA in English Creative Writing and published her debut novel, a Young Adult Fantasy entitled The Frituals in fall 2018. When not writing, Costello is working in the visual arts as a photographer and director.

Visit her at www.katelyncostello.com or on most social media spaces @authorkatelyncostello.

www.ingramcontent.com/pod-product-compliance
Lightning Source LLC
Chambersburg PA
CBHW050840030726
47503CB00007BA/2248